Stuart Campbell is a full-tim[...] [...] of Edinburgh now living in [...] worked as an English teacher and Adviser in the Lothians, and as a part-time manager with Health in Mind, an Edinburgh-based mental health charity. He has previously written for the BBC, the Guardian and the Scottish Book Collector. He is the editor of *RLS in Love*, an anthology of Robert Louis Stevenson's love poetry, and author of *Boswell's Bus Pass*, a travelogue of modern Scotland following in the footsteps of Dr Samuel Johnson and James Boswell, as well as the novel *John McPake and the Sea Beggars*. Stuart Campbell is married to Morag and has four grown-up children.

Also published by Sandstone Press

RLS in Love
Boswell's Bus Pass
John McPake and the Sea Beggars

THE
AERONAUT'S GUIDE
TO
RAPTURE

Stuart Campbell

SANDSTONEPRESS
HIGHLAND | SCOTLAND

First published in Great Britain
and the United States of America in 2016
Sandstone Press Ltd
7 Dochcarty Road
Dingwall
Ross-shire
IV15 9UG
Scotland.

www.sandstonepress.com

Editor: Robert Davidson

The publisher acknowledges support from
Creative Scotland towards publication of this volume.

ISBN: 978-1-910124-93-2
ISBNe: 978-1-910124-94-9

Cover design by Mark Ecob
Typesetting by Iolaire Typesetting, Newtonmore
Printed and bound by CPI Group (UK) Ltd, Croydon CR0 4YY

To Emily, Tom, Alice and Sandy

ACKNOWLEDGEMENTS

I would like to thank these friends for their support and expertise: Sylvie Schramm (19th century Paris), Donna Weidenfeller (American language), Andrew Greer (Vietnam war), David Nelken (Italian culture), David Raitt (aerodynamics) and both Jim O'Sullivan and Roy Henderson for their critical insight, gentle advice and encouragement. I also acknowledge my debt to Richard Holmes' *Falling Upwards: How We Took to the Air*.

ACKNOWLEDGEMENTS

PROLOGUE

Nothing will ever quite equal that moment of total hilarity that filled my whole body at the moment of take-off. I felt we were flying away from the earth and all its troubles and persecutions for ever. It was not mere delight. It was a sort of physical rapture... I exclaimed to my companion Monsieur Robert – 'I'm finished with the earth. From now on our place is in the sky! ... Such utter calm. Such imensity! Such an astonishing view.'

Dr Alexander Charles who made the first flight in a hydrogen balloon on 1st December 1783.

I had missed the flight. The happy occupants of the basket waved to those of us on the ground, not realising that I was meant to be one of their number. Despite my annoyance I waved back. How could I write about balloons if I had never been on one?

The Satnav had failed me completely. The postcode had led me through several housing estates and dumped me in a supermarket car park. I almost managed to convince myself that balloons were often launched from such places and that it was, at that very moment, being inflated beyond the industrial waste bins and would soon materialise above the cars like a sulking genie from *The Arabian Nights*.

1

I had read many accounts of early pioneering flights and wanted to experience for myself the small intimations of rapture that seemed to be a recurrent theme of the early pioneers. Thomas Baldwin in his *Narrative of a Balloon Excursion from Chester* in 1785 was so carried away by a sense of euphoria he could only write about the experience in the third person, '*A tear of pure Delight flashed in his Eye! Of pure and exquisite Delight and Rapture.*'

As an antidote to chronicling the squalor of Victorian London's poor, Henry Mayhew treated himself to a balloon flight from the Vauxhall Gardens with Charles Green. He describes '*floating through the endless realms of space, and drinking in the pure thin air of the skies, as you go sailing along almost among the stars, free as the lark at heaven's gate and enjoying, for a brief half hour, at least, a foretaste of that Elysian destiny which is the ultimate hope of all.*'

Not only Mayhew but Edgar Allan Poe, Charles Dickens, both Shelleys, Jules Verne, H G Wells and Ian McEwan had all somehow managed not to miss their flights.

My own experiences of anything approaching rapture had been confined to endorphin rushes after sustained exercise and pleasurable moments attained during my earlier flirtation with Buddhism. I was too much of a coward to emulate Aldous Huxley and R D Laing and chase the dragon or whatever it is that drug addicts do. I did though have a residual memory of a brief morphine-induced euphoria prior to a knee operation many years back. Auto-erotic asphyxiation held little appeal. Not at my age, and anyhow I vaguely recalled that it was mainly Conservative politicians who resorted to such measures.

It had to be a balloon flight. If my characters were to have a hard time, which is the lot of most characters, then perhaps their fictional tribulation could be resolved by a shared all-absorbing mystical experience that sucked in and transformed the reader. Anyway that had been the hope.

Immodestly I thought that I could write a conclusion to my narratives that would be transcendently beautiful, and which would conjure the sort of pleasurable afterglow that can accompany a half-remembered dream.

A man's dog tugged at my trouser leg. 'Lovely, isn't it?' he said, pointing at the multicoloured balloon as it hovered above the houses on the edge of the park.

'Yes,' I conceded through clenched teeth, watching jealously as the balloon cleared the trees. Perhaps Louis XVI had been right when, fearful lest balloon travellers should be lost in unknown regions, he proposed that only condemned criminals should be permitted to climb into the basket.

'Wouldn't get me in one of them though.'

'Nor me.' Lying was easier than explaining my disappointment.

As I grumpily clicked my seat belt into position I looked through the rear-view mirror at the speck of the balloon climbing above the Pentlands; a mascaraed tear in the eye of a clown; a tiny spheroid globule straining at the tip of a scientist's pipette.

URSULE
FRANCE 1864

CHAPTER ONE

She had fed the beasts and persuaded the newborn calf
to suckle from the bottle. She had to prise apart the
animal's lips and rub them gently with the teat before
it understood. It had sucked and sucked until the bottle
was empty. She had held the bottle higher so that it could
drain the last drop. Without her noticing, it had grown
dark in the barn.

Her father ruffled her hair, blew out the lamp and sent
her to her bed. Her mother too had looked up and smiled
before resuming her knitting. A good day. And many more
to come, good days stretching to the outer edges of her
childhood. Tomorrow she would meet up with Angélique
and the pair of them would finish the house they were making in the hay.

It was hard work flattening the stalks that always sprung
back into their original shape. Ursule spat out the husks.
'Not on the carpet,' said Angélique and the pair of them
collapsed laughing until their sides ached. Dust stuck to
their faces and smeared them like savages. Angélique had
brought some hard-boiled eggs and bread. They sat and
gossiped like their elders and talked about Pierre the boy
on the neighbouring farm whom they both pretended to
love. Meanwhile the dragonflies hovered around the edges
of their conversation.

They both knew that Pierre preferred Ursule. He had, after all, snatched a kiss when they met accidently down by the river, but all good things were to be shared with one's friends. All three would live together in a big house. There would of course be children though Ursule had not given any thought to how this might be achieved. There was always a solution for everything.

Gradually her father became more distant and smiled less often. Her mother no longer knitted clothes for them all but sewed and sewed until her fingers were red raw. Then Gérard would come and take away her work, leaving another mountain of cloth in front of the cold hearth.

Angélique disappeared from her life for reasons she never understood. Soon there were no more calves to be fed, and there was no more grain in the barn. The large door swung open and creaked and groaned throughout the long nights.

And then she was sold to Gérard.

She had never seen a man so tall. Behind his back the neighbours called him le Géant. He filled all of the space in the room. He and her father conferred, and then she was sent to pack. Her mother could not look at her and instead addressed her shoulder explaining that she was, after all, nearly sixteen and had to make her own way. Money was owed to le Géant who would look after Ursule and give her a trade. Of course she could visit her parents as often as she liked. She would find life and excitement in Paris. It was a grand city full of possibility.

At first le Géant had treated her well. He was, after all, her new tall uncle. They stayed in a small apartment in Place Royale with a view over the park. She would stare at the neat boys rolling hoops and the parade of large perambulators being pushed by upright women in black. She was never certain that the carriages actually held children;

perhaps the servants were just practising for children as yet unborn.

One night she woke in her truckle bed screaming, trapped in a dream in which she pulled back the small lace curtains and saw that each pram held a dead faceless baby. Le Géant shouted to her to be quiet and go back to sleep.

The next night he suggested that she should join him in his bed so that he could comfort her if the nightmare returned. She had often crept into her parents' bed and thought this would be a good arrangement. She felt safe for the first time in a long while when she nestled against his warm strong body.

She clung to the edge of the bed in the aftermath, sobbing and in great pain. Why had he done that to her? Why would her uncle want to cause her such hurt? Le Géant grew angry and said he would give her a reason to cry if she didn't shut up. So, the pattern was established. She had no idea where he went during the day. She would keep the room tidy, take his clothes to the wash house where she was well treated by the older women. She would haggle for meat and vegetables in the market and cook them as best as she could. Her best was rarely good enough. 'Why does this smell like a Prussian latrine? Was it your useless mother who taught you to cook pig shit?'

Once he took the meat from his plate in one fist and crammed it into her mouth until she was gagging. He then rubbed the plate and the remaining gravy into her face and hair.

'Learn to cook, whore!' He stormed out of the apartment and to Ursule's relief was so drunk on his return that he fell where he stood in the doorway and slept until morning.

Sometimes an ill-smelling older man, Eugène, would return to the apartment with le Géant. She would be given a few sous and sent out to the grog shop on the corner.

Eugène would put his forefinger and thumb to his mouth before counting out money into two unequal heaps on the table. Sometimes he would catch Ursule staring at the transaction and wink at her with an expression that frightened her. Once le Géant called her over and made her sit on Eugène's lap like the child that she was. Eugène placed a hand under her skirt and she fled to the recess in the far wall. Le Géant laughed. 'Later,' he said. 'Patience my friend. All good things can wait.'

Although Ursule conscientiously washed le Géant's clothes, prepared his food to the best of her ability and swept the apartment, she continued to spend much of each day staring out of the window at the park and its visitors.

She had names for all of the regular strollers: Jacques, the old man who would pause and wave his stick at the sky for no apparent reason. Marthe and Maxime, two thin housemaids who would stroll arm in arm before sitting on their favourite bench. If it was occupied they would loiter, glancing repeatedly at the intruders until they moved away. Madame Piquenez would strut with self-importance as her four small dogs fussed and sniffed their way along the gravel paths.

As dusk fell the gas lamps were lit and the park clientele changed. While the nurses were tucking their charges into bed, single women and groups of men would pass through the gates. The glow from a score of cigars would enable Ursule to follow the men as they hunted for companions. She noticed too how laughter sounded louder in the dark. Turning away from the window she would listen anxiously for Gérard's return.

Best of all were the nights when he didn't return at all, leaving her to savour the sound of carriages passing in the darkness. Who were they carrying? Spies? Government officials with despatches from the front? Lovers returning from illicit encounters? Sometimes the horses sped over the cobbles with the fast rhythms of a polka, at other times they moved slowly in a tired waltz.

Le Géant returned mid-evening. This was very unusual. He stood on the threshold. 'Get your coat, you need a drink.'

He strode ahead and she struggled to keep up. He waited impatiently for her at the door of le Refuge and then pushed her into the smell of men and smoke. Their arrival was met with loud cheering. Le Géant nodded his head in acknowledgement of the applause. A small part of Ursule was gratified to learn that Gérard was so well received by his friends. Perhaps she had misjudged him. Perhaps she should try harder to make him happy and meet his needs.

'Behold the prize!' proclaimed le Géant, indicating Ursule with a flourish. She felt embarrassed but not displeased to be referred to in this unexpected manner. Yes, she really must try harder. The room was dark and thick with smoke and she felt her eyes smarting. When they adjusted to the light she recognised Eugène. She nodded at him but he responded with a sneer. Another man with a large beard and small eyes banged his crutch on the stone floor expressing either frustration or approval, Ursule couldn't tell. The landlord placed a tray of glasses on an upturned barrel and uncorked a brandy bottle.

Le Géant took to the floor. 'Comrades,' he said. 'Times are hard, the Prussians are at the gate. We must look after each other. As our socialist friends tell us, we must share our goods. I am willing to make the ultimate sacrifice. This young woman here can be yours, for a price! Now who will offer me ten francs? A bargain, I assure you.'

Ursule smiled, assuming that le Géant was jesting at her expense. She could forgive him his miscalculation. It was good, after all, to see him in such fine spirits. Several hands were raised.

'Fifteen,' said Eugène.

'Twenty!' shouted a youngish man whose face seemed to have been sown together with a scar.

'Come on now, look at her young flesh!' Le Géant lifted Ursule's dress. The crowd whooped their approval. Ursule was confused.

'Twenty-five!'

She tried to rise from the table but le Géant pressed down firmly on her shoulder. 'Sit there, slut,' he muttered for her ears only. Again she tried to stand, again she was restrained.

'Thirty!'

'Any advance on thirty? Come on, gentlemen, it's your last chance.'

'Thirty and my dog!'

'Sold to the owner of the large stomach in the corner!'

Le Géant removed his hand from Ursule's shoulder as he pointed out the winner of the auction. Instantly she rose and fled towards the door. Eugène extended his leg and tripped her but she maintained her momentum and tumbled into the street.

Running fast through the cold night calmed her sufficiently for her to consider returning home. After all there was more than a chance that he would return too drunk to make a fuss. She would, however, sleep fully clothed.

Gérard pulled back the covers and towered over her, his face grotesquely lit by the candle dripping wax into her hair.

'It was a joke, who in their right mind would pay money for you anyway? Scraggy runt of a woman, of no use to man nor beast. You forget that I rescued you from your past. Without me your parents would have starved. And you with them. Look at you. Curled up like a baby with your thumb in your mouth. You make me sick! Thank God I know real women who would give their eye teeth to spend a night with me.' With that he walked out of the apartment, slamming

12

the door after him, rocking it in its frame. In her mind's eye Ursule saw le Géant holding court, surrounded by women with faces like harlequins who nevertheless were gentle and welcoming to him in a way she could not manage.

She had seriously considered not returning after the incident at le Refuge, but where would she have gone? Perhaps in her naivety she had failed to understand le Géant's robust humour. She knew little of the world. Perhaps she deserved to be sold. She had, after all, transgressed. She had betrayed him.

CHAPTER TWO

She never understood how he had found the journal. It had been hidden in a small gap left by the ill-fitting grate. She had slipped the pages into the crack, leaving a tiny corner the size of a protruding fingernail so that she could retrieve it when it was safe to do so.

'Adulterous whore! If the devil himself came to the door you would invite him in and fuck him behind my back. Did you bring soldier boy here? Did you? Did you?'

He circled her throat with his hand and moved her round the room, knocking a table aside in their miserable dance. He only released his grip to turn over the next page in the journal. 'He is not my husband,' he read in a simpering falsetto voice. He moved away from the light of the gas lamp and moved towards her again. It seemed to Ursule that he filled every inch of the room, a monster squeezing all light and air from their living space.

'I'm the man who rescued you from penury and your pathetic parents. The man who keeps you in luxury. And what do I ask in return? Answer me, answer me!' He slammed his fist into the bureau, smashing the slatted cover. Ursule shook her head, not by way of answering his question, but out of fear of what was to come.

'Exactly, nothing, nothing, just the hope that you might comfort your benefactor between the sheets now and again.

But no, you are too busy with soldier boy's cock. Slut! Fucking slut!' He threw the journal into the fire, a few pages detached themselves and fluttered onto the hearth.

Now apoplectic with rage le Géant looked round the room for suitable missiles. Ursule cowered in a corner as he aimed the crockery at her. The cups smashed against the wall with a noise that he found momentarily gratifying, especially when he noticed a thin stream of blood trickling down her face.

Ursule for her part was strangely detached from the proceedings. The crockery seemed to move through the air in slow motion, giving her time to reflect on the provenance of each cup. The first three were part of a set that Gérard claimed to have bought in the market. Ursule had always hated the faux Chinese pattern. Next was the bowl that for some reason her mother had added to her bundle when she left the farmhouse for the last time. She assumed it had some family significance but had no idea what. Then it was time for her beating.

By chance Ursule avoided Gérard's flailing fists as he lunged across the small space, knocking over a plant stand. He caught his foot on the rug and sprawled on the floor. Ursule then darted behind the upended table. He went one way, she the other in a tragic pastiche of a playground game. He picked up a full bottle of wine and, after a moment deciding if it were best deployed as a cudgel or missile, he opted for the latter and took aim. Ursule ducked as the glass shattered against the pale wall.

For a split second le Géant assumed victory was his as he apparently watched her head explode into a cascade of dark red blood. But the whore was still alive. He had little time to absorb the significance of this fact as Ursule, emboldened by sheer panic and a primitive instinct to survive, sprang on him and clawed at his eyes. Howling with pain and unable to see, he groped his way across the floor, slid on the glass and skidded into the dresser that promptly fell on him. Assuming that Ursule had somehow recruited a previously unseen ally, he lay stunned. Ursule snatched the smouldering journal from the hearth and, without pausing to gather her coat, fled from the room and ran into the street.

She ran blind and lost into Boulevard de la Contrescarpe. A cab driver pulled sharply on the reins to stop his horse trampling the young girl who seemed particularly eager to be killed under its hooves. The animal strained at the yoke and reared up on its hind legs, a pugilist spoiling for a fight. The single passenger reacted angrily to being jolted against the side of the carriage, and readjusted his hat. Several young men, about to take their place at a table outside of le Chat, waved their canes lustily, half in admonishment, half in encouragement as Ursule rushed past.

'The filly's in the first race at Longchamp.'

'Ten francs says she will win!'

Obliged to pause by the crippling stitch in her side, Ursule looked over her shoulder but le Géant had long abandoned the pursuit, preferring to drown his sorrows, cut his losses, and plot his revenge in the smoky comfort of le Refuge.

After negotiating the sewer works in Rue de Rivoli she entered le Jardin des Tuileries, and, despite her anxiety, was calmed by the sense of space and tranquillity. L'Allée des Mûriers led her past a fountain and towards a bandstand where a knot of young soldiers was lounging, waiting for the early evening entertainments to commence. They all sported the chocolate brown of the local battalion. She ran closer and stared in the vain hope that Louis was in their number. He wasn't but the men welcomed the scrutiny of a single woman in the gardens.

Ursule realised that she had fled from the apartment without her shawl. She pulled the two sides of her chemise together, aware that it was providing a focus for the young men's gaze. One by one the gas lamps were lit. Their orange hissing flames imparted an aura of decadence and mystery over the assembling crowd. Strolling couples arrived with their arms wrapped round each other. Black hats were ostentatiously doffed in exaggerated gestures of greeting. To applause, a band started playing. Ursule watched transfixed as the pairs formed and glided between the tables whose occupants raised their glasses.

She became uneasy when two men, after nodding conspiratorially at each other, forsook their table and approached her. The taller of the two bowed from the waist. The other blew rings of cigar smoke in her direction and looked amused as she coughed.

'Bonsoir, Mademoiselle,' he said, tapping the ash onto the gravel. 'Are you unaccompanied this evening?'

'Yes, but...' Ursule lost her words as she recognised the leer in the speaker's eyes. She had seen the same expression on le Géant's face in the days preceding his suggestion that she join him in his bed and snuggle up for warmth.

'I'm just leaving...'

'With us, I hope. Does Mademoiselle have a room close by? We will bring wine.'

She turned to leave but one of the men was standing on her dress that was trailing on the ground. She tried to pull it free but he kept his foot firmly planted where it was. He smirked, enjoying her discomfort. His friend guffawed and lit another cigar. Panicking now, Ursule made to move but only succeeded in tearing her dress. The men cheered and gawped at the freshly revealed calf and thigh. Their laughter attracted the attention of other male revellers who hurried over to enjoy the spectacle. Now trapped in a raucous circle of baying men, she became aware of two uniformed members of the préfecture pushing their way through.

'What's happening here?' asked the older of the two officials.

'I was importuned, officer,' said the man who had first

spoken to Ursule. He touched the brim of his hat with the tip of his cane.

'Importuned, officer,' chorused the others.

'A common prostitute. Look at the state of her.' Ursule tried to pull the remnants of her dress further down her leg. 'And not a day over seventeen if I am a judge of womankind.'

One of the men pinched her behind and vanished back into the crowd. The official looked sternly in the general direction of the culprit.

'Come with us, Mamzelle,' he said. He and his colleague each pulled an arm behind her back, then pushed her head downwards with a shove to her back before propelling her out of the crowd and out of le Jardin to the waiting police cab. She was thrown onto the floor of the carriage. Her first thought was one of relief on realising that there were no windows. At least le Géant would not see her.

★

At the office of the Préfecture, the receiving official, without glancing up from his ledger, quickly ascertained her name and the fact that she was of no fixed abode.

Her cell already had three female occupants. One of the women was asleep on a bench with her face to the wall. Her long straggly grey hair almost reached the floor. Her two companions were identical twins, plump with mongoloid features. They both stood in front of Ursule and announced their names.

'Mirabelle.'

'Nina.'

Ursule noticed that Nina elongated her name. She had a cleft palate.

Ursule introduced herself and the twins smiled. It was difficult to tell their age. Perhaps the same age as herself. They glanced at each other and both placed a finger on her face as if to ascertain that she was real. Ursule, knowing that she was in the company of gentle spirits, willingly stood still for the inspection. Satisfied, the twins giggled and then sat cross-legged on the floor opposite each other, and continued whatever game Ursule's arrival had interrupted. She too slumped onto her haunches, stretched out her legs and tried to make sense of what had happened to her. She touched her cheek and felt coagulated blood. One of le Géant's missiles must have found its mark after all.

She felt safe in the cell. What she wanted above all else was for Louis to break down the door and carry her away to a new life. He would soothe her, comfort her, look after her. They would live together. Her warm fantasy flipped itself on its back. He had been killed in battle, his body was in a ditch, the maggots in his eyes. She stood up and paced the cell. The twins looked up at her.

Ursule was aware that the cell's other occupant was waking. The woman pulled herself into a sitting position on the bench, stretched, yawned loudly, picked something from her head and apprised Ursule.

'Well, child. What terrible crime has led you here? Who have you murdered? Did you garrotte your parents? Did you poison your lover?' She idly inspected several straggly strands of her own hair.

'I was walking in le Jardin...'

'We all need money. You need a different trick. Like this.' She clicked her fingers and the twins abandoned their game and stood to attention alongside the woman who Ursule now realised was probably their mother.

'La mer,' said the older woman and the twins with arms outstretched, started undulating their torsos, head and neck in the movement of waves.

'Le bateau.'

Mirabelle got down on all fours while Nina sat astride her and pulled on imaginary oars.

19

'Les pirates approchent!'

Both girls scanned the horizon with their hands on their foreheads before producing imaginary telescopes which they skilfully adjusted.

'Bravo!' shouted Ursule.

'The authorities assume I am a madam selling my girls. There are few magistrates in all of France who have not enjoyed the same spectacle as I try to convince them that my simpleton daughters are not whores. Tomorrow we will do the same for the Prefect. I am Camille, artiste and acrobat. She bent forward, pulled a hand through her hair then bowed from the waist with the palms of her hands flat on the floor.

'I'm Ursule, and I don't know what I am...'

During the night Ursule lay awake shivering with the cold. The stone floor was hard. Camille had offered her the bench but she had declined. Her torn clothes were not ideal prison wear.

'Girls, keep our friend warm,' said Camille. The twins moved, one each side of Ursule and nestled into her side, sharing their body heat.

'Now, tell me your story,' said Camille.

'I am not a good girl.' The pitch black of the cell made it seem to Ursule as if she was thinking aloud rather than confiding in a comparative stranger. 'I have run away from the man who looked after me, fed me and gave me clothes. He was not always a good man but he gave my parents money for me when they were poor. I miss my parents, I don't know where they are.'

'Did he beat you?'

'Yes, but I deserved it. I did not make a good home for him. Perhaps I should go back to him.'

'Never!' Camille shouted so loudly both twins started in their sleep, relaxed then tightened again their grip on Ursule.

'But I betrayed him. I saw a boy from my window and wove spells of happiness round him. I would think of him when I should have been preparing food for Gérard. He found my journal, the diary in which I poured out my heart. Gérard will beat me. I think he might kill me.'

'Do you still have the journal? Show it to me. I have a candle.

Reluctant at first, Ursule eventually relented and removed the charred pages from her chemise where she had hidden them after running into the street. She flattened the pages with the edge of her hand and passed them to Camille who had lit her candle in expectation.

The first few pages were filled with spidery drawings of the view from her room overlooking the gardens. She had sketched the huge perambulators and drawn the small boys with their hoops. Camille skipped through the next few pages which contained no words or drawings just dense patterns with sharp black edges: spirals that fled to the bottom of the page, tall shapes that could have been apartments with black windows towering ever upwards. Ursule winced as she realised that each touch of her pen testified to the pain and fear that had characterised her life with le Géant.

Across another page flowed a black swirl that could have been a river in flood, equally the small vertical lines could have been arms sinking before the torrent. The only truly identifiable drawing was of a small cradle in the corner of a room. It was being gently rocked by a hand that emerged from the side of the page. What did it mean? Was it the cradle in which she had slept in the farmhouse? She had no idea. Camille too looked puzzled.

'You'll see him soon,' said Ursule who was slightly hesitant to turn the page in case the most precious image of all had faded to nothingness.

It was still there, still there. It was Louis when she first saw him from the window. And then a page full of questions.

21

Who are you? Where are you going? What is your name? Will you pass this way again?

Camille smiled. 'Ah,' she said, running a finger over the outline of a slim boyish figure sauntering through the garden. 'What a handsome fellow, I think I'm falling in love too.'

Ursule looked at the drawing on the next page. It showed herself on a park bench, her elbows on her knees and her head in her hands. Her hair obscured her face but it was apparent from her position that she was miserable. Camille read aloud:

Today I did a silly thing. After cleaning the house and putting away Gérard's clothes I went into the park for the first time. I thought all the ladies were looking at me, then I thought they were sneering. At least I could look into the prams that passed but I still didn't see a single baby. I dare hardly admit to myself that I was hoping he would pass that way again. But I wanted to see the young man. I waited but he didn't come. I went home feeling stupid and guilty. Gérard stared at me oddly in the evening and I couldn't look him in the face.

The next page featured no words only a variant of the first drawing. This time the bench seemed bigger and the slumped figure smaller.

On the next page again the figure and bench had moved to the bottom right-hand corner and were tiny. It looked as if the whole blank page was pressing down on Ursule. Insignificant and worthless.

This was followed by a child's drawing of a huge sun complete with smiling face. As the face was so large Ursule had written her account in the margins, managing only two words or so where the sun's ears almost touched the edges of the page. Camille continued:

I saw him enter the gardens. I wanted the ground to open up and swallow me, I knew I was blushing brighter and

22

*brighter as he came close. I was shaking and felt foolish. I
tried not to stare but looked at him out of the corner of my
eyes. He was taller than I thought and so slim. And then he
sat next to me. HE SAT NEXT TO ME! I turned to stone,
embarrassed and hating myself.*

*'Are you all right Mademoiselle?' he asked. 'You are
shaking and yet the day is warm. Are you unwell? Do you
want my coat?'* As these last words were squeezed under
the sun's chin, a small arrow indicated that the narrative
continued on the next page. Camille squeezed Ursule's
arm.

*He said he had seen me at the window of the apartment
opposite he had thought of waving but that might be seen
as forward he made a point of glancing up whenever he
came into the garden and felt disappointed when I wasn't
there his name was Louis and he came from Lyon where
his father was a bookbinder he was twenty years old he had
come to join the National Guard he wanted to serve his
country his parents had tried to dissuade him from leaving
for Paris it was dangerous he would be killed but it was
something he had to do the Prussians were advancing on
Paris he wanted to stop them and was waiting to be called
to the front he said the prams were too large and looked
stupid just rich people flaunting their money he said he
asked what my husband did for a living I said that Gérard
was not my husband then I got flustered and to my horror
began to cry he put his arm round me.*

Camille smiled and handed the pages back to Ursule.
'Bravo,' she said. 'Bravo! Tell me about the boy. Did you
kiss? Did you make love?'

'No, nothing like that. We spoke. He told me he was
going to fight the Prussians. But I think of him all the time.'

'You must find this boy. You must seek every byway
until you find him.'

'I want to, Madame, I want to.' She was aware that

23

Mirabelle was patting her reassuringly as if she had been listening and had understood every word.

'Tell me, do you have a man you love?' asked Ursule.

Camille replied with a sound that was half snort, half spit.

'I will tell you my tale but I don't want to frighten you, or give you nightmares. I loved a man, Alain, he was called. From Aix en Province. A hurdy-gurdy player. We travelled to all the fairs and entertained the farmers. As he played I would turn summersaults. I persuaded the men to go down on all fours and I would tumble and cartwheel my way over their backs as light as a feather. We drank the cider in Bretagne and the wine in Alsace. We had a simple carriage and a horse, Victor. The living was good. The farmers let us stay in their barns or else we slept under the stars. We would play at weddings and feast days.

'When the money was short Alain would play the cards, not gambling you understand, he played tricks. He would go to the tavern, find a seat on his own and start to make the cards climb his arms and stand on end. Soon others would become curious, and then they were hooked. He would produce the chosen card from under their tankards, from inside their vests, from the lining of their hats. Once they were charmed and mesmerised, he would challenge them to guess the card they themselves had chosen and put into their pocket. At first he would let them win, shrug and play the good loser. Then the stakes would rise and before long he would climb back on the wagon with bundles of money. We would find a quiet spot, near a river if possible. Alain would light a fire over which I cooked the rabbits we had caught earlier. Then my hurdy-gurdy man would start to play and I would sing. Together we would charm the stars. And drink, and lie together in the warm light of the dying fire. Such was our life of love and plenty until...'

24

'Until what?' asked Ursule who was herself lying, not next to Mirabelle and Nina, but next to Louis and the warm embers of a fire.

'Until one of the farmers, a beast called Gustave, very drunk and furious at having been deceived, followed the sound of the hurdy-gurdy until he found us. He slit Victor's throat. We heard strange noises from the horse as it collapsed. Alain went to investigate and met the same fate. Terrified, I ran into the night but Gustave caught me, tossed me over his shoulders and took me back to his farm where he must have drugged me.

'As I regained consciousness, I was aware that he was tying a rope round my ankles. I tried to struggle but could only squirm across the dust yard like some sort of crippled creature, a dying mermaid perhaps. His salivating dogs got excited and would have eaten my face there and then had he not kicked them aside. After all, he had a better fate in store. As my nightmare unwound I cursed his soul to hell but he just knelt on me and slapped me until I shut up. It's difficult to shout when you are choking on blood. Anyway, he hoisted me to my feet and made me walk with tiny mincing steps to the edge of the well. He pushed my head onto the lip, and after tipping me over, lowered me down the sides, dangling on the end of a rope. A fallen angel being slowly returned to the pit. I tore my fingertips as I tried to hold onto the stonework but it was pointless. I was being lowered towards the water in which I would drown. Mercifully the summer had been hot and the foul water was shallow. After he had dropped the rest of the rope onto my head I managed to stand up to my knees.

'That night I watched the tiny circle of sky grow darker. I punched the stonework until my knuckles bled. I howled for the man I had lost and for the blood of the man who had killed him. When I next looked up, I saw that a single star had wandered into the dark circle. It was there for me. It

25

was my light. I undid the rope from my ankles and stretched my muscles. I was Camille the Acrobat. There was no well deep enough to contain me, especially one as narrow as this. With my back to one of the sides, I stretched out my legs and clamped them tight. By carefully adjusting my position, I could move like a crab upwards. My sinews were ready to snap and my back was scraped red raw but I climbed. Slowly I climbed.

'Two hours later I dragged myself out of the well and slumped exhausted on the ground. While recovering in the shadow of the well, and wondering how best to extract my revenge, I heard footsteps. Gustave was approaching. His voice echoed as he tossed some crusts into the well, "Bread, whore. Don't die on me just yet. I haven't finished with you."

'Surprised at the lack of any sound or movement from the well, he leaned over the edge. A fatal mistake. I upended him and tossed him down into the darkness. I am strong you know,' she said, stretching her thin arms and tightening her biceps. 'He must have landed head first.

'I caught my breath in the darkness. In the distance the dogs barked and an owl flew through the night close to my face. Perhaps it was the soul of Alain. I followed it across the fields and was passing a barn when I heard sad human cries. I was not alone, there were other souls here in this Hades. The sobs and cries sounded like echoes of my own misery. I pulled back the plank that was holding the two barn doors together and out tumbled these two young angels. They clung to my skirt like babies. So, when the sun sank I had a lover and a horse. When it rose again, there was just me and these two.' Camille gestured towards Mirabelle and Nina. Both were sucking their thumbs, still nestled into Ursule. 'Together we stumbled out into the day, and we are still together, aren't we girls?' They nodded. 'They had been kept as slaves and fed on scraps. That's all they will tell me about M. Gustave.'

26

At the mention of his name both girls looked up anxiously at Camille. 'It's all right, girls, you are never going back. I will look after you.' Lowering her voice she continued. 'Their past is a mystery. He may have been their father, he may have been their whore-master. Now they are the reason I stay alive. I sometimes think that Alain wanted me to have them. Perhaps he struck a bargain as he left this world.'

Camille fell silent. Ursule too reflected on how these bargains might be struck.

After an interval during which Camille seemed to recover from her relived trauma, Ursule asked, 'What will happen to me now?'

'An appearance before the magistrate. Can anyone vouch for your good character?'

'I don't think so.'

'At all costs we must avoid your name being added to the Vile Book.' The twins nodded.

'Is that for vile people?'

'No. All prostitutes, all importuners, must be registered, but we will come up with something.'

Inspired, Camille clapped her hands together. 'Sisters,' she said. 'We need a diversion.' Mirabelle and Nina stood to attention waiting for their orders. 'Sudden death!' said Camille, clapping once more. Mirabelle started to pace around the cell in a distracted manner of a malfunctioning mechanical toy, kicking the straw out of her way. Nina followed her at a short distance. Mirabelle stopped as if struck by an unseen assailant and clutched her throat emitting an alarming series of gurgling sounds. Ursule rushed to intervene but Camille motioned for her to stay still. By now Mirabelle's eyes were on stalks. Her whole body contracted, her knees collapsed and she fell into a seizure, foaming at the mouth and drumming her feet on the ground. Ursule was certain she heard her head hit the stone floor. Meanwhile,

Nina, having embarked on an unearthly wail, knelt at her sister's side to loosen her clothing, then suddenly declared, 'She is dead! She is dead!' elongating the words across her deformed palate.

Camille observed the performance with an impresario's eye. 'Bravo,' she said. The sisters stood to attention once more and bowed from the waist. Ursule applauded.

'Our show will start at midnight,' declared Camille. 'There will be an audience of one, the turnkey, Jean-Claude. He will come alone, the others will be asleep. You must hide by the door, and when your chance comes, disappear and run like the wind.'

Camille kicked the straw into a corner. The twins did likewise. Camille told Ursule she must sleep if she was to enjoy the drama later.

Her straw nest made her think of Angélique and Pierre but her arms had not retained the heat from the sun, and her belly was lacking both the boiled eggs and the bread. The straw smelled not of the farm and the warmth of the beasts but of things stale and rank. She envied the twins and their syncopated breathing, lying entwined without a care in the world.

Camille tapped Ursule on the shoulder and she woke. 'The show starts in ten minutes,' she whispered. 'The scene is set. We're just waiting for the missing member of the cast.' It was quickly agreed that Ursule would crouch on the floor at the end of the bench nearest to the door. The moment she was in position, Camille let out a blood-curdling shriek, half banshee wail, half that of a mother finding that her firstborn had been strangled. Footsteps sounded in the corridor, keys jangled and the door opened. Before the unfortunate gaoler could close it behind him, Nina had thrown herself round his legs, pleading for his assistance. Meanwhile Mirabelle had embarked on her nightmarish circuit of the cell. When she stared directly at the gaoler and performed the salamander trick with her eyes, the attendant stood in slacked jaw astonishment and moved towards her without any idea of how best to intervene.

Ursule left the room on all fours and stayed in that position until she had passed the reception desk and reached the external door. She flung it open and ran into the night.

CHAPTER THREE

She only paused when taking one more breath seemed an impossibility. She had no idea where she was. There were no lights flickering from windows. In fact there were no windows in the buildings that towered above her. There were no gas lamps in the street. It was as if she had dropped off the edge of the world into a dark place where no human being had ever ventured. In the absence of any light she could only move forward by edging her way along the brick wall. For a moment she thought she was in that odd state between sleeping and wakefulness where it was just possible to manipulate your dreams, impose some order and steer them back into the world of everyday consciousness. She certainly wanted to leave behind the bizarre perception that she was some sort of fugitive who had just escaped from prison. Who were the odd creatures clinging to the edges of her memory? Twins? An acrobat? She had had similar dreams before when Gérard had been her gaoler.

The light swinging towards her was not, however, indicating the end of a tunnel that showed a way out of her dreams. It was being held by a dark figure in a cloak tapping a stick on the road as he approached. Ursule shrank against the wall and watched the nightwatchman pass. He was muttering to himself. The guttering cone of light thrown by his lantern showed that the buildings were boarded up on both sides. The whole area was awaiting demolition. Gérard had often sneered that what he called the old Paris was no longer fit for a businessman of his stature. 'Tear it down,' he would say. 'Tear it down.'

After walking for two blocks Ursule crossed into Place de Valois. A fire was burning in a gap where recently a building had stood. Several figures were hunched around its flames. Shivering from the trauma of the day and because of the plummeting temperature, Ursule moved closer. Like a small child waiting to be asked to join in someone else's game, she hovered on the fringes of the heat. One of the men beckoned for her to come closer. She acquiesced and joined the huddle. The others ignored her. The man offered her a drink from the bottle which he took from his greatcoat. She shook her head. 'No, thank you,' she said.

'What politeness. What demeanour!' commented her self-appointed host. A large man, he dragged her towards him and forced the bottle into her mouth. 'Don't be ungrateful. Don't refuse a beggar's grog!' Choking, she had no choice but to swallow the liquid that made her burn. The man tilted the bottle until the dregs slathered down her chin.

'Now show your gratitude, whore!' With one arm round her back he grabbed her breasts until she cried out with pain. She ducked beneath his arm and fled. The pounding in her ears drowned out her attacker's taunts and vitriolic abuse.

'Louis, Louis,' she shouted.

The days and nights that followed were bleak. With neither money nor clothes she joined the growing legion of Paris' dispossessed, and gravitated to the northern arrondissements where the factories spat flames into the sky and a degree of heat into the streets.

The country was at war. Posters depicting fat bellicose Prussians were on every lamp post. Boy soldiers in pristine uniforms stood in knots on street corners. As weapons had to be fashioned, the anvils rang and the smoke from myriad small forges watered the eyes of passers-by.

When she first found the hot air vent on the corner of Rue de la Paix and Rue des Dames it had already been colonised. Nevertheless she elbowed her way into the midst of the vagrants, most of whom had settled down for the night. Her need for warmth was stronger than any instinct of self-preservation. This impulse was in turn misinterpreted as a sort of courage by those of her new companions who were still awake, and she was grudgingly accepted.

She found an early champion in an elderly man who willingly moved his own heap of rags and blankets to one side so that she could squeeze in beside him. She thanked him and he smiled. She asked him his name and he produced a piece of paper with PASCAL written in bold letters. He touched his mouth and shrugged. Ursule nodded her understanding.

His lack of speech proved no obstacle to his ability to express his views and opinions. He indicated each of her new companions in turn, making it clear if they were trustworthy, habitually drunk or mad. His facial contortions when he pointed at a younger woman on the outer edge of the encampment, a series of grimaces supported by a mime during which he banged his fists together, left her in no doubt whom she should avoid.

He next rubbed his stomach and assumed such an exaggeratedly sad face that Ursule laughed despite her wish not to cause offense. Pascal smiled and then pulled an even more exaggerated version of the first expression. After a moment he assumed the pose of a hunchbacked beggar and held out his hands for money. Ursule understood. 'Is begging the only way?' she asked. Pascal's ambivalent expression, and the fact that he glanced towards the younger woman, indicated that there were other ways to make money. He licked his fingers before moving a log in the brazier until it spat out stars and sparks. He then held out both hands to her, clearly inviting her to speak.

'I have brought all this on myself. I was being kept in a nice apartment by a man who took me off my parents' hands, clothed me and gave me pocket money.' Pascal's quizzical expression suggested that he knew this was not the full story.

'Yes, he beat me, but I deserved it. He found the journal in which I had written about my young soldier.' Pascal nodded his encouragement. 'Since then I have been in prison. And escaped!' Pascal applauded. 'I never thought life would turn out like this. As a child I would run and play in the fields and have dreams. I loved the animals, I loved the darkness and the smell of the night. I would plan my future. I would marry and be happy.' Pascal gently touched her arm. 'More than anything else I want to find my soldier. He will look after me.'

In the silence that followed, Pascal took out a faded photograph and smoothed its creases with the back of his hand. The picture showed rows of vines stretching to a distant point. He traced a path through the vineyard with his finger, and then pointed animatedly to himself. Not fully understanding, but overcome with tiredness, Ursule watched as Pascal then shaped some of his rags into a pillow on which she gratefully lay her head and slept.

She had never known such hunger pangs. The end of the street was obscured by mist and the sounds of the city were muted. A news boy, probably disorientated, wandered past, urging non-existent pedestrians to buy his paper and read of Napoleon's latest military triumph.

Pascal indicated that Ursule should follow him. She walked behind him and noticed that his rheumatic limbs made him sway like a matelot. As they moved towards the commercial centre, she became ever more conscious of her torn clothes. Their progress was hampered by innumerable sullen shopkeepers depositing their garbage on the streets. Ursule's stomach heaved as the rank smell of offal from the fleshers mingled with the rancid stink of skin offcuts from the tanners. Dark liquids sluiced across the paving stones.

Pascal had chosen the route carefully so that they were always just ahead of a cart collecting the waste. When he took too long rummaging through a promising heap of scraps and rotting food, the cart would catch them up. The horses tossed their heads as if sharing the disdain of their masters. A squat workman threatened them with his shovel. 'Human vermin, human shit, it's all the same to us. We can take you now, or take you dead.'

Pascal growled but persisted until he had retrieved a large coat from a heap spilling into the gutter. He draped the new acquisition around Ursule's shoulders and shook a fist at the squat man who wanted the coat for himself. Next he darted into an alley and re-emerged with a misshapen loaf. He rubbed it against his sleeve to remove traces of a dark coloration. Ursule stuffed the bread into her mouth.

Ursule followed Pascal to what was presumably his preferred begging pitch in the shadow of Pont Neuf. The pigeons reluctantly left the parapet as the newcomers established themselves. It was soon obvious however that begging together was not going to prove successful as the sight of an old man next to a pretty young girl merely provoked the passing bankers and merchants to a feast of innuendo. Ursule said she would set out on her own. Pascal mimed his heartache and extracted a promise from her that she would return to the camp later.

Initially Ursule had some success, and several small coins soon nestled in her palm. It was obvious though that older men hoped that her acceptance of a few sous was a precursor to another, more carnal transaction. When she shook her head, indicating that the exchange only worked one way, they would threaten her, or, as happened on one occasion, shake her violently.

As Ursule wandered, seeking a new patch, she made the mistake of stopping outside a flesher's in Rue Turbigo.

She stood open-mouthed in front of the fat hares hanging skewered through the neck, their pelts still sleek and their eyes still unglazed. On the slab was a haunch with white veins of fat. Adjacent was the offal, snaking and twisted into plaits, its dark earthy smell filling the shop. Lorraine sausages, the size of a child's forearms, linked into a giant's necklace. She shivered at the unwanted association and she moved her gaze to the meats.

The cold delicacies had been arranged in order of size: pale Boulogne links swung next to their smaller blood-red relatives from Salon which in turn nudged the finer herb-filled delicacies from Bretagne.

By now her head was spinning and her stomach ached as if she too had been skewered. Perhaps she should, after all, go with a man into an alley and give him what he wanted in exchange for money. The trouble was that the precise nature of what this man might want eluded her. She could choose a man who looked clean and friendly. After all, she now had proof in Louis that not all men were obsessive and violent. Ursule realised that she had absolutely no idea what she would be expected to do. She could not see how the brutal coupling with le Géant was an activity that could possibly take place in an alley. Nor in fact did she associate le Géant's bestial grunting and thrusting with pleasure in any form. Why would a man, even if he was clean and kindly, wish to take part in such an act?

Eventually Ursule succumbed to a different temptation. For several days she had been fighting the urge to return to the garden where she had first seen Louis. There was just the slightest chance that he too was seeking her. Equally she had to face the prospect of being apprehended by the ogre who probably still lived in the same apartment.

She walked quickly for an hour or so keeping the Seine on her right. As she hurried, she rehearsed various scenarios in her head. They would fly into each other's arms, he would lift her off her feet and swing her round. He would be embarrassed and feign not to know her. He would smile apologetically and nod in the direction of the beautiful woman whom he had left for a moment to admire the view.

To minimise the possibility of being recognised by le Géant, she sank further into her newly acquired overcoat as she entered the gardens. If le Géant were to see her talking to her young soldier, he would rip his limbs from his sockets, of that there was no doubt. She looked around her and felt marginally disappointed that there were no women in black pushing the prams that may or may not have held babies.

When safely hidden by a tree, she looked up at the window of her former home, half expecting to see le Géant waving his fist at her. He wasn't there.

At that moment she felt a blow and braced herself for the worst. Instead of the worst she realised that a small child had careered into her in the vain pursuit of a hoop that was still wobbling its way down the slope. Seconds later the child's mother arrived. She shot a disapproving look at the woman hiding for some reason in a man's coat, rescued her mewling child and retrieved the hoop from a lilac bush.

The pounding in her heart increased when she saw Louis in his blue uniform with his back to her. For a moment she could neither breathe nor move. Then she ran towards him shouting his name. When she was within touching distance of her love, Louis turned round, intrigued by the noise. It wasn't Louis. It wasn't Louis. The man was twenty years older. His hair was white. He looked quizzically at the oddly attired young woman running towards him and instinctively rested his hand on the hilt of his sword. Ursule slowed and made as if she had recognised another man standing some yards further away.

The afternoon light was fading as Ursule slumped her way back down the hill. She glanced at the distant yellow pinpricks of the gas lamps incrementally lighting the affluent parts of the city. Couples who moments earlier had been walking with their arms around each other, took to walking separately as they approached the gates. A man ironically tipped his hat at her. At that moment she hated Paris, its coldness, its vileness.

When she woke stiff and cold in the morning she stretched her arms then hunched and released her shoulders. The space next to her was empty. Pascal had simply rolled up his rags and walked into the night. She sat up in case, for some reason, he had moved to the other side of the pitch but there was no sign of him. She hoped, with little real conviction, that he was on his way to the vineyard in the picture. Feeling bleak, she looked at the human shapes next to her. Fallen bodies covered in makeshift shrouds. An unwanted battle image. Louis lying in a field with his dead comrades. One of the bodies was sitting up facing her. It was Henriette, Pascal's bête noire.

Henriette rarely left the pitch during the day, preferring to clutch at the trousers of passing men, most, but not all of whom, swore at her and kicked her away. She was mouthing something at Ursule, her face contorted. Ursule looked away but the broken eye contact only served to further provoke Henriette whose curses were now audible.

'Sewer slut... garbage... young whore...'

She was striding across the bodies of the fallen, some of whom groaned as her feet trod on their ribs. She squared up to Ursule, hands on hips, then stooped to pick up Ursule's small bundle of possessions. Sneering, she hurled it down the street. Ursule pulled herself to her feet and stood with her face inches from Henriette's. For a moment they both stared at each other. Ursule saw jealousy and bitterness in the eyes of her adversary but her inspection was short-lived as the older woman spat in Ursule's face. Ursule spat back which was the last thing that Henriette expected. The two women grasped each other and tumbled into the cobbles like eager lovers unable to wait for the comfort of a bed. The other occupants of the space woke and watched the fight with total indifference.

'Where is your whore-master now?' rasped Henriette. 'Did you make love to the mute under his rags? Did you fumble with his cock? You should join him in his vineyard!' She threw back her head and laughed open-mouthed until Ursule punched her in the teeth. Spitting blood, Henriette retaliated by trying to squeeze the life out of her smaller opponent. Ursule, who had some experience of extricating herself from unwanted embraces, wriggled free while Henriette fought for her breath and fingered the space recently vacated by her two remaining teeth.

Ursule quickly retrieved her bundle, and as she ran down the street felt through the cloth for the rounded edges of the journal. It was still there. She felt something else through the cloth. Opening the draw strings she took out two gold coins. She quickly replaced them lest someone was watching her. Pascal must have put them there. She felt disbelief that the old man could have had such a fortune, and even greater disbelief that she should be the beneficiary of his unsuspected generosity. It had been a long time since fortune, in any shape or form, had smiled on her. Suddenly the day felt less cold. She needed clothes and she needed somewhere to live.

Still wrapped in swathes and wisps of hope, she started to climb towards Montmartre. She would seek lodgings in the north of the city. The district was busy with the incomers displaced by the demolition and rebuilding of central Paris. It should be a good place to be anonymous.

She walked for several hours, holding on tightly to the coins and the small dream that she might be able to take back some control over her life. At Avenue Trudaine she passed a family with their possessions in a handcart. A saucepan poked its handle through a heap of clothes, a picture of the Virgin Mary nestled on top of bedding. The two children were taunting each other until their father stopped the cart to cuff both their heads. He abandoned his chastisement only when he saw that a precariously positioned wooden box was about to tumble into the street. The woman pulled her shawl tighter. Several soldiers passed in the opposite direction. They strode with an urgency sustained by patriotic thoughts of liberating France from Prussian tyranny. Louis was not in their number.

Grog shops grew ever more frequent. A fat drunkard stood in the street whistling and shouting obscene comments at any woman who passed by. He reserved his most graphic sexual invitation for Ursule who looked down and walked faster. The encounter brought le Géant to mind. She felt cold once more. Le Géant could be in any of the drinking dens, holding court among his retinue of fawning sycophants, bemoaning the evils of unfaithful women and extolling the joys of revenge. She made a point of walking in the shadow of the cart whenever she saw that they were about to pass another tavern.

She saw a line of clothes stretched between a grog den and a shop selling brushes. A thin woman beseeched Ursule to stop and buy. 'I have four children to feed and a wastrel of a husband.' The smell of drink was overpowering. Ursule chose a camisole and a faded dress. They would do. The woman's obsequious gratitude suggested to Ursule that she had overpaid, but it didn't matter. Why should she be the

39

only recipient of good fortune that day? She walked into an alley and stepped out of her torn and now badly stained dress. As she stood balanced on one leg she realised she was not the only woman in a state of dishabille in that narrow place. Mercifully the lovers to her left were too preoccupied to notice an intruder. She decided her over-large coat looked acceptable now that her lower legs were covered. She pirouetted in front of the still delighted vendor who clapped her approval at the transformation.

'Are there cheap lodgings nearby?' asked Ursule.

'If you can live in a cupboard try M. Barroux, 17, Chemin des Boeufs. He's ancient but harmless.'

The building smelled of damp and decay. The narrow staircase spiralled its way upwards through the pitch black. On the top landing Ursule groped her way until she found what could have been a door. She knocked and waited until a sliver of vertical light suggested that someone was approaching. On the threshold stood the smallest man Ursule had ever seen. Initially M. Barroux assumed Ursule was his daughter, greeted her with tears of gratitude in his eyes, and then gently berated her for not having visited her old father for so long. Despite the confusion the transaction was speedily concluded and the tiny man opened another tiny door on the landing that revealed the cupboard about which she had been warned.

The rent for her tiny room would leave her little for food but Ursule felt safe in the cramped space. From the single window she could see two windmills, now abandoned and rapidly disappearing under vegetation and stray vines. If she concentrated, the city ceased to exist, only a vista of fields that could have surrounded her childhood farm.

No sooner had she lain down on the tiny bed than M. Barroux knocked on her door and asked her to join him for a glass. Although tired, she acquiesced and joined him at the hearth that still emitted an aura of warmth despite the fire having died. He poked at the embers with his stick, only succeeding in raising a small cloud of dust that settled on her shoes.

'Rumours of a siege,' he announced by way of a greeting. 'They say Napoli took a hell of a beating at Sedan. A chest wound some say, others tell of him hiding in a barn and crying like a child. The sheep and cattle are being herded into the city. It won't end well, mark my words. Do you speak any German? They are recruiting spies, you know.' Ursule shook her head.

As the dusk filtered into the room M. Barroux gestured animatedly while expounding his ever more elaborate theories of war.

Frequently the final half of his sentences eluded him. He stared at the cold hearth before returning to a conversation he had not had in the first place, addressing Ursule as if she were the spectre of his dead wife.

'Why did you have to leave me? Why?' He seemed genuinely affronted as he resurrected the details of his wife's death. 'You said you were fine, but I heard you stifling your cough; why did you deceive me? You said it was the rheumatics, you said it was the rheum. You were lying all along, you should be punished.'

He waved an admonitory finger at Ursule. 'You were scheming all the while with Masson, the coffin maker, lining his pockets behind my back. You didn't have the decency to say goodbye. You just went away with neither a word nor a note.' With a final shake of his head he fell asleep. Ursule took a blanket from the bed in the corner and placed it round his shoulders.

Despite its smallness her own room was cold. She put her arms round herself for comfort and warmth. She moved her hands down her sides in slow reassuring movements as Louis might have done had he been there. She climbed into bed moving the bedclothes to one side with her foot which meant that she did not have to relinquish the hold on her sides. She lay under the full weight of her young lover. He was immeasurably lighter than le Géant. She felt his warm breath on her neck. She couldn't make out his words but they were soft and caring. 'Tell me that again,' she said. But he didn't. There was just silence apart from a drunken burst of song from the street below.

Unable to sleep, she took out the journal. She must add to it and not make her sadness worse by lingering over the drawings of Louis. She waited as her crayon hovered over a new page. She had no idea what she would draw and watched bemused as the crayon, seeming to make its own decision, sketched a watery sun, the silhouette of a church tower, and, in the foreground, tall vines in whose midst she saw the stooped figure of a small man who was clearly smiling.

CHAPTER FOUR

A black locomotive had stopped on the viaduct at the end of the road. Steam leaked from every orifice, an animal in its death throes emptying itself of its life force. Young soldiers, boys really, excited at the prospect of joining battle, hung from the windows of the first carriage, waving their caps and making obscene gestures at Ursule and her workmates standing outside the laundry. Ursule's stomach lurched as she thought of Louis.

Young Félicité returned the gestures, which provoked the volunteers to a semaphore of obscene lunges and thrusting, leering and pouting in a way that reminded Ursule of the gargoyles that clung to the sides of Notre Dame. Giselle raised her dress and improvised a cancan down the edges of the street until one of the older women cuffed her ears.

With the security of somewhere to live, Ursule had eventually found work at Madame Gascogne's wash house. A huge two-storey building, it was the cathedral of all wash houses. Women would rest their baskets on the upper balcony and look down onto the steamy landscape below. It was the only wash house in all of Paris to use the new-fangled mangle imported at great expense from America. Only the most trustworthy of staff were allowed to turn the handle. The rest toiled in the lower stalls that resembled cattle pens. There were rumours that some foreigner had invented a steam-operated mangle but that seemed extremely unlikely. Madame Gasgogne ruled by tyranny. At any moment she could emerge from a cloud of steam like a Wagnerian valkyrie and summarily dismiss the nearest hapless worker just to encourage the others.

During the day Ursule's eyes ran constantly and the sweat stained her chemise. Her main function was to empty the vats of boiling water into the troughs while the women good-naturedly nagged her for her tardiness. Rolling up their sleeves, they would settle old scores and beat their husbands' shirts with more enthusiasm than the task demanded. 'Here's for your drunkenness, here's for sneaking into the wench's bed behind my back. Here's for being a useless layabout. Here's for spending every last sou I earn on absinthe...'

Eventually the locomotive cleared its lungs and attempted to move. Its wheels skidded on the rail sending it into further paroxysms before the troop train slowly dragged itself off the viaduct.

As Félicité slouched back inside, Ursule looked up and down the street, knowing that it was only a matter of time before Gérard discovered her place of work. She jumped as a building at the far end of the road fell in on itself and disappeared under a cloud of dust. Haussmann's relentless march through the bones of old Paris showed little sign of abating.

Her moment of reflection was shattered by shouts from the women who had already returned to their business of rinsing clothes and exchanging gossip. Madame Gasgogne, built like one of the oxen she claimed to have tended in an earlier life, had Benoît, the water boy, squealing under one of her massive arms. Her sodden, now semi-transparent clothes bore witness to the heinous crime perpetuated by the fourteen-year-old. Benoît, who had a reputation for idling and was frequently suspected of stealing undergarments, had tripped and emptied a large vat of cold water

44

over the valkyrie. Drenched and outraged in equal measure, the huge woman was now intent on drowning her captive. Benoît for his part squirmed and thrashed his legs as his head was held under the soapy surface of the rinsing trough.

Initially the other women howled with mirth but Ursule was growing increasingly anxious as seconds passed and Benoît's attempts to escape became more and more subdued. Madame Lerat, the bookkeeper, had left her office and was haranguing Madame Gascogne but to little effect. 'Let the boy go. You've punished him enough!'

Madame Gascogne was unaware of the blows inflicted by the other women who were now equally alarmed. She seemed to be in a trance, her eyes staring into another place. Her arms were locked rigid, and the bubbles from Benoît's last snatched breath had stopped breaking the surface.

Ursule, realising that a more drastic intervention was warranted, stopped punching, and instead bit into her adversary's forearm. At first Madame Gascogne seemed oblivious to the fact that someone was now firmly attached to her arm by the teeth. Eventually though she howled with pain, relinquished her grip and released Benoît who collapsed on the wet floor gasping for breath. Rubbing her forearm from which the blood streamed, she scanned the faces searching for her assailant. Seeing Ursule, she launched herself at her new victim. At the last moment Ursule took avoiding action and stepped aside. This sudden sleight of foot caused Madame Gascogne to collide face first into the side of the metal bath. She slumped to the floor unconscious.

At first no one moved. 'Is she dead?' asked Bernadette, who rarely spoke on account of her southern accent that provoked endless mocking imitation.

'Smelling salts!' shouted Madame Lerat.

'This isn't a salon for posh folk,' said Félicité who fetched a pail of bleach, soaked her 'kerchief in its noxious contents and thrust it under Madame Gascogne's nose.

Startled into consciousness, Madame Gascogne dragged herself into a sitting position. Ursule stood waiting for the inevitable storm which was not long in coming and which, predictably, broke with full force. 'You animal, you blood-sucking fiend from hell! I run a good laundry, I don't want the police closing me down on account of a dangerous lunatic like yourself. How *dare* you bite me?' She moved towards Ursule who backed away.

The other women, now fearful that their part in the fracas would also bring punishment down on their heads, murmured in agreement.

'Troublemaker,' pronounced Bernadette, now confident that she spoke for them all and would not be mocked. Ursule, knowing full well that there was nothing she could say by way of exoneration, hastily retrieved her shawl from the communal bench, and without making eye contact with the other women, left the laundry for the last time.

Gérard, le Géant, had his snitches. Money no longer changed hands, the threat of emasculation always worked. It was well known that the innkeeper at Limoges had never again satisfied his wife after Gérard, suspecting that his beer had been watered, had grabbed the Jew by the groin and twisted until the man fainted.

It was Vincent who told him where Ursule now worked. Vincent had lived well making clocks until his left hand was lopped off by the sword wielded by a Mexican soldier during a minor colonial skirmish. Vincent hoped that he might be rewarded for information about Ursule's whereabouts. But no, le Géant threw back his own tumbler of absinthe, and then finished Vincent's for good measure. He wiped his lips on his sleeve, belched and strode into the street.

He knew Madame Gascogne, at least they had lain together at some point, if not communicated, as their conversation had consisted solely of grunts of varying intensity.

As he turned the corner into Rue Corneille, he summoned a vague, satisfying memory of Madame Gascogne's large ample body, not like that of the skinny runt Ursule. Unsurprisingly, given her trade, she smelt of soap, something of a novelty among the women le Géant normally bedded.

As he passed les Caves, one of his pimps took the pipe out of his mouth and nodded a greeting. Le Géant ignored him, preoccupied now with a fantasy infinitely more satisfying than the recollection of Madame Gascogne's breasts. Revenge. How had she dared to draw blood from his cheeks with her childish bitten nails, and then wriggle away from his grasp and flee into the night? No one ever treated le Géant that way, certainly not a woman, not that she merited the term, a mewling vixen perhaps, a woman, no.

His entry into the wash house would be spectacular, there was no doubt about that. After all, he had a reputation and would not tolerate half of Paris laughing at him behind his back. They would talk of this night for a long time to come. He would turn the baths red with Ursule's blood.

He was close and could already make out the lighted window and hear raised voices. He would soon give them reason to raise their voices. The door was open to let out the heat. He grasped either side of the door with his hands, his head brushing against the lintel, and stared into the steam. The shapes slowly assumed human forms. 'Where is the skinny whore who dared raise a hand to Gérard?'

He stormed into the crowded room, kicking over the full buckets placed in a row by Benoît who had eventually recovered from his near death-by-drowning.

He went to the open oven door and grabbed the red hot poker. 'Bring her to me and I will brand her treacherous little arse. She will never sit again. Bring her to me, witches, or I will do the same to you!' One of the younger girls squealed with her apron at her mouth and retreated into the back room.

Madame Gascogne emerged from the turmoil. 'Ah Gérard, it is you. I see your temper has not improved. If it's Ursule you want, I sent the vicious little cow on her way.' She held out her arm to show the bite marks. Unimpressed, le Géant grabbed at the lines of washing as if he was picking fruit and flung the assorted clothes into the faces of the women who had not managed to escape. With a final roar, he turned on his heels and left. Fortunately, Vincent had also told him where Ursule might be living.

Barroux was waiting for her at the top of the stairs. The last thing she wanted to do was talk but the old man was insistent. His hearth was cold and his spirits low.

'The city is closed,' he confided. 'The gates are shut. The Prussians found some boys playing in the fields beyond the forts and cut their heads off. They put them on stakes.' He grimaced, staring at the line of heads. 'It's true. I read it in the newspaper. No woman will be safe if we capitulate. Mark my words. I saw the placards today. "Starvation before Rape". Cowards are paying to be smuggled out of the city. They say there are bodies in the Seine with their tongues cut out. Mark my words, now that the Prussians have put a ring of steel around the city the butchers will round up the cats and dogs. Pampered pets will disappear from the posh apartments. The strays will hunt in packs for protection from the carving knife. We will eat like beggars. Keep an eye on your children or their flesh will fill the bellies of the aldermen. There's no escape, you know...'

With Barroux sunk into his own bleak world, Ursule retreated to her bed where she pulled her shawl over her nose against the cold. She was comforted by the warm breath on her face. She was a child again in the Normandy farmhouse of her childhood. Her parents were asleep in the adjacent room. Tomorrow she and Angélique were going to gather berries then lie in their straw house and have a

48

feast. Perhaps they should invite Pierre. What if he kissed her again? Angélique would be jealous and the day would be ruined.

'Quick! They're coming! The Prussians!'

Ursule woke up. Someone was coming, of that there was no mistake.

Opening the door onto the landing she peered down the ill-lit spiral of stairs. Several flights below she could hear le Géant abusing Eugène who was draped over the bannister complaining that his lungs were about to burst. He was trying to keep his voice down but the words 'Useless turd,' forced through clenched teeth, wafted towards her. Le Géant then threatened to hurl his breathless companion to his death if he didn't resume the climb.

Ursule ran back into M. Barroux's apartment, slamming the door behind her. This was a mistake she knew, it would alert her pursuers. Barroux rose to the occasion and, despite his lack of stature, moved a large chest beneath the small skylight. He urged her to reach her arms up and push against the pane of glass until it yielded and she could open it fully. He then placed a suitcase on top of the chest that enabled Ursule to haul herself through the aperture onto the flat part of the roof. She looked around her.

The chimney stacks were in silhouette. The moon was high and a cat brushed against her legs. She stepped past the first stack, noisily dislodging a slate as she did so, and ducked behind the next in line. The brickwork was warm and oddly comforting. As the night was still, the smoke wandered upwards in idle swathes. She placed her hand over her mouth to stop herself coughing. Despite the danger, she felt calm. Perhaps she was about to die, her brains dashed onto the street below. It would be quick. It didn't matter. As an alternative to contemplating her death, she chose to concentrate on the distant landscape of tiny lights and dark shapes. Happy distant summers lit by legions of fireflies were nothing compared to this. She thought too of her father outlined against the night, prodding his rake into the patchwork of glowing embers of burnt stubble.

The symmetrical lines of gas light traced the Grands Boulevards where the theatres and dance halls rang with gaiety, the more random lights marked the taverns and grog shops where people laughed, flirted, played cards and drank to forget tomorrow. Small pulses of flame revealed the forges and factories working through the night turning out steel that would become weapons and engines for the coming war.

A slowly moving line of dark shapes and light from a firebox showed the progress of another troop train clanking to the front. She thought of Louis and felt cold.

Someone was bellowing. She recognised the voice and took a step backwards. Ursule saw that the skylight was now barely visible, its place taken by the top half of le Géant's torso.

Completely stuck, he roared like an injured bull. His arms seemed unnaturally close to his shoulders as he tried to extricate himself. There had been times, although she had always felt guilty about them, when Ursule had lain in bed fantasizing about a moment exactly like this. She could easily retrieve the dislodged slate and slice it into his fat neck leaving him to bleed onto the roof.

Before she could pursue the thought further, he suddenly dropped from sight as if he had fallen through an executioner's trapdoor. She pictured Eugène hanging onto his legs, a small helpless sexton ringing church bells moments before the ropes snapped and he was crushed by a dome of falling bronze. But no, Eugène was next to appear in the skylight.

Ursule cowered closer to the chimney stack as the small angry man climbed onto the roof and started running from side to side looking for her. Eventually he stood on the edge of the roof and stamped his feet like a spoilt child. Once his tantrum had subsided, he returned to the aperture and lowered himself down. Ursule heard le Géant's angry voice trailing away as he presumably called off the search and left to find consolation in absinthe.

Barroux gave her brandy and cursed the Prussians for hounding the cream of French womanhood across the rooftops of the city. She explained that, sadly, she could no longer stay in her room and would have to find other accommodation.

'I will personally stick a bayonet up Bismark's arse if he sets foot in Paris.' Ursule watched as the old man mimed the act he described. 'I will crush his testicles in my fist! Sorry, Mademoiselle, but these things happen in war.' Finally his eyes closed and he lapsed into a dream which was, judging by his constant jerking and groaning, a continuation of the bellicose fantasies that had exhausted him in the first place. Ursule left some coins on the dresser, collected her few possessions, picked up the journal and left.

After crossing the Seine she plodded along the Rue de Rivoli. In the damp darkness someone touched the hem of her skirt. She walked faster to shake off the urchin wanting her attention. But he was not for shaking. In exasperation she stopped to give the child a piece of her mind when she recognised Benoît from the wash house.

'Mademoiselle Ursule,' he said, 'Why are you out walking on your own? It's not safe for a lady like you.'

'Oh, Benoît,' she said, 'it's good to see you. I trust you have not taken any more unwanted baths.'

'No Mademoiselle, but why are you here?'

'It's a long story and not a very happy one.'

'I think a man has made you unhappy and you have nowhere to stay.'

Ursule looked at Benoît as if for the first time. He was older than his years.

'I know somewhere better for you to sleep, come with me.'

Unable to think of a reason not to follow Benoît, she let herself be led through a warren of lanes and alleyways. At one point they both had to step over the body of a man sleeping in a position that suggested he had been crucified and nailed to the ground.

For a moment Benoît seemed unsure which direction to follow. He paused and looked over a small wall before proceeding with more certainty. Ursule recognised les Papillons, one of le Géant's preferred haunts. She hurried past but not before she had been critically appraised by a phalanx of lecherous men swaying their way into the tavern.

Ursule recognised the outskirts of Montmartre. After more twists and turns, Benoît led her down a lane that ended at a locked gate which led into a courtyard. Benoit leaned against the heavy gate while poking his fingers into the lock. It yielded and they walked down the side of the building plastered with gaudy shreds of old posters. At the far end he repeated his locksmith skills and ushered Ursule into a small dark storeroom that smelled of sweat and perfume. Benoît pushed her gently downwards until she sank into a large heap of soft material.

'Curtains,' he said by way of an incomplete explanation. 'I will leave you now, Mademoiselle, but you are safe here.' He squeezed her hand and slid out of the door.

Overcome with exhaustion and a sense that she was powerless to chart her own course, or make meaningful choices, Ursule drifted into a sleep pleasantly punctuated by snatches of song and gales of laughter that bled through a wall.

An accordion was playing somewhere. She thought of Camille's hurdy-gurdy man and hoped that the acrobatic woman and her girls were safe. She thought of the travelling players that would come to her own village. Her mother had expressly forbidden her from mixing with the gypsies and vagrants but she and Angélique had once sneaked down to the river where multicoloured tents covered the field. There they found their own pied piper, an old man with a penny whistle who was leading the children over a magical obstacle course of his own choosing. 'Perhaps we will be taken to the land of the fairies,' squealed Angélique. Ursule had certainly hoped so.

CHAPTER FIVE

'You! Strumpet! Can you sew?' Ursule took a moment to remember where she was, and then focused on the silhouette of a large man who had entered the room by a door she hadn't noticed.

'Is there no one in this godforsaken city who can sew?' His question was hypothetical and was not specifically addressed to Ursule. His intonation was melodramatic as befitted one of the new breed of theatrical impresarios who were increasingly colonising this part of Paris.

'I can sew,' said Ursule, dragging her hand through her hair.

The stranger looked down and feigned total surprise on seeing a prone woman several feet beneath him. 'Then get your backside in here, for God's sake!'

Blinking in the strong light, Ursule was propelled down a long corridor and into a large room crammed with whom, she rightly assumed, were actresses in various states of distress and indeed undress. Bizarrely at least two of the women were perched on a narrow bench holding up their skirts and screaming for no apparent reason.

'The rat's dead, you stupid women! Get off that bench and calm yourself.' Calm did not seem a realistic option for most of the women present.

'Pierrot throttled it with his bare hands. Look, it's lying there in the corner. Pierrot, show them.' This last instruction was a great mistake as a smirking Pierrot lifted the rat by its tail and advanced towards the actresses, all of whom surpassed their previous levels of hysteria.

Meanwhile the impresario, addressed as le Patron by the women who were still capable of semi-rational speech, approached Ursule with outstretched arms holding a tumble of silk skirts and underwear. 'They are all torn,' he explained. 'The silly trollops stood on them as they took fright at the sight of our poor M. Ratty.'

He ushered Ursule into a side room and pointed out the sewing implements contained in a wicker basket. 'Sophie hasn't been seen since yesterday, lying drunk in some stew I imagine. Useless, useless woman.'

In the absence of any further explanation, Ursule assumed that she was now a temporary seamstress in the employ of the Théâtre des Variétés which was the name emblazoned across the framed posters on the walls.

In many ways, these were some of the best days Ursule had known since her arrival in Paris. Martine, also a young seamstress, suggested at the end of work that they venture together onto the new boulevards. They had linked arms and sung their way to the Jardin du Luxembourg.

They grew quiet and slowed their pace as they absorbed the transformation that had occurred in such a short space of time. A long line of carriages stretched as far as the eye could see. Martine had approached one of the horses and patted its head until the coachman woke from his sleep and threatened her with his whip. They had both recoiled and scurried to the other side of the pavement.

A small man in a frock coat approached and stood for a moment appraising them. Fingering his moustache, he approached Ursule. 'You, Mademoiselle, come with me, you are the chosen one. You can bring your pretty friend as well. My purse will stretch to two of you.'

Without thinking, Ursule slapped the man across the face, knocking his hat to the ground where it lay in a fringe of ginger hair. Apoplectic, the man bent down to rescue his wig which he held reverentially as if it were a dead pet. Hysterical with laughter, Ursule was grabbed by her friend and bundled down the street. Eventually they had to stop for breath which, on regaining, was instantly spent again on unrestrained gales of mirth.

Geneviève, a large Negress, had also taken to Ursule. She treated her like a daughter and insisted that her fellow actresses address her adopted child with a degree of deference when they approached her for repairs to their costumes.

Initially her fingers were slow and she made mistakes but gradually the old skills returned. Her mother would have been proud of her.

The women would become increasingly demanding as the hour approached for them to perform. Yvette, a dwarf whose features were obscured by a full mask of make-up, stamped her feet in agitation as Ursule laboured over a seam for Racine, her first customer.

'Be patient!' urged Geneviève, 'You look like a child wanting a piss, wait your turn.'

Ignoring the older woman, Yvette snatched the unfinished garment from Ursule's hands and threw it on the floor. By way of retaliation Racine delivered a hefty slap that lifted Yvette off her feet

'You shrunken toad! I will fart in your face later!' Yvette dropped the chemise, folded her arms and pouted. She fully appreciated the horror of the threat as her main function during the afternoon performance was to hide under Racine's bustle and emerge during a scene of tender courtship.

The days passed quickly. Ursule enjoyed working to a backcloth of gossip, rumour, hysterics, laughter and the occasional fight between the women, which invariably ended in tearful reconciliation.

Sometimes she would sneak into the theatre and watch the spectacle from the back of the stalls where the smoke would sting her eyes. She had enjoyed, but not understood, the last tableau that she had witnessed. Several of the actresses were waving happily from a large wicker basket held by thick ropes suspended from the ceiling. They led the audience in a raucous chorus of *La Marseillaise* before Mademoiselle Monferrand, the leading lady, having peered over the edge of the basket, embarked on the solo ditty that Ursule had heard being rehearsed many times:
'See how the plain is glistening
With bright helmets in a mass
Impalement would be dreadful
On those spikes of polished brass.'

On cue, one of her fellow travellers clapped a hand to her brow and squealed, 'Alas! We are losing height. Soon we will be ravished by those Prussian spikes. We will have to throw the ballast overboard!'

'But we have no ballast. What can we do?'

A red-faced man in the stalls staggered to his feet and bawled, 'Get your clothes off and throw them out!' Having heard the one cue they were waiting for, the occupants of the basket proceeded to divest themselves of petticoats and undergarments that they tossed into the baying crowd. To prevent a riot, the proceedings were brought to a close by a judicious lowering of the curtain.

'Where do you sleep, child?' asked Geneviève, stepping out of her costume and untying her hair at the end of a long day.

'In the curtain room,' said Ursule.

'Cold and flea-ridden. There is a better place. With a bed.'

Geneviève led the way into the deserted theatre space

and onto the stage from which the props had not yet been cleared. A horse's head made of papier maché, discarded items of underwear, a marionette that Ursule had to look at for a second time to ensure it was not, in fact, a small emaciated child, and a carpet of visiting cards which had earlier rained down from the boxes like rotating sycamore leaves, each a testimony to lustful expectations.

Ursule's eyes smarted under the impact of cigar smoke that still clung to every surface and insinuated itself into every uncovered pore. Geneviève stepped down from the stage and pushed against one of the front boards revealing a large space used for storing costumes. In the far corner there was indeed a bed. They both crawled into the space. 'For special performances,' she explained. 'When the magistrates are distracted and the punters pay, we entertain them with scenes of sin and voluptuousness.' Ursule nodded as if she understood.

The total darkness of her den nurtured her that night and the many that followed. She dreamed of Angélique and their improvised home in the hay. She dreamed of her bed in the farmhouse and heard once again the murmur of her parents' conversation in the room below.

One night she dreamed of Louis, heard his quiet approach, heard him push open the tiny cupboard door, felt his warm body as he snuggled next to her, felt his warm breath, felt his hand on her breasts, her stomach, and then felt the joy as he explored her.

But something was very wrong. He was too insistent, too rough, he didn't speak, there were no endearments. No words were whispered. She had not at that point ever lain with Louis but she knew this was not him. She woke in a sweat, and this time, derived little comfort from the dark. Her heartbeat was audible as she opened the cupboard and peered into the gloom of the empty theatre. Her sense of logic told her it had been a nightmare, she was sure of it.

She moved her hands down her body as if checking for unwanted signs of her nocturnal visitor.

When she reported for duty in the crowded dressing room she could not concentrate. Geneviève noticed her inattention and gently chided her. Ursule redoubled her efforts to make the buttonhole wider but only succeeded in jabbing the needle into the palm of her hand. She yelped in pain. Geneviève approached and put an arm across her shoulder. 'Le Patron?' she asked.

Neither Ursule nor any other of the women were troubled again by le Patron's advances. His Germanic origins had come to the attention of the authorities who were determined to root out anyone with a vaguely Prussian-sounding name on the assumption that they were spying for the enemy.

When the Garde Nationale burst into the stalls during a particularly affecting and sentimental death scene, the audience assumed they were actors and hooted with laughter. Geneviève lowered the handkerchief that moments before had been mopping her fevered brow, and watched bemused as the soldiers apprehended the unfortunate Wilhelm who was playing the minor role of a eunuch. His protests only served to further fuel the hysteria. The auditorium was filled with shouts of bravo and the many hats that were thrown triumphantly into the air.

As the soldiers manhandled Wilhelm down the aisle, his breeches slipped. One of the audience stood and roared, 'He's no eunuch! He's got balls the size of a stallion!' The soldiers and their captive left to the patriotic strains of *La Marseillaise*. The cast succumbed to a collective fit of the vapours. Ursule had looked up from her sewing and wondered what the commotion was.

Yvette was the first to become unwell. She convulsed, clutched her stomach and ran from the room, but not fast enough. The sick dripped through the fingers of the hand she had placed over her mouth in a failed attempt to stop the inevitable.

'Hideous dwarf! Clean that up, and open a window! What a smell,' shouted Claudette, fanning the air immediately in front of her nose. The others followed suit.

The following morning five of the women failed to show. Pierrot, who had assumed control after Wilhelm's unfortunate capture, was incandescent with rage. 'Lazy whores, if you stayed away from the gin you might manage to turn up. What am I supposed to do? The lunchtime crowd are in already.'

Sure enough, coarse male laughter was audible from the adjacent auditorium. Someone was impersonating a bull. Others joined in.

'Listen to that farmyard!' said Pierrot, 'They will burn the place down if they don't get what they came for. You!' he said pointing at Ursule. 'Put that dress on and get out there with the others.'

Ursule protested but to little effect. 'Do what I tell you or you will never get another sou from me.'

'Do what he says,' said Geneviève, holding the dress open for Ursule to step into. 'Just stay at the back and keep your eyes on me. When I kick, you do the same.'

Ursule stood mute as one of the other women rouged her cheeks and pulled back her hair. The woman then thrust a hand down the front of Ursule's dress and tugged her breasts until they almost spilled out.

'Give them what they want, duckie! Show them your tits and they won't mind if you dance like a cow.'

Petrified, Ursule let herself be pulled onto the stage. Blinded by the gaslights, deafened by the music and the lustful baying from the crowd, she staggered behind the line of women.

She recognised *La Marseillaise* as the tune blared from

the pit. She tried to sing along but the words wouldn't come. She then stepped on the trailing dress of the dancer in front. To the unrestrained delight of the hooting crowd, they both tumbled to the floor. Ursule had completely removed the other woman's dress, and was herself lying on her back with her legs in the air. The audience became hysterical in their appreciation of the mishap and the sight of more flesh than they had anticipated even in their most carnal of imaginings.

Back on her feet, Ursule tried to rejoin the line of dancers while the recently defrocked woman shot into the wings to a mounting crescendo of raucous approval.

Stricken with panic, Ursule felt her legs become heavy. The music became a slur of sound, and she thought she was about to pass out. Gasping for air, she raised her eyes above the blinding halo of gas light and, in that small second in which time stood still, she realised she was staring at le Géant.

She could see the man, his face contorted with spittle on his lips, leaning out of the nearest box as if trying to pluck her from the stage.

He was holding some sort of cudgel. She realised that in his rage he had torn one of the arm rests from his seat and was about to launch it in her direction. In slow motion the missile tumbled though the air and connected with the head of the dancer standing next to her. Felled like an ox, Ursule's companion sank groaning to the floor. The crowd had never had such fun. Money was thrown, hats were tossed onto the stage. Commotion and chaos threatened the very fabric of the building.

Le Géant was no longer there. He had left the box.

Ursule ran through the curtain that Pierrot had wisely lowered lest a riot ensue. Knocking over a heap of black canes prepared for the next turn, then ploughing a direct path through a wall of top hats, she left the building.

Two elderly women in widow's weeds tut-tutted as Ursule ran past clutching the folds of her stage dress and weeping tears of black mascara. They looked behind to see whatever monster was pursuing her, shook their heads and continued their disapproving gossip.

CHAPTER SIX

Ursule turned into Rue du Faubourg Montmartre and ducked down beneath the line of parked cabs and bored horses. She skidded momentarily on the sewage leaking from a drain, crossed Boulevard de Clichy and turned into the Cemetery.

She knew that le Géant was following her. She flattened herself against a large sarcophagus and looked sideways towards the entrance. There he was. He looked even larger in his state of rage, flailing his arms as if they were sickles. He kicked a vase of faded flowers over a low wall and knocked angrily on a tilting merchant's tomb, insisting that the dead resident surrender Ursule into his care. He peered into each grilled window to see if she was lurking inside.

A small group of mourners moved to harangue him for his lack of respect then had second thoughts once they saw the size of the man they were about to berate. Frustrated, le Géant grabbed a large stone Madonna by the throat, threatening dismemberment if she did not tell him where the slut was hiding. A flock of pigeons took to the air.

Still clutching her dress, Ursule ran down one of the narrow avenues. Perhaps it was the sound of her shoes on the cobbles, perhaps he saw movement out of the corner of his eye, but he saw her. Uttering a sound that was neither quite a triumphant roar nor a shout of discovery, he took a diagonal path towards Ursule, then stood facing her across a three-deep phalanx of tombs and monuments. If he tried to take the direct route, she would be able to put more ground between them both. But seeing no alternative, he straddled the first obstacle, a wrought iron railing surrounding an elevated grave, then paused to see if his quarry was still in grabbing distance. There was no sign of her. He vaulted over the next tomb in his path, knocking over several framed pictures of its dead occupant.

Ursule was now standing in an adjacent avenue. He moved one way and she the other. A macabre game of chess that le Géant was determined to win. He had no choice but to run to the next intersection and then take a right angle which should put them on the same path.

When he reached the spot where she had been standing moments previously, she had gone. Shaking his fist at the unseen God who was normally addressed with more deference in this hallowed place, he let fly a torrent of abuse.

'Where is the justice here? Why won't you deliver to me that whore from hell, that painted harridan, that adulterous fornicator? Come out and face me!' This last was addressed not at God but at Ursule, who, having not the slightest intention of complying with this particular demand, had kept her head down and ran towards the adjacent intersection. Stepping into the next row she found her face inches from that of a stone angel. 'Louis,' she murmured, 'help me!'

Le Géant was getting ever closer to her place of concealment. There was nowhere else to hide. If she ran, he would see her, if she stayed, she would be discovered. To her left was a horizontal marble tomb with a full-sized man in pious pose lying on top. She quickly joined him and assumed the same pose. Her dress mimicked the white of the marble. She heard his fast breath as le Géant approached. Within seconds he stood muttering with his back to her. She could have leaned forward and touched him. There was something painfully familiar about this unwanted proximity. How many nights had she lain inches from the same man, not daring to move lest the very act of breathing provoke him into violence? In an instant he was off and running again.

Ursule, knowing full well that he would eventually retrace his steps, rolled away from her stone companion and crawled several yards towards a small sepulchre. It was tilting and subsidence had loosened its iron door.

She prised it open and crawled into the fetid, damp interior. She curled into a ball and waited for what she felt was her inevitable discovery.

Ursule was fully aware of the irony that she was in the best possible location to be murdered. She wondered if the original occupant was buried beneath her, or if his bones were piled at the other side of the dark space. Who was he? Would he welcome the company or would he resent her intruding into his last resting place? Would he molest her just as le Géant had done? Was she going to be victimised in death as she had been in life?

CHAPTER SEVEN

Louis cowered in the dark. For what seemed like hours, the ground had been shaken by the horses thundering past in a nightmare of flesh, hunger, strings of saliva and panic. An endless tableau of frightened beasts, many wounded or blinded. Some of them still carried their dead riders flopping from side to side, all their bones now broken and not just those smashed by Prussian axes. Some of the horses trailed bayonets like grotesque souvenirs from a carnival. Others had fallen onto their front legs and had died where they stood, providing additional obstacles for those still alive.

This was surely their revenge on those hungry soldiers who had feasted on the flesh of fallen horses. Louis had watched bemused as Marceau, a labourer from Chenonceau, had thrust his knife into the bloated belly of a dead beast. He was no flesher and the blood and guts had tumbled out over his hands. He held them out for inspection, as if expecting his fellow soldiers to rush to his aid, gently chide him for his lack of expertise, and clean him with fresh towels as his mother would have done.

It was Léonard who knew how to slaughter. He moved his fingers expertly along the flank, and having felt for the end of the ribcage, plunged his knife in up to the hilt and dragged it along until he had carved out a significant portion of meat. A surprising lack of blood this time, thought Louis.

The men had fallen ill during the night, clutching their

sides and vomiting until they were emptier than they had been before slaughtering the horse. Even then Louis had wondered if eventually the men would eat each other.

He was uncertain how much more battering the small hut could take from the dispossessed herd. Several of the planks in the wall had already sprung open letting in sufficient light for him to see more clearly the relentless torrent of wild horses. Their way out of the valley was blocked by the mountain of abandoned equipment on one side, munition wagons, gun carriers, carts confiscated from obdurate peasants, and the river on the other, roaring unceasingly through the ravine.

Some horses had launched themselves into the void above the tumbling waters, falling in graceful slow motion, fighting against the tide before surrendering without demur to the relentless current. Their bodies would eventually circle each other in the whirlpools, nose to tail in an endless dream.

The silence was disconcerting, a prelude perhaps to another assault. Louis stepped out of the hut and looked westwards to where the battle had taken place. Thin pillars of smoke were climbing weakly into the sky, each a small supplication to the gods of war asking for respite from the carnage that had killed upwards of eight thousand men.

The mud sucked at his boots, reluctant to let him go; an invisible legion of grieving mothers and lovers on their knees, clutching at the legs of the men, begging them to return from the dead if only to say goodbye.

★

Ursule stayed in her sarcophagus until daylight. She knew she could never return to the Théâtre des Variétés. Gérard's spies would be assiduous in their attempts to curry favour with their master.

Colder than she had ever been in her life, she emerged

into the graveyard. The mist was lying on the ground, creating the illusion that she was walking through clouds. This impression was reinforced by the sight of a stone angel on her left whose pedestal was no longer visible. Perhaps he would look after her.

However, she was not alone. To her left she saw an old man advancing stealthily towards a pigeon with a makeshift net in his hand. Despite her anxiety lest le Géant was still lurking in the graveyard, her curiosity was undeniably roused. The bird, sensing threat, waddled and flustered its way towards the shelter of a granite stone. The man started to make gentle cooing noises which merged into softly spoken imprecations to climb into his net. Eventually the bird dragged itself into the cold air and landed some twenty yards further on. The man threw down his net in exasperation and cursed.

'Can I help you?' asked Ursule. The man looked at her.

'I've got two already,' he said pointing to a cage surrounded by a halo of feathers.

'Are you going to eat them?'

'Of course not. Are you stupid? The government are paying good money for these birds. It's the balloons, you see.' Ursule clearly didn't. 'They take off with the mail and a basket of pigeons so the folk in the rest of France can write back. They put tiny notes in a tube tied to their feet. Technically they should be racing pigeons, but who's going to tell the difference? This pair must be worth at least ten sous each. That's food and grog for me. It's big business you know. They're looking for young women like you at la Gare d'Orléans. Can you sew?'

It occurred to Ursule that this was the second time in recent memory that she had been asked that question. She had no idea that the one talent she had always taken for granted might one day stand her in such good stead.

'Yes, I can sew.'

'Then get down there quickly. It's the balloons, you see.'

All Ursule could see was that the conversation was going round in circles.

'What do you mean?'

'They need girls to sew the balloons,' he explained with growing exasperation. 'They have a contract to make one every ten days or else penalties will be incurred.' Pleased with his use of this official phrase he waited for a reaction.

'I will go there now.' As if it was now missing the attentions of the old man, the pigeon hopped back, well within net range and cooed seductively. The man crouched down and set off in slow pursuit.

Outside of les Halles Centrales she was accosted by a man swathed in bandages. He held up a jar before her eyes, holding two decaying objects. 'Them's my ears,' said the man. 'Lopped off by a Prussian barbarian.'

Another hawker interposed himself between her and the earless beggar. He waved a newspaper. 'Read all about Eugénie's orgies. Detailed pictures drawn by our finest artists!'

The queue extended out of the waiting room and into Boulevard de l'Hôpital. The young matelot charged with marshalling the crowd of potential seamstresses was out of his depth. A sturdy matron plucked his cap from his head and balanced it on top of her already tottering coiffure. She easily held him at arm's length as he struggled to retrieve both his headwear and his dignity. Most of the women waiting in front of Ursule were in more sombre mood as befitted their determination to do their patriotic duty.

Ursule had noticed that most women in the city had abandoned their crinolines in favour of more sober garb. After all, la France was at war, and their Emperor had meekly surrendered like the pathetic coward that he was.

The women were taken in batches of ten to a stuffy room, formally the baggage hall, where they were allocated a table, two pieces of calico, a large sewing needle and, of course, thread. Their instructions were to join the lengths of material with stitches so close together that the supervisor would be unable to insert his pinky between them.

Several women failed their examination within minutes of starting on the task, and left with bad grace. One of them made a point of nudging Ursule as she stormed out, hoping to make her miss a stitch. The attempt failed and Ursule waited patiently until the supervisor with the overworked pinky nodded, indicating that she should progress to the next line of women who were queuing on the platform nearest to the station entrance.

Ursule had visited la Gare d'Orléans in the past when she and Martine had finished their quotas of sewing, or when the theatre was dark. They had stood, innocents abroad, staring open-mouthed as passengers and porters wove hurried patterns between the platforms and the waiting cabs. They had listened to the babel of greetings and bellowed instructions. They had read the luggage labels that conjured exotic and distant destinations: Bordeaux, Arcachon, Biarritz, Pau and Tours. They had gazed at the black monstrous locomotives sending pillars of steam into the ornate roof.

Now the vast arena was eerily quiet. Three parallel lines of trestle tables stretched the length of the furthest platform, apparently disappearing into the distant tunnels housing the defunct locomotives that had not breathed since the siege had been raised. Upwards of thirty women laboured at each row of tables. Next to them, men were weaving together the wicker baskets that would eventually carry their human load into the skies. From the girders in the roof hung calico streamers, as if part of a welcoming ceremony for a visiting emperor. They undulated slowly. The exotic smell, Ursule later learned, was from a potion of oil, litharge and rubber being mixed in a giant's pudding bowl by an army of men stripped to the waist.

Most astonishing of all was the sight of three huge, bloated carcasses lying prone next to each other. The balloons, for that is what they were, were being inspected by a team of workers, each of whom had his ear pressed against the tightening material listening for escaping air. Their hands moved over their patients with a surgeon's care.

'Table four,' said a rotund man with a huge moustache. He pointed to a gap between two women hunched over their sewing machines. Neither woman looked up as Ursule squeezed in between them. She had no idea what was expected of her. Rather than appear idle, she fiddled with her own machine as if inspecting it. Eventually the older woman rescued her. 'That's your section,' she explained. Ursule realised that all of the women were working on the same piece of material that stretched the length of the platform. 'Don't hold us up or there will be hell to pay.'

'Hell to pay,' repeated her companion.

'They have to pay fifty francs for every day's delay, and it comes out of our wages, doesn't it, girls?' The others assented gloomily.

In her anxiety to play her part in the gargantuan task, Ursule caught her cuff under the needle and realised she had now sewn herself into the fabric of the balloon. The first woman laughed out loud. Then her companion, then the women on either side. The shared hilarity attracted the attention of the supervisor who fussed ineffectively in the background while the women extricated Ursule's cuff from the machine.

She thanked them and the ice was broken. She soon settled into a rhythm compatible with the efforts of her co-workers.

The cavernous hall sent the sailors' shouts back to the perpetrators with interest. The winching machinery punctuated all conversations. The matelots hauled on the ropes with an enthusiasm that reflected their chosen profession.

71

The leaden skirts of the balloons elongated themselves from the platform floors like sullen, half-drowned witches being dragged from the ducking ponds. Once dried they would be lowered and inflated. The mechanical fans sucked the air from the hall and forced it through the fabric orifices until the sleeping giantesses reluctantly stirred. Initially the balloons assumed an elliptical shape then haughtily pulled themselves up to their full height like offended dowagers. Ursule stared in disbelief at the size of the balloons as they swayed above the workers. Madame Godard, the bench supervisor, moved down the line towards her.

'No one will escape Paris if you keep gawking instead of sewing.'

Ursule apologised and reapplied herself to the section of seam for which she had sole responsibility. 'Sorry, Madame. They are so big, I had no idea.'

Madame Godard looked up and down the hall to see if her husband, Eugène, the Director of Aeronauticals, was approaching. He was obviously busy elsewhere.

'Go on,' she said, 'we can spare you for ten minutes.' She pointed with her eyes to the swaying balloon which Ursule gratefully interpreted as permission to leave her station to observe the launch.

Ursule watched as the men released sufficient air to enable them to manoeuvre their sluggish prisoner away from the iron roof girders and out through the arch that opened into Place Girmond. A crowd had assembled. Whether they were casual onlookers or were about to perform a vital function she had no idea. To counter the late afternoon gloom, the square was flooded with light from the headlamps removed from the redundant locomotives. The trailing ropes were secured while the wicker basket was positioned beneath the beast floating with a degree of disinterest above the square.

The giantess was then persuaded to lie on the ground while the snaking gas pipe was pulled from its shelter and positioned above the basket and beneath the canvas. The sound of hissing took Ursule back to the crowds at the Théâtre des Variétés expressing their mock displeasure as the villain of the piece twirled his moustaches and eyed his next victim. The canvas grew ever tauter, the network of ropes tightened round the bloated belly, and once more the monster assumed an upright position. The balloon was eager to shuffle off the mortal coils that held it earthbound. Several of the sailors were practically lying on the ground to restrain its natural impulse to escape.

Things happened quickly after that. Two men in black frock coats approached, a footstool was placed against the basket and they climbed aboard, and each man took a rope as if testing it for strength and stamina. Another man approached with a small trolley holding sand bags which he draped over the edge in the manner of a fishmonger slapping his best wares onto a slab.

As the light was fading into dusk, other men stepped forwards holding oil lamps. Their approach was synchronised. Again Ursule thought of the Théâtre des Variétés and in particular of an operatic lampoon during the course of which a trio of villains, dressed as footmen, stalked the unfortunate hero, but this performance was more spectacular than anything she had witnessed from the wings. The cast grew and grew. Another trolley was wheeled on stage. A basket of pigeons was handed to the aeronauts. Yet another lackey handed over a silver tray containing champagne and three glasses. The cork was shot into the cheering crowd. The men toasted each other. Finally three black bags were hoisted aboard. On cue, the crowd parted to let pass M. Fauconnier, the principal celebrant. He approached the men in the basket with a practised solemnity, doffed his hat and then stood back. The cry went up, 'Let go of the ropes!' Liberated from the bonds that bound it to the earth, the bulbous monster stretched itself and rose elegantly into the sky. Ursule nearly toppled backwards as she strained to watch the balloon disappear over the rooftops.

She resumed her place at the table in the hall. Her new companions nodded their understanding that Ursule had witnessed her first launch.

'Some never land,' said Virginie, a young girl with a startlingly bony face and spindly arms. 'They are never seen again.'

'Shot down, most likely,' added Clotilde. 'It's the Krupps, you know, the biggest guns in the world, they say they can fire into England.'

'Don't say that. The French country folk rescue them and hide them from the Prussians. They are treated like heroes.'

'Her sailor flew from Place Saint-Pierre a month ago, and not a word since,' explained Clotilde in a conspiratorial whisper to Ursule. 'Perhaps the angels take the very best,' she said more loudly for the benefit of Virginie.

'Do you think so, Clotilde?'

'Yes, Virginie. Sometimes the balloons fly so high they find themselves on the edge of heaven. That's when the angels lend a hand.'

Virginie silently pictured her Jean-Paul trying hard to find a gap in the cloud so that he could keep an eye on her.

'Why do they use sailors?' asked Ursule.

'They don't get seasick,' said Clotilde. 'Look up there, they're practising.' Ursule looked up into the girders where a basket was being violently shaken by a man on the platform at the other end of a rope.

'Have you heard the latest plan?' asked Virginie. 'Well, they've been training eagles to pull the balloons through the skies. It's simple. You place a piece of fresh meat on the end of a stick and hold it in front of the birds...' For a moment the women all shared the same mental picture.

'What if the meat drops off the stick?' asked Annette. The others nodded sagely.

'And guess what,' continued Virginie undaunted. 'They are thinking of tying all the balloons together and making them carry a giant sledgehammer that they will drop into a big crowd of Prussians.'

'And how do you get a crowd of Prussians?' asked a sceptical Dominique.

'Well, that's the clever bit,' said Virginie, growing more animated by the moment. The others paused and looked at her.

'They hide an orchestra in the baskets and then, as they get close to a Prussian camp, they all play Schubert and… Who's the other one they like?'

'Wagner.'

'Yes! Exactly. They love that music. It drives them mad with patriotism and they lose all common sense. They will run from their tents to see where the music is coming from, and that's when we let go of the giant hammer.' By way of demonstration she banged her fist down on the workbench, causing a tray of needles to jump into the air.

At midnight the supervisor blew loudly on a whistle. The noise startled Ursule.

'Time for bed,' explained Clotilde. 'Are you staying at the Grand Hotel?'

'Sorry?' said Ursule who realised that she had not given a thought to where she would sleep that night.

'Not to worry. First class accommodation, isn't that right, girls?' The others assented. 'Come with us.'

Ursule followed a dozen or so of the women to the end of the platform. After a moment's pause, several candles were lit and the party walked into the entrance to the nearest tunnel.

Despite the fact that the locomotive they passed had been idle for several months, the air was still pungent with smoke. Ursule's eyes were slowly adjusting to the darkness.

'Home sweet home,' declared Clotilde, stopping beneath the first of several carriages that had been abandoned in the tunnel.

'Share with me,' pleaded Virginie. 'I hate travelling on my own.'

A little perplexed, Ursule followed her up the steps and into the small compartment. Virginie closed the door behind her, lit two candles and stretched out on the upholstered bench. She indicated that Ursule should do likewise on the opposite seats.

'Lots of blankets,' she said, leaning to pick up a large bundle of balloon silk and giving it to Ursule.

The girls lay in the darkness.

'Do you think Clotilde was right about the angels?'

'It seems highly likely,' said Ursule tactfully. 'Where shall we go tonight?' asked Virginie. 'Rome or Venice? You get to choose.'

'Venice, please.' One of the stage sets at the Théâtre des Variétés had featured St Mark's Square and a rubicund gondolier. It was probably the most exotic image that Ursule had ever seen. She pulled the blankets up to her chin and breathed in the smell of calico which seemed equally evocative of foreign lands. Virginie blew out the candle. Ursule moved closer to the back of the bench to better accommodate Louis.

CHAPTER EIGHT

Louis heard the footsteps on the stone flags. He heard the farmer remonstrating with the Prussians. He heard loud voices and then the sound of the cellar door being thrown back. Daylight flooded through the hole and glinted off the bayonet that preceded the soldier conducting the search as he carefully climbed down the steps. Louis had no weapon, and in any case was too ill to offer any resistance.

'Raus! Raus!'

The four of them shivered in the courtyard. Their hands were bound behind their backs and they were blindfolded. If anything Louis almost welcomed the end. Having traipsed across fields of the dead, once stumbling in a ditch and landing on top of a decomposing sergeant, he had had enough. Cold, hungry and in deep despair, if this was the end, then so be it. He had long abandoned naïve fantasies of a better life. The final comforting image to be jettisoned was of the young woman whom he had first seen smiling at him from a window overlooking a park. She belonged to a different world, the unreality of which was beyond belief. It had been smudged out of the canvas that at one stage depicted his dreams of a life more normal: promotion in the army, marriage, family, companionship, and all of the other beguiling lies that had exacerbated his loneliness once he was left for dead in the maelstrom of battle.

As he sheltered from the horses in the hut, he had speculated about his own death. In particular he was intrigued by the fleeting fragment of consciousness that might register unimaginable pain and loss in the flash of death as a bullet entered the brain. He had once been felled by a stone, hidden in a snowball, hurled by a boy from the neighbouring village. Instantly unconscious, he had absolutely no recollection of any awareness of the moment of impact. Presumably a bullet would be the same. The difference was that he had absolutely no expectation of being hit by the stone. Now he knew that his life would be snuffed out at any moment, and that knowledge, he noted with surprise, had no emotional component.

'Prime your weapons!' He heard the synchronised clicking of a dozen rifles.

'Take aim. Fire!'

★

'You can send messages, you know.'

Ursule paused her hand on the wheel of the sewing machine. 'What do you mean?'

'Messages. If there is anyone out there you are missing, parents, a lover, I can arrange for letters to be included in the bags they take with them. Jacques, my young boy, the love of my life, is the sailor who takes the bags to the balloons. You must have seen him the other day. Tall, extremely handsome. He will do anything for me. If farmers find bags in the fields they must, under pain of death, take them to the post. They are handsomely rewarded. Of course, sometimes the bags are captured by the Prussians, but what can you do?' Clotilde shrugged.

The clever thing is that messages come back wrapped in tiny tubes tied to the pigeons' feathers. And, here's something. Jacques tells me that they have found a way to make the messages so small that they cannot be read with the naked eye, but when they are taken from the birds they can make them big again. A machine makes them appear on a wall and anyone can read them.'

As if in response to Clotilde's explanation, a commotion broke out in the vast hall. Each matelot put two fingers in his mouth and whistled. The women stopped sewing and banged their palms on the table. The workers, perched on ladders to position the strips of cloth on the girders, hit the metal with whatever tools were at hand. Ursule looked up and saw a tiny startled pigeon swooping through the air, desperate to find a way to escape. 'Lazy bird!' shouted Virginie, pointing her finger. 'Do your duty, deliver the messages to our countrymen.'

As the bird finally disappeared through the entrance arch and into the Parisian skies, the entire workforce clapped their hands and chanted, 'Death to the Prussians! Death to the Prussians!' Eventually M. Godard rushed up and down the tables flapping his arms at the women as if he was himself an errant pigeon, ordering them to resume their labours.

That night in their first class apartment, Virginie suggested their destination should be Milan. Ursule was less certain, preferring Madrid. 'We can lie in the sun all day and I can make us money by dancing in the cafés in the evening.'

'The Spanish men are too short and hairy, I would sooner have a tall Italian on my arm.' The women lapsed into silence, each pursuing their innocent fantasies.

'Tell me about your soldier boy,' said Virginie.

'Well, he's quite tall but not so tall that kissing him would be difficult. He has wonderful sad eyes. Look, I have a drawing here. Light the candle.' Ursule felt for the journal that had become a second skin round her stomach. She flattened the sketch book and turned the pages until she came to the one she sought. 'It's not very good but I'm not an artist.' She ran her finger round the outline of his face, smudging the charcoal. The candle flame was multiplied by the several reflections in the carriage windows.

'He looks lovely but he is quite thin.'

'I know but I would make him big meals and put flesh on his bones.'

'Would he enjoy elephant casserole?'

'What?'

'Haven't you heard, they are starting to eat the animals in the zoo? Jacques tells me he tried gazelle the other day. A bit fatty, he said.'

'I will make him tiger stew so that he can tear the heads off the Prussians.'

'And I will bring along some monkey paté so he can swing from the trees and hurl coconuts on their heads.'

Both women laughed so loudly that the occupants of the adjacent carriages variously asked if they could come to the party, or begged them to keep quiet and let them sleep.

★

'Look at the middle one. It's all down his legs! I won! I won! Let's shoot him now for stinking the place out.' A smirking soldier tore off the blindfolds from the three prisoners. Louis took a while to adjust to the sunlight and considerably longer to adjust to the realisation that he was still alive. He stared bemused as each of his captors handed money over to their companion who had most accurately forecast the outcome of the mock execution.

Having had their sport, the Prussians reverted to the drudgery of herding the prisoners through the carnage of the town square. A woman, her arms resting on the ledge of an upper window, spat into the street. A horse emerged from an alleyway, collapsed onto its front legs and died. A cart loaded with captured weapons had become stuck in the mud and debris. Its driver waited impassively. Two peasants dragged a dead soldier by his legs towards another cart already laden with an unruly cargo of corpses. A soldier's head, only just attached to its neck, bounced off the cobbles and left them stained with blood. An urchin clutching a Prussian pointed helmet was being chased half-heartedly by a fat soldier who in a different place would set off in a similar pursuit of his grandchild.

There was a hold-up somewhere. The long snake of prisoners came to a stop. Up ahead one of their number, on refusing to move another inch, was summarily executed. He had made a choice that Louis fully understood.

As they left Sedan it seemed that all colour had been drained from the world, as if colour was an extravagance unaffordable in war. The hair, faces, uniforms and boots of the prisoners were grey with mud. The fields and remaining hedgeways were grey. The fast-flowing waters of the Meuse, whose banks they followed, were grey. The mood of the men was sombre and grey. The expressions on the guards' faces suggested that they too had been vanquished in the battle, and like their charges, hankered for comfort or colour of any sort.

With no visible shelter apart from the fringe of trees that framed the loop of the river in which they were penned, the prisoners squatted, crouched or simply lay down in the mud and shivered.

The man nearest to Louis was rocking backwards and forwards, holding his knees. 'Jesus God,' he muttered, 'Jesus God... Jesus God.'

'Shut up, for the sake of Jesus God, Mary and Joseph or I will pull out your tongue and eat it!' The soldier rose to his feet and stood over the rocking man with clenched fists.

'Leave him,' said Louis.

'I'll have your puppy tongue as well, you young bastard, with salt and pickles...' The image conjured by the angry prisoner had the unexpected effect of mutating his aggression into acute hunger. He slumped back onto the ground and stared into the middle distance.

★

Ursule rarely left the station. She enjoyed being mothered by her older companions, all of whom readily involved her in their discussions.

'My daughter ran off with a Jew,' said Annette. 'My man tried to find them both, to make amends, to beg for a fresh start but there was no sign of them. Vanished. My man died of a broken heart soon after.'

'It's always men, isn't it?' pronounced Delphine, accidently stabbing a needle into her thumb.

'What do you mean?'

'You know, they cause so many problems. They seem strong but most are just like small boys.' She abandoned her discourse to concentrate more fully on sucking her pricked thumb.

'Did you hear about the Palais de Saint-Cloud?' asked Jeanette, inspecting the seam she had been working on.

'No.'

'Completely destroyed. By our own forces. Can you believe it!'

'No!'

'Yes. A miscalculation apparently. We are doing the Prussians' work for them.'

'Guess what I've just seen?' Virginie quickly removed her bonnet and took her place between Annette and Ursule, hoping that her lateness had not been noticed by M. Godard.

'What?'

'The menu outside of Gustave's. For an entrée he's offering Civet de kangourou.' Can you imagine?' She started to bounce up and down in her seat, her hands transformed

82

into paws. The others howled with laughter. 'Not to mention le Chameau rôti a l'anglaise.' She sunk her head into
her shoulders and instantly grew a hump. 'And as for the le
Chat flanqué de rats…'

M. Godard instantly noticed the commotion and moved
to quieten the mirth. His intervention only served to make
the women more hysterical. Ursule put her hand to her
mouth fearful that she might be sick with laughter.

Once the women had settled back into their routine there
was another interruption. Raised voices at the entrance to
the station made most of the assembly line look up. The
matelots were struggling to restrain a mountain of a figure
who was forcing his way into the workshop. The guard
dogs clung to his breeches but he hit them both hard with
his club and they whelped away. Mortified, Ursule realised
that le Géant was approaching. She stood up, transfixed
with fear. Virginie was the first to make the connection
between the huge and very angry figure and the tale of woe
that Ursule had shared with her one night in the carriage.
She shoved Ursule to her knees and pushed her under the
work table. The other women rose, several machines fell
to the floor as they moved away to avoid the fury that was
approaching. M. Godard manfully blocked le Géant's path
but was swept to the ground.

'Where is the whore? Where is she?'

CHAPTER NINE

Le Géant's progress was hampered by the fact that he was now carrying two matelots on his back who were ineffectively pummelling his head. Enraged by his initial failure to locate Ursule, Gérard shook off his assailants and swept through the hanging balloons as if they were theatre curtains and he was the star making a dramatic entry stage left. Eventually, in response to its manhandling, one of the deflated balloons left its moorings in the roof girders and collapsed onto le Géant who was soon completely submerged beneath a cascade of fabric. His shouts became muffled as he fought against his latest assailant. At least ten matelots threw themselves onto the undulating mound of man and balloon. Now at risk from suffocation, le Géant became gradually more subdued. The matelots soon gained the upper hand and, after peeling away the layers of silk, they reached the gasping form of their quarry and managed to wrap him in the ropes of which there was a plentiful supply. Now in an upright position, Gérard seemed to be regaining his strength. The effort was evident in his face as he strained against the ties that bound him but they held firm and he was frogmarched towards the entrance.

Ursule had not dared to look at the proceedings until the very moment when le Géant was being bundled past the table under which she had hidden. She peered out.

They made eye contact. The veins stood out on le Géant's forehead and his eyes bulged but the matelots managed to sustain the forward momentum and continued to propel their captive onwards. Eventually his shouts merged with the habitual street noises.

Even M. Godard felt some sympathy for Ursule who, shaking with fright, was clearly unfit for work. The women reassured him that they would tend to her and he eventually returned to the mundane inspection regime which he understood.

A collection was held and Virginie volunteered to leave the station and purchase smelling salts.

'No, she needs *aqua vitae*,' said Clotilde. A bottle was passed down the line and duly administered. Ursule could only assume that, as a parting shot, le Géant had somehow succeeded in setting her innards alight. She coughed and retched.

'I came this close to sticking a needle in his eye,' declared Michèle who had garnered a reputation for a degree of shyness and timidity that normally precluded contact with any of her co-workers. Her neighbours on the table looked incredulously as she mimed not only piercing a human eye with a needle but then proceeded to demonstrate how a gimlet could be used to effect complete decapitation.

'A kick in the groin would have stopped him in his tracks,' said tiny Béatrice who almost toppled over as she too demonstrated her preferred method of assault. 'Always worked with my man,' she added.

Ursule tried hard to compose herself, and attempted to align the seam in front of her but she was shaking so badly she had to give up. Virginie motioned for her to sit back while she took responsibility for the additional yard of calico.

★

Some of the prisoners seemed incapable of any movement. It was as if they believed, and perhaps hoped, that if they stayed still for sufficiently long any residual life would slowly drain out of their cold bodies and leech into the mud. The rest would be oblivion. Their eyes were expressionless. Soon it would be over.

Once every other day a heavily guarded wagon would enter the compound. The sleek well-fed horses exuded superiority. They picked their way through the prone bodies as if reluctant to sink their hooves into human flesh from a fear of contamination. A fat Prussian steadied himself and hurled a small flurry of loaves into the crowd. Some of the men rose to their feet, a sea of hands followed the movement of the bread as it sailed above them.

Two men wrestled over a loaf. They swore and gouged each other's faces. 'Let go, you piece of shit, it's mine.'

'I saw it first,' said the other with a schoolboy's petulance. Eventually the loaf disintegrated into several pieces that sank into the mud while the men fought themselves to a standstill.

As Louis watched the feud with indifference, he felt a touch on his shoulder. He turned to see a bald man in a greatcoat staring down at him. 'Are you hungry?' he asked. Without waiting for the obvious reply, he told Louis to follow him. 'I need a fit lad to keep watch.' Pleased at the thought of a diversion, Louis shrugged and stood up. The older man looked him up and down. 'Bertrand,' he said, offering his hand.

'Louis.'

Bertrand led the way through the somnolent and slouched ranks of enlisted men in the direction of the river. He breathed noisily and, judging by his lopsided gait, was carrying an injury. Despite the considerable difference in their age, Louis found that he had to break into a half-trot to keep up with the older man. One of the guards eyed them with an expression somewhere between indifference and suspicion.

'Going for a shit in the woods,' explained Bertrand.

'This is my batman. He wipes my arse.' The guard nodded. 'Doesn't speak French,' explained Bertrand. 'Strange people, the Prussians.' They had reached the thick line of bushes that ran parallel to the Meuse.

'See,' said Bertrand pointing to the opposite bank. 'Crawling with guards waiting for the poor sods who try to wade to freedom.' He cackled. 'Good idea not to provoke them. Now, your job is to watch them like a hawk and warn me if they start taking notice.' Louis breathed in the damp ferny smell of vegetation. It was familiar but he couldn't place it.

As Louis crouched down in the bushes and started his observations as instructed, Bertrand lowered himself down the bank and started foraging in the greenery that extended to the water's edge. He returned moments later clutching an armful of leaves. 'A meal for two,' he explained. 'The secret,' he said, 'is to chew the leaves as slowly as possible. Keep them in your mouth for as long as you can.'

Louis, having decided that his new companion was completely mad, was intrigued nonetheless. How could he have failed to recognise the smell of wild garlic?

★

His father had sat at the kitchen table and explained how he had been asked to bind a complete set of Molière for the mayor. 'Good money,' he said. 'You might get that dress after all.' His mother smiled and served the ragout, redolent with garlic. Louis dropped his knife and was rebuked for his table manners. Then he was told to go and look for his younger brother who had obviously found a distraction en route to the table.

The smell of garlic also summoned l'Auberge Savoyarde in the street next to the cathedral. There were prints of

Harlequin on the walls, a songbird in a rusty cage and tall plants in the corner with thick, green, dust-covered leaves. The inn was always chosen for special occasions. His older sister had just announced her engagement to Frédéric, who owned a silk factory. 'A great catch,' said his father in an aside to his mother as he opened the first of many bottles. Having been forbidden to eat breakfast, Louis was salivating at the smell of the roast boar, the oyster pie, and the sweetmeats.

Frédéric wiped his mouth with his napkin, turned to Louis and asked him what he wanted to be. 'A soldier,' he replied. A palpable silence descended in the room. His father lay down his cutlery. Frédéric thrust his fingers into his snuffbox and snorted the brown powder up his nose. Never had a wall clock ticked so loudly.

'Who do you miss most?' asked Bertrand, scratching his behind.

'What do you mean?'

'Your parents, a dog, a girlfriend?'

Louis took another two leaves and chewed them slowly. The sensation of a filling stomach was very pleasing.

'I don't know. It all seems like a different country, a different life. The strange thing is, the person I miss most I hardly know…' Bertrand nodded. 'We only spoke once or twice. In a park. In Paris. I can't get her out of my head. No, that's not quite true. During the battle I became like an animal. I thought of nobody but myself. I would have killed my sister then to save my skin. I would have killed my father.' He paused as the weight of what he had just admitted caused him pain.

'Afterwards I felt guilty at not having kept her face in front of me. I betrayed her somehow. And then this emptiness…' The leaves tasted bitter and he spat them out. 'She was living with a beast who might have killed her by now. They say Paris is under siege, they say the Prussians are slitting the throats of people as they sleep, they say…'

'They say a lot, my son,' said Bertrand, placing his arm round the boy's shoulders. 'We must go back. I think the guards on the other side of the river have noticed us.' They walked back side by side across the undulating furrows of mud. The dusk was already spreading its mist over the ground.

There was significant movement in the centre of the compound. The grey figures were agitated. The sound of raised voices, commands and curses filled the air. They paused hoping they would not be noticed but two Prussians with fixed bayonets were already striding towards them. 'Stay close to me son. I will be your talisman, your lucky charm,' said Bertrand.

The foremost soldier grabbed hold of Louis. His companion remonstrated. 'Let him be. He's with me.' The other Prussian swung his rifle butt at Bertrand's head and knocked him to the ground.

As he was frogmarched towards a line of waiting wagons, Louis tried to look back but could see no sign of Bertrand. 'Talisman,' he muttered.

★

Ursule stared out of the carriage window into the dark tunnel. She could only see her reflection. 'Le Géant will come back, I know he will.'

'He doesn't know you're here. No one will tell him,' said Virginie.

'You don't know him. He has spies who know everything.'

'By the time he finds out we will be travelling through the Alps, the dawn will be breaking over the mountains. The guard will ask if we would like coffee and croissants. Your young man will be waiting at the next station…'

'No. No.' Ursule was in no mood to share Virginie's well-intentioned fantasy. She banged her fist into the upholstered bench releasing a shower of dust that made both women cough.

Virginie moved to the other side of the carriage and embraced Ursule. 'Don't worry, little one, don't worry.'

★

Louis was also in a railway carriage, or more accurately a cattle truck, with at least thirty other prisoners. They were packed so tightly no one could move their arms.

'I want a piss!' shouted one of the men.

'What's stopping you?' One of the guards, standing on an elevated dais at the end of the carriage, waved his rifle in the general direction of the speaker. 'Let the waters flow. Keep your friends warm.'

With no warning, the truck was shunted violently. Louis felt his chest being crushed by the displaced mass of his fellow prisoners. The movement stopped. The human tide ebbed in the opposite direction. The locomotive was skidding. Warm steam wafted over its cargo. Slowly the wheels gripped and the trucks jolted forward.

'Where are they taking us?' Louis' question was addressed to the prisoner whose head was a shoulder's width from his own.

'They've built camps in Prussia. We're between the devil and the deep blue sea. You can either die of starvation in the mud of France or be exterminated in the Kaiser's backyard. At least I'll get to see the world, I've always wanted to travel,' he added bitterly.

'Oh Jesus God, forgive me my sins, fold me in your arms and take me away from here.' Louis could feel the breath from the petitioner on the left side of his face. He turned his head and saw tears of desperation in the man's eyes who then started to whimper like a lost infant.

'Prussian bastards! Bastards!' From the middle of the truck

a man's torso rose like a cork from a bottle. Now head and shoulders above the rest, but with his arms trapped at his sides, he spat at the guard behind Louis. His saliva was thrown back in his face by the momentum of the train. The guard laughed.

★

As always a small yellow glow in the carriage announced another day. Stretching, Virginie asked if her travelling companion had slept.

'Like a log,' lied Ursule.

Ursule took her place at the trestle table and pulled a section of cloth towards her.

'I've got my needle ready if he comes back,' said Michèle before the others shushed her.

As Ursule bunched the seam together, she was aware of the whispered gossip inspired by the events of the day before.

'...he was the size of a monster...'

'Do you think he's that big all over? I mean she's so tiny...'

'Shhh, don't let her hear.'

Ursule was on high alert. Her brain had raced through the night. Her course of action was clear. Rarely had she felt so certain about anything.

CHAPTER TEN

The launch was scheduled for three o'clock but the preparations were well under way. The canvas had already been dragged from the platform and arranged in the square. M. Godard was nearing a crescendo of self-importance, tutting and clucking, issuing orders and small rebukes to his women, none of whom took the slightest notice. But as always, they were caught up in the tension and excitement that preceded any launch.

Under a pretext of going to the store for a roll of tape, Béatrice scurried to the station exit and returned with the news that she had overheard one of the matelots declare that the wind was set fair. She had no idea what the phrase meant and had assumed it was bad news until the others enlightened her. Several carriages swept into the station and disgorged their important guests. The top hats bobbed above the horses' flanks.

'Jacques says they will be carrying a government minister with a message from the Emperor,' said Virginie. 'He wants all of the country folk to take up arms and pitchforks and move towards Paris and break the siege.'

The women nearest to her cheered and attracted the disapproving attention of M. Godard who flapped a hand in their direction.

As the balloon was inflated, it gradually obscured the

light that streamed in from the station entrance. It seemed to Ursule that dusk had come early. Several additional gas lamps were lit above the women's tables so that they could still see to sew. The shouting intensified.

'It's too windy,' confided Clotilde who always prided herself on understanding the complexities of the launch. 'Mark my words.' She pointed towards the entrance. 'See the matelots straining to hang onto the ropes.' Ursule glanced towards the bulbous shape and could indeed see several small figures who were seemingly fighting in slow motion with an ogre.

'My Jacques says it's today or never, the minister has to leave Paris today or all will be lost.'

Ursule told the others she was feeling sick and made her way to the entrance. She was almost knocked sideways by the pigeon carrier who was strutting towards the basket, all the while jerking his head forward like one of his charges. Next the ballast sacks of sand were manoeuvred into the square on a cart pulled by two men. The matelots had linked arms to restrain the crowd of well-wishers and the plainly curious, for whom a launch was always the day's highlight. Only by moving their legs sideways could they deter the small army of urchins who were keen to exploit any gap in the human chain.

With a vicious hiss the gas pipe broke free from its handlers, reared up in the air and snaked its way towards the nearest observers. The crowd gasped, those nearest screamed. After a struggle the errant pipe was eventually surrounded, subdued and led forcibly back towards the heart of the square where it was fed once more into the vast belly of the balloon. Sated and needing a lie down, the balloon toppled onto its side, spilling the basket and its contents onto the ground. It then slouched its way towards the apartments on Boulevard de l'Hôpital.

The supervisor of operations blew loudly on his whistle

and the matelots duly fell in line along a trailing rope and, leaning backwards, digging their feet into whatever gaps they could find in the cobbles, played tug-of-war with their adversary who was apparently determined to greet the customers sitting outside a café on the edges of the square. The patrons fled, upturning their chairs as they moved quickly to avoid being swamped in canvas. After a sudden surge of reinforcements, the tug-of-war team gradually gained the upper hand. The balloon offered further token resistance before surrendering to the inevitable and, with noticeably poor grace, let itself be dragged back into the centre of the square.

After sulking for a while, and thereby luring its handlers into a false sense of security, the balloon decided to play again. It hauled itself to almost its full height, huffing and puffing, causing consternation among the groundlings. It straightened its stays, pushed out its chest and did its utmost to escape upwards. Like giddy waiters, the matelots ran into each other, dropping their trays and spilling the drinks. The monster was rapidly becoming untameable. Once more the wicker basket was upright but its contents including a compass, telescope, barometer, a bottle of champagne, and sacks of mail were spilt on the ground. The urchins gathered armfuls of cargo and melted back into the crowd.

Ursule glanced to her left and saw a matelot release the pilot balloon which shot upwards and then changed course, narrowly missing the rooftops. Irrespective of this inauspicious sign, the preparations for departure continued with a maniacal intensity.

No sooner had a pair of steps emerged from nowhere than the minister of state was being encouraged to lift his leg over the side of the basket. As this manoeuvre was proving beyond the capacity of both his pride and his arthritic limbs, he was unceremoniously tipped into the basket by a willing matelot. Next the pilot, a M. Putois, whom Ursule recognised from the descriptions given by his many female admirers, swung himself into the basket, and doffed his hat to the excited crowd.

The cry went up, 'Release the ropes. Release the ropes!'

Ursule sprinted past the defensive line of matelots, past the entourage of officials vainly shouting sycophantic encouragement to the minister of state, and launched herself at the basket now some four feet off the ground. The occupants seemed too preoccupied to react. Those on the ground, too slow. By now Ursule had both arms firmly draped over the edge of the basket which rapidly ascended out of the square.

She closed her eyes and gave in to an overwhelming sense of joy. The shouts from the crowd suddenly sounded very distant.

Neither of her fellow travellers had realised that someone was clinging to the outside of the basket. The Very Important Man noticed her first and tugged M. Putois on the arm while pointing at Ursule.

'My God, we've picked up an angel already,' said Putois. 'We're normally a bit higher when that happens. Get aboard if you intend coming with us.' He motioned to his companion to help pull Ursule into the basket.

'I'm afraid the champagne didn't survive the launch. I think that according to the Napoleonic Code you should be shot, but the regulations are somewhat ambiguous regarding aeronauts. Well, Mademoiselle, you are hereby appointed chief scout. Take the starboard side and look out for Prussian encampments.'

At that moment the balloon lurched sideways as if tugged by an unseen hand towards the buildings on the far side of the square. Ursule braced herself for the inevitable collision but at the very moment when the basket was about to intrude into the drawing room of a third-floor apartment, the balloon decided to behave and corrected itself, and the basket swung away. Ursule caught a fleeting glimpse of an old lady holding a cup and staring open-eyed at the apparition through her window.

'Close shave,' said Putois.

Unsurprisingly, there were no Prussian encampments on the rooftops. She half expected to see le Géant stuck in a chimney, squinting upwards and shaking his fist at her. Unless he had been turned into one of the many pillars of smoke, he was not there either.

Gripped by a euphoric sense of unreality, Ursule stared at Paris beneath her. Astonished by the unexpected symmetry of the Grands Boulevards, astonished by its ant-sized people, she looked towards the meandering Seine. How could the spindly bridges support their load of carriages? Was each of those tiny dots really a boat? She was mesmerised by the balloon's elongated shadow sweeping across the landscape below them as if she was watching a black crayon plotting a path on a map.

'Ballast!' shouted Putois, 'we're going down. Two bags over the side!' The Very Important Man just stared.

'For God's sake, do what you're told! Why are politicians so useless?'

Putois picked up the bags himself and tossed them over the edge. 'It's your fault, Mademoiselle, had you really been an angel this would not have been necessary.' He glanced over the edge in time to see the bags explode in the park below. 'No one hurt. I'm losing my touch.'

Despite Putois' best efforts, the balloon continued its descent. 'Oh, the ignominy, the shame.' They seemed to be landing prematurely in a clearing which, judging by the stumps of trees, had once been a sizeable forest. Ursule vaguely remembered M. Barroux talking about how the Bois de Boulogne had been cut down to give the artillery a clear view out of the city towards the Prussian lines.

'Look out below!' shouted Putois as he jettisoned a large sack of sand. The sack exploded next to a startled young man who waved his fist at the occupants of the basket, and then looked round for his female companion who was running, clutching her skirts, towards the edge of the wood. Ursule thought of Louis.

Putois had succeeded in stabilising the balloon which, after a moment's hesitation, rose steadily upwards once more. The Very Important Man was gripping the edge of the basket with his eyes firmly shut. His face was green. Putois muttered to himself after scribbling some calculations based on the reading from the red barometer. He dropped his pencil and grabbed one of the side ropes as the balloon seemed to spin on its axis. The basket creaked as the unforeseen gust of wind twisted the frail craft and sent it in a completely different direction from the one it had been following.

'North be damned!' said Putois who stared at the approaching countryside through his telescope. The Very Important Man vomited over the side. Ursule felt again a frisson of the pleasure she had experienced earlier. She had a strong sense of being released from all responsibility. She could exercise no control over events. She was literally being propelled at speed towards her destiny wherever that might lead her.

Their passage over a copse released a flurry of crows that fled squawking into the twilight. Strange disconnected sounds rose towards them: cattle lowing, children's voices from a village, a dog barking, the croaking of frogs. Oddly, they heard strains of music emanating from one of the farmhouses over which they sailed. A ballad or love song, she thought. The sounds only served to intensify the silence of their flight. They were travelling in a different realm.

The entrance to this realm was marked by a series of vast mirrors which reflected the very last rays of the sun. 'Pools of water in the peat bogs,' explained Putois, answering her unasked question.

Ursule leaned out of the basket to touch a cloud. She would never have dreamed that such a thing was possible. She unfolded her hand looking for traces of the magical air that she had grasped, but there were none. As they ascended, the clouds took on a different quality. They played tricks with her eyesight and stopped her seeing clearly. They were teasing her, but playfully. She thought of the public séance conducted at the Théâtre des Variétés by the Great Salvadore. She had watched half terrified through a gap in the stage curtain. At the moment of communing with the dead, vapour, 'ectoplasm' he had called it, had oozed from his fingertips. It had a bitter smell and loitered in the stalls long after the show had finished and the audience had retreated to the adjacent Salon d'Absynthe. Soon the clouds were beneath them.

Once, at the bullying behest of le Géant, her mother had attempted to sew a quilt. She had held the satin folds against her daughter's cheek. They were soft, but not soft enough for le Géant who later threw the cloth to the floor and trampled it under his shoes. This quilt stretched to the edge of the world. Ursule wanted to step out of the basket, wrap herself in the clouds and sleep for ever.

As they climbed, the light faded and the night clamped down. Not since her childhood had Ursule seen such a black sky. 'That's Jupiter,' said Putois. As she stared at the vastness a single shooting star fell between the constellations and died. She knew she had experienced this moment before. At the end of a shift at the station, she had volunteered to help the matelots whose job it was to inspect the balloon fabric for the pinholes that could jeopardise its flight. Once she was completely draped under the calico, a lamp would be shone, and if she saw the pinpricks of light she was to say. She had once almost fallen asleep under the warm weight of fabric, half dreaming that she was among the stars. And now she was. Looking down where the earth had been, she saw several small fires.

'Charcoal burners,' explained Putois.

It was M. Putois who roused her. 'Mademoiselle, you will be cold. Thankfully I have not yet jettisoned the blankets.' He gave her one and told her to crouch on the floor of the basket. The Very Important Man had already claimed his corner where he sat asleep with his knees on his chest. He was still clutching his portfolio of important papers in case they were about to be stolen by a malevolent troupe of demons who just happened to be passing through the firmament. Putois lit a small oil lamp and suspended it from the lip of the basket.

'With any luck a light in the sky will be seen by the Prussians as an omen of their downfall.' Putois then produced a bottle of Burgundy and two glasses. 'Home comforts,' he said. 'A bottle survived. A gift from the gods. Eat, drink and be merry, for tomorrow, who knows... Salut, Mademoiselle. Now, as I am still deciding whether to have you shot, court-martialled or, given the nature of our craft, keelhauled, perhaps you should tell me your story.'

For the next two hours Ursule opened her heart and told Putois of her trials and tribulations. Whenever she paused, concerned that she might be boring her audience, he begged her to continue.

'Well, Mademoiselle, the jury has deliberated and the judge has decreed that you are not to be thrown overboard, as you are guilty of no crime apart from an excess of goodness. As a consequence, your sentence is commuted to exile in a place as yet undetermined.' With that, he kissed her on the head and stood to read his instruments. The balloon fled across the night sky.

★

Louis too attempted to read his fate in the stars. The omens were not auspicious. Even before the defeat at Sedan, the French troops had motivated and dispirited each other in equal measure by repeating rumours about how the Prussians treated their prisoners. It had become a competitive sport. Being tossed into burning vats of oil was a recurrent rumour only matched by tales of enforced cannibalism. Louis now assumed that the truth was less spectacular. Prisoners were routinely frozen to death en route to the homeland. The efficiency was undeniably impressive. Dead bodies alongside a railway track would attract little comment in the months after the war.

Louis suspected that many of his fellow soldiers in the truck were already dead but it was impossible to tell as they were so tightly packed. It was certainly a long while since the wounded had begged for help.

The tears streamed down his face. They were initially prompted by the bitter wind that lashed the open truck but were now also a manifestation of the profound sense of despair and loss he felt. It was not so much particular memories that caused him pain, although more than anything he wished he could be reconciled with his parents, rather it was an unfocused awareness of all that he would not be able to do; a sense of a life short and essentially unlived. If his life was about to be snuffed out, then what had been the point of it in the first place? What was the point…? What was the point…? The rhythm of the phrase was echoed in the movement of the wagons as they sped over the tracks towards Prussia.

In an instant the rhythm was shattered. The sky caught fire. Hot coals flew overhead like meteors. His truck left the track and climbed upwards to impale itself on the one in front. The sound of splitting timber. Steam and fire. Screams and shouts. The crush of bodies. A cry went up, 'Vive les francs-tireurs! Vive les saboteurs!'

The guards fired their rifles into the air then clambered out of the truck and ran towards the front of the train where the broken locomotive was in its death throes. The bodies of the crew lay alongside the track. Lanterns flashed incoherent messages into the night.

Louis' first awareness was of the cold rail against his face. He was aware also of men stepping over him and he could smell the burning trucks. He crawled towards the edge of the embankment, slid to the bottom, then stumbled into a stream. He waded through the water until it became too deep then climbed out into a field. He saw several sheep but no signs of any other escapees. Logic told him that if he followed the railway at a distance, he would be moving away from the border. He breathed deeply, the first shoots of the morning sun were lighting the distant trees.

Ursule had never seen a sight as beautiful as the pink clouds beneath the balloon. Both the moon and the new sun were visible. She had not realised such a thing was possible. M. Putois was preoccupied adjusting the valve cord. The Important Man, still hunched in a corner of the basket, scowled at her. Ursule was aware that they were climbing higher. At first the ascent was exhilarating. The pink clouds now looked very distant and had lost some of their colour. Perhaps they were going to get a closer look at the moon before it faded away, thought Ursule; she would like that. She would study it carefully and add it to her journal later. She felt for the notebook still wrapped against her stomach. Good, it was still there.

Ursule was feeling very cold, so too was the Important Man who reached across and took all of the blankets. M. Putois was becoming agitated. 'The valve won't open,' he said, tugging at the cord that was suspended from the mouth of the balloon. 'As the day gets hotter, we will climb and climb. We could set a new altitude record, but we would also be dead.'

101

To Ursule's great concern and to the acute consternation of the other traveller, Putois pulled himself onto the edge of the basket. 'Back soon,' he said, before hauling himself onto the hoop from which the basket was suspended and which itself tethered the network of ropes that encased the balloon. He then proceeded to clamber from the hoop towards the mouth of the balloon. The angle was so great that he had to entwine his legs around the ropes to stop himself hanging in the void.

'God save me!' implored the Important Man who was certainly not used to being ignored by the deity.

'What can I do?' asked Ursule.

By this time M. Putois was balancing on the hoop and reaching into the balloon. 'Got it!' he said, tumbling back through the hoop and into the basket. He clasped Ursule in his arms. They both stood still, listening to the sound of escaping gas and the increasingly alarmed cooing from the pigeons.

'That's too much,' said M. Putois, looking up at the entrance to the balloon. 'Hold on, we're going down.'

The Important Man shrieked in terror. Ursule braced herself against the side of the basket. 'Ballast!' cried M. Putois, 'Over the side with it!' He and Ursule managed to drop several sandbags over the edge but failed to halt the rate of descent.

'What else?' asked Putois, hurling the empty wine bottle and the blankets over the side. He then snatched the portmanteau from the Important Man and tossed it to the winds. 'My papers!' howled the Important Man, watching incredulously as the bag obligingly opened and distributed its contents evenly over the rapidly approaching forest.

With a jolt the basket touched the tree tops and balanced precariously. Unthinking, the Important Man stepped out of the basket, still muttering, 'My papers! My papers!' and slid through the upper branches until he landed with a broken ankle on the ground. Limping, he set off across the field in pursuit of the papers dancing just out of his reach like so many teasing imps.

'I think I know this wood,' said Ursule. 'And those fields are familiar.' M. Putois raised an eyebrow.

At that very moment, freed from the weight of the Important Man, and nudged by a wind that sprang from nowhere, the balloon righted itself and tottered once more into the sky, just managing to clear the hedgerows and a copse.

Louis had noticed the balloon's flight and had observed its distant descent with curiosity.

M. Putois pointed at a church tower and the outline of a village. 'Time to visit the locals,' he said, tugging once more on the valve cord. 'Don't forget the pigeons.'

'I won't,' said Ursule.

INTERLUDE ONE

I flicked through the pages of the *Metro*. The café was empty and the coffee was cold. Despite my best efforts, whatever article I read morphed into a critique of Ursule's narrative. Was Émile Zola turning in his grave at the Panthéon? Not content with plundering his novels for convincing 19th century names, I had unashamedly borrowed the launderette fight scene from *Nana* and the deranged horses from *Le Débâcle*. Furthermore, where was the rapture?

Where was the rapture? Why was I not punching the air in empathetic celebration of her near escape into a distant realm? Why had I settled for gentle relief, and the undefined hint of better things to come, rather than pure, unbridled euphoria in the skies?

Basically, why had I given up on my metaphor and unhesitatingly brought Ursule back down to earth, the source of all her unhappiness? Furthermore, having made that decision why did I not bite the narrative bullet and ensure that 'journeys end in lovers meeting' instead of dangling the limp possibility that Ursule and Louis might just miss each other?

I could so easily have incorporated the well-documented moment, redolent with narrative possibilities, when a French balloon had actually snared itself on telegraph cables and come down on a railway line carrying Prussian prisoners. Ursule and

Louis could have enjoyed a stunning reunion. I could have attempted to capture their shared moment of earthly joy in an impressive demonstration of magical realism.

What would Dr Alexander Charles have said about my apparent shying away from the pursuit of rapture? It was a sort of cowardice.

Another narrative possibility I had eschewed was to consume Ursule in flames. This would have been a type of symbiotic consummation, an aerial apotheosis based on the fate of Madame Blanchard, whose balloon was observed in 1819 reappearing from the clouds in a sheet of flame. It was too late now, I had had the chance and let it pass. And had I really written 'Ursule leant out of the basket to touch a cloud'? What nonsense. Only write about what you know! Embarrassing.

Like many people I was in the habit of reading the *Metro* from the back, starting with the sport. When I arrived at the inside page I was confronted by a six-inch full colour image of, yes, a yellow balloon under the headline TEARS OF JOY? I was being pursued by bloody balloons. In the bottom left of the picture, where realistically the basket might have featured, was an adolescent face whose lips were fixed on the thin neck of a party balloon. The sub-heading cast some light. GOVERNMENT BANS LEGAL HIGHS. It occurred to me that might have been a better title for this book. The article referenced a webpage which warned me against drinking too much cough syrup, OD-ing on herbal Viagra, K-Kane, XTC, Snow Blow, Speedway, Hawaiian baby woodrose and Magic truffles. I noticed that none of the above were on the blackboard menu.

Was I deluding myself? Perhaps these experiences, triggered by snorting ground fertiliser up your nose, were, in their own way, as transcendent, as mystical and as spiritually significant as the mental state I was trying to evoke through my balloon narratives. Surely not. Was it really just the pursuit of fame and transient excitement that drove Laurent de Gusman in 1710 to rise into the air on the back of a wooden bird filled with air as depicted in an engraving? What about Francis Goodwin who, seventy years earlier, had tried to achieve his dream by tying himself to a team of wild geese?

There was a quote I had encountered somewhere which described a balloon flight in terms that would not be unfamiliar to those souls seeking chemically induced rapture. It was from John Wise who in the 1840s had hoped to establish the first aerial service across America and described the 'high' of ballooning. 'The blood begins to course more freely when up a mile or two – the gastric juices pour into the stomach more rapidly – the liver, the kidneys, and heart work with expanded action in a highly calorified atmosphere – the brain receives and gives more exalted inspirations.'

While seeking to capture a sense of exulted inspiration in my narrative I also wanted to capture a type of epiphany that went far beyond physical exhilaration. I wanted to bottle a yearning for fulfilment, a profound hankering for mystical sublimation, which would be of a different order from any temporary high, legal or otherwise. Both may have had their origins in dissatisfaction with life as it is, but it was the former I wanted for my characters, and arguably for myself.

Perhaps things would have turned out differently if I hadn't missed my own flight.

DEXTER
VIETNAM 1965

CHAPTER ONE

The excited men had hunkered down on the perimeter of the airbase, one by one abandoning any semblance of taking part in a discussion. They all talked at the same time about the welcome that would envelop them when they set foot in the Country. Picnics and parades, concerts and fireworks. That Star-Spangled Banner would sure be waving o'er the land of the free and the home of the brave. At home the BBQ would groan under the weight of fatted calves while willing girls, hoping to catch sight of the hero, put their heads above the fence to gawp at the porch festooned with ribbons.

Dexter Warberg lay back in the long grass and smiled at the fantasies that had sustained his buddies throughout the war. He stretched up lazily and lifted the grey metal movie canister from the archive shelf in his head, took out the spool and blew off the dust. It was the one that he reserved for special moments such as this. The label said *Coney Island Amusement Park '55*.

Jake and Dexter saw the dwarf smoking a cigarette. He had his back to them when Jake swept the pork pie hat off his head and ran off with it. The dwarf tossed aside the cigarette and set off in pursuit of the laughing boys, his miniature legs pounding the sidewalk. Eventually the boys turned down Maple Street and dropped onto the sand. They lay side by side, consumed with mirth, quite unprepared for the storm of attrition that was about to break round their heads.

Having taken note of the precise point where the boys had dropped off the boardwalk, the dwarf took a running jump and landed on top of them both. Winded by the impact of the midget man, neither boy could react. The dwarf alternately pummelled both their faces with balled fists. Eventually he sat astride Jake's chest while Dexter tried to haul him off. He eventually succeeded and all three lay in the sand. Knowing they had met their match, Jake and Dexter quickly got to their feet and prepared to run again. It was Jake who first noticed that the dwarf, no longer intent on maiming the boys, was in fact laughing, his makeup dissolving into long black streaks reaching down to his chin.

When his mirth subsided, the dwarf retrieved his hat, replaced it back on his head and solemnly declared, 'Bad boys!' He spoke in a deep voice with a strange accent. 'German,' said Jake later, though Dexter doubted that his friend knew anything about accents.

'How did you get to be that small, Mister?' asked Dexter.

'God's revenge,' said the dwarf, 'God's revenge on my son-of-a-bitch father and his whoring ways. The sins of the fathers and so on. But I have lived, boys, I have lived. Have you heard tell of the Boston cannonball? Well that was me, boys. Apprenticed to the Zacchini, I have been shot from the mouth of a cannon more times than you have eaten hot dogs. I have faced the stars, I have flown over President Johnson. Old LBJ himself.' He held his rescued hat reverentially, out of respect for the memories he was about to share on the sand.

'I was sold to the circus by my evil father, sold for forty dollars.'

'Do they use gunpowder?' asked Dexter.

'And blow a man to smithereens? No. It's compressed air with a little gunpowder, just to make it look real. But I won't tell you the secrets of the trade. I have sworn oaths of secrecy.' He lowered his voice conspiratorially. 'If I betray my code of honour my throat will be slit during the night.'

'Why did you leave, Mister?' asked Jake.

'My back is broke,' said the dwarf rubbing his lower spine. 'The net didn't hold. I think it was done on purpose. Sabotage. They were jealous of me, see. I was the best. A lot of politics in circuses. I was a young man, what could I do? I offered myself to the military, for secret missions, willing to be blasted over enemy lines, the Flying Spy, but they turned me down. Too short, you see, no exceptions can be made. So now I play the clown and make folks laugh and then I make them cry.' He replaced his hat, stood up, brushed himself down and admonishing his listeners with a repeat of 'bad boys', hauled himself back onto the boardwalk and waddled back towards the arcade. Jake and Dexter serenaded the departing clown with a series of discordant notes produced by blowing on the grass stalks they held between thumb and forefinger. Jake almost choked with laughter.

With the spool carefully replaced, Dexter reflected contentedly on the days that had preceded this moment. All the superstitious touching of dog tag, water bottle and watch; the sacrilegious signs of the cross, the ritual double-checking of carbines and the ruthlessly enforced taboos of not talking about the Date of Estimated Return from Overseas had worked. Christ it had worked! Beth and Maryanne must be twenty now, two years younger than him. Soon he would be strolling along the boardwalk. The conquering hero kissing each in turn then drinking the Bourbon. First Beth and then Maryanne touch the scar on his abdomen. They all look at the lights across the bay. A tugboat hooter acknowledges them.

The first shells crump into the fuselage, nothing to worry about, not to a boy reared on the roller coaster in Stacy

111

Park. The missing bolts always made for a more interesting ride. He had kept several of the rivets he found on the sand in a box by his bed. The Lockheed C-130 whined then screamed like when the strange man took Mary Lou's hand near the Palace. The canvas straps garrotted him as the plane tilted. Jody, who had only stood up to stretch out the cramp, flew towards the cockpit, arms and legs like a spider fish. A single tongue of flame pushed its way through the floor.

'Tell the fire eater to get back on his feet for Chrissake. Get those kids outa here. That's real dangerous.' The kerosene smelt strange, more bitter than that used to flush Charlie out of the tunnel, except that he never came out. Never. And then the rush of hot jungle air, rotting and sweet from the door of the plane. John G, the loadmaster, is braced against the exit, his wind-inflated uniform transforming him into the brother of the Michelin Man who towered above the Parade. Or the bloated VC floating face down in a green, rain-filled crater. The Colonel punctured him with a stick, the putrid air rose like a bad genie and sought out their faces. Charlie shrank and withered until he slipped under the slime, leaving a thin ribbon of bubbles.

'Get outa here, mother fuckers!' screamed John J. 'No time for fucking chutes. Time to die boys!' The stalling plane reared, bucked and hung suspended for an infinitesimal second between its forward momentum and the inertia of gravity. The jungle turned a cartwheel. John J beat at the flames fondling his legs. 'Fuck! Fuck! Fuck!' He grabbed the Colonel's seat belt and wrenched it through the buckle. He pulled the larger man to his feet, frogmarched him to the open rear door and threw him like a puppy into the warm pond of the night. A miasma of kerosene blew through the fuselage. A screaming crescendo of engine noise rendered Dexter and the other passenger incapable of decision. Each surrendered in turn to their furious jailer. Dexter was the last to leave the plane. John J grabbed him by the scruff of his neck as if he were in need of rough discipline.

Now he was back on the Island roller coaster for the first time, his stomach straining against the ligaments, bile in his mouth. The blur of lights in distant Manhattan. Tumbling in slow motion through the hot, scented night. Distant flashes of fire burnt holes in the dark sky as the mortally wounded plane buried itself in the jungle and the treetops speared upwards.

The branches tore at his uniform. His pants were ripped as if by a medic eager to expose a gaping wound. His left eye was gouged by something sharp and his cheeks were flayed.

The jungle found his unexpected arrival hysterical, insects chattered, birds hooted and sundry animals bayed with pleasure. He pushed his tongue onto his upper lip and tasted the salty blood from his eye. The jungle then decided that the disturbance was something of an anticlimax and went back to sleep.

Suspended from a branch by the webbing from his uniform, he hung helpless as a toddler.

Weeks after his arrival, his platoon had found the small corpse of a Viet Cong soldier tortured to death and strung up by the arms. On that occasion Dexter had climbed the tree and cut him free. The decomposed body covered in rags fell like wisps of smoke. Now it was his turn.

Dexter freed a hand, found his knife and cut the strands of fabric holding him. He fell through the vegetation like garbage down a chute. Slumped and covered in insects, he lay still and consciously chose spool number twelve. It had to be number twelve. Both parts of it.

The Jump had always dominated Coney Island. New Jersey's answer to the Eiffel Tower, his old man said. But his old man was wrong, there could not be a similar structure in the whole known universe. Brought in from the New

113

York World Fair of '39, his daddy said. The Eiffel Tower of Brooklyn, a yellow and red steel construction, rose 250 feet above the boardwalk. The boys would spend hours each day craning their necks to see the orange and white parachutes suspended from twelve arms at the very pinnacle. At the throw of a switch the lucky riders would plummet in billowing freefall towards the shock absorbers below.

But you had to be measured to be allowed on. Dexter used to hang by his fingertips from the stair to make himself stretch. Ma used to tell him he would grow arms like a monkey and would end up going to a zoo rather than the school. He had no complaint with that idea.

'You're kind of small, too young, come back in a decade. Find a cure for the rickets that are stuntin' your growth, son. Audition to join Dixie's Troup of Travelling Dwarves, but meantime, vamoose! Diapers leak on seats and stain the canvas. Step aside, boys, make way for the real men... Welcome, Sir. Welcome. If memory serves me right, you came here with the army years back. Best parachute trainin' in the world, they said.'

Dexter and Jake heard the same routine every day but they persisted. They knew that Antonio swigged from the brown paper bag mid-afternoon. Please God, make him so boozed up one day that he just lets us on. No questions asked.

They always tried to identify the 'screamers' by scrutinising the queue. It was a difficult challenge. The frailest invariably showed most courage; the burly and boastful were more likely to squeal like pigs as they plunged downwards.

'They both wet their pants,' said Antonio, nodding towards an unsteady couple clearly pleased to have survived the drop.

When the ride closed because of the high winds the boys would watch forlornly as the collapsed chutes nudged against the empty gondolas. When the tower was struck by lightning the boys would smell the ozone.

Jake assumed the role of historian when he suspected that the gawking tourists were vulnerable to his charm. 'Roll up, ladies and gentlemen, roll up, gaze on the mighty structure that was used to train our brave boys during World War II. The whole tower was dismantled after the New York World's Fair in 1940 and transported here for your benefit and admiration.' He would accompany his enthusiastic narrative with grandiose gestures.

When in his stride, he would unashamedly make up facts. 'Over one hundred thousand rivets were used in the Tower's construction, fifteen men gave their lives to build this wonder, and my buddy here...' he pointed dramatically towards Dexter, '...caught a tiny baby that had fallen from the car. They had no right to smuggle a baby on board, but my buddy here flew through the air and caught the child with his fielder's glove. He was, and still is, a freeman of Coney Island on account of his extraordinary courage. He will sign autographs for a dime.' Antonio shook his head and said nothing.

Antonio lived in fear of jumpers. Although there had been no jumpers, a kid from freshman year in high school claimed to have seen one. 'He dove like a bird,' he said. 'Head first onto the boardwalk, he just kind of folded into a sea of blood. I got some of his brains on my jacket.' He held out a sleeve for inspection. 'That's your own snot,' said one of his sneering peers. The kid got chased round the schoolyard and slugged in the mouth. But Antonio would take no risks. No one was allowed to ride alone. Singles had to be paired up with each other. Failing that one of the operatives would share the seat.

It was Jake's idea that they solve the height problem by making stilts, short ones just six inches high, easily hidden under pants scavenged from the garbage bins in the Heights.

115

They took turns to practise on the boardwalk, tottering like whores. Fixing shoes to the wood was the challenge. They stuffed them with stones, jammed in half-bricks but nothing worked.

Jake was the first to see the tailor's dummy lying on the sidewalk outside Macey's waiting to be collected. They nudged each other and stared at the rounded torso and the androgynous pink groin. Dexter wondered if Maryanne looked like that under her dress and panties.

'See the feet,' said Jake. 'They're screwed on.' But not for long. Laughing at their good fortune, they ran back to Dexter's home, each hiding a wooden foot under his vest. Two nails, one up through the sole, and one through the back of the heel was all it took.

Jake's question, 'You or me?' sobered them both. Only one of them could use the stilts. 'Paper, scissors, stone,' suggested Dexter.

'Scissors, scissors, stone, stone, paper, stone, you changed, you cheated, no I never, yes you did!' The boys wrestled on the carpet. Dexter's forearm fitted neatly across the soft flesh of Jake's throat. The younger boy signalled defeat with his eyes.

'I was always the lucky one, Jake, I was always the winner. Like now. I'm sorry, Jake, I'm sorry.'

His old man's overcoat came down to his ankles. Jake had suggested they should charcoal a moustache but they settled for a woollen scarf, probably the only scarf ever seen in Coney Island in August. Jake kept his distance as Dexter limped towards the pay booth.

Antonio welcomed him with a pastiche of the greeting normally reserved for New Jersey Mafiosi when they swaggered into town for R and R. 'Step right this way, Sir. Sure is the finest ride in all of the US. No charge, Sir, free as a bird. We normally prohibit smoking once in the parachute seat sir, but rules are made to be broken.' Dexter nodded

116

and attempted what he assumed was an approximation of a worldly wise swagger. The overcoat lurched off one shoulder.

Antonio opened the small gate and ushered the unnaturally elongated small boy towards the culmination of all his aspirations; the climax to all his dreams.

In one movement Antonio grabbed Dexter by the scruff of his neck, lifted him until his false, now inward-facing feet dangled clear of the ground, walked him with arms rigid for several yards and dropped him by Jake who was ill with mirth.

Dexter, the grown boy of twenty-two, put his thumb in his mouth. He opened his eyes and appraised the vegetation that had cushioned his fall. A bower of green glistening leaves was threaded with brown tendrils, one of which was now supporting a tiny beetle with pincers like the metal arm in the grab-a-candy arcade machine. A second insect was trying to drill into his head but he couldn't summon the energy to swat it away. He closed his eyes again and breathed in the rich, choking smell of wet earth.

CHAPTER TWO

Dexter dropped the bright blue insect into his mouth and teased it with his tongue before swallowing.

He must get on with the day. It was probably mid-afternoon. He rolled out of the bivouac, relieved himself, his urine steaming back up at him from the undergrowth. He felt the weight of the jerry can collecting rain water. He put it to one side and positioned an empty can in its place. He was well supplied. It had taken him a while to locate the crashed aircraft which had broken into two. The cockpit section had been incinerated. Nothing remained of the captain, co-pilot, navigator or flight engineer, all cremated in their canvas seats, along with buckles and jackets, dials, glass windows, levers, gauges, handguns, first aid kit, intercom, mess tins, helmets, life jacket, flares, joy stick, the emergency instructions printed on tin, rivets, the lucky bear given to the co-pilot by his son; everything picked clean by the flames.

The rear section located half a mile away was virtually intact. He had briefly considered using it as his base but it didn't seem safe somehow. Charlie might stumble across it. Eventually he had bundled up the unused parachutes hanging like shrouds from the open door along with the jerry cans. As he stepped down from the plane he caught sight of a letter lying among the detritus of the crash. It was addressed to Ann O'Sullivan, 12043 Bracklands Woodville, Connecticut.

It was the letter that was on his mind now as he repositioned the silk awning so that it would channel the rain into the empty jerry can. He felt compelled to check that the letter was safe, stealing it was just the sort of sneaky stunt that Victor might pull. He ducked back into the shelter and poked at the folds of the parachute that served as his mattress. He located the corners of the envelope, pulled it out and ran a finger across the address. He had never been tempted to read its contents, they were secret words between a man and his girl. The one thing he knew was that the letter would reach its destination. He wouldn't make the same mistake again, no sir.

The platoon, newly arrived at Da Nang, had known he was guilty. Guilty as sin. Who else would have been so stupid? No one else would have dropped the mail on the track between the latrines and the tent and then watch helplessly as the Commando G-392 ground the missives into the churned mud. Like the first time there had been consequences, but this time no one had died.

As the address on the envelope had been obliterated, Joe's letter from his sweetheart was accidently opened by the captain who read out the words of love and sex that ran down the page in a silly girly falsetto voice. Joe snatched it back and smoothed the page flat. John-John feigned tears as he read the news that his dog had died. He didn't even know that he had a dog. Zak who did have a dog that he loved more than life itself, and which was now apparently dead, torpedoed like the quarterback he was, into John-John's midriff. But they all knew who was to blame. They held Dexter down and rouged his cheeks with gun oil, then tugged at his pants to do the same with his ass, but he had wiggled free as they laughed and called him their slave for

119

the rest of the day. That had been easy. Swift justice. Why had he not been beaten and punished after the Jake thing? Why didn't he just kill himself after it all happened?

'Nope!' he shouted. 'I will not go there! Not yet, soon, soon, when I'm good and ready.' He swung himself out of the hammock. Most of the time he was immune to the screaming cacophony of the jungle, but now he was deafened. He was being smothered by a malicious and malevolent environment. Shrieking birds competed with the mechanical insistence of the crickets. He was trapped in the boiling innards of a vast green machine being driven to breaking point and lubricated by sweat. But he would not go there. He would not go there. He had seen how his fellow grunts anaesthetised themselves with dope and made their war mellow. His method was different but effective. Long before Vietnam he had cultivated his gift of memory as his drug of choice. In the months after the Jake thing he had sorted and catalogued specific memories which could, in the short term, postpone unsolicited moments of panic and dread. The method only worked for a while and there was always a reckoning. But that would come later.

Where was canister 14? Had he put it back in the wrong place? No, there it was. He handed it to the projectionist.

While the staccato numbers counted down on the screen Dexter realised that he may have gotten confused over the content. What was he about to watch? The Brooklyn Dodgers bitter sweet 2 – 0 victory over Pittsburgh Pirates as they prepared to leave Ebbets Field in '58? Could be, but he wasn't certain. Reassembling a carburettor for the first time and getting a dollar from his dad? No. Breaking into the fairground at night with Jake, sitting on the painted horses, sick with laughter? No. A good memory right enough, but probably number ten or thereabouts. Pushing the raft made of a stolen pallet and jerry cans into the dark waters off Coney Pier? He shuddered. Definitely not.

He felt a surge of excitement in his stomach as the first images appeared. Movie number fourteen was usually reserved for the pitch-black night when dead colleagues called out to him, begging for help, for cigarettes, for mom, sometimes for dad. The memory that worked when all else failed.

There he was, lying under the Coney Island boardwalk with Beth and Maryanne. A girl under each arm, a lord of life at the age of fourteen. They would giggle as couples paused and kissed, unaware of the smirking youngsters beneath their feet. Sometimes they would silently count to three and then roar like bulls, startling the lovers into flight. Once too, Hobo Joe had stopped directly above them, his boots blocking the slivers of light that filtered through the cracks. They heard him uncorking his bottle before he continued his argument with someone who had left him many years ago. What had he said? 'I'll whip your ass if you look at her again, you squinty-eyed son of a bitch!'

And what had Dexter shouted in a high pitched voice to impress the girls? 'Oh Joe, come back to me, come back, my sweetheart!'

Joe took off down the boardwalk shouting 'I'm on my way, Dolly, I'm coming, honey.' The three of them howled until Maryanne couldn't get her breath, which made them laugh even more. And then the girls showed him how much they liked him.

They were still there when the first light of dawn picked out the ripples on the water. The tide was in and the sea was nudging its way towards their legs. Maryanne panicked, 'Geeze, Dexter, my ma will kill me.' She grabbed her shoes, emptied the sand from them and fled homeward along the narrowing ribbon of beach. Beth said nothing. Both she and Dexter knew that Maryanne's mother would not notice that her daughter had been out all night. The recent influx of sailors into New Jersey would have kept her busy.

Dexter yawned, stretched and lowered himself onto the ground. Movie number 14 was becoming indistinct as the sound of the sea merged into the perpetual tinnitus of insects. It was time to inspect the bodies.

'Colonel George, Sir.' It was difficult to look up thirty metres into the glare of the sun but by shading his eyes he could see more clearly the picked-clean skull slumped onto the officer's shoulder. There had been some slippage but the bodies had not yet embarked on their final journey to the jungle floor.

When he had first found the colonel he had been disconcerted by his resemblance to Christ. In the searing light the dead man's features morphed into the image of the Sacred Heart that Dexter's mother had pinned to the pantry door. The crown of jungle thorns had slipped. Dexter had dropped to his knees barely able to look at his Creator. Perhaps his sentence was under review. Perhaps the Court Martial convened by the Holy Trinity had decided that the initial sentence had been too lenient. Colluding in the death of a friend compounded by abject cowardice deserved more than exile to a war in the Far East. He braced himself but there were no further pronouncements. Case adjourned.

When he next summoned the courage to pay reluctant homage to his commanding officer, things had changed. He was no longer a Christ figure but a comic scarecrow dressed in army fatigues, mocked by the birds perched on his skull, picking at his sockets.

The other dead man, bent double over a branch, had always been deserving of less attention. His comical posture, that of a discarded puppet, served to reinforce his irreverence. Dexter had found him tedious in the cargo hold of the C100. Boastful and sneering at the same time, he had competed with the abominable noise of the aircraft, and left spittle on Dexter's ear as he filled it with bravado tales of rape and brutality. Death suited him.

More recently Dexter's relationship with the Colonel had improved and he would, on occasions, confide in him.

He saluted, 'Nothing to report, Sir. No sign of Victor. By my reckoning we've been here for six months now, Sir. Do I have permission to speak, Sir? Thank you, Sir. Sometimes, Sir, I feel real lonesome. No mail. No word from home. I worry about my folks, and I know it's maybe selfish but I miss hearing about the Dodgers. Sometimes I fall asleep playing the games in my head. Perhaps no news is bad news, Sir.

'I did what you said, Sir, and covered my arms in mud, it sure kept the critters at bay. And the thing is, Sir, though I know you'll get us out of here and back to the Country, with respect, Sir, I don't see how it can be done. The cliff you boys chose to crash into is sheer, like glass. No toeholds, nothing. And with the rains and all, the river is fast. It's like the Grand Canyon, not that I've seen the Canyon, Sir, but my old granddaddy, he used to tell me about the waves and the steam. It's the same, Sir, so help me.

'Sir, I don't mean to be disrespectful, but I can't hear what you're saying, Sir. I think one of those goddam bugs has crawled into my earhole.'

Banging one side of his head against the palm of his hand, Dexter turned to walk back to the corner of the jungle that was his. He paused. There was something else on his mind.

'One more thing, Sir. I've got my purple heart, Sir. You and I know that they give them out like candy, something to tell the folks at home, let them brag a bit with the neighbours. "My boy's a hero and he's making our country safer," and similar baloney that the hairy-faced peaceniks scoff at. Well, Sir, that aside, you and I know that I done a brave thing in the tunnels. What I'm saying, Sir, is I'm not a coward, Sir. When they hauled me out of that hole by the rope round my ankles, and I dangled spinning upside down from that tree. And you laughed, Sir; you said I was a brave, brave boy. And I saluted you, Sir, my upside down face next to yours.

'Thing is, Sir, I know I should try and swim that river. I swam a lot at the Island, drowned three times according to my folks. But Sir, it's the piranhas, I can't face them, Sir. I took three of those yellow tree frogs down to the edge the other day. You know the poisonous ones, they was squirming as I tossed them into the river and the water boiled, Sir, it was a witch's brew of blood and pus. I'm not a coward, Sir, but I can't swim in the water, Sir.'

'Can't swim in the water,' Decker muttered as he fanned the mosquitos away from his face. He spat one out of his mouth, and then ducked as a swarm formed a shimmering mask round his head.

There was a time when he could swim in the water. Dexter and Jake had previously made excursions into the creek. The pickings on Gravesend Bay were good if you wanted to find something that would float. On this occasion charred and rotten beams from a harbour somewhere nudged up against rusty car innards, half a door and a zinc bath. The oil drum was well lodged into the sand and it had taken both of them a while to work it free and lie it on its side. 'Heavy as a hog,' said Jake. 'It must be half full, it'll never float.' He wiped his tarry fingers down his pants.

'Your ma will kill you,' suggested Dexter.

'And yours,' he said, rubbing the residue into Dexter's vest. The two boys fought for a while then rested against the drum. 'Need to empty it,' said Jake.

'We need Antonio's wrench.'

The boys raced each other towards the Parachute Tower. A young couple joined at the waist with their arms entwined read the safety notice. '...take no responsibility or liability for accidents, death or other unforeseen circumstances...' After unnecessarily elongating each syllable the man scoffed

124

and spat his gum onto the boardwalk. Two seagulls arrived simultaneously from nowhere. Antonio, sheltering from the sun in the kiosk, wiped his brow with his handkerchief. Jake ducked under the fence and crawled on hands and knees past the window towards the awning where the toolbox was kept. The padlock was off.

It took both of them to carry the heavy greased wrench back to the beach. Dexter took charge and tightened the jaws round the rusted drum cap as he'd seen his old man do many times in the garage. The cap eventually surrendered under the boys' combined weight and popped out onto the sand. It was followed by a flow of gloopy black sludge that formed an ever-widening pool. Dexter sat down and pulled off his sneakers. He stood in the black oil and watched his toes disappear. He stood on one leg and flicked a long thread of oil at Jake who retaliated by stamping in the black mess, sending tongues of oil onto Jake's pants. Shrieking, they picked up dripping handfuls of black sand and rubbed them in each other's hair. 'We're the minstrel boys,' said Dexter, strumming an imaginary banjo.

'And dear ol' Dixie's our home.'

They rolled the drum to the water's edge and pushed it out into the bay. It floated low down in the water which reached their knees. Jake patted an errant beach ball back to the woman in a swimsuit who had been dispatched to retrieve it. He grinned at Dexter who had also been distracted by her large bosom. And then there was no sand beneath them, just water. Both boys held onto the rim of the drum but there was little purchase. They were floating away from the shore. The shouts and laughter from the sunbathers became muted and then stopped altogether. Jake tried to clamber onto the drum which responded to his efforts by rotating beneath him and returned him to the water. Jake was the weaker swimmer. He clung to Dexter and both boys sank. 'Just float,' spluttered Dexter when they next surfaced. Reluctantly Jake let himself be slowly steered towards the beach. They were helped ashore by a large man in a Hawaiian shirt who removed his pitcher's glove before offering his hand. 'Never trust water, boys,' he said.

Soon afterwards they lay side by side on the sand with their eyes closed against the sun. 'You swim like a fish out of water,' said Dexter.

'But man, we floated that old drum for miles,' said Jake. 'We damn near made the other side.'

'Some day,' said Dexter. 'Some day.' The memory shrivelled.

Dexter stood completely still. He siphoned out the buzzing, squawking, cawing, shrieking and whooping and listened for the tiny sound of cracking twigs that would reveal Victor. Nothing.

The path back to the bivouac was well trodden and familiar. Even so, he concentrated on every foot of the way, looking for tiny telltale signs of disturbance that might reveal the presence of a new trapdoor. He knew he was miles from Cu Chi but old habits die hard.

Eventually he inspected the parachute thrown over the sloping A-frame of branches. He knocked out the pools of rain water weighing down the silk, and crawled inside. As he hunkered down he reflected on the recent one-way discussion with the Colonel. Was his silence significant? He snorted, thinking that his lack of response was more easily explained by the fact that the Colonel had been dead for the last six months. Even so. He would not like to incur his displeasure. Perhaps he shouldn't have boasted about his bravery underground.

He hadn't felt so brave the first time he saw a soldier winched out of the tunnels. He and Dan had squabbled earlier about which of them would go down first. Dan won, and winked as he placed his dagger between his teeth and ducked into the pit. They heard the muffled sounds of gunfire and had hoped that Dan had killed the VC in the darkness of the tunnel.

As a boy, Dexter would wait with his pals outside Ebbets Field, trying hard to interpret the noise from the crowd. That was a home run surely. Was that the last strike to win the game? So too when they heard the gunshot, there was a discussion about whether it had been from the standard issue Colt 45 or a foreign weapon. JC had pointed out that Victor was just as likely to have stole the gun so they would just have to wait. His words proved to be prophetic when they hauled Dan out. He had no face and dropped blood on the ground like the sides of meat in the Brooklyn factory where his papa had once taken Dexter for a treat.

The memory disconcerted Dexter. He felt his heart pounding and hoped that the noise would not alert the silent enemy who had perhaps approached, and was now braced to force a stake into his ribcage.

He lay motionless until convinced that he was alone, then brushed the silk with his hand. It was his sweetheart's face, not that he had met her yet, but he would, and her face would be as soft as the fabric he stroked. It was his sweetheart's breast. His finger and thumb sought out the harder shape of her nipple in the sown seam. After a moment he stifled his fantasy and looked nervously out of the bivouac, half expecting his old man to emerge from the jungle, belt in hand, preparing to leather his son the way he had when he found him reading *Playboy* in the cupboard under the stairs.

He had loved that dark, warm place and frequently hid there when in trouble. Once he had gone missing and his mother, having searched high and low, contacted the police department. The cop seemed massive with a badge the size of a star. He issued her with a warning when the small, snivelling boy was hauled out from behind the new hoover and the spare bedding. Why had he hidden there in the first place? He couldn't remember but guessed he had been in trouble for some minor misdemeanour, and had been told to wait until his old man came home.

Perhaps he had sneaked out to meet Jake and venture onto Surf Avenue, past the bowling lanes and down Stillwell Avenue to gape at the photos outside the tattoo parlour.

'Jees, a whole Elvis rippling down your arm.'

'I fancy the schooner, and an anchor, and the bell, cool.'

'What about a mermaid?'

'Nup, the bottom half's a fish.'

Perhaps they had gone to look at the Rocket Ships, the Whale Boats or the Dark Ride. Perhaps he had taken the brown pennies from his mother's purse against the time when they would be tall enough to attempt the Jump. One day too they would enter the Tent of the Deformed, and gasp with delight at the woman with an ear in the middle of her forehead and the man with white, white skin, hair and eyes.

Jake said it had been closed years back. 'And anyway, it's not right to stare at folk born that way.'

'We belong together, Mr Rat,' said Dexter, dragging the entrails from the thin, still twitching carcass and flicking them into the jungle. He stuck the bamboo skewer up its butt, manoeuvred it until it emerged from its mouth and placed it across the flame. There were now three of them in a row.

'I suppose you is a rat, a Nam rat, different from those fairground rats that scuttled over our legs in the dark. Never thought I'd be eating a rat but life is full of surprises. Don't you go using all my gasoline now. Two for me and one for Jake: boy never did have much of an appetite.

'Perhaps it was you I seen in that tunnel. When I put my head through that trapdoor bracing myself for a stake in the throat, perhaps it was you I seen. Beady eyes and whiskers a-twitching.

'Funny thing, see, I never had no problems with tunnels. Small and wiry. "Have you any Mexican in you, son?"'

'No, Sir, I just didn't grow much after things happened at home.'

'Do you have any fear of enclosed spaces?'

'No, Sir, I spent days once in a dark, dark cupboard.'

'Well, son, you have just been volunteered to become a tunnel rat.'

'Down you go, son,' said the colour sergeant. 'Get your ass in gear and get down the hole.'

The tunnel entrance had been uncovered by the heavy earth movers that had cut swathes through the undergrowth. The grunts followed in their wake, elated by the open space and the possibility of respite from the snipers. Respite too from the sunken mortars that could rip off their limbs like wings from a Kentucky Fry. The earth movers would absorb the impact, the shredded tracks might fly above their heads but the crew would emerge dazed and goddamning whatever motherfucker Victor had buried the device with his trenching tool. There would be a welcome delay as C-rations were taken; each mouthful chewed in slow motion to elongate time. The grunts would sleep standing up against the stranded vehicle.

The trapdoor had been scooped up with the black earth and the vegetation. A grunt stood above the hole about to toss in a grenade when his arm was held by the sergeant. 'Not now,' he said. 'It's time to bite the bullet. Here's your big moment, boy.'

Dexter knew the drill. Drop into the dark, crawl a few yards, lie still, listen to the blood in your ears and then back out of the tunnel. He had heard the reports from the others. 'It's cold, Sir, cold as a witch's tit, Sir. Victor's gone on his holidays. Gone to Cambodia, Sir.' But Dexter wanted to do the job properly. If Charlie and his cronies were in the bowels of the earth he would find him no matter how deep he was hidden.

His fear made him bite harder on his knife than he had intended. His teeth hurt. His torch showed that the tunnel came to a dead end just a few yards further on. He knew there would be another trapdoor. Inching forward on his elbows, he was aware that the tunnel was narrowing; he was a perfect fit. There was no room to move his arms behind him to reach his pistol should he need it. The tunnel walls were closing in and squeezing the breath from him. How could earth smell so strong? The cloying dusky smell of overripe vegetation, something rank and animal, something human, the tang of sweat, excrement. Charlie's shit. Roots caressed his face as if trying to identify him from its contours, before strangling him once the soft flesh of his throat had been located. He was hot and breathing so fast that the knife dropped in front of him. He held it and picked at the edges of the trapdoor, a surgeon probing the edges of a wound. If it was booby-trapped these would be his last moments on earth. He might have crawled willingly into his own grave.

CHAPTER THREE

He and Jake were ten years old. The recent storm had moved the sand and revealed a new space under the boardwalk near West 12th Street. It needed further excavation. The boys would lie side by side facing the sea and talk and plan and plot.

They had given names to all of the tugboats that ploughed relentlessly up the bay. Old Boiler, Mrs Dugdale and Rust Bucket. They could easily swim across the current and wave to the skipper who would take them aboard, give them dry towels and show them to their bunks. They would have to work their passage of course. They could paint the cabins, clean the galley. They would travel to India, Africa, Nantucket.

Some days they would bring their rations, soda and cookies, which would have to last them until rescue came. On one occasion the cookies fell into the sand which gave them a problem. Their survival depended on those cookies so they licked off the sand and spat it out. Dexter felt the grains in his teeth.

Best of all was when it rained. They watched from their dry shelter as whole families, after initially defying the rain, decamped with hampers and towels.

Once they found a rag puppy dropped by a small girl who was hurrying to keep up with her ma and pa. They thought briefly of handing it in to the cops but then recognised it as a prize from the tombola stall. Old Henry was notoriously stingy with his prizes, especially the puppies. They would look after it for a few days and then sell it back to Henry. Jake said no, he would think they had stolen it in the first place and whip their backsides. No, best keep it.

It was fall, and the sand was damp at the point where it reached the underside of the boardwalk. They were both shivering and had to do something to keep warm. It had been Jake's idea to start the tunnel. Progress was slow until they found their rhythm. Jake lay on his side and pushed the sand down towards Dexter who pushed it further back. They took turns to dig until the tunnel was long enough to accommodate them both, one behind the other.

'We need to shore it up,' said Jake. 'Else the sides will collapse.'

The rest of the day was spent gathering wood washed in by the recent storm. Dexter found the crate with Anchor Beer stencilled on the side. They quickly broke it into planks which they added to the heap of fence stakes, sticks and branches.

'Invite me to the barbeque, boys,' said Hobo Joe.

'You bring the chow,' said Jake.

Hobo Joe held his bottle in its brown paper bag at arm's length and toasted the boys before lurching down the sand.

Staggering under the weight of wood, they ducked under the boardwalk and dragged their load to the narrow apex they had excavated earlier. They used the planks to make a floor, and then they wedged the sticks upright hard against the underside of the boardwalk. They lay behind each other as the day grew dark.

'We could stay here for ever,' said Jake. 'They'll never find us.'

'We'll need candles,' said Dexter. 'Ma keeps them under the stairs.'

Next to the trapdoor a small alcove held several candle stubs. Victor would only use them sparingly lest they sucked out the sparse air that leaked from the diagonal ventilation shafts sneaking down from the jungle above.

Dexter found a grip on the door and prised it from the floor of the tunnel. He had heard tales of false openings through which the trespassing grunt would fall and be impaled head first on spikes; or slither into a snake-filled pit. Or drown in a deep earthen tank of shit.

He shone his torch into the void. He could see the earth several feet down. Lowering himself headfirst into the hole he hung suspended for several seconds before letting go and landing awkwardly on the floor. He lay bruised and breathing fast. His torch showed a bend in this lower tunnel towards which he inched. The hot rancid air suggested that the tunnel was not abandoned.

The floor sloped steeply. He moved crouching for several minutes. Having memorised the slight bends in the next twenty yards, he switched off his torch and stopped. Whose breath was he hearing, his own or that of Victor in the dark? He waited and then lay down again on the floor, inching his way forward. Realising that he owed a death to Jake made him calm. He knew a ninety-degree bend was ten yards away. When he reached the turn he rested his head on the soil. If his adversary was to fire into the void there was a good chance he would aim at where the bulk of his body would be had he not been crouching. He listened again but could only hear the blood in his own ears. He was not in a hurry. He would wait for as long as it took before Victor lost his nerve and fired first. He switched his torch on and off as quickly as he could. There was no gunfire, no eardrum shattering explosion. As the dark returned he tried to make sense of the afterglow image that stayed with him for a millisecond.

The shadow scorched on his retina told him that the tunnel

sloped downwards in a straight line for approximately fifty yards or so. Elbowing his way downwards in a side-to-side rocking movement he became, in that instant, Jonny, the Negro Midget. Jonny would have his audience in stitches as he waddled down the aisle before hoisting himself into the lap of a stranger, carefully chosen on account of his preoccupation with a girlfriend rather than the show. Like an overgrown malevolent toddler, he would nestle into the man's armpit and pretend to sleep. The man would instantly leap to his feet with Jonny's small arms wrapped round his waist holding on for all he was worth.

Eventually Dexter felt his face pushing against something soft, a blanket perhaps. Thinking for a moment that he too had crawled up against a stranger, he braced himself for the shot that would end his life. Again no shot came. He felt the material, it was a curtain of some kind. Switching his torch back on he saw that the sacking served to block the tunnel from whatever lay beyond. Light was seeping round the edges.

Light was seeping round the edges of the tent. Jake had suggested that if they crawled closer and removed a peg they could lift a corner of the canvas and peep under and stare at Ryan's Exotic 'demoiselles from Gay Paris' who were resting between shows. The ground along the bottom of the canvas was thick with cigarette butts. Dexter had pulled one of the restraining pegs back and forth until it surrendered like a stubborn wooden carrot. By keeping one side of his head against the earth, he could just look into the space. He could though see nothing apart from the sagging underframe of a settee hard up against the canvas. After staying motionless for long enough to convince Jake that he was witnessing a feast of naked flesh and a sea of discarded undergarments, Dexter re-emerged, rolling his eyes in what he hoped was a simulation of sated lust.

Jerking his head slightly to dislodge the sweat about to drop into his eyes, Dexter peered under the curtain. The small chamber was lit by several candles. The stench of sickness and decay was overwhelming. A wizened figure, lying on a bed, made eye contact with him as he drew back the curtain and stood up in the space. He saw another figure, and another. All stared impassively. Saline drips hung from the ceiling. In a corner, assault rifles were stacked together. As he stood transfixed he became aware of someone else in the room. A small woman was staring at him. Dressed completely in white, she made no sound, nor did she flinch under this stranger's gaze. She was young, seventeen or so, thought Dexter, as tiny and thin as a bird. And beautiful. He nodded respectfully at his enemy and withdrew back into the tunnel.

'I figured you were dead, boy,' said the Sergeant. 'I'd started dictating that letter back home to your mom, telling her how brave and unflinching in your duty you was as you engaged with the VC in a manner that inspired the whole platoon. Now get your ass out of that hole and get saddled up with the others.'

A sinew of rat meat lodged itself between Dexter's back teeth. He probed it with his tongue but it refused to come loose. He tried with two fingers but it was not for moving. He was already anticipating the moment hours later when he would find it in his mouth, a tiny thread of meat that he would then savour. The stash of C-rations he had salvaged from the half fuselage had not lasted long. He had stacked the small tins outside the bivouac and rationed himself to one tin a day until the contents rotted and smelled bad. He had emptied the fat writhing worms onto the ground.

Feeling relaxed he thought he might just treat himself to movie number 4. He sat leaning against a tree and waited for the show to start.

135

The carpets always stung your feet when you got out of the baths. No one knew why. It was always a matter for discussion. Soaked with disinfectant, some said. Others said it was the itch from dirty folk from the Gut. There was general agreement that Ravenhall was the best. The water was cleaner, the steam was hotter, the hot dogs and fries were beyond compare, the soap dispenser was always full. Jake said they should take extra and sell it but the lifeguard was watching. No other baths had a passageway under the boardwalk to the beach. The purple stamp on your wrist would last for days if you didn't wash. Dexter's ma said it looked like he had iodine all over his skin to cure some infection, and she kept a clean home. All the boys tried to get the locker room next to the girls' changing room because of the knot hole through in the wood, though Ed said he got his eye poked from a large woman on the other side. One thing was certain, swimming sure made you hungry.

Fried knishes, corn on the cob, fried dough, cinnamon, sugar and candy, shish kebabs, sausage links, sauerkraut, fried oysters. It was the smell of roasted peanuts that hurt most.

When the old man collapsed on the boardwalk that time, Mikey left his stall and rushed to help. Jake leaned over and helped himself, stuffing his mouth with hot nuts. His cheeks bulged and burnt. As they ran away, Jake's pockets overflowed, leaving a trail that the keystone cops would not have missed. They ran onto the beach and shared their spoils. Clutching their bellies, they started pelting each other before settling for a nut-spitting competition. Dexter won. But he always did.

Sensing an unbidden dark cloud forming in his head, Dexter spun through the other memories that he could call on. The roulette wheel slowed ominously at memory 11 then, to Dexter's relief, found the energy to click the dice across two more wedges of the board. It stopped with the Buick.

'Learn the motor, son,' said his old man. 'Take the beauty to pieces, part by part and label them all when you're done.' His father pointed towards the Invicta crumpled beyond repair, newly arrived in the yard. 'And don't be giving me that sulky face.'

In a moment Dexter was suffused with admiration for the engine's complexity. Through the clouds of his own preoccupations, he was now staring at the inner workings of a universe completely different from the one he knew with its endless guilt and unhappiness. It was a universe he would conquer.

The front fender was easy as it had been partially dislodged by the crash. He soon located a spanner that enabled him to detach the headlight assemblies. A larger spanner was needed to remove the radiator support. The grille assembly was buckled and resisted all his efforts, until he combined the finesse of a stevedore with the patience and precision of a surgeon. Eventually it too rested on the floor. The battery was easy once the positive cable and associated wiring had been dealt with. Removing the hood hinge from the rusted fender bracket taxed his ingenuity. Utterly absorbed and sweating profusely, he turned his attention to the radiator. After disconnecting all the hoses, the contents washed into his shoes. With an innocence long forgotten, he enjoyed the sensation of the cold brown water cooling his feet.

Dexter froze, there was movement somewhere. The jungle fell silent. Not a leaf stirred. Knowing that he was exposed and vulnerable, he crouched and ran into the immediate undergrowth. He had the knife with a rat's carcass skewered on its tip but no other weapon. His pistol had jammed during solitary shooting practice a month back. Despite taking the weapon to pieces, it was beyond repair. He had subsequently found several machine guns in the plane wreckage but they had fused together in the heat of the fire and were quite useless.

Was it a VC, like himself lost and stranded, separated from his platoon? An animal, a wild dog. A ghost? The restless soul of his enemy? Charlie believed in ghosts. That's why the VC always retrieved their dead.

His platoon had returned to the scene of a firefight. They saw the blood-marked trails where the villagers had dragged the cadavers to lie them alongside their ancestors. The numbers of dead combatants were the only indicator that they were winning the war. On orders from on high, they had dug into new graves to confirm the body count. Decomposing corpses stared open-eyed at the violators of their eternal rest.

Rick, a loud-mouthed grunt from Louisiana, had urinated into a newly exposed grave found on the side of a hill near an abandoned village. The others, despite his urging, were reluctant to do likewise. It was unlucky. The dead men would rise, would find them in the darkest hours and cut their throats as they slept.

The dead certainly returned to haunt Dexter's sleep that night. 'It wasn't me! It was Rick,' he shouted from the depth of his nightmare. He sat up in his sleeping bag. Had the other members of the patrol heard him? In that instant he felt disloyal. He was a schoolboy betraying his pal rather than take his punishment at high school.

He had last set foot in high school five years ago. The best part of two thousand days. In that time he had been wounded twice, set fire to numerous small, apparently deserted villages, spent one whole night submerged in a ditch, taken part in several firefights, explored dark tunnels, been unbelievably bored waiting for something, anything to happen, been bitten by dogs, endured nightmares and slept standing up during the day, had two men die in his arms, been complicit in the death of an over-enthusiastic

138

platoon leader, written scores of letters home, and run his bayonet through a small VC fighter. Two thousand days. Two thousand nights.

If he did his duty he would be spared and go home. If he was a good boy his Mom would hold him in her arms, Dan Willowby from next door would turn up with the Bourbon bottle to toast the conquering hero. He would go to college. He would graduate *cum laude* while the band played the *Star-Spangled Banner*. He would celebrate his twenty-third birthday with Maryanne who would finally give herself to him. Sated, they would cruise the bars on the boardwalk. The same bars he had been too young to frequent when he enlisted.

Now he just hid in the jungle and listened to his own heartbeat. Waiting for whichever ghost had returned from the dead to snatch his soul. It would be the small VC, of that there was no doubt. When the blade entered under his ribcage, they had stared at each other frozen in the moment. The VC looked at him with disbelief and hatred. He emitted a long gurgle, not breaking eye contact. Then he fell. The knife was stuck. Dexter placed his foot on the man's torso and heaved until the blade came out. Eventually one of his platoon found him and smacked him heartily on the back. 'Let the motherfucker rot in his own voodoo hell.' That phrase again.

An insect sucked at the sweat on his forehead. He endured its slow progress down past his eyes and along the bridge of his nose. He couldn't swot it lest this, the smallest of movements, would betray his presence. He desperately wanted to urinate and eventually did so, deriving a small comfort from the relief and the warm wet sensation in his groin. Gradually the jungle came to life again, the birds shrieked and gossiped. The threat had receded. Charlie had gone home. Dexter emerged cautiously from his hiding place. 'I will tell the Colonel tomorrow,' he said out loud before creeping once more into the silk bivouac.

Within minutes, night descended. The sudden onset of night in South East Asia was a phenomenon that still surprised Dexter. Cocooned in the darkness, he was soon on the verge of sleep. Eventually he managed to switch off the magic lantern show of dead VCs and hungry ghosts, and returned to those happy first days in the garage. He had known all along that the carburettor would prove a real challenge to his newly-honed skills and so it proved.

By way of preparation he had studied the relevant section of the *Shop Manual Supplement* that his father had passed to him once he realised that his son was serious in his endeavours. They worked well together. Jake was still a bleak presence for both of them but there was an unspoken understanding that his shade would not intrude into either of their heads so long as they concentrated on the task in hand. Jake would stay in the yard, kicking his heels outside of the garage, waiting to tug at Dexter's coat when he ventured out.

But that was for later. Just now it was important to disconnect the vacuum supply and delivery line, the choke heat pipe, the fuel line, the spark control line, the fast idle cam, the fast idle screw, the throttle return screw... As the detail of the mechanical operation became blurred and sleep took hold, Dexter enjoyed the exhilarating physical sensation of his body leaving the earth. In his euphoria he was rising through the air completely at peace with himself and the whole world.

When he woke the feeling was still with him. He savoured it as if trying to recreate the taste of a recently finished meal but its precise texture remained elusive. First light came suddenly and he felt the raw earthy smell on the back of his throat. Someone threw a switch and the birds squawked and chatted to each other. Dexter unwrapped the waxy leaves from the leftover slivers of rat. He washed in the water which had collected overnight in both the jerry can and the improvised bower of umbrella leaves. As agreed with himself, he had to report to the commander.

The Colonel seemed to acknowledge his approach. A slight incline of the head. No more. The other figure was predictably indifferent to his presence.

'Morning, Sir, sorry to disturb, Sir.' In response to the unheard instruction to stand at ease he relaxed into his report. 'Movement, Sir, I think Charlie was sniffing round last night. I lay low, Sir. No alternative, no weapons. You're right, Sir, I guess I should have been braver, crept up and strangled him with my bare hands. I'll do better next time. I won't fail you again, Sir. I'll smoke him out, Sir, I'll find the sucker, string him up by his black pyjamas. I'll get on his tail right away.'

Dexter saluted and made to leave. As he did so he paused in front of the other figure slewed in the vegetation. 'Scuse me, soldier, have we met before? Unless I'm much mistaken I think you were at Abraham Lincoln High School. Third grade. You were neighbours to Jake. Yes, that's him. God bless his soul.' Dexter crossed himself.

'No,' he said defensively. 'What? Don't you be saying that! It was an accident. I reckon everyone knows that. You better wise up, dumb-looking hoodlum, or I'll climb up there and bust your ass, so help me. I told him we were too far out, but you know Jake... No, that's not fair. I'm warning you, soldier. Don't push me. You're a useless piece of dog shit! I'm telling you! Stop hiding up there, brown-nosing the colonel.' He held his fists in boxer stance, 'Just you and me, come on!'

Disappointed that the dead man seemed reluctant to take up the challenge, Dexter turned on his heels and left, muttering his way back into the jungle.

Realising that he owed it to the Colonel to hunt down his enemy, he decided to start from the point where he thought he had heard Charlie the day before. He tucked his knife into his belt and picked up a metal bar he had rescued from the wreck and hidden with other potentially useful objects in the vegetation.

Progress was slow as he inspected the undergrowth looking for broken leaves that could have been left by his quarry. He looked too for the bobbing antennae of the RO leading the way, and the other platoon members who should have been spread out on either side like an accordion. He felt they were there somewhere, just hidden from each other. He was fully aware that Charlie would make booby traps from sharpened bamboo pulled taut and attached to a hair trigger.

On his first patrol he had heard the cry from Ret, a farm boy from Oklahoma with a love of horses, the only soldier he had really spoken to since leaving the Country. He found him perfectly skewered through his abdomen by a stake, probably poisoned. In disbelief and denial, Ret had tugged at the stake with both hands. Two grunts had rushed forward while the others crouched and scoured the trees for signs of ambush. The two-metre long bamboo prohibited any sideways movement. Ret jerked forward like the clown-faced robot in Astroland Park. He was as scared as any human being could be, begging for help and howling with pain.

The grunts pulled unhelpfully like audience members hauled up on stage to test the illusionist's claims. The claims were valid just as they had been when Dexter and Jake had put their hands where the magician's torso should have been. Jack swore afterwards that he had seen the thin body of the charlatan wrapped round the back of the trunk. Dexter said that the legs were false, the man had been lying flat with only his head showing to the public. The man had slipped them a dollar after the show and put his finger to his lips. Jake and Dexter had fought for the coin outside the tent. Dexter got to it first.

'Pull the motherfucker out of me!'

The RO radioed for a chopper but there was little point. He knew his men would be invisible from the sky and the flares were all used up. Ret was staring at the blood pouring from his stomach. His pants were red. Like a small boy who had soiled himself with excitement, he called for his mom. He slumped forward, unable to fall. The sergeant retrieved his dog tag.

Dexter closed the memory down and concentrated on his immediate surroundings. Gradually the jungle was thinning and giving way to paddy fields. The water was sour, the dikes were unkempt. And then Dexter saw him. He was standing on the other side of the flooded field. Short, even for a gook, and dressed in the ubiquitous uniform of the VC. Dexter pulled the knife from his belt and splashed into the water. His adversary just stood there with his hands on his hips. Dexter could have sworn that the man was laughing at him. In his eagerness Dexter floundered and fell into the water. As he pulled himself upright there was no doubt about it, the gook was indeed laughing and pointing animatedly.

Realising the futility of wading through the fields, Dexter climbed back onto the dike and started to run towards his foe who ran in the opposite direction until he reached an intersection diagonally opposite Dexter. Both men paused and looked at each other. As Dexter ran, so did the gook. A game of chequers. A ridiculous mating ritual. A dance, the choreography of which both men understood. Dexter feinted to the right and the man mirrored him by moving left. Both men paused and stared at each other. They understood that the game was over. The stalemate had to be resolved. The gook nodded to Dexter as if they were opponents in a martial arts tournament. He then slowly pulled out a knife. Both men stepped into the water. The gook seemed to be high-stepping like a pantomime villain.

143

Eventually they stood facing each other barely five yards apart. Again the gook bowed. Before Dexter had time to fully take in the absurdity of the situation, his legs had been whipped from under him and his head had been forced under water. Sheer blind panic filled each unbearably elongated second. Finding the strength in his terror, he finally managed to throw off his adversary. 'For fuck's sake, Jake,' he spluttered, 'you take things too far, man,' he wiped his forearm across his mouth. 'You never know when to stop.' He spat into the wet sand. 'You could have drowned me.' The gook started to say something but Dexter spoke over him. 'Shut up talking! You know how I feel about water, and yet you held me under. You just don't get it. I've said I'm sorry, but you won't let it go, you won't let it go.' Now exhausted, he sank to his knees.

CHAPTER FOUR

'I know it sounds crazy, Sir, but when I looked up he was gone. But I almost had him, Sir, tricky little fucker gave me the slip, Sir. It won't happen again, I promise you that, Sir.' Dexter paused, the Colonel seemed attentive as if giving him time to collect his thoughts. A brightly coloured bird landed on his skull.

'Can I talk openly, Sir? Thing is, Sir, I can't sleep, I get these dreams, perhaps I miss the boys. Are they all dead, Sir? Perhaps I shouldn't ask that. Classified information. But I do worry about Zak. His wound looked real bad. I held his belly together as we carried him to the chopper. He asked me to tell his girl he was fine. Her name was Ruth. But thing is, Sir, I don't know how to contact her. I feel I've let him down. She's maybe waiting on the farm holding their dreams, watching for him coming down the track. Maybe she's been baking. We used to get cross with Zak, Sir, when we lay in the dark and he talked about her apple pie. They had an orchard he said and she would hold those bright red apples in her apron. 'Shut the fuck up about those apples and that pie!' I said that, Sir, and now I regret it. Do you think someone could get the word through, Sir?

'And I know this sounds bad but sometimes I worry about the gooks. Could be a court martial offense, I know that. Sympathising with the enemy in my head, Sir. I know most of them were lousy little sons of bitches wanting us dead but you know, Sir, I still see them in my dreams. That line of prisoners with their mouths and eyes taped together, I know, see no evil, speak no evil, they all had an arm on the shoulder of the one in front. "The blind leading the blind," is what the captain said. Were they shot, Sir? I figure they probably deserved it. One of them was crying, I know, a cowardly fucker, but he looked about twelve, Sir. They don't shoot boys do they, Sir?'

The coloured bird flew away from the colonel's skull. 'And I worry about the villages, Sir. I figured they were harbouring the VC and hiding weapons and had to be raised to the ground, I know all that, Sir... I worry too about that soldier we saw at Hue, you remember him? Crouched in a hole stuffing a bible into his mouth. Eating God's words and then he vomited, all those holy words, all the commandments, all those psalms lying in the dirt. Thing is, Sir, I know why he did that. The bible's a sacred book, but I've figured out why he did that. Do you think God's an American, Sir? I'm not so sure now. Wash my mouth out.

'And I kinda worry about going home, Sir. I was hearing those peaceniks were putting flowers down the barrels of soldiers' guns. Why would they do such a dumbass thing, Sir? We've given our lives so the folks can live good lives, raise their kids without fear. I will stick the flowers up their backsides, Sir, if they come near me when I reach the Island. And I heard tell that a boy set fire to himself outside of McNamara's office. No need for that, Sir.

'Sir, I know this is most likely my weakness I'm sharing with you, and I should really talk to a chaplain but, you know, that's just not a possibility just now. And I have another dream, Sir, it comes mostly in the morning after the bad dreams. And it's a good feeling but I don't know why. I'll tell you anyway, if you boys are not in a hurry. It was way back, maybe a year, up in the hills. A scout came

146

back and told us that gooks had been spotted moving into position over the ridge. It was late in the day and no one wanted to move their butts. Anyway the Captain shouted at us, calling us lazy mother-fuckers, so we set off. We crawled and crawled through the vegetation until we got to the ridge and peered over. And do you know what we saw, Sir? Four small boys were playing, crouched down. They had placed little squares of silk over sticks like tiny tents. They held down the edges of the silk and lit Zippos underneath them until slowly, slowly the tiny tents lifted into the air and floated above the ground. The boys squealed and pointed. We were only yards from them but we did nothing, just watched, and then we crept away down the ridge, smiling to ourselves. We told the Captain the gooks had vanished.'

Making the money had been easy. Victor the shoeshine had to see a lady, he said. The boys always hung around his stand and begged him to tell tales of life on the railroad, and how he bummed his way across America. He would pause, shake the brown rag, and stretch his back with hands on hips and start. 'Did I ever tell you boys about the bag of dollars I found on the bank of Wichita Creek?' He carefully folded the rag and placed it on the enamelled sign that advertised his services.

'It was hot, damned hot and I just wanted to flop my hot ol' body into that water. I laid my shirt, pants and shoes on a fallen tree and dove into those cold waters. I swam with the frogs and the eels. There were 'gators too but I never saw them.

'When I stood on the bottom with my arms resting on the water, I could feel my feet sink into the sand, and then my ankles. I sure had a struggle to get myself out of there. I coulda been dragged down deep into the devil's own parlour.

'Anyhow, I was swimming a while like a hound dog with my head outa the water, then I felt mighty cold and made my way back to the shore, and you'll never guess what had happened. Yessiree, some critter had stole my clothes and my shoes and left ten dollars in a newspaper by way of payment. Well I was pleased as you will well imagine but I was stark butt naked. I had to hide in the woods and sleep under the leaves with my hand clutched tight round those dollars. I was cold and shivering and hungry.

'Next night I got close to a farmstead and peered through the window at those lucky folks eating hot stews, and just behaving like ordinary happy families. And then the old man would blow out the lamp, and he and his missus would climb the stair to their bed. Well I waited till there was no sound and then gently prised open the window, and lowered my naked body into that room still warm from the stove. An old dog raised its head then slept again. I scooped the stew with my hands straight from the pot and by the light of the moon looked for clothes. I found some fine dungarees on a hook and a pair of boots by the door. I was so grateful to feel that rough cloth on my cold body that I decided to leave all those dollars on the hearth. And I vowed there and then not to want much from this old life, and always 'preciate having clothes on my back. Well, boys, I don't want to leave that special lady waiting any longer, so you take over. You know what to do, and if you make more than a dollar then you keep the rest.'

They knew what to do all right. They must have watched Victor shine a thousand shoes, or maybe a thousand and one as a man had once rested on his crutches and put his best, his only foot forward for a shine. 'Half price to you, Sir,' said Victor.

Jake and Dexter knew how to keep the polish from clogging the small holes in brogues, how to use the chamois and not to spare the spit.

148

Jake had the pimp's gift of persuading complete strangers, indifferent to the sand on their shoes, to surrender to his buddy's ministrations. As a final winning flourish, Dexter would wipe his elbow over the front of the shoe and peer into it looking for his reflection. The nickels and dimes rang loud in their pockets as they stood in front of the mechanical fortune teller. Her head poked out of a box, the join shrouded in a shawl. As the first dime nestled somewhere near her metallic chest, her garish mouth opened, she emitted an ominous guttural roar and vomited a small piece of card into the waiting tray below. Jake waved the YOU WILL BE A RICH MAN card above his head and out of reach of Dexter's attempt to take it from him.

Dexter for his part was less than pleased with the BEWARE OF WATER card that had been his prize. YOU WILL TRAVEL FAR AND WIDE was as close as he ever got to the promise of a good time. Due to a malfunction, Gipsy Meg also managed to spew out a blank card that intrigued both boys. 'You've no future,' said Dexter gleefully.

'There's too much about to happen to print on a card,' countered Jake.

'Loser, loser!' Jake held his pal in a headlock before releasing him as he saw the adjacent Love Machine and the neon invitation to FIND OUT WHAT KIND OF LOVER YOU ARE. The legends flashed up on the screen. WELCOME ABOARD, BIG BOY. SAVE IT FOR ME, HONEY. The boys smirked and jostled, pretending to understand the stream of innuendos. Many years later the leering Saigon whores would whisper similar words at the war-weary boy soldiers.

The insect had found its way into his groin. Dexter pushed his hand down his pants and cursorily inspected the tiny fluorescent creature before crushing it. He had fought his way along the river bank before on two occasions but had never gone further than the bend where the water fell over the rocks into a miasma of steam.

'"Face your fear, face your fear," the man said. I can face the fear but I will not put so much as a foot IN the fear.'

He clung to the fantasy that at some point the whole damn river might disappear into the ground if he followed it for long enough. It might just plummet into subterranean caves or be sucked into the porous rocks with the cellular honeycomb structure of sliced bone. Then he would march out of his prison, cross the rice fields and stride towards the flat plains and certain rescue. He would be a hero in his home town. GI RETURNS FROM THE DEAD. Interviews on NBC. A tearful reconciliation with his ma and pa.

All things were possible on the other side of the river. He understood now the peaceniks' song. This was the River of Jordan, and Dexter was travelling the banks to find where it flowed to the sea. Soon the clear waters would cleanse his soul, and Jake would step out of those cold waters, hug his buddy and forgive all his transgressions. He stood still and listened intently for the gook who might be on his trail. He resisted the urge to flail once more at the helmet of mosquitos stuck to his head. From the noise he knew he was close to the waterfall and the towering rocks. If he followed the dwindling tributary, cut inland and then turned back to the river, it might not be there. Gone underground. The rushes were shoulder-high and razor-sharp. His boots were full of water. He knew he would find bracelets of leeches around his ankles when he took them off. He hated leeches and with good reason.

Two years previously at the camp outside of Bien Hoa, the soldiers had passed round the Zippo, taking it in turns to flick the flame at the bloated parasites until they withered and let go of the flesh. That tiny firefly light had been enough. Hank folded forward under the impact of the sniper's bullet. There was then an elongated millisecond between the image of Platoon Leader Burnside hanging in the air above them, and his slow motion fall. The jungle was sliced into separate frames by the strobe of incoming shells.

In the House of Horrors on Surf Avenue, Jake would milk the strobe for all it was worth, assuming a quick succession of frozen poses, each more menacing than the last. A Frankenstein stumbling in the dark, a child murderer closing in on his victim.

A boot on the end of a free-flying leg smacked Dexter on the head and left him unconscious. When he opened his eyes the firefight had moved on, Puff the Magic Dragon had been called and flares lit to guide it to the latest harvest of broken bodies.

Each flashback served to peel away another layer of whatever resilience he had cultivated. Dexter stood in a clearing and shivered despite the searing heat. His presence had disturbed the birds hiding in the adjacent foliage. Indignant, they rose upwards, shrieking hysterically, gossiping wildly, telling tales of his whereabouts. He watched their jerky ascent from twig to branch to bough then shielded his eyes against the rasping sun. Sometimes he hankered for the plain, no nonsense seagulls running along the Coney Island boardwalk, scavenging the trash, dragging impossibly large cartons from the bins.

Once in the fall at Sea Gate, he and Jake had stumbled on a harvest of dead gulls lying ramshackle along the rind of seaweed and flotsam of cans and plastic. Some were splayed, some were half buried beak first in the sand. All were inelegant in death, robbed of power and purpose. Jake had picked up one of the birds by its wing and waved it above his head as he moved towards Dexter who retaliated in kind. He held his chosen bird by a scaly leg. He was surprised by its weight. The boys circled each other, whirling their bird weapons in a choreography of feather and sand. Dexter was the first to let go. He launched his bird which for a moment rediscovered the power of flight and wrapped its wings round Jake's face. Jake dropped his bird, and ran down the beach brushing his cheeks and spitting out sand as he fled. Dexter thought he might have been crying but couldn't be sure. He caught up with him sitting on an overturned beer crate. 'I hate dead birds,' said Jake. 'I mean, what's the point? One minute you're in that blue sky, looking down on the folks below, then you're real dead with insects eating your eyes. It's gross.'

'But at least they flew, we're never gonna fly, we'll never feel that freedom.'

'And shit on who you like. Just hover over any old bastard what annoys you, and just let go. Open that bird ass and paint them snotty green from on high.'

'Who would you target first?'

'I'd shit on Walmart's bald head. Splatter his pate. Make him wipe it off with his equations.'

'And then Riso, "If I see you boys hanging round these mirrors again, I'll whip your asses till they bleed." See him running round that arcade, bird shit in his eyes, smearing it on his goddam mirrors. All his customers wanting their money back. Probably get closed down by the health department.'

Spontaneously, both boys made faces at each other. Jake pulled at the flesh beneath his eyes exposing blood-red inner skin. Dexter pushed both his cheeks towards his nose, one higher than the other, while aping the speech of the truly deformed. Suddenly bored, Jake broke away and ran down the beach, flapping his arms in slow motion like a huge seabird intent on lifting itself into the air and wheeling over the bay towards the Manhattan skyline smudged by the heat haze.

He could still hear the river, fainter now, perhaps he had been right and the water was draining away into tunnels and caves far underground. He moved forward, picking a path warily, pulling off the sticky tendrils that latched onto his flesh and clothes. The triangular flaps of cloth hanging from his uniform repeatedly snagged on bushes. He no longer noticed the ribbons of blood scratched on his torso. He blinked the sweat out of his eyes which left them stinging. Sometimes he wondered if endlessly breathing in hot air would scald his lungs. He breathed onto the palm of his hand to see if it was even hotter on its way out. It seemed so.

He had long ago stopped noticing the smells of this alien country. In the early days he would step out into the night, a new boy still enjoying the novelty of sleeping outdoors in a foreign land, in a foreign war as yet unseen. In those far-off days he could distinguish between the hints of vegetation: incense, musk, a bitterness, a sweetness, something rotting. Testing each scent on his palate like his old man at Christmas when he poured brandy into the glass that Dexter had first thought was a goldfish bowl. Later the whole country smelled of rotting fish and cooking fires. Now the air was just hot.

'Shit!' said Dexter when he saw that, rather than doing the honourable thing and draining into the centre of the earth, the river, to spite him, had flowed into the flat plain, rolling the opposite bank towards the horizon. The water was calm, gently suckling the ribbon of sand that separated the rushes and reeds. The water too seemed endless, a whole nightmare landscape. He knew an anxiety attack was about to knock him over. His chest hurt and he was snatching at his breath. The sky was spinning. 'Breathe real slow,' his buddy had told him as they lay side by side in the shell hole while the napalm burnt overhead and dying men screamed. 'Real slow,' he had insisted, squeezing Dexter's hand at intervals that corresponded with the ideal rate of breath intake and exhalation.

It wasn't just the breathing. He must also distract himself from the certain belief that he was about to die. He must concentrate on the detail of his surroundings. Deep plastic green vegetation, sharp pointed leaves, green bayonets bursting into flowers at their tip. Those peaceniks again. A large red beetle trailing its mucus up a tall stalk. A trickle of opaque sap on a single reed.

The worst had passed. A degree of calm had returned. Altering his focus, he looked further along the river. At first he thought it was a shed that had slumped into the water. A fisherman's hut or a VC lookout post. It was a boat, a sampan partially drawn up onto the bank, big enough to hold a single man with a pole, a farmer perhaps whose land lay on the other side, a Buddhist monk returning from retreat, or Charlie with a woven basket of grenades, and cigarettes looted from dead GIs.

The deck was just under water but the stern was floating free. It was a test, one last chance to rewrite the past and give it a happy ending. He owed it to Jake.

Dexter stamped through the shallow water as if he had returned to the wet Coney Island streets and was staying dry by landing hard and fast in the dead centre of each puddle while Jake tried to push him off balance. He felt nervous, elated even, but it wasn't something he couldn't control. He stood on the deck of the sampan and wobbled briefly with his arms outstretched. He reached down and picked up the long bamboo pole and pushed it down into the newly muddied water. This was easy. He laughed out loud. If he kept his nerve he would soon be on the other side and reunited with his patrol who would give him beer and roll-ups, more C-rations than he could eat, and a cake from Zak who, grinning, would cut out a huge wedge, carefully avoiding the red icing-decorated house. He would sleep among his buddies who would watch over him, so pleased that he had returned. This water held no fear. This was safe water.

Jake was staring into the dark with a hand up to his eyes. The Island lights were growing fainter as those in New Jersey shone brighter. The pallet rocked beneath them. The oars stolen from the Marina proved unwieldy. They were too big and there was no way of attaching them to the wood. By way of compromise, they each took one oar and attempted to manoeuvre it with both hands. Jake dug too deep with his, and was almost pulled into the water. Dexter also lost his grip and watched as it sank out of sight.

They had given no thought to the return journey. Their arrival on the shore of Brooklyn would be big news. A ticker tape parade seemed unlikely but an interview on Walter Cronkite's *CBS Evening News* was not out of the question. He would be forgiven when the newspaper men called, their flashlights lighting up the porch, microphones thrust towards his ma, 'When did you realise your son was a hero, Mrs Dexter?' The magazines would pay, they were sure of that. They would have to fight the girls off at school. 'We'll play it cool,' said Jake.

'I wouldn't want to upset Maryanne,' said Dexter. 'I mean she's stayed with us through thick and thin.'

'Amen,' said Jake.

Jake saw the tug first, or rather the tumbling white wave that preceded it, rising out of the dark. 'Geeze!' he shouted. Both boys had been lying down, their hands clutching at the edges of the wood as the swell was making them both feel sick. Jake stood up with difficulty and waved at the massive craft bearing down on them. 'Look out mister, getouta the way!'

A claxon sounded. Dexter had no memory of the collision. What he could remember was Jake gripping his hand in the moment of impact. His friend's bony fingers clung to him, and he let him go. In that instant he betrayed Jake, he forsook him, he let him go.

Dexter fell backwards into a warm prism of sunlight and water. He flailed briefly before breathing the river deep into his lungs. He saw the figure with arms folded, staring at him. He blinked and it had gone. An elongated moment of choking despair was followed by total blackness.

CHAPTER FIVE

'Sir, I tried, goddam, I tried. Call it cowardice if you like, I'm willing to face a court martial if you reckon you've had enough and that an example needs to be set. But you must understand, Sir, it's the water thing. The river thing. I get bad dreams, Sir. What's that, Sir? You're giving me an ultimatum? Another three weeks to find a way out of this hellhole or face the consequences. OK, Sir, message understood.'

The Colonel's skull had slumped a bit further towards his rib cage, imparting a degree of solemnity to his pronouncement. Dexter looked at his companion. He was grinning, Dexter was sure of that.

'Something amusing you, soldier? Do I know you? Did I see you on the bridge? Did I see you drag that woman out of the hut, her kids clutching at her skirt? Did I see you going through that old man's belongings? Did you tug at his gold tooth as he lay dead with his mouth open? Did you smack that young soldier round his head with your rifle 'cuz he was crying, and call him a cowardly fucker? Was it you who torched the first hut, and then kissed your Zippo as the flames swallowed the straw and the folks inside? Did you use those VC bodies as stepping stones, pushing their heads deeper into the mud? Did you rip the tape from the prisoners' mouths and feed them dirt? Did you shoot Sergeant Jones in the back of the head in the heat of battle? Tell me, soldier, did you start this whole goddamn war? Was Agent Orange your idea?' And then, shaking with rage and pointing animatedly, he screamed, 'Did you drown Jake?'

Dexter grabbed the tendrils that snaked up towards the object of his fury. He tugged at them like the bell-ringer in the church. The soldier flailed and shook before his rotting body slipped and tumbled through the vegetation. He lay collapsed in a heap at Dexter's feet. Two small funnels of angry insects erupted from his eye sockets.

Dexter knew he must have swum back to the Coney Island shore in the dark but he had no memory apart from stumbling up the beach towards the boardwalk. Shivering and sobbing he stood on the stoop and banged the door. 'Who's there?' asked his mother after an interval during which she had retrieved her dressing gown from the laundry pile and armed herself with the bat the boys used for stickball.

'It's Dexter, Ma. Let me in.' He was still banging at the door when it opened. His mother caught his fists in both her hands and held her boy close despite her anger.

'Where in God's name have you been? I thought you were sleeping. You're soaked.'

'It was my idea, my idea, I killed him.'

'What are you talking about, child?'

'Jake, he's drowned. I let him go, I let him go!'

'You don't know that he's drowned, maybe he swam back just like you,' said his mother, trying to make sense of what she had just heard.

'He's drowned, Ma, he's drowned. I let him go.' Dexter sank his head into his mother's soft middle, craving for the time when she could make all bad things, all unwanted dreams, all bullies disappear.

158

'Let's go see.' Dexter's mother pulled clothes on over her nightwear and led her tearful son by the hand out of the house. A neighbour, woken by the sound of the door slamming, shouted something. They ran over the boardwalk and onto the beach. His mother muttered all the while. Dexter couldn't tell if her murmurs were veiled threats of punishments to come, or imprecations to a god to whom she only spoke when times were hard, or she was consumed with anger at the accumulated small injustices of her life.

It was still dark and the wind was up. Dexter stumbled into a hole dug and abandoned by yesterday's carefree holidaymakers, almost pulling his mother into the pit with him. They ran through the water's edge shouting Jake's name but the sound was smothered by the wind and tide.

'Jesus, Dexter, Jesus! We have to raise his folks. You go back and get them here.'

Every time he fell, the crust of sand adhering to his sodden clothes got thicker and heavier. When the stitch skewering his chest subsided into bearable pain, he limped up Mermaid Avenue, pulling himself along the railings outside the church until he came to Jake's place. He pounded the heavy knocker into the door and shouted through the mailbox but there was no reply from inside. Jake's ma and pa hit the bourbon heavy some nights, and this must have been one of them.

In despair he stepped back into the road, picked up the half-brick that had marked the pitcher's spot and hurled it at the upstairs window. The missile passed cleanly though the pane and disappeared into the room. Moments passed before a shot gun poked through the shattered glass, followed by the unshaven bleary face of Jake's father. 'Well, I'll be darned,' he said, having identified Dexter.

Soon man and boy were running towards the beach. Hobo Joe raised his bottle to them as they passed. A small dog, delighted by having something to do in the dead of night, joined them, snapping at Dexter's heels.

Jake's father scoured the shoreline, which was just visible in the light of a full moon, and ran towards the stooped figure.

'There's something over there,' said Dexter's mom, pointing at a black shape floating on the tide in the shallows. It looked like black sodden rags but it was Jake. His father ran into the water, fell, and then rose again to haul the small body up onto the drier sand.

Since the event happened Dexter had tried to destroy the black canister that held this, the worst of movies, but it proved indestructible and would play at unannounced times to an audience of one. The titles on the shelf had been organised thematically by the over-diligent, fanatical curator who held sway in his head, and he now had no alternative but to watch the next spool. It was contemporary but mercifully short.

The tiny Vietnamese woman sank to her knees and leaned forward to pull the corpse from the flooded bomb crater. The platoon stood embarrassed on the other side, their weapons pointing at the ground. Not a word of bravado passed from any of their mouths. All in that instant saw their own son, their own kid brother, the neighbour's kid, floating upside down in the fetid water. The woman clutched the body to her chest and looked up at the sky as if hunting for someone to curse and blame. The soldiers too squinted into the furnace sun and saw no one.

'Three weeks to find a way out of this hellhole or face the consequences, yes, Sir, no, Sir, three bags full of fucking shit, Sir.'

Dexter stepped out of the bivouac and kicked at the embers from the previous night's fire. His sense of geography was downright poor. The GI's lot was not to ask the precise whereabouts of their next mission.

'Charlie will torture the truth out of you. It's amazing how having your balls cut off loosens the tongue,' the fat sergeant had said while wallowing in the discomfort of the latest cherries to arrive at the camp. 'They eat them,' he said. 'It's a Nam delicacy.' He continued snapping his gum from one cheek to the other as if finding the testicles hard to chew. 'Fine with garlic.'

Dexter thought Cambodia was not far away and had heard talk of the demilitarised zone but apart from that he had no idea. He wouldn't face the river again, of that there was no doubt, which left the mountains.

On most days the mist hung low and brooding on the hills that held the crashed plane and its cremated occupants. On the occasional clear day he could see the sun glinting off distant bare rocks. He would try; there was no alternative.

He filled two of the canteens rescued from the plane wreckage. The water was warm but he was quietly confident that he would encounter streams on the ascent. The only problem he foresaw was that his boots would deteriorate further. The leather was paper thin in places and would be cut to threads by sharp rock. There was though a solution. Although it would be an act of consummate insubordination to remove the Colonel's boots, he could surely requisition the boots that belonged to the Colonel's irritating companion. The soldier, who had almost admitted being responsible for this whole damn mess, deserved no less. It was the least he could do to atone for this debacle.

With this thought at the forefront of his mind, he made his way back to the dead men. After cursorily saluting the Colonel, he knelt down by the decaying and collapsed body of the other soldier. He put his hand over his mouth to stop himself from gagging and was mildly surprised, having assumed that he was long immune to the stench of death.

161

'Need to get yourself some deodorant, soldier, I think maybe a rat has crawled up your backside and died.' He easily removed the boots which proved to be a near perfect fit.

'Walking in a dead man's shoes,' he pronounced before starting the ascent through the trees.

At first he made good progress by using the trunks to balance himself as he negotiated the not quite vertical slope. Eventually though he felt breathless, and reached the point where the trees were no longer able to cling to the hill. The cliff was sheer. He looked over his shoulder and felt his head swim as his eyes took in the sweep of the land on the other side of the snaking river. Turning back, he jammed his foot into a crevice and, after searching for a handhold, pulled himself upwards. The next crack was at a ninety-degree angle to the previous one and necessitated him spreading his legs to their limit. He felt the strain on his shaking calves. He pulled himself upwards until the rock face bulged outwards, and his cheek was hard up against the hot stone. He closed his eyes against the stinging sweat and the blinding light.

This too had happened before. 'Christ!' said Dexter.

The metal felt cold. Jake was above him, shouting something he couldn't hear. This was meant to be The Great Event, the assault on the Parachute Tower, the thought of which had sustained them both through the entire winter. Others had done it before them. Olly Craven said it took him four hours. The Schlecker Brothers had to be rescued by the cops. Someone said that Zak Schlecker had wet himself with fear, but no one dared say that to his face. Others claimed to have done it, but there was no proof.

Jake had said to climb at dusk just after Antonio went home but before it got so dark they couldn't see. If they climbed when the boardwalk was full of tourists someone would see them and raise the alarm. They would be grounded for weeks.

They had practised for the big event by climbing up the scaffolding that covered Maggie's bakery shop. One of the neighbours thought he was being burgled and called the cops. The fat cop parked his car in the middle of the road and gave chase to the boys who had dropped off the building and fled.

Dexter and Jake ran down the Bowery, cannoning into the display of buckets and spades carefully arranged outside JP's hardware store. Old JP himself came out and waved a fist at the two small figures. Jake got to the boardwalk first and threw himself underneath. Dexter followed moments later. The fat cop passed overhead and the boys lay there convulsed with laughter.

They had planned the ascent for weeks, identifying which points in the latticework of girders and metal straps would give their feet the best purchase. They would have to climb crab-ways rather than attempt the most direct route. They were though wise enough to recognise the risks inherent in wet or windy conditions. They did consider roping themselves together but reckoned that would only increase the likelihood of them both plunging to their deaths.

The metal felt cold. Jake was somewhere above him and was shouting something he couldn't hear, then he started screaming. This was not how The Great Event was meant to pan out. Dexter could see Jake's legs dangling above him. This made no sense. His legs were flailing; he was not standing on a girder. The screams grew louder. Dexter felt sick to his stomach as he inched his way towards Jake who was suspended by a wrist caught in the intersection between two spars. His screams grew louder. Soon the pair of them were crying.

Spread-eagled against the rock face, Dexter could feel the sniper's cross hairs focusing on the small of his back. Maybe the strange VC who had materialised on two occasions was just playing games with him, waiting for a moment like this when he could just pick him off. He braced against the impact of the bullet but nothing came. It gradually dawned on him that he was totally, completely stuck. His fingers had tightened into the crevice and he couldn't move them. His biceps were trembling. The angle of his legs was unsustainable and he could feel them cramping. Looking up into the sun he saw two motes that materialised into birds circling, waiting to peck out his eyes. He closed them tight for a moment, then opened them and looked down. He had no idea how high he had climbed. If he fell he would dash his brains on the ground or skewer himself on the trees.

No cops now. No angry parents masking their relief with anger. No Antonio shaking his head. No Jake. The birds were circling closer. The pain in his legs was unbearable. The hammer in his head was about to burst through the thin membrane of bone. His fingers loosened and he fell.

If Jake's wrist snapped then he would fall through the mesh of spars and bounce off the metal onto the boardwalk. He would dislodge Dexter as he fell. The pair of them would die. It was unclear who heard them first. Antonio had long gone home. Most of the tourists had slunk towards the bars and the lights away from the sea.

The cops were not best pleased as they laboriously climbed the structure to rescue the boys. As he nursed his broken wrist, Jake said that he had slipped on a girder covered in seagull shit.

'Goddamit, Sir, I sure as hell don't know how long I lay there. Last thing I recall was letting go. I must have blacked out as I fell. Something damn spooky, Sir. When I came to, I saw him again, you know, the VCI told you about before. Just squatting there watching me. When I looked again, he was gone. Spooky, Sir. I know the mind plays tricks in this heat, but he was as alive as you are, Sir, well, that's not

164

quite what I mean, what with you being dead, Sir, no disrespect, but he was there. I know what you said, Sir, "three weeks to get out of this hellhole or face the consequences," well, I've tried my damnedest, Sir. If I was a fish I would have swam that river, if I was a bird I would have stretched my wings over that mountain, but I'm just a grunt, Sir, a twenty-two-year-old GI, and I'm plain stumped, Sir.'

Thick hot rain fell onto the bivouac. The silk sagged under the weight of the downpour. The roar of rain smothered all other jungle sounds. It sounded like sustained applause. The jugglers bowed from the waist. The midgets hit audience members at random with foam bats. The wind generated by the rain matched the swirl of the carousel chairs as each swung their captives above the crowd. A glimpse of legs and skirts, a flurry of bright clothing. And then as quickly as it started the rain moved on. There must be another way. There had to be a way out.

Dexter always slept badly. It wasn't just Vietnam; it went back way before that. The days and nights before Jake's funeral were the worst he had known. Jake's father had come at midnight beating on the door. He had several buddies with him all snarling with drink. A lynch mob come to Coney Island. Dexter's Ma refused to let them in. A baseball bat was forced through the splintered wood panel. From a crouching position halfway up the stairs, Dexter watched the smooth wooden head, a large eyeless worm in a cartoon, poking its way into the hallway. Eventually it was withdrawn and the posse disappeared, muttering revenge.

'Maybe you should go away for a few days, son,' said his ma, 'just until things die down.' But neither of them could think where he could go. The folks on his father's side in Kansas had always seen themselves as superior and wouldn't welcome a young, scared lodger, and there was no one else.

Although unable to face the funeral, Dexter found himself drawn to Washington cemetery on a bleak November afternoon. He watched the proceedings from a distance. There was a shed on a knoll where they stored the tarpaulins and digging equipment. From there he could just make out the hymns. He ducked out of sight when Jake's pa jerked his head over his shoulder as if sensing that his son's killer was close by. That was one of the moments that frequently woke Dexter.

He was ostracised at school. Names would be shouted until he found himself under a maelstrom of fists, taunts and saliva. Jake would have fought with him, would have been on his side, he knew that. The whole class would turn his back on him when he entered the room. An impressive piece of choreography, as if a long line of open books were closed at the same instant. On the chalkboard were the words, 'HE LET JAKE GO.' His notebooks either mysteriously disappeared or were covered in vile words and drawings too. Mess and dead things were placed in his bag by unseen hands. Gum was pressed into his clothes when he had no alternative but to squeeze past a crowd. The teachers did their best, and sometimes let him work in the Principal's outer office where the secretaries would also give him a wide berth. If they saw him first, Maryanne and Beth would turn on their heels and return down the corridor the way they had just come. On one occasion he plucked up the courage to approach them outside the math department. 'Terrible smell,' said Beth.

'Must be the drains,' said Maryanne, sniffing the air and puckering up her so sweet nose. These words too would drip like poison into his sleep. Eventually he stopped going to school altogether.

The truant officer went through the motions. 'Your boy's gotta attend school, Mrs Dexter. It's the law.'

'My boy's not fit for school. Those pieces of shit jist torment him. He's too sick to make class.'

166

'He's gonna work with me.' The unexpected pronounce-ment from Dexter's father surprised them all. Although a man of few words, they were always honoured, and his son soon found himself in the unfamiliar surroundings of the garage his father ran with a partner.

For the first fortnight his father had no idea what to do with his gangly uncoordinated son. Bored with sweeping up the tide of cigarette butts, metal shavings, rust and flecks of chrome, Dexter had taken to hiding round the back to read about Captain America in *Tales of Suspense*, or flick through the well-thumbed copy of *Playboy* retrieved from the back seat of a Buick.

'Familiarise yourself with the automobile, son,' was the extent of the direction his father provided. To his surprise, Dexter began to feel at home in the salvage yard where the wrecks, piled on top of each other, spoke of broken dreams, of promises dashed, of money squandered. He touched the fender of a Buick Roadmaster Riviera and rubbed the oil between his fingertips. He put his fingers to his nose. The crumpled chassis still had an elegance, a sense of superior-ity. He climbed on the hood and pulled himself through the open window of the Chrysler resting above a 1950 Town and County Newport with white tyres and wooden trim like a three bar gate. A getaway car. He held the steering wheel, glanced at the black and white newsreel footage, eavesdropped on the conversation between Carlo Gambino and Frank Costello in the back seat, and breathed in the cigar smoke.

'The punk had it coming to him.'

'Damn right.'

Balanced precariously on the metal sculpture of wrecked automobiles, was the maroon torso of a Chrysler DeSoto Deluxe. If he strained he could hear the business jargon, the talk of takeovers and mergers. Gold cufflinks on a white sleeve glinting as part of the handshake, a deal sealed.

Parked on its own, newly arrived, was the plump corpse of a Pontiac. The hood was concertinaed as if the crushing machine had started its business prematurely. A family on their way to a picnic in the County Park. The rugs, the blue and white gingham table cloth, the wicker basket containing potato salad, Stokely's finest pickle, Hawaiian Pineapple cake and the iced Nescafé. And the crash that came from nowhere.

When bored with the scrapyard, or when his fantasies failed to blot out thoughts of Jake, Dexter would take off and wander the Island. On hot days he would head for the beach and the total anonymity of the crowd. He would zigzag his way through the fat male bathers pulling on trunks behind screens, and women, already wearing bathing suits, squirming out of dresses. He stepped over couples lying like spoons on the sand. He threaded his way past families staking out their patch of conquered territory. He brushed aside the slowly floating beach balls that bounced serenely from head to head. He carefully avoided the squatting fathers trying to coax football scores from plastic transistor radios. At best he was an indifferent observer passing the time that would otherwise strangle him, at worst he was utterly detached from these alien forms, a silent, panicking scream moving through a landscape devoid of all colour or meaning.

He would loiter on West Thirty-First Street and watch the younger kids jumping from the rooftops onto the mattresses below. At night he would drift towards the Bowery to watch the spontaneous dancing and feel the edge in the air.

There were always fires on Coney Island. A combination of arson, neglect and vandalism meant that the fire wagons were ever present. He would follow the smoke and lose himself in the gawking crowd as another pavilion was reduced to ashes and cinders. All fires smelt different. Some were sweet. Some were acrid and bitter. All represented a development opportunity for one of the sharks profiting from the life-ruining misfortune of others.

Early in the fall of '61, he watched a fire from the Boardwalk. As the sparking rafters of the drug store collapsed inwards, he saw Hobo Joe in the shadows, staring at the flames, waving his bottle towards whichever demon he saw skipping through the white heat. Dexter bundled Joe into his arms and dragged him protesting onto the Boardwalk. As Dexter's clothes were still smouldering, he ran through the darkness, over the sand, and dove into the water. The shock of the cold made him remember where he was. This was Jake's territory, he didn't belong there and so dragged his legs back onto the dry sand as fast as he could.

When he got home his mother took him into her arms, but the distress and inarticulate love she felt for her troubled boy could only find expression in anger. She slapped him repeatedly round the head and he shrank beneath the raining blows. Then she relented and, breathing in the smell of wet burnt clothes, held him so close to her bosom, he thought he would suffocate.

On occasions Dexter was drawn to places he associated with Jake, not from any sense of nostalgia but from a need to punish himself further. Jake and Dexter would often hang out near Joseph Greenstein's stall, the last Coney Island Strongman. A tiny man, stripped to the waist, with a corkscrew moustache, he would twist horseshoes with his bare hands and wrap a girder round his neck. The crowd demanded more. Individual punters would check the authenticity of what their eyes had shown them by examining the discarded chain-links before declaring Joseph to be a deserved holder of his five world records. Meanwhile his equally tiny wife, Leah, would parade among them with a tray of elixirs guaranteed to turn shrivelled men into bears, potions that would restore hair, virility and winning ways.

This one would 'grow their parts' she said with a wink, this one would mend a broken heart.

She hadn't changed her patter when Dexter stood once again at the back of the crowd. On this occasion, carried away on the wings of her own hyperbole, she waved a small vial, the Lazarus bottle, and told her audience that two drops rubbed behind the ears of a dead man would make him open his eyes.

'That's not true!' shouted Dexter. 'The dead are dead, no witchy lady's gonna bring them back with a rub from her bottle of snot.' The crowd grew quiet, Joseph put down the metal bar and moved towards the heckler. 'You be careful what you say, boy! Don't you go disrespecting my Leah.' As he got nearer he recognised Dexter and was minded of his tragedy. 'Slip along, son,' he said quietly. 'Make no fuss. You're right, no potion's gonna bring back your little buddy.'

His mother took the news that he was going to enlist stoically. She knew that at the age of nineteen his life was already permanently blighted in Coney Island. She knew that the shadow of guilt was waiting for her son behind every street corner, and in every store.

The radio bulletins left no room for doubt. Their whole life, everything they held dear, was under threat from the communists. She had watched the newly recruited young men swaggering their way down the Boardwalk at dusk, with a girl on each arm. The stallholders competed with each other to offer the lowest prices to Our Boys. Uncle Sam pointed without discrimination at everyone, the bag lady and the gent, who passed beneath his bony finger and bright blue eyes.

'Make a new start, son,' she said, holding him tight. 'Make a new start.'

The beating rain stopped as suddenly as it had started. He

170

had been daydreaming again about the Vietnamese boys playing with their Zippos and the handkerchief of silk. Two of them held the edges between thumb and forefinger as if they were handling butterfly wings, the other two held the Zippos steady. The yellow flames rose like tiny genies with crossed arms. Sensing the merest tension in the silk the boys opened their fingers. For a moment nothing happened. Then, almost imperceptibly, the silk rose at least two inches of its own accord, then six inches, then several feet into the air. The boys cheered, then wrestled with each other for a moment before competing to be the first to retrieve the floating gossamer square of silk.

A growth spurt during the summer after his fourteenth birthday had hastened the day when he could stare Antonio in the face, or at least in the chin. He had thought of treating Maryanne but it had to be Jake who joined him on the wooden steps. Soon they were both strapped into the harness beneath the 'chute.

Slowly, slowly, they were winched into the sky, barely able to absorb the scene of their childhood unfolding beneath them. Beyond the tiny figures on the beach, he could just see the v-shaped wake from a dog swimming to freedom and a tug moseying through the channel.

The Palace viewed from above seemed diminished. It had never occurred to Dexter that the building might actually have a roof; that it did not in fact pierce the heavens, a pleasure dome with a direct route into a celestial realm. There was even a tangle of aerials and a triangular corner of corrugated iron that had been wrenched upwards by the vandalism of an ancient storm. He had not been aware of the wind on the Boardwalk earlier but now it made his eyes smart. Perhaps they were tears of excitement.

He and Jake swayed backwards and forwards in an attempt to rock the cradle that held them, but it ignored their best efforts. Davy, the one-armed former football player, balanced on the cross-beam and snapped the metal bar tight across their laps. He recognised the pair of them. 'I hope you like the ride, boys, it's like your first woman, you dream of it for years and then it's over in seconds.' Moments later their stomachs plummeted. He had been right about the woman thing.

All the young rookies in the platoon pretended they had slept with most of the girls in high school, boasting of how they had graduated from heavy petting in the drive-thrus, to full blown intercourse in the cornfields, in the basement with the babysitter, in the laundromat when the attendant turned a blind eye, in the back pew of the church while the preacher droned on about sin and retribution until the Halleluiah Chorus filled the building, and angels came down. Dexter had not joined in the competition as he knew that he wouldn't be believed. He had been disconcerted the first time he heard the phrase 'motherfucker', surely not.

His first R and R in Saigon had been much anticipated. The men had given him the lowdown. Dragon Suzie with the python thighs, the Chinese witch who could dislocate her jaws to be more accommodating, Whistling Jade whose privates performed ventriloquist tricks. They queued on the stairs, wiping the sweat from their faces, despite the languid, disinterested spin of the fan hanging by a wire. A lizard swithered its bulbous eyes and then darted into a crack in the wooden boards. Dexter looked for telltale signs of life-changing ecstasy in the faces of the grunts who emerged at intervals from the curtained space. Tightening his buckle, Tomas put his thumbs up and winked at him as he sauntered back down the stairs.

As his turn came and went Dexter knew that Davy had been right. The expectation had far exceeded the reality.

It had been the same with the parachute jump. He had

thought about it many times since and it still made little sense. Although the descent, the delicious moment of free fall from the top of the blue and yellow scaffold before the silk blossomed, was exhilarating beyond anything he had ever experienced, it somehow paled alongside the slow ascent; the unbelievable moment when the parachute, in the face of all logic, went upwards.

CHAPTER SIX

Dexter held his hand up to blot out the sun. He was only partially successful as the rays spilled through his fingers. His arrival at the feet of the dead men had been announced by an entourage of courtiers and panderers in the guise of parakeets and parrots, all eager to curry favour with the Colonel.

'Permission to experiment. Want to use my initiative, Sir. If you don't object to me borrowing a parachute, Sir, I think I can engineer a means of escape. If I can take a chute then I think I can fly over that river and make my way to our own folk. I suppose I'm talking about constructing a balloon, Sir. I understand what you're saying, Sir. Yes, Sir, probably a dumb idea but we've nothing to lose. I want to start right away, Sir, if that's ok. 'Preciate it, Sir.'

Dexter saluted the Colonel who seemed like a man with other things on his mind, like being dead, thought Dexter.

He walked the half mile or so back to the broken fuselage. The path seemed alarmingly well trodden. He was annoyed at himself for leaving a trail of broken twigs and elephant grass sufficiently flattened to alert any half-vigilant VC. On the other hand, the two halves of the plane were steadily sinking into the undergrowth and were less visible than in the days following the crash.

He knew where the parachutes were stored and easily

opened the metal hamper. Once released, the chutes assumed a life of their own as if revelling in the sense of space after their confinement. He chose the largest, presumably designed to soften the landing of a M102 howitzer or Jeep onto the floor of the jungle. Bizarrely he was minded of his mother struggling with the sheets at the laundromat on West 10 Street.

Clutched by tendrils and mauled by thorns, he carried his ungainly bundle through the vegetation. The material felt so soft he didn't want to tear it with his calloused hands. Maryanne once wore a silk blouse to a prom. He had stroked it during a slow dance, partly to feel the firm outline of her breast, but also because he was fascinated by the material itself yielding like talcum powder under his touch.

Someone was tugging at the other end of the ropes trailing behind him. Suddenly rigid, he paused and looked back. He just caught sight of a small figure retreating into the undergrowth. He dropped his burden and took out his knife.

'Come outa there, motherfucker! Come outa there!' The bushes swayed slightly. Dexter moved in a slow, tight circle, holding his knife out straight, ready to lunge at whatever spirit was haunting him. 'Fuck you, fuck you!' he screamed. After waiting for an age, trying to interpret every squawk, every shriek of birdsong, he lowered his knife, bundled up the parachute, tucked it under his arm and made his way back to the bivouac.

Inside, calm again, he made his plans. He would need a sufficiently large stretch of land to spread out his potential balloon. The real challenge was to devise a way of raising the silk off the ground so that small fires could be built underneath. It would need to rest on a bamboo framework of some sort. The main danger was that the whole flimsy structure would catch fire. Would it carry his weight? How far might it carry him? Was any of it possible?

He woke restless into the same inner discourse. Only this time, his mind still heavy with sleep, he was discussing the possibilities and solutions with Jake. This was no different from the fantasy planning sessions that preceded the assault on the Tower, and the subsequent voyage into the bay. Invariably it was Jake who came up with the solutions. That was always the way. It was Jake who found the loose piece of fence that gave them unlimited entry to the Pavilion. It was Jake who worked out the nightwatchman's blind spots that enabled them to stay in the Aquarium long after it had closed.

'You'll need to check it in case it's torn, but repairs will be easy, man, look at the resin oozing from these trees. Collect it in your mess tin, heat it and smear it on the joins. Have you still got your blade? Good. I reckon you'll need perhaps twenty bamboo canes stripped down and pushed into the earth. You'll have to clear the ground first. Be a gardener, drag out the weeds, and tear out the shrubs. Remember to collect all of the cords into the middle, don't let them drop into the flames...' Jake's voice faded into the morning light. Dexter stepped out of the tent, listened to the low distant roll of thunder and saw faraway flashes. He had no idea if nature or man was responsible. He looked directly overhead for sign of an incoming wave of F4 Phantoms bristling with armaments, hell-bent on obliterating whatever VC troop might be engaging with an isolated platoon of increasingly scared Americans.

At Loc Ninh he had been the first to spot the incoming cavalry, all guns blazing. Too exhausted to cheer, the men waited for the comforting crump of shells into the jungle. The markers had placed the flairs accurately but from nowhere a wind had snatched at the yellow smoke and dragged it like a thin blanket back towards the Americans. Retinas burned and ear drums shattered as the explosion vacuumed up the scorched air and wrapped the men in its fatal cowl. In a blind panic Dexter had fallen into a flooded crater where he wallowed in terror, uncertain if he was dead or alive.

When he surfaced he saw the shredded body parts of his former comrades draped over the bushes like a hobo's washing. The rancid hot air tore at his throat. He held onto his sides and howled, begging his mother to come and get him. His mother failed to materialise, unlike several members of platoon B who gently led him away.

Dexter shivered. Perhaps the war was over. He had no idea. Clearly the balloon must take off from close to the river if he was to cross it successfully. From his last ill-fated excursion he remembered a clearing near the water which should meet his needs.

Carrying the parachute through the undergrowth was again problematic. The silk repeatedly squirmed out of his arms like an errant toddler. Holding the bundle in front of him made it difficult to see and he twice fell, face forward. The second time, part of him was tempted just to lie there swaddled in the material, to pull the blanket over his head and wait for better times.

The savannah grass was much taller than he had remembered. It would need to be tamed. After spending a sweat-soaked hour flailing in vain at the vegetation, he threw aside his improvised sickle and trampled as much of the grass underfoot as he could. After no more than a moment's hesitation it sprang back into life.

Dexter returned to the rolled-up parachute and wrapped himself in it. He had had enough. 'Shrimp Boat, Soft Shell Crab, Filet Platter, Chicken Basket, Shrimp Rolls,' he intoned from memory, reeling off one of the signs from the Busy Bee Hamburger Stall. Jake countered with, 'French Fries, Hot Pizza, Knishes, Hamburger Basket.' Dexter brought up the rear. 'Italian Sausage Heros, Fish Sandwich, Cold Drinks, Fried Shrimp, Pizza, Hot Corn...'

Feeling better, he succeeded in tugging up several armfuls of the grass but it was as fruitless as tugging single hairs from a giant's chin.

A day later he returned with a can of kerosene drained from the crashed plane. Trying hard not to splash his own arms, he liberally dispensed the fuel in a series of arcs across the proposed take-off site. He remembered how, every Easter, his mother would drag him to mass and he would breathe in the stifling incense as the intoning priest clanked the censer against its chain.

Crouching, he took out his Zippo, momentarily mindful of the Vietnamese boys who were his present inspiration, and touched the flame against a single strand of coarse grass. After a moment's pause, the fire snaked up the stalk and kissed its neighbour which kissed the next one until a blotch of flame was working its way through the patch. First the small rodents escaped, then a petrified rat ran into his leg before blundering on its way. He half expected to see tiny VC women with rags and babies in arms shuffling their way out of the flames. But they didn't come. The smoke precipitated a premature twilight. Perhaps he had ignited the entire country more effectively than a fleet of B52s dispensing Agent Orange and instant death to every creature, human or otherwise. But the river stopped the flames on one side and a rocky outcrop on the other side proved equally resistant to the fire.

Dexter lay back and watched the spectacle. He was already thinking about the next challenge. Once he had spread the balloon across the prepared patch, he would have to find a way of elevating it sufficiently to light a central fire without igniting the fabric. He would though have to wait until the smouldering ground had cooled. Perhaps he should report in to the Colonel.

'Not a bad day, Sir. Progress made. Yes, I figure the fire

might have drawn attention to ourselves but, you know, it was a risk worth taking. Sorry if you disagree, Sir, but it's done now.

'There's something on my mind, Sir... this whole war, Sir. I don't intend hanging round here much longer but I can't go without sharing some thoughts with you, Sir. It's a whole world of hurt. You know that, Sir. And the bottom line is, well, should we be here? I know the planet will be taken over by the commies if we don't make a stand. We all love our country, no one loves the US of A more then I do, Sir. We've put a man in space, we've got the best army in the world but the gooks keep coming back. You knock them down like skittles but up they jump. They live in the trees, they live in tunnels underground. And all that matters is the body count. Drag the corpses out of their graves so we can count them. Knock the widows out of the way. "Sorry, mam, we've got to see how many of your folk are in that there hole. Your husband, you say, and your son, but what about the others? We hope you've not hid any more bodies in there. I sure hope you and your sisters haven't been stacking up the dead just to deceive us poor gullible Americans."

'I get homesick and lonesome, Sir, we don't get no more letters these days. It's not a complaint, Sir, I suppose, after all, you're dead and there's a limit to what you can do. What will my mom think, am I KIA or MIA? Missing, I suppose. But I've got a plan, Sir. Soon I'll be out of here, and I'll knock on my door, and that little old lady gonna cry and fall to her knees and hold my legs. "It's OK, Mom," I'll say. "I made it. I just had to come home for your roast beef, corn on the cob and mashed potato." And all of that Jake stuff will have been forgotten. I will be forgiven. Jake's da will tell me that his son was just the first of hundreds of young men to be taken from the Island...

'Do you have any messages you want me to carry back to

179

the World, Sir? You got any relatives worried about you? I'll send you all the back issues of *Stars and Stripes* I can find, so you'll know whose all gotten out of here and who didn't make it.

'I worry about this country, Sir. When I first arrived, a cherry, a newbie, I thought I had arrived in paradise. The sun was shining on the mountains, the farmers were in their fields. I hadn't seen a water buffalo before. There were palm trees and monkeys. Was this a zoo? A holiday camp? Maybe I had been an early casualty, perhaps I had died and gone to heaven. You must agree, Sir, the Vietnamese women are the most beautiful in the world. Not that I have much experience in that area, Sir. Long black hair, tiny waists, lovely eyes always smiling.

'But that all changed, Sir. The next time I saw a water buffalo it was in a crater made by a 500-pound bomb. At first the grunts didn't notice its bloated body floating towards them as they laughed and dove in the water. I just stayed on the edge, Sir. You know I can't handle water on account of what happened. Maybe their swimming and fooling about made a wave, I don't know, but that old buffalo just plain exploded. Its guts were in the air and falling on the men who raced to escape. And the smell wouldn't go away, it sort of hung around in your nose. Every breath smelled of dead buffalo. And the smell just stayed. 'Cept it was men, not buffalos.

'Don't get me wrong, Sir, I've made some great friends in Nam. I've sung songs with the soul brothers, I've smoked dope with an ex-cop from the Bronx. I met a man who had been a Hell's Angel in the World, crying at the sight of a dead puppy. I saw a blind soldier rescue a man whose leg had been blown clean off. Holding the man round the waist while feeling all around for the missing limb. And I've seen how good men have been changed into animals, taking scalps, tying them round their bellies. I've seen how the skin has been ripped from soldiers' bodies by the thorns, and their flesh pitted like burgers. And I've seen good men go crazy, hollering like babies and sucking their thumbs. And I've seen so-called heroics done by men who want to die, charging a whole platoon of VC, guns blazing from the hip, cursing and singing. Soon they get their wish as a hole exactly the size of their heart is punched through their rib cage. And they find peace. I saw a man on a stretcher with no face just a hole in the bandages for his cigarette. And I saw a man who had been shot in the groin, his pecker shot off. Can you imagine the homecoming as he wraps his arms round his wife?

'And the Cong have changed, Sir. Those beautiful women are less beautiful now, they'll give you sex for a packet of cigarettes and then stab you through the heart. I'm twenty-two, Sir, but I'm an old man in this war. We made children walk point for us and show us the mines and booby traps. What happened to the Nine Rules, Sir? I committed them to memory, Sir. Remember we are guests here; treat women with politeness and respect; always give the Vietnamese the right of way; don't attract attention by loud, rude or unusual behaviour. I've sure seen some unusual behaviour, Sir...

'These people had nothing when we came, but they've less now except diseases in their bodies and anger in their souls. I'm not figuring on ticker tape when I get home, Sir. But I want to tell folk what I've seen. I understand the Amish better now, Sir. They understand more about living a good, clean, simple, God-fearing life than all those generals in the Pentagon. But I've got a busy day tomorrow, Sir. I appreciate you listening to me but it's my last day here. I've got plans to lay and schemes to see through. I don't reckon I've gotten through to you, Sir, but you have a good one, Sir.'

As he left he glanced disdainfully at the Colonel's now completely diminished companion.

Dexter woke with the first rays of dawn. He listened for a moment to the wall of bird and insect sound before stepping out of the bivouac. He felt excitement, a euphoria that connected with other more distant times.

Sometimes Jake would sneak out of his house while everyone else slept. He would make his way through the still slumbering streets and then throw a handful of gravel at Dexter's window who, when he appeared, would give a thumbs-up, and emerge moments later, pulling on his jacket. The air felt fresh and full of unspecified promise. The boys mock-punched each other by way of enthusiastic greeting. The day held adventures.

Some of the traders, with an eye on an early influx of visitors on the first train, assembled stalls in front of their shops. White plastic windmills started to rotate unbidden in response to an unfelt breeze. Cheap wind-up hurdy-gurdies lined up alongside hand-puppets, fast asleep. The traders greeted the boys with a howdy and a wave, and then returned to sweeping the garbage off the sidewalk. Not all of the trash cans had been emptied, old fruit and greasy paper seeped onto the street. A friendly pack of dogs nosed its way towards the beach, collectively sniffing up the old smells from yesterday and the new ones being conjured by the early morning activity.

Both boys had listened to the overnight storms and knew that the shoreline would yield rich pickings. And so it proved. Jake just beat Dexter to the plastic helmet half hidden in the sand. He emptied it and pulled it over his head before moving towards Dexter with the exaggerated gait of an alien sprung from the pages of whichever comic the boys were sharing. Eventually, unable to see, he tore off the helmet and hurled it out into the ocean where it bobbed for a while, then sank. Coming in on the tide was a red canister. 'It's a bomb,' said Jake.

'A nuclear bomb,' suggested Dexter. 'The whole island is going to blow unless we can save it.' Choosing not to take off his sneakers, Jake waded out towards the rotating object.

'It's a fire extinguisher,' he said. They dragged it ashore and Jake held it under his arm like a bartender determined to douse a fire that had spread from an ashtray. 'Might be worth a lotta money,' said Jake. 'Get it refilled.'

They weren't done yet with the fire extinguisher. After hiding from the midday sun under the boardwalk Jake resumed hitting the salvaged canister with a small rock. The repetitive ringing was infuriating Dexter. 'Quit that,' he said.

'It's almost coming,' said Jake who had succeeded in levering up a small edge of metal from the middle of the red cylinder. Dexter showed renewed interest as his buddy removed a panel, and carefully lifted a tube from the interior. There was a nozzle and beneath it a button which would normally have been activated by the action of pulling the pin on the extinguisher. Jake pressed the button and recoiled as the pressurised air tore a trench in the sand. 'Jesus!' said Jake, threatening to point his newly discovered weapon at Dexter.

The boys fought until Jake let go of the extinguisher whereupon it snaked of its own accord across the sand underneath the boardwalk. 'Jesus, just look at that,' said Dexter. They set off at a quick crawl to retrieve their wild toy that eventually became exhausted and surrendered and then died. Jake held it in his hands admiringly.

Dexter knew the memory was particularly relevant to his present situation but couldn't work out why.

He stood and appraised the scorched patch of land. He could have sworn that new green shoots were already pushing their way through the burned grass but that wasn't possible. He did a rough calculation and decided that he would need between fifteen and twenty bamboo branches if he was to hold the parachute off the ground and stand any chance of heating the air beneath.

183

He remembered that bamboo was plentiful a mile or so further downstream. He walked along the edge of the river trying hard to ignore his beating heart and rapid breathing, sure signs that he was becoming uneasy and anxious. So long as he walked at an angle, the water would not intrude into his peripheral vision. There were problems with this as he frequently stumbled on the rocks or sank into the sucking marsh, and he was increasingly aware of a crick in his neck as he squinted at the boiling sun. He was also trying to banish the intrusive, insistent memories of Jake floundering in the water. That was a different time, a different life. He started singing to blot out the thoughts. He shouted out the full repertoire of the Rolling Stones. Yes, he knew it was all over now, yes, time was still on his side. He turned up the volume. Of course he wanted to be her lover, baby, he wanted to be her man.

Back in Cam Ne he had stood behind a grunt who was throwing flames into a village to the rhythm of *Play with Fire* which was reverberating loudly in his head.

Soon after pushing his way into the wall of bamboo, he realised that his blunted knife was useless. He threw it to the ground and rubbed both fists into his smarting eyes. Predictably it was Jake who came up with a simple but effective solution. If the poles were bent over until they touched the ground and then wedged into the roots of the other trees, even a blunt knife would cut at the point of maximum tension. The plan worked and was only compromised by the occasional rogue pole snapping erect and slapping Dexter hard. Rubbing the wheals on his forearm he counted the number of poles. Twelve. Almost enough.

Staggering under the weight of the wood, he moved back towards the launch site.

The VC always seemed to be carrying bamboo, tiny women carrying bundles across their shoulders as if on the way to private crucifixions. Tiny men whose bicycles balanced enough wood behind their saddles to build a whole village. If they cycled really fast, their overburdened bikes with wooden wings would take flight and climb slowly into the clouds.

He dropped his load on the edge of the cleared land. Exhausted, he decided not to return to his bivouac. His journey had started and there was no going back. Instead he stood and wrapped himself in the parachute that would soon be transformed into the balloon that would transport him back to the World, away from this foreign land. He hopped towards the jungle, a strange, swaddled pharaoh last seen in a school history book, a chrysalis waiting to release the insect that would fly away from this place. He sought some shade and decided to avoid the worst of the midday sun. He was hungry but food could wait until he arrived at his destination. A life without C-rations beckoned.

The morning's exertions had left him feeling stiff and he stretched.

'Touch the sky,' his instructor would say. 'Frighten the gooks with your size, be supermen in the land of the pygmies. Tower above Charlie until he shits himself with fear.' Nothing could have turned out to be further from the truth as experienced by Dexter. If Charlie had been intimidated by the soldier giants, many of them black as devils, he sure did a good job of hiding his fear. As he reflected on the size of his enemies, he looked across at the burnt patch. To his astonishment four of the bamboo poles had been planted equidistant from each other the length of the plot.

He must have dozed off. Disbelieving, he ran to the nearest pole and moved it from side to side. It had been sunk at least a foot into the ground. A perfect depth if it was to play its part in supporting the parachute/balloon. He had not the slightest recollection of planting the poles before he took a nap. He looked round at the jungle shimmering in the heat haze. It made no sense, but few things had in the last three years. What was one more inexplicable occurrence alongside the accumulated oddnesses of war?

The vets told tales of dead men returning to their platoons, saluting their colleagues then melting back into the jungle. Men claimed to have seen angels hanging from the trees anxiously pointing out dangers ahead. At Plei Me a forgotten radio had burst into life of its own accord. The oddnesses nurtured superstitions. Hardened grunts sought refuge in private worlds of secret touching, making signs of the cross, and dressing in a particular order. When unwritten rules were transgressed, small untold rituals had to be enacted to placate whichever minor gods were in charge of arbitrarily choosing who was next to die. In this case, Dexter chose to believe that he had in fact sunk the poles himself but that the heat and sheer exhaustion had conspired to erase the memory of having done so. He had best complete the task. Only by wrapping his whole body round the poles like a baby koala could Dexter force them into the ground. He thought of the candy barley poles sunk into the necks of the garish horses onto which the small kids hung for dear life as they were whirled fast on the undulating carousel. Once he and Jake had seen a child fall from his mount and sprawl to the edges of the fast spinning disc. It was Jake who had got Old Jessop's attention. He slammed on the brake and the whole contraption squealed as it slowed. The boy's father picked up his mewling child then went to remonstrate with OJ who gave as good as he got and threw the 50 cents fare at the apoplectic father. The coins rolled off the carousel into the dust from where they were retrieved by Dexter. They bought a toffee apple with the money, if his memory served him right.

When all of the poles had been planted, he stood, as if in the middle of a palisade, and checked the symmetry of his construction. The sweat running into his eyes blurred his vision. He was back at Fort Dix on the firing range. At the press of a button, full-sized tin cut-outs of VC soldiers would spring up and his task was to fire his pistol at whichever snarling face first presented itself. No sooner had he fired at one, than another sprung up behind him. He whirled round and fired from the hip. Soon all fifteen were lying on the ground.

Now different figures emerged from the edges of the circle: his mother fleetingly waved at him; Walt, their neighbour in the Houses, was shaking his head ruefully as if he had caught Dexter doing something bad, which was often the case; the shoeshine wagged a finger at him, an ironic admonishment; next to emerge was one-armed Davie; then the strange woman in white he had encountered underground. What did she want? The Colonel put in an appearance, his skull and features fully restored. Dexter span round. The fairground dwarf, still rubbing his back, barely came up to the halfway point on the pole; Zak, his wounded friend, trying hard to stop his entrails falling to the ground, looked at him balefully. The other stations were occupied by former platoon members who variously stuck their middle fingers in his direction, or just looked through him, preoccupied with staying alive. Finally, and most vivid of all was Jake. His buddy just smiled. 'Soon,' said Dexter, 'soon...'

He ran forwards and tripped on a trailing vine. He lay with his face pressed into the undergrowth still redolent of smoke. When he lifted his head he saw only the poles.

CHAPTER SEVEN

He had underestimated the challenge of spreading the parachute evenly across the bamboo framework. He started at the centre and then stretched the thin silk towards the outer ring. He became tangled in the trailing ropes and then blinded as the bundle he was carrying high above his head collapsed and smothered him. The one section he had managed to secure snagged and fell off its flimsy support. 'Fuck,' said Dexter. He had lashed an extra pole against the one in the centre and started again. This time he had more success, and eventually found himself in the middle of a virtual tent. It was swaying slightly but seemed to be holding up. He collected the ropes into the middle and looked up into his balloon. It felt cooler and somehow safe, and, for the time being at least, was proving an effective barrier against the insect hoards flicking at the exterior. The glaring sun was equally unsuccessful at finding a way in and had to settle for flooding the inside with a diffused opaque white light. Like a mariner checking his sails, Dexter patted the points where the nylon sagged but overall everything was holding.

Very occasionally Dexter's father would return from the garage with gifts for his son and wife. There was a giant toy panda which was as big as Dexter. His mother said it was a stupid present: there was no room for it in the apartment. Eventually she became so resentful of the bear's innocuous presence that Dexter acquiesced to its removal and subsequent donation to the thrift store. He distinctly remembered his mother pushing the bear ahead of her down the stairs. No way to treat a bear, thought Dexter.

The most enduring present had been a small model balloon consisting of a rigid plastic globe in a mesh of string that supported a tiny wicker basket. The globe was painted with vertical blue and white ellipses. Dexter had climbed onto the top of his wardrobe and secured it to the ceiling as close to the centre of the room as he could manage. His mother used to complain that it was only collecting dust, and she had enough to do keeping body, soul, him and the house together without wasting time with a feather duster.

At night it was the last thing he would look at before sleeping. As the room grew dark its precise features would fade and he would project his soul into the tiny wicker basket and sail out of the room, over the houses, over the fun park and off over the ocean. Sometimes he managed to steer the balloon towards the street where Jake lived. He would hover and then drop a rope up which Jake climbed. Soon clouds would roll in and obscure their view as they peered over the edge of the basket and they were enveloped in the thin smoke of mist.

Dexter felt drowsy but was disinclined to rest. That would come later. He was eager to move to the next stage of his escape. He would need fire to heat the air inside his balloon. The scorched earth beneath the canopy was a helpful reminder of how easily he could summon flames. The jungle floor provided rich kindling as the monsoon rain barely penetrated the very lowest echelons of undergrowth.

He soon had armfuls of sticks, desiccated vegetation and

189

crumbling stalks which he divided between three separate heaps quite close to the central poles. He checked that the outer skirts of the balloon touched the ground, ensuring that the area to be heated was comparatively self-contained.

He was enjoying the womb-like feel of the tented space. The early days under canvas in Nam had felt good too. New comrades, friends, the occasional weirdo. Shared tales from homelands that sounded exotic and distant to Dexter. Texas, the prairies, the Rockies, Chicago. On the third night after arriving he had held his audience spellbound with descriptions of Steeplechase Park. Every last man became a child again, each revisiting their chosen fairground memory, rodeo or circus.

He ducked out again into the intense heat and looked at the tops of the trees for evidence that he had a favourable wind. Although the air felt sultry and stagnant at ground level, he could detect the upper branches swaying slightly in the direction of the river. Soon he would soar skywards and float above the treacherous waters until he gradually lost height and landed in another world. His chest ached with excitement.

He gathered the ropes together and laid them carefully on the ground. At the last moment he would tie them tightly round his waist, sense them tensing and then feel their firm grip when he was lifted off the ground as if by a friendly giant. He patted his pockets, checking that the knife was there. That was the extent of his luggage. Travelling light he thought. His head filled with songs again. *You Can't Hurry Love* merged into the *Last Train to Clarksville* and then ended with *These Boots are Made for Walking*.

His hands shook as he knelt before each of the three heaps and applied his Zippo. They caught instantly and crackled with serious intent. He could feel the heat from the fires and moved towards the ropes. No sooner had he gathered them together than the fires, almost simultaneously, died.

Disbelieving, he stared at the embers. 'Son of a bitch,' he said. 'Fuck, fuck, fuck!' He stuck his thumb in his mouth and pouted for a moment then sprang into action. He would need to build larger fires. How had he ever thought that those would be big enough?

Now frantic, he ducked out once more and swept into the jungle, emerging with armfuls of twisted sticks and small branches. On returning from his third foray into the undergrowth, he paused. He was being watched. He knew it. He dropped his bundle and took out his knife. Crouching down and moving backwards he scanned the jungle. 'Come on out!' he shouted. 'Miserable commie bastard, show yourself!' No one showed. He looked angrily at a small flight of birds heading into the sun, and tried to calm himself. He was hot, maybe dehydrated. These things happen.

The pyre in the centre of the balloon reached nearly a yard up the central pole. He would try again. All would be well. The dry fuel caught instantly and he had barely time to take the Zippo away from the source of heat. He was bending down to retrieve the ropes when he saw that the flame was almost licking the sagging underbelly of the fabric. He tore off his T-shirt and used it to beat the flames. He flailed angrily at everyone who had ever slighted him, he lashed out at the peaceniks, at Bozo, at the high school students who had shunned him, at every goddam NCO in Vietnam.

He had failed. He was going nowhere. Furthermore his hands were burnt. He looked round for Jake, either as someone to blame or as a source of commiseration. Jake had failed him again. He hunkered down and, holding himself in his arms, rocked on his heels and emitted a low noise: half sob, half keening.

Dexter couldn't face the Colonel. They had said their farewells. He didn't have the courage to report on the aborted mission. He would spend the night inside the parachute tent that resolutely refused to change its status to that of balloon. At least he had put out the fire. In any case the light was fading. As the night dropped on the jungle like a dead hand, he curled into a foetal position and closed his eyes. He took canister 7 down from the shelf.

Crouched on the third step from the bottom of the stairs, he listened as his parents talked about him.

'He shoulda gotten over it by now.'

'He won't talk about it. He's beating himself up. Have you seen the wallpaper by his bed, all written over? Jake, Jake, Jake, big letters, small letters.'

'And his arms, I can't bear to look at them. He's cut the letters deep in the flesh. Boy needs a doctor.'

'Perhaps I'll take him away for a few days. Camping. Just him and me. The Alleghany River.'

And so it came to pass.

They said very little on the journey. His old man had borrowed a 1953 Buick waiting for collection. The owner was away for a few days. 'Jist test driving it for him,' he said, pulling off the road.

The powerful torchlight cut swathes into the forest until his dad chose a break between the trees to pitch the tent.

As he lay in his sleeping bag, Dexter was overwhelmed by the total blackness of the night. 'Can I light a candle, Pa?'

'Wise up, son, you'll burn the tent down. Now go to sleep.'

The following day they made their way to the river. His father had not been fishing for years and sustained an enthusiastic monologue about the choice to be made between a spinner bait, a crank bait or a jig. Eventually, unable to stand his son's silence anymore, he turned to him. 'For Christ's sake, Dexter, make an effort. Your buddy drowned. It wasn't your fault. The coroner said it was an accident.'

'Ok, Pa,' said Dexter, aware of the pain he was causing his old man. 'I know, I know.'

Partly reassured, his father assembled his rod on the clay bank and then attached the bait. He held the spinner in his hand and showed it to Dexter. 'See this,' he said, lightly touching the whiskers hanging from the lead. 'Those bass can't resist a pretty skirt.' Dexter grunted. His father turned over the blades in his palm. 'See these blades? They flash and the fish can't say no. The gold ones are best for murky waters.' He launched the line towards the opposite bank. 'Now, if the fish takes it, you don't want to tug or you'll lose it. Let him get familiar with it, let him turn it round, give it some slack.'

For the next few hours they each settled into their separate, solitary worlds. Dexter found the river difficult. After a while he couldn't look at the water and screwed up his eyes towards the sky.

When jolted out of his reverie by his father's excited shout, he could only see bright light through a veil of mosquitos.

'Don't stand there, lend a hand.' The line was bent taut as a bow and the slim fish wrestled with the fresh air before it was landed on the bank where it twitched and jerked. The fish was Jake. Dexter looked away as his father administered a sharp blow to the fish's head. It was still.

'Where are you going?' asked his father, exasperated and annoyed that his son seemed incapable of sharing his moment of triumph.

'Just going for a leak.' His father shook his head.

Both father and son wanted to reach out to the other but neither could.

Realising that a strained silence would end badly, the older man consciously chose to talk, even if it was destined to be a one-sided discussion.

193

'Wonderful piece of equipment,' he said later as he prepared to cook the fish. 'The Primus stove was invented by a Swedish man, Frans Wilhelm Lindqvist, a mechanic in Stockholm. Best thing since the wheel. The secret is turning the kerosene to vapour by pushing it through heated pipes, and then lighting it when it mixes with the air. But you need this pump here to generate the pressure.' Despite himself Dexter expressed interest in the process. The subsequent explanation and related questions became an oblique metaphor through which they both expressed their affection for each other. The fish tasted good, and the darkness that followed within minutes of them crawling into the tent proved less troublesome to Dexter.

'Dumb! Dumb! Dumb!' Dexter sat upright and berated himself. He had slept longer than usual. The sun was streaming into the bivouac. 'Did you learn nothing? Dunce, ignoramus! You need pressure. It's no damn good lighting a fire in the fucking jungle and hoping for the best. Dumbass, jerk! Stoopid!' He smacked his palm against his forehead and glared at the condensation dripping from the interior of his shelter. 'You need to heat the fuel under pressure. Did you learn nothing from your old man? You got to vaporise the fuel. Now get your sorry ass back to that plane. And put those skills I learned you to good use!'

'Yes, Sir!' said Dexter, agreeing to carry out his own instructions.

He strode through the jungle, ignoring the tendrils grabbing at his legs and face. 'Motherfuckers! Get out of the way!' The birds squawked and gossiped their approval as he fought his way to the site of the crash.

'Now you need a fuel tank. A small ammunition case should suffice. And the pipework is essential. There should be plenty of pipes in that ol' wreck. Now here's the clever thing! That pipe has got to twist and turn on itself so that the vaporisation is maintained by the flame once it's up and burning. Jesus, Dexter, you're one smart dude... I know, I know, that's all down to my old man. He learned me real good. Better than that damn school.'

He approached the wrecked aircraft with caution. Since he had last visited, the jungle had wrapped its green arms more tightly round the half fuselage. As he leant into the open hatchway, Dexter was assailed by a tight ball of insects. After spitting them from his mouth and rubbing his eyes, he noticed that the interior was a writhing mass of snakes.

Armed with a strut from the undercarriage, he waded into his latest enemy and thrashed at the squirming, many-headed hydra. He hurled some of the snakes into the jungle while others feinted and darted at him with slivers of tongue. He took out his Zippo, readjusted the flame until it wandered languidly some six inches from the nozzle, and moved it towards the snakes who, sensing that they were beaten, slid away into the deeper interior of the aircraft.

The aeroplane smelt bad but Dexter couldn't place the cause. It occurred to him that perhaps not all of the passengers had jumped and that one of their number may be festering under a seat somewhere. He had no wish to check his hypothesis having seen enough rotten, tortured human beings to last him a while.

The rear of the plane was largely intact. An unopened packet of Marlboro lay on the decking along with the wrappers from C-rations. Dexter lifted the metal seats that lined the interior and rummaged inside. Soon he found what he was looking for. He lifted out the toolbox and whistled as he explored its contents. 'A real treasure trove, man!' He removed a wrench. 'Now. That's a tool Ol' Antonio would pay good dollars for! Man, look at that, a pair of knurled-handle and smooth-jaw angled-nose slip-joint pliers. Now what is the army doing with something as fine as that? Jesus! Metric nut drivers. And look at that rivet buster. Well, I'll be darned.'

Having chosen a slotted square-shank screwdriver, he tore away the canvas webbing on the inside of the fuselage and soon found the piping he was looking for. 'Pass me the tooth pliers, buddy.'

He had soon cut several lengths which he lined up outside of the plane. He ducked back inside and soon located the ammunition boxes. He chose the smallest. 'Now for the million dollar prize! Where am I going to find me a foot pump?' He flipped open all of the boxes down one side like a contestant on a game show.

'Don't hide from me. I know you're in there somewhere!' He tossed their contents into the middle of the passageway: flotation devices, a heavy compass, 'might be useful,' medical supplies, 'I could sure use a shot of morphine,' mosquito nets, heavy duty batteries, a black chain with grappling iron attached, black tape, 'I'll take that.'

'Yes, siree!' He lifted out a pristine foot pump still in its box. 'You're smarter than the average bear!' He held the pump at shoulder height so that the photographer could get a good shot of the trophy. 'This is just the first of many triumphs,' he explained modestly for the benefit of the journalists eager to capture his every word.

His spoils were heavier than he had realised, and he assumed it was only a matter of time before both his arms left his sockets with a final tear of sinew and muscle. He eventually dropped his load close to the parachute that was still resting on its bamboo poles. He ducked under and saw that someone had apparently completed the task of clearing away the burned debris from around the central poles, and replaced it with fresh kindling. The ropes too that he had inadvertently scattered in his panic to put out the fire, had been carefully gathered together and indeed plaited.

He scratched his head. It was just possible that in his

tired state he had worked on after the last disaster, but he didn't think so. Logically, he could either embrace the unlikely scenario that once again he wasn't alone, or simply ignore the evidence of his eyes and maintain the pretence that nothing had changed. He consciously chose the latter option. And why not? The only truth he fully understood after fighting in Vietnam for three years was that he knew absolutely nothing about how the world worked, about his fellow man, about justice and morality. Nothing. How hard would it be then to assimilate this latest illogicality into a belief system based on an unquestioning acceptance of life's absurdities and contradictions?

Once that puzzling development had been relegated to the back of his brain, Dexter could fully concentrate on the logistics of escape.

To maximise the pressure difference, he would have to wait until the heat started to drain from the day. He would leave the earth when the sweat dried on his skin and the crickets became hysterical at the approaching dusk. That would give him the best part of eight hours to construct the burner.

As Dexter planned, he talked constantly to himself, chiding, reassuring and checking. He also spoke to Jake. 'Soon, old buddy, soon. I sure hope you packed the food, and a change of clothes. I sure hope you left a note for your Da. And I hope you checked the ropes as I told you. Now remember, we mustn't get too close to the flames. Timing is everything. Get it wrong and we get incinerated, one last BBQ for Charlie.'

He poured a scoop of cold water over his head and then started to lay the piping in an approximation of the position it would eventually occupy. He also placed the tools in order of their likely use. 'Look at that, Pa,' he said, stretching.

He was reluctant to bend the piping into shape. There would be no problem flexing a length across his knee but

197

there was a danger that any bend might constrict the flow of vapour. Anticipating this, he had uncoupled a dozen or so clamps from the innards of the plane. If the pressurised air was to enter the fuel tank from the top, he would have to saw two lengths of piping and deploy a couple of the clamps to prevent leaking.

As he examined the pump, he again experienced a sense of disbelief at his good fortune in locating such a vital component. Perhaps Lady Luck was on his side again. As he mentally saluted the fortune-telling robot at the fair, he realised that the bore of the pipe was larger than the outlet tube from the foot pump. He quickly solved the problem by wrapping the black electric tape tightly round the join.

The ammunition box presented its own challenge. It would not be easy to pierce the strong casing so that it would allow entry to the pipe. When he hammered a screwdriver into the side, it only reluctantly buckled but stayed intact. On closer examination he located a small seam that suggested a point of potential weakness. After a sustained assault, he felt the pleasing sensation of the tip of the screwdriver entering the box. The hole was quickly enlarged and eventually he could press the pipe home. Any moment his old man would wander from the office built into the side of the garage and inspect his son's work. 'Keep it tight, a little at a time. Well done. Now you gotta build the heat tray.'

He had wisely brought along one of the metal compartments that had originally lined the toolbox. It was sufficiently robust, could hold a fair amount of kerosene and wouldn't leak. If the fuel was to vaporise, it would be crucial to expose several feet of the piping to the source of heat. This could only be achieved by manipulating the piping into a structure that turned back on itself at least twice, thereby exposing the maximum length of piping to the flame without it becoming unwieldy. 'Clever thinking boy, neat solution.'

He placed the pipe from the fuel tank on the lip of the tray on its longer side. His plan would be to connect this pipe into the middle point of a second pipe that straddled the tray at right angles. This piece of tubing would, in turn, feed into vertical pipes at either end, thus ensuring that the fuel circulated in two directions, effectively doubling the exposure to the heat. If these vertical pipes then turned back on themselves, it should be possible to pierce a connecting pipe at its lowest point and devise a nozzle from which the vapour would escape. The resulting flame would have sufficient heat, height and intensity to raise his balloon into the skies and into another world. Overwhelmed by the symmetry of the solution, he and Jake hollered in unrestrained joy.

Cursing setbacks while noisily acclaiming each small success, Dexter toiled through the midday sun. The jungle provided the perfect audience, babbling and whooping its own animated commentary. Several tiny red birds swooped down to get a closer look and then flew away.

Eventually the time was right, the hour had come. He stood still, almost paralysed with adrenaline, sniffed as if inhaling dope, wiped his nose with the back of his hand and checked that the ropes were sufficiently close to be grabbed at the moment of ascent. He crouched down and held the Zippo close to the nozzle. He steadied his wrist with the other hand. The small red worm of flame insinuated itself and then snatched at the thin jet of fuel. He stepped aside and picked up the ropes but it was too soon. The far side of the balloon had become snared on an adjacent pole, leaving a gap through which he could see the jungle. He put down the ropes and gently untangled the material as if it had been an infant's tousled bedding. Other gaps appeared. An errant gust of wind must not be allowed to destroy the plan. The billowing rippled its way round the far edge and then ceased.

The heat was now palpable. He looked above for signs that his balloon was inflating. Nothing so far, but then he detected the merest hint that one of the many folds and creases was straightening itself, becoming appreciably smoother. This phenomenon was replicated at intervals until it was gloriously obvious that the fabric was swelling. The quilted ceiling was slowly transforming into a tight white dome. The transformation was not even. Some sections became taut while other segments still hung slackly, reluctant to play the game. As his eyes swung from one side to the other, checking the fabric, he became aware of an unmistakable sense of power, partly in himself, partly within the small environment of the balloon. For such it now was. He felt the tug on the ropes and in his mounting joy almost forgot to step either side of the thick knot where the ropes had been tied together.

He and Jake were strapped into the parachute ride. OJ checked the fastening, threw some affectionate abuse at the boys, signalled to his pal in the small kiosk who pushed the lever away from him. There was a jolt and in the same moment they stopped rocking in the cradle and, gripping the metal struts ever tighter, realised they had left the ground.

Dexter had left the ground. Fearful of moving lest he disturb the subtle equilibrium, he held his breath, then exhaled gently. If exaggerated, this movement too could jeopardise the ascent. The ropes bit into his groin but this didn't matter. With astonishment, he watched as the scorched circle beneath him shrank and gradually merged into a much wider space. He looked up. The tight dome still seemed motionless. He looked down again. The circle was now much smaller and was surrounded by undergrowth. 'Holy fuck!' he muttered. Nothing in his life had afforded him such elation. The feeling was physical, almost sexual in its intensity.

Only once did he tell his Ma that he had dreamed that he had left his small bed and slowly risen towards the ceiling, from which vantage point he had looked down on his clothes and possessions strewn about the floor. His Ma had gotten cross at this point and told him never again to eat cheese before he went to bed. But he knew then she was wrong. He knew it was real, he knew that he had, on the very cusp of falling asleep, left his bed and hovered near the ceiling. The moment when the blankets fell from him had been the best part of the whole experience. He felt pleasure in his stomach in a way he had never felt before. After Jake it never happened again, he remained tied to the earth. In later years he thought his ma had probably been right. It had been the cheese.

But Dexter again felt the same sensation in his stomach. The earlier event had been but a dress rehearsal for this moment. An intimation of a future joy. The ropes were rigid in his hands and they creaked slightly, but his balloon made no other noise. He was rising from the earth, rising out of the war. He was being hauled skyward by an unseen hand. He had wondered if death on the battlefield would be like this. A glorious moment when the medics stopped pounding his chest, injected no more morphine, stopped the superfluous mantra of encouragement and the pointless imprecations to hang in there. He was leaving. He'd never believed in angels but, Jesus, something was happening here.

Why had no one told him the jungle was so beautiful? He climbed slowly past the mottled wood of ancient trees aching to reach the sun. His noiseless elevator made no stops through the vegetation undulating beneath him in folds and curves of sensual green. Deep greens and paler greens nestled together.

The river that had held such terror meandered benignly through the landscape: an innocuous silver skin long discarded by the serpent. A chain of smaller lakes and ponds

201

marked its course until it was sucked into an electric haze of heat. Dexter was possessed with joy, vindicated, forgiven, consumed with rapture.

He had passed to the other side. He had crossed the river. To mark the sanctity of the moment the caretaker threw a switch on the sound system, the cacophony of birdsong become gradually muted as the power ebbed from the jungle. The very silence was rendered deeper by the celebratory insistent bark of a wild dog. Dexter nudged his face into the thin wisps of floating cloud, emissaries bringing messages of hope, outriders protecting the ecstatic traveller.

So too, Jake rose from the waters of the bay, his body slack and relaxed. The wetness drained from him in streamers, his eyes open and smiling. His shoes had fallen back into the sea. The loss made him lighter, more amenable to the ascent. Dexter held firmly onto his hand and did not let go.

INTERLUDE TWO

What do they mean, the weather's not good enough? There's not a bloody zephyr in the sky? Not a cloud. This has happened three times now. Get on the website, said friends in the know. It's a scam. They never fly. Just read some of the comments about the small print, and arbitrary changes to agreements. Seven cancelled flights and you're out. Forget about getting your money back. Put it down to experience. Try the ombudsman. Phone the Met Office next time. Quote chapter and verse. Tell them about the anticyclone settling over the country. Do they even have a balloon? Is it a figment of some marketing executive's fevered imagination? Yes, they have a balloon, I've seen it with my own eyes. I just failed to catch it. What do you mean? Where is it now? I suppose you're right. It could have been taken down to Southern England. Better weather certainly. Perhaps it's out of commission. Punctured by the beak of an angry crow at altitude. Sold on eBay. Bugger! Bugger! Bugger! My specific disappointment with the cancelled flight merged into generalised doubt about the Vietnam narrative. In some ways it felt worse than *Ursule*. Apart from anything else I had learned nothing and had written, 'Dexter nudged his face into the thin wisps of cloud'. For goodness sake. Even if I hadn't yet managed to book a balloon flight there was no excuse for that. Did I really think that clouds floated past like diaphanous butterfly wings or little puffs of ectoplasm in a child's cartoon? Perhaps Dexter should have gathered them and kept them in his hat. I would certainly go back and excise the sentence and its equivalent in *Ursule* during the rewrite.

My doubts about the latest story again went deeper than irritation with the occasional errant sentence and un-American sounding phrase. I had invested a lot of emotional energy in the story but once more it had left me dissatisfied.

Doubts about the overarching themes of the novel sent me scuttling back to my sources. Mayhew provided some confirmation that I had been on the right tracks. In *The Illustrated London News* of 18th September 1852 he declared that, 'to feel yourself floating through the endless realms of space, and drinking in the pure thin air of the skies, as you go sailing along almost among the stars free as the lark at heaven's gate, and enjoying for a brief half hour, at least, a foretaste of that Elysian destiny which is the ultimate hope of all.'

So why the dissatisfaction? Dexter seemed pretty happy when he climbed above the river. Surely it was euphoria of sorts? Isn't that what I wanted? The final moments of the narrative suggest an expiation that goes far beyond the absolution that he craved. On balance Dexter seems to have attained a state of release that is more permanent and significant than Ursule's. That had certainly been the intention, and at least I resisted the urge to bring him back to earth.

Perhaps I was just experiencing the sense of anticlimax that is to be expected when a satisfying all-absorbing task is finished, and a void opens up.

Was it possible that I was missing both Ursule and Dexter? This was ridiculous. They are not real. On reflection it was Mayhew's final phrase, 'a foretaste of that Elysian destiny which is the ultimate hope of all,' that came closest to the cause of my dissatisfaction.

It had never been my intention to couch any sense of spiritual transcendence in a specifically religious context. Perhaps I had to face the possibility that the balloon-shaped elephant in the room was, despite my conscious intent, religion. But there was more. Perhaps my naïve pursuit of rapture, albeit clumsily expressed in the flight metaphor, had at its core something more specific than religion. It was death.

DANTE
PALERMO, SICILY 2015

CHAPTER ONE

'Father, I've been touching myself inappropriately,' said the woman.

'Don't we all?' said Dante Corsini unthinkingly. 'Shit! Shit,' said his brain. 'Wrong words, Father, wrong words.' He conjured a severe cough from nowhere as if he could somehow erase them as they hovered in the damp air of the confessional box. He sat upright, coughed again, softer this time, and nervously put his rosary beads to his lips. A stupid habit but one that went with the job. 'Sin no more, my sister. Go and pray for me.' He moved to close the shutter.

'But you haven't given me any penance, Father, does that mean you don't really think it was a sin?'

'No, I...'

'Because I too wonder if the church is right to condemn such a natural, relief-giving activity. Is it true that God makes a kitten die every time someone masturbates? Where does he get all the kittens from? Do the nuns run kitten farms?' Exasperated, he pulled back the shutter and stared through the grille but she had gone. He heard her stifled laughter as she ran out of the church. He stepped out of the box. No one else was waiting, no witnesses who might have told him who had run down the side aisle and out of the door.

Her voice had been familiar. Not a young person, but someone who should have known better. He went back into the confessional and resigned himself to waiting in the dark for another fifteen minutes or so before retreating to the canonica for a night cap.

It had been a hard day that had started with him driving into the hills to administer the last rites to the Widow Fantini. The witch had scowled at him constantly as if he were personally responsible for the cancer that finally got her. If only, he had thought. If only he had such power, a few more folks would be getting bad news soon. He then instantly regretted that thought as well. What was happening to him? In his sixties he should be becoming kinder, mellower, saintlier. He snorted.

Over the last forty years he had progressively developed an unreasoning hatred of saints. It had started harmlessly enough with him expressing minor reservations about Saint Violetta to Bishop Cellini. The bishop had raised a patronising eyebrow but had let the young priest rant on. Violetta was manifestly mad, barking, by any medical definition, delusional, and the tale about the frogs was plain stupid. What sort of role model would pluck out her eyes and plunge into the Tiber?

When the parish had been ordered to pray for the recently dead Blessed Adolfo Maretti he had refused. The bad old bastard had abused half of the altar boys in the district. 'Less of a saint than my arse' was the phrase that got him into trouble with the authorities.

He thought of the woman in the confessional again. What age was she? Was she married? Did he know her? Was she clothed when she indulged in inappropriate actions? Was she in public at the time? Appalled at this line of thought, he stood up and pulled the entrance curtain to one side, preparing to leave. He would not stay a moment longer.

Through the side door he saw Signora Belcastro, a tiny

210

shrunken woman limping down the aisle. She was almost certainly coming to confession. No, he wasn't going to stay. Signora Belcastro had been coming to confession every second Friday for the last twenty years. Her script never changed. It was always a detailed account of the same moment that had blighted her life. Martino, her husband, would always beat her when he came home from the osteria. He would unbuckle his belt before he opened the door of their house. He was usually right to beat her, she conceded. Sometimes the small scullery was very untidy, she should have tried harder. She was not a good cook but some of her culinary failures were so stupid that she deserved to be punished. Once, for goodness sake, the cabbage was hard and raw. Of course he was right to spit it onto the table, then punish her. She would run her fingers down the new wheals as if each ribbed line of flesh was a message from the church reminding her to be a better wife.

Once when he fell asleep after complaining of a painful forearm, for which he also rightly blamed her, she heard him choking but did nothing about it. She killed him by not venturing in to clear the vomit from his airways. God knew she was to blame and so now did Dante. She just wanted to die so that her foul soul could endure the perpetual torment which was now its destiny.

She claimed to have chosen Dante Corsini from all of the priests in Sicily. He first saw her during the procession to honour Santa Rosalia at Monte Pellegrino some twenty years previously. She had darted from the cobbled lane leading up to the sacred cave, and fastened herself limpet-like to the side of his cassock. Unable to shake her off, and in danger of dragging the woman in his wake, he stepped to one side and asked angrily what she wanted. 'Hear my confession,' she said. The bishop had paused and shook his head when he saw that Dante was to blame. That man should never have become a priest. The woman was probably a fallen

211

mistress whom he had smuggled into the canonica. She was probably pregnant, another bastard to be adopted and hidden somewhere. It all took so much money.

During the subsequent High Mass in the sanctuary carved out of the cave where Santa Rosalia appeared, Dante saw Signora Belcastro squashed between one of the novices and Father Alunni who was visibly squirming. He remembered thinking it was probably the first time in eighty-five years that Father Alunni had been in such close proximity to a woman. She was staring at Dante, and he was sure that she winked at him.

She duly appeared at Santa Caterina's a few days later. His heart sank as he saw her gurning away in the front row. And another wink. Over the weeks that followed she tested his commitment to the confessional seal by making up extravagant sins including infanticide, regicide and attempted suicide. What was the common Latin root, wondered Dante, *cide, cide?* Yes, that was probably it. When he failed to baulk at the litany of incrementally lurid crimes, she decided he could be trusted with the account of the husband and the vomit.

No, he was not going to stay and hear the tale again. He left the church by the side door. He would get a row from the sacristan for not locking it but he didn't care if whole armies of Sicilian bandits in a fleet of supercharged Fiats descended and looted every pietà, every collection box (always empty but he suspected they would burn well), the vestments, yes especially the hideous vestments. Would they sell on eBay? he wondered, and, for all he cared, each of the eleven Stations of the Cross? No, perhaps they could be persuaded to leave number eight. He had always had a soft spot for Mary Magdalene depicted as if she were one of the many prostitutes who frequented the harbour. He had himself on one occasion, when he was a young and even more tormented priest, sought solace there.

212

As he crossed the piazza, a stray football was kicked in his direction by one of three boys who were using two spare café chairs as goalposts. Dante stepped over the ball thereby hiding it completely under his cassock. He then feigned puzzlement as he pretended to look for the ball. The boys soon caught on and, after a few moments of deference, tried to dislodge the ball by aiming kicks at Dante's clerical garb. He then lifted the cassock up to the knees, flicked the ball onto the instep of his left foot where he balanced it, while hopping in a circle on his right leg. The boys were impressed and if he was honest, so was he. Sixty-five but the old skills had not left him completely. If God had either compassion or a sense of humour he would have, there and then, wound back the years and let him play with the boys as equals. But no. While three of the boys shouted, 'Bravo, Padre,' the oldest stole the ball from Dante's instep and flicked it into the air intending to trap it in the small of his back. Dante barged into the thin boy, sent him sprawling and skied the ball over the adjacent workman's hut. 'I was provoked, referee,' he said to nobody.

As he climbed Via Carini he heard the music emanating from the building on the corner. The former abattoir had been converted into communal rooms which the locals could hire. Through the gap in the lace curtain, he recognised a dozen or so of his older parishioners moving in slow motion to a waltz tune. The dance club had been one of his better ideas. Apart from anything else, it seemed to him that the endless round of funerals had stalled somewhat as the frail and aged had swapped their infirmity for an energetic nostalgia, and in one or two cases, lust. Old Remo, for example, had his back to the door and the widow Donatella firmly in his arms. Shaking his head, Dante acknowledged his own jealousy. While other parishioners scoffed at the idea of geriatric coupling, and feigned distaste, Dante could understand the joy of facing the final journey to oblivion in the arms of another warm and loving human being. Their old bodies were rejuvenated, as they shared laughter on finding out which bits still worked and which didn't.

He suspected that most of his bits still worked but in a more unpredictable and perhaps less sustainable manner. By a chain of connection not difficult for him to fathom, he thought again about the woman in the confessional. One of the biggest disappointments he had experienced on entering his sixties was discovering that his lustful inclinations had not noticeably declined. Having struggled with priestly celibacy for most of his adult life, with one or two fleeting exceptions still much revisited in his memory, he had come to look forward to a more serene phase in his life when he could finally embrace a principle that had always struck him as ridiculous. He could accept the other less desirable corporeal changes: hair loss, indigestion and the unwanted growth of a belly with breasts attached, with a degree of equanimity but it seemed that God was determined to make his life miserable to the very last.

It was God's sick joke of course. An essentially vengeful Old Testament God had never forgiven Dante for the sermon, delivered a decade ago, to a full congregation at Santa Caterina's, during which he had railed against the church's obsession with sex. What type of deity would raise the Satan of guilt in the bedrooms of young people finding their sexuality for the first time? What type of God would censure natural thoughts flowing through the heads of healthy, well-adjusted people trying to make sense of life and relationships? What sort of God would equate the use of contraceptives with child murder? This last had proved a provocation too far for some of the older worthies who had left noisily. Father Demetrio, broken equally by rheumatism and bitterness, led the exodus. He leaned against the baptismal font to compensate for the momentary abandonment of his stick which he was waving like a weapon in the general direction of the pulpit. 'Heretic! May you burn in the fires of hell!'

Dante warmed to his theme. 'Sex is a gift from God, not a dirty secret to be strangled and denied. Sex brings joy and life. Sex is laughter and delight, it is the great liberator from tedium. Sex spits in the face of Death...' By this point most of the congregation had left.

The bishop, a kindly man who had always had a soft spot for Dante, mainly because he reminded him of his own illegitimate son begotten of a maid whom he had befriended during a retreat at San Giovanni, temporarily removed Dante from the parish. He said that he had probably fallen under the influence of the Beatles and had lost his way. 'Some of the Beatles' music is very good,' he had ventured as a token of his modernism but soon realised he had himself overstepped the mark by gently singing, 'All we need is love.' He had coughed and sentenced Dante to spend two months in a remote monastery.

Furthermore, Radio Maria, the church's own station, had immediately cancelled its invitation for him to deliver a homily in the 6.30 am slot. A pity, as he would at that point in his life have welcomed a career in the ecclesiastical media.

As he waded through a tide of mail in the vestibule of the canonica, he remembered that Francesca, his housekeeper, was away on another pilgrimage. They never worked. When would she learn? On one occasion her sciatica had worsened to the extent that she had changed shape completely and walked sideways like a crab. 'God works in...,' she had started until Dante waved his finger at her. Where had his patience, his saintly tolerance gone?

There were several requests for Masses for the dead. He made a neat pile of the 10 euro notes attached by paper-clip to the pleading letters. A glossy brochure offered him the retreat of a lifetime, an opportunity to replenish the ecclesiastical batteries, a tonic for the soul, and a unique opportunity to reflect on the reasons why he joined the priesthood all those years ago. A good question, thought Dante.

He had been fast-tracked at school. At the age of seven he had been chosen from all of the altar boys to officiate at a concelebrated High Mass in the cathedral. His mother had been so pleased. She had organised a festa in the piazza: wine and cannoli for all the neighbours. He remembered the horror of dancing with the dowager Fabbri, she had smelt horrible. What was the name of the girl who had played footsy with him throughout the meal under the long trestle table? Among the other reasons for joining up, he supposed, there was his complex and changing relationship with God. Even at a young age he never understood why was it that both Judaism and Islam generally condoned railing and ranting at God. Why was it acceptable in other faiths to point out the folly of believing in Him, and criticise Him for the arbitrary nature of His grace and favour, while Christianity demanded unthinking sycophancy?

Luciana was the name of the footsie girl. Luciana, what became of her? Next then, several bills, and a round robin from a very tedious priest who had been presented with a choice between a thorough defrocking and missionary work in Liberia. Dante thought it ironic that it was the missionary position that had got him into bother in the first place. A tiny handwritten envelope intrigued him. More so when he discovered it was empty. Something compelled him to sniff it. It was her perfume, it was the scent of the woman from the confessional.

He was relieved that Father Adolfo with whom he shared the canonica had not returned from whatever duties he had contrived, and from which he would invariably combine maximum pleasure with minimal emotional engagement. Adolfo had a virtual monopoly on blessing ships.

At one time he had been chaplain to the small fishing fleet that sailed from Scoglitti. He was revered by the sailors who had attributed the return of a fishing boat, lost in the Adriatic for three days, to the devout intercessions of Father Adolfo. In his cups, one of the survivors swore that he had seen the clergyman walking on top of the stormy seas towards the stricken vessel. Adolfo had dismissed the rumour with a modesty that suggested this sort of feat was well within his capability.

The bishop had quickly appreciated that Adolfo was just the man to handle the tribe of unruly fishermen who, at best, adhered to a brand of Catholicism that owed more to witchcraft and superstition than to the subtle realignment of faith as published in the latest papal encyclical.

Increasingly, being chaplain to the fleet became a burden to Adolfo. The penultimate straw was officiating at the funerals of three brothers who drowned off Maremotu, and whose decomposed bodies were found on the rocks weeks after their disappearance. The last straw had been the suicide of Matteo, a young fisherman of whom he had grown particularly fond.

Unable or unwilling to engage at this emotional level, Adolfo had gradually moved upmarket and now peddled his blessings among the yacht-based Mafiosi and captains of industry who sailed into Palermo. He had a novelty value in the eyes of the rich who would invite him to dine with them and entertain their guests with tales of demonic possession, exorcism, hysterical nuns or mediaeval methods of torture, which latter topic was increasingly becoming one of his specialities.

Dante could take Adolfo in small doses. The man was outrageously clever and provided a provocative foil to Dante's increasingly pessimistic view of life and the priesthood. Sometimes it even felt like the early heady days in the seminary when the young novices would argue late into the night over articles of faith and the odd dubious interpretation of the gospels. The main difference was the prodigious quantity of drink that Dante and Adolfo could now consume when in argumentative mood.

Dante had in fact just poured himself a large grappa, a gift from a grateful parishioner, when the bell rang. As it was past ten o'clock, Dante feared the worst. And so it proved, as he opened the door to Riccardo, a drug addict who would have been long dead had Dante not frequently sheltered him in the back bedroom of the canonica, much to the petulant disapproval of Francesca.

'What now, Riccardo? Why are you disturbing an old priest at this hour? Can't you see he just wants to lay his old bones into a comfortable bed?' This was the absolute truth. More than anything, he wanted to devote his attention fully to the not unpleasant challenge of placing the provocative woman. He wanted to do so in bed, confident that any speculation would contain a pleasingly lustful element that might, if he was lucky, colour any subsequent dreams.

'I have just seen the Devil,' moaned Riccardo. 'He had my child in his jaws.'

'What are you on?' asked Dante.

'Just despair, my drug of choice.'

'You know I can't stand it when you get like this, sorry for yourself. Come in, for goodness sake.'

Out of habit, Dante straightened out the covers on the aged settee. Riccardo would not have noticed had he been ushered onto a seething nest of vipers. Dante sat in his armchair at ninety degrees so that he could maintain as much eye contact with Riccardo as felt right for them both. It had been a struggle to persuade the diocesan committee to fund his counselling course. They had tried to explain to their difficult priest that the art of listening with compassion was a gift from God and not a skill that could be learned in the dubious company of social workers and other quacks.

Eventually they had acquiesced. The course had at least confirmed his good habits and made him more aware of his bad habits such as falling asleep when bored or tutting judgementally whenever a saint's name was gratuitously invoked.

Riccardo was in his late twenties but seemed decades older. Tall and gaunt, he reminded Dante of the thirteenth Station of the Cross where Christ's broken body is carried down from the scaffold. He was living on the streets, and until recently could be found at the corner of Via Roma with a filthy but undeniably mournful Labrador.

On one of his rarer moments of resourcefulness, Riccardo, realising that the sad dog was infinitely better at eliciting alms from passing tourists than he was, trained the beast to beg without the obvious support of a human being. After discreetly tethering the dog to a lamp post with fishing wire (invisible in twilight), he would leave him behind a begging bowl with a bone motif, a lit candle, a tiny statue of the Virgin Mary and a sign round his neck declaring I AM A GOOD DOG WHO TRIES HARD TO LOOK AFTER A VERY TROUBLED MAN WHO SOMETIMES DRINKS TOO MUCH.

Often Riccardo would return to find the dog guarding a small but not insignificant pile of coins.

After a fortnight, during which time the dog had made sufficient money for Riccardo to buy a haircut and shave, essential prerequisites if searching for casual work in hotels and bars, the dog disappeared, presumed stolen. It was never seen again despite Riccardo conscientiously searching the Palermo streets with an expression infinitely more mournful that that of the lost dog. It was during one of these searches that he and Dante first met.

In recent years Riccardo had developed a series of involuntary twitches and tics as if trying to dislodge whichever devil was squatting on his shoulder at any one time. Dante had encouraged him to confront each of these personal demons at one time or another: his anger against his father, his profound self-loathing, his fear of death, but they always returned to torment their host.

Now he twisted the edge of the settee cover as if wringing out his soul. 'I see the executioner in my dreams, every night the scene plays over and over in my head. I have tried not to sleep, sometimes for days on end, but it never works. The shutters fly open and he stands there in black…' Dante always thought of *Don Giovanni* at this point in Riccardo's tale.

'My mother screams and knocks over the coffee pot. The liquid scalds my little brother who cries. My father just stares as if resigned, relieved even. I sometimes think I see a smile on his face as he looks at the man in black with the gun.'

Dante joined Riccardo on the settee and put his arm round him but said nothing; he knew the tale must run its course. He wished the grappa was not in a cupboard across the room as the tale was about to reach its climax.

'"Giuseppe, you betrayed us," says the man in black, stepping down from the window and placing the gun to the back of my father's head. He moves it slightly as if to make it nestle better in my father's hair. Then he pulls the trigger and my father's head explodes. All I could think of in that moment was how Mamma had saved to buy those curtains, and how cross she would be when the blood won't come out. She had kept the money in a biscuit tin in the dresser.'

Riccardo seemed quite calm as he uttered these last words and stared without movement into the middle distance. Dante kept his arms round the gangly man then held him tighter until the sobs finally came. Riccardo curled into as much of an approximation of the foetal position as was possible given his size and the constraints of the settee.

Dante patted his shoulder comfortingly. 'This dream will pass, Riccardo, each telling is like an exorcism, its details will fade and you will find peace again. You are a good man. Your father's murder had nothing to do with you.' Dante noticed that Riccardo was obsessively rubbing his knees as he tended to do at this stage in their ritual encounter. The next stage was to encourage Riccardo to lie down on the settee at an angle with his legs on the floor. This was easily achieved. Dante then covered him with the drape taken from the armchair. He kissed the top of his head and blessed him.

He heard Father Adolfo fiddling with his key in the lock. Eventually his fellow priest swayed into the room, only just suppressing a belch which morphed into a phrase half greeting, half good night. He glanced at Riccardo, muttered something uncomplimentary and climbed the stairs a little unsteadily to his bedroom. Dante waited until he heard the toilet flush overhead, checked to see that Riccardo was asleep and also took his leave.

As he pulled the bedclothes up to his chin, he remembered that he had been saving a particular train of thought for the moment between wakefulness and sleep. What was it? As a boy, this moment was often reserved for action replays of the football he had played during the day. In the seminary, he would imagine his mother's proud conversation as she boasted to the neighbours about her son's vocation. As a priest, newly assigned to his parish, he would conjure and knead ethereal metaphors that would constitute the centrepiece of his next sermon. In his dotage, the sublime metaphors had given way to earthlier, sexual speculation about the younger members of his congregation. And older women too, if he was honest. Oh yes, the woman in the confessional. He experienced a pang of self-loathing as he took stock of the sad decline in his fantasy realm. But there was nothing else for it. He listened again to her words that had been intended to shock, or titillate. If the latter, then she had succeeded. But who was she?

He flicked through the appointment diary in his head and scanned the faces at whichever baptism, funeral or wedding he had presided over in the last year. Who was that sitting at the far end of the table? Was it her? No, it was the younger Morelli sister. Nice looking, but it wasn't her. Was she an employee of the diocesan office? Unlikely, most of the office staff were either superannuated nuns or spinster harridans. Had he met her in the supermarket, had they exchanged words on the bus? And then he saw her.

He had been persuaded against his will to accompany Adolfo to a party of his newly acquired powerful friends. The yacht belonged to a Russian banker. The lackeys served vodka and caviar with impressive efficiency despite being weighed down by yards of gold braid. The oligarch clearly had a monopoly on uniforms destined for the Ruritanian army. 'It's not what you know...' said Adolfo, correctly interpreting Dante's facial expression as one of deep cynicism.

Why on earth had he gone along? Perhaps he had recently fallen out with Adolfo, a not infrequent occurrence, and had been trying to make amends. It was definitely her. She had cornered him. Even then she had seemed familiar; this was not their first meeting. In her late forties, very attractive with an unnaturally deep voice. 'Why was he a priest?' That had been her opening gambit. He had instantly risen to the challenge, choosing to hide the truth in a veneer of irony. 'To make the world a better, more compassionate place, to offer comfort and succour to the poor and needy.'

'Succour,' she had replied, lingering over the word as if trying it for size. 'Might you succour me Father?'

'I might,' he replied, staring directly at her, 'unless I thought you were beyond the pale.'

'But isn't that for God to decide, not one of His servants, one of His minions?'

'Better God's minion than Satan's plaything.' He knew he had miscalculated, and given her the advantage.

222

'Do you think I am one of Satan's playthings? Do I look like anyone's plaything? Do I look like one of your playthings, Father?' The question was accompanied by her gently pushing her finger into his chest.

'No, not at all,' he stammered, completely defeated. 'Not at all.' She twisted her finger, then withdrew it and turned to join the other guests. He stood there deflated and watched her laughing at whatever conversation she had gatecrashed on the other side of the room.

His dreams, when they came, were not of the lustful variety he had perhaps hoped for, having partly solved the identity of the self-fondling woman. When a young boy, he had been admonished by the priest in confessional for offering up his dreams as evidence of depravity and moral turpitude. The priest had said that without the release of dreams we would all go mad. By way of a caveat, he suggested that spending overlong when awake trying to recapture the precise details of lustful dreams was probably a sinful activity and therefore best avoided. This left Dante wondering how long he could reasonably spend thinking about already fading dreams. He decided that ten minutes could be justified on the grounds that, not being yet fully awake, he could not be expected to self-censure instantly. Additionally, given that, by their nature, dreams faded at the same rate that consciousness returned, he could realistically be permitted to concentrate as hard as he could, while he could.

His dreams that night were a mix of the familiar and the bizarre. He mounted the pulpit in Santa Caterina's in front of an expectant congregation to deliver his sermon during the eleven o'clock mass. The church was surprisingly full. Adolfo as always was leaning in the vestry doorway so that he could gather verbal kindling for the fiery debriefing over grappa. He was delighted to see both of his parents in the front row, even though they had been dead for at least two decades. The small scrubbed boy squashed between them was himself. The bishop was there, the pope was there. Silvio Berlusconi was there next to two surprisingly young prostitutes. There was however one very empty seat on the end of the third row. Who was missing? Who had failed to turn up to hear one of the finest sermons this side of heaven? There was an expectant pause, someone coughed. Dante, having placed both hands on the pulpit, then crouched down to create the feeling of intimacy with his congregation: a trick he had borrowed from a visiting Franciscan friar in the past.

For their part, the good people in the church leaned forward so as not to miss a sainted word from his holy lips (even his sleeping self winced at the choice of adjectives). Dante breathed in deeply and opened his mouth. But no words came out. Not a sound. He had no idea what to say. There wasn't even the shadow of a memory about the profound message he was going to deliver. His mouth stayed open. The congregation stared and stared and then one by one each face became that of an animal. By and large, the front row turned into sheep, behind them were several cats. Towards the back of the church he saw Riccardo's Labrador Orlando raising his mournful eyes to the impostor orator. Dante wanted to tell Orlando to stay where he was, as his owner was desperate to find him, and had already taken a solemn vow not to exploit him ever again, but still his words wouldn't come, and in fact Orlando was the first to leave. Slowly at first, the other animals left their seats and crowded into the aisle. Soon the pews emptied like water down a sink and Dante woke with a pounding heart and an overwhelming sense of imminent disaster.

Adolfo shuffled into the day room in his pyjamas. In fact he was wearing a red surplice that had once belonged to a priest visiting from Nigeria. Whenever Francesca looked askance at him wearing a sacred garment, he would bless her, and invariably she would mutter her way back to the kitchen. 'When does the wretched woman get back from her pilgrimage?' he asked Dante who was coming down the stairs.

'Thursday, I think,' said the older priest, running a hand through that part of his head where hair last grew. 'Or Friday...'

'It's a disgrace,' said Adolfo. 'I shall write directly to the Holy Father. It is a nonsense that clerics of our standing should have to make our own breakfast when there are monasteries stuffed full with underemployed nuns who would sacrifice their best rosaries to be able to look after deserving menfolk.'

Dante smiled.

Adolfo was looking at Riccardo sprawled across the settee. 'And why is it that whenever I come down in the morning I have to share my space with whichever tramp you have rescued off the streets? Honestly, Dante, it's this sort of spontaneous charity that gives Catholicism a bad name. I can't even scratch my arse in my own front room.'

'Do you want a coffee?'

'Please. But I know what your subtle solipsist game is.' Adolfo waved a finger at Dante who was already in the kitchen. 'You think your time has finally come now that St Francis of Assisi himself has taken up residence in the Vatican, or rather in a humble hut somewhere in the vicinity of the main car park. Mark my words, it will end badly. How long do you think the Holy See will tolerate a pontiff who genuinely believes in helping the poor? And who only possesses one pair of shoes? Believe me, they will bring back that bad old German, the Führer waiting in the wings. Tomorrow belongs to me!' These last words were sung in a loud Germanic accent. Dante put a finger to his lip as he handed Adolfo a small cup. 'Don't wake Riccardo, he gets little enough sleep as it is.' Both men glanced at their comatose guest.

'He needs real counselling, not just the friendly ear that we provide.'

'Speak for yourself,' said Adolfo. 'He needs a flea in his ear and a kick up the backside!' He mimed this last action and spilt his coffee into the saucer. By the way, did you ever find his dog?' He put down the coffee and embarked on an elaborate pantomime that involved lifting each cushion, and looking behind the settee. 'Orlando, Orlando, where art thou? Your master needs you. I've got a lovely bag of bones for you, fresh from the catacombs, no sorry, *dog*acombs.'

Dante had indeed spent a day dog hunting. He realised now that dogs rarely ran or indeed walked through the streets and byways of Sicily. All they did was sleep, lying on pavements where they fell, exhausted by the heat. Invariably they lay on their backs immodestly flaunting their bollocks to all innocent passers-by. Sometimes they lay in packs. Sometimes they lay with stiff legs pointing skywards as if dead. He had paused at the cathedral as a wedding spilled into the piazza that was liberally covered in sleeping dogs. The photographer had made no attempt to waken them. An interesting photo album, he thought.

'Admit it, admit it, it makes you feel good, doesn't it? Helping the homeless, giving refuge to the dispossessed. Perhaps you had a vocation after all. St Peter will soon need a new tally book having run out of pages to record your good deeds. You get lots of gold stars for looking for stray dogs.'

'Better than supping with the money lenders,' retorted Dante, aware that the conversation, although light-hearted at the moment, hovered round some painful truths for them both. '"Blessed is he who drinks cocktails with oligarchs", I don't remember that one. And look at the size of your belly, stuffed with dainties and complements.'

'It's a fine belly, a friar's belly, the belly of a jolly man who can always be trusted with other people's money. A belly under which small animals can shelter... Orlando, Orlando are you there?' Adolfo put down his cup and pulled out the waistband of his pyjamas to better search for whatever household pet might have sought refuge there.

'Careful,' said Dante, 'you might find something horrible lurking down below.'

'My God, you're right! A rat, I think, perhaps a gerbil, it's difficult to tell these days. It's certainly neglected, whatever it is.'

'Enough,' said Dante, 'we have souls to save, bishops to placate and I've got an old woman to bury this afternoon.'

'How many deaths have the diocese now formally attributed to the insupportable boredom of your worthy sermons?'

Dante moved to the settee and put his hand on Riccardo's shoulder. 'Time to wake, sleeping beauty.'

There was no response from Riccardo as he was dead.

CHAPTER TWO

'Feel for a pulse. Lay him on the carpet. CPR.'

'What?' asked Adolfo, unable to move.

'Put him on the floor, pound his chest. See if we can get his heart started.'

Dante held Riccardo under the arms and pulled him from the settee. Adolfo eventually reconnected with the world and did likewise with Riccardo's legs. His mouth fell open. He was undeniably, incontrovertibly dead.

'Jesus Christ!' said Adolfo who picked up the empty grappa bottle and the blister packs that until yesterday contained the anti-inflammatories that had been prescribed for his gout.

The involuntary evocation of his Saviour's name reminded Dante that his day job required him to respond in a particular way. 'Phone for a fucking ambulance! I will administer the rites.'

While Adolfo did as he was told, Dante went to the cupboard behind the TV and brought out the last rites bag embroidered with a cross and a Latin motto. He crossed himself and then put his fingers to his lips. He opened the small vial of unction and started to anoint Riccardo. 'In nomine patri...' he heard the words coming out of his mouth but they belonged to someone else. Someone who actually believed that this posthumous intervention might change the mind of a God who had already decided that eternal purgation in the fires of hell was the most suitable punishment for the dead man who had, after all, committed suicide… 'All right, on second thoughts, I will commute the sentence to several centuries in purgatory… In nomine Patris…' Dante clenched his fists as if he had scored a winning goal but his emotion was anger. He looked up and howled. Adolfo rushed to console him. 'They're on their way,' he said.

'Why did you do that, Riccardo? Why? Things were getting better.' Dante's anger had transferred itself from God to the dead man. 'Why didn't you wake me? Stupid, stupid man! More names are being given daily to the authorities. The tide has turned. Your father's assassin would have been found. You have no answer, do you?' Struck by the absurdity of his own question Dante relented and kissed Riccardo's forehead. Adolfo knew his fellow priest well enough not to intervene.

The door had opened without either priest noticing. Francesca, the housekeeper, refreshed if not cured of her rheumatics, had returned. Sensing some untold catastrophe, she had crept forward until she met Riccardo's unflinching gaze. She dropped her ancient leather suitcase and screamed. 'A dead man in the canonica. It's all your fault, Father Dante, bringing home every lost soul you find on the streets. Turning this sanctified place into a hostel, a doss house and now a morgue. Wait until word reaches the bishop. The building is possessed. Satan has made his nest here in a holy place. We need an exorcism!' She crossed herself repeatedly, faster and faster until it seemed she had a propeller on her chest.

'For God's sake, Francesca, stop doing that and be silent!' said Adolfo. The housekeeper started to sob loudly but wisely retired to the kitchen before she witnessed the full extent of the priest's anger.

229

Soon the paramedics arrived, and soon after, they departed with Riccardo's body on a stretcher. Dante opened the curtains to watch them load their burden into the back of the van. The process was also closely watched by a small boy holding a red helium-filled balloon on a taut string. Stepping into the street for a better view of his first dead body, the boy let go of the string and, with Dante, watched the balloon meander up the side of the building. It brushed against the second floor window as if wanting to peer in, then resumed its upwards amble before disappearing over the rooftops.

'Use the side chapel,' urged Adolfo. 'Riccardo was a down-and-out. Who is going to come to his funeral? Get it over with and move on. A pity in many ways they repealed the edict about saying Mass over the body of someone who committed suicide. When was that? 1983. Who was pope then? That weakling Jean Paul probably. Cause, knowledge and gravity. The three criteria, and your man Riccardo meets them all...' He bit skilfully into his cannoli, rotating it at the same time to prevent further stains on his cassock.

'Enough, Adolfo,' warned Dante who was not going to rise to the bait. Today was not the time to play their habitual game of adopting stereotyped positions that neither of them actually believed.

With near perfect timing, Francesca shuffled into the room. She had reclaimed her stick which she had consigned to the attic, prematurely confident of, if not a miraculous cure, then at least significant remission from her condition. As a consequence, her face had reverted to its default position of scowl mixed with general disapproval. 'For you, Father.' She handed an envelope to Adolfo. 'Probably an application from the town's tramps applying for permission to stay in the canonica. They've heard the grappa is good.' She shot a look at the two priests that would have frightened hardened criminals, deployed her stick to

230

execute an elaborate three-point turn and left the room.

'I think she's glad to be home,' said Dante, opening the envelope. Bemused, he held up a fat wedge of euros. 'What the...?' Adolfo took the empty envelope and read the words on the back: FOR RICCARDO'S FUNERAL.

Initially the funeral director had been reluctant to commit the horse-drawn cortège. Had the passenger been a senator, a senior police officer or indeed, someone well connected with the underworld, then there would not have been a problem. But a pauper! His firm would be a laughing stock. Dante made quite clear that he had contacts in the Vatican curia who would ensure that Signor Cortes and his obsequious colleagues would never again preside over a funeral in this or any other diocese. He made a knowing reference to a recently deceased local businessman whose body had been found hanging from a crane in the docks, and observed that horses' heads were more plentiful these days given the recently revived taste in equine flesh fostered by some of the classier restaurants. Signor Cortes bowed deeply and promised that all necessary arrangements would be put in place. Rarely had a lie given Dante such satisfaction.

Dante endured another sleepless night. Not only was his head over-exercised by the money and the possible identity and motivation of the benefactor, but he was also grieving for Riccardo. Irrespective of the strange circumstances that had arisen, the young man, of whom he had grown very fond over recent months, had taken his own life. Probably fondness and exasperation in equal measure. The same combination he had noticed in the many parents he had supported when their own sons had become lost and wayward. Could he have done more? Were there signs he missed? He had genuinely tried to hold the hope for someone who, for a while at least, was incapable of holding it for himself. He could hear Adolfo calling into question his motivation, and in his forensic way, teasing out sinews of self-interest and ego. But no, he was confident that his engagement had been genuine, spontaneous and untainted by any complex motive. He just missed him.

On their second or third meeting, and after the ritual blurting out of the graphic facts of his father's death, Riccardo had provided more background. His father attended San Gaetano's parish in the old quarter of Brancaccio and gradually came under the spell of Father Guiseppe Puglisi, the anti-mafia campaigner. He could recite from memory the parodic Lord's Prayer which Puglisi recited from the pulpit to lampoon his enemies.

'O Godfather to me and my family, You are a man of honour and worth. Your name must be respected. Everyone must obey You. Everyone must do Your will for this is the law for those who do not wish to die. You give us bread, work; who wrongs You, pays. Do not pardon; it is an infamy. Those who speak are spies. I put my trust in You, Godfather. Free me from the police and the law.'

Riccardo would smile as he remembered how his father made him learn the prayer, and how he was once punished for reciting this version during a school service. He smiled too when he described his father returning from Mass during which Guiseppe had forbidden the children present from dropping out of school, thieving, drug dealing or selling contraband cigarettes. But his face would cloud over when he recalled the circumstances of the priest's death: shot outside his church with a single bullet fired at point-blank range by Filippo and Giuseppe Graviano. Riccardo's father, despite his mother's wishes, had decided to make a stand and had put a sign in the window of his hardware shop, making clear that never again would he pay the pizzo. He urged his fellow shopkeepers to do likewise. He was murdered three days later.

Adolfo had agreed to concelebrate the High Mass for

the dead despite his initial reservations. 'We are entitled to some of that money,' he reminded Dante who ignored him. A small choir had been retained and the sacristan had agreed to welcome any mourners who might attend. Both priests had officiated at Masses in the past where it had seemed that the only member of the congregation was the body, and it seemed likely that this would be the same.

Francesca hobbled into the front row where she planted herself, and shot a vituperative look at Dante. Three street workers from the St Vincent de Paul Society put in an appearance, and a sophisticated couple, he in double-breasted suit, and she hidden by a veil, sat halfway down the church at the end of an aisle. Ready to start the ceremony from the front steps of the sacristy, Dante was wondering who they might be when he was distracted by a commotion at the church door. The sacristan had raised his voice and seemed to be denying entrance to a small crowd of potential mourners. Adolfo gestured at the sacristan who relented and let pass into the church at least ten dishevelled men and several dogs. They hovered in embarrassment at the back near the baptismal font and then filed into a row. Two of the dogs, delighted at being out of the sun, and feeling a rare disincentive not to fall asleep, roamed the aisle. One of them cocked its leg against the marble font and relieved itself. Francesca had stood up and was about to remonstrate when Adolfo motioned for her to sit down and behave.

'In nomine Patris...' The service was under way. Adolfo moved to the coffin and released clouds of incense with each clank of the censer against its chain. The choir stood and sang *Ave Maria*. One of the men at the back also stood and joined in with a gusto rarely heard in that place. He had a beautiful voice which unfortunately had the effect of inspiring the dogs to emulate his effort. 'All we want now is an appearance from effing Francis of Assisi,' whispered

Adolfo. The man sat down when his peers started laughing loudly at him.

As Dante raised the host above the small and increasingly inattentive congregation and muttered the words 'Body of Christ,' he braced himself, knowing full well what was about to happen. And so it came to pass. His head was instantly filled by voices of doubt as if assailed by devils. A babel of half heard mocking laughter filled all of the space in his head. It had been several years since he had been able to savour the innocent, intense, serene moment that came with the symbolic raising of the host. He had first felt these transcendent spiritual epiphanies in the seminary. He had interpreted them as divine confirmation that he had chosen the right vocation despite the counter indications of his flesh and heart. By the same logic he was now being told, without ambiguity, that he had embraced a life of self-delusion and spiritual fraud. So intense had these black moments become, that of late he was avoiding opportunities to celebrate the Mass at all. Adolfo had noticed but said nothing. This was, however, something he had to do for Riccardo. He would see it through. Still shaking, he invited any communicants to approach the altar rail. One of the men from the back, accompanied by his dog, came forward. Dante blessed the dog and placed the wafer in the man's hands. He had the unwanted thought that perhaps the man had not eaten for days, and perhaps he should give him several. Francesca was next in line and embarked again on the religious hand-propelling that so irritated Adolfo.   After a pause, the veiled woman walked slowly down the aisle and stood opposite Dante. Instead of offering her cupped hands to receive the host, she pulled back her veil and put out her tongue to receive the body of Christ. Dante nearly dropped the chalice as he realised it was the woman from the confessional. She had her eyes closed but opened them just as Dante approached with the wafer in his shaking hand. He managed to place the bread on her tongue but not without his index finger making the slightest contact with her mouth. She lowered her veil and turned back. He was dumbfounded and stood without moving until Adolfo gave him a small nudge. He felt himself hyperventilating as he returned to the altar and prepared to give the final blessing before the hired pall-bearers prepared to remove the coffin with all due ceremony. Dante was a man whose compass had been wrenched from its moorings and tossed into the sea. All he had to do was hold things together for sufficiently long for him to make it back to the sacristy and deal with whatever turmoil waited for him. Instead he again approached the altar rail. Even the men at the back looked up with a degree of expectancy. 'Riccardo was murdered. This was not a suicide; this was delayed murder. This sweet, innocent man was as good as dead from the moment when he witnessed his own strong, principled father killed by those people whose name we are not allowed to mention, Sicily's sickness, the men we pretend no longer exist in our society, the families who are always served first at restaurants, the strangers we dare not cross just in case they are relatives. Forget the show trials, the grovelling informers, confessions and prison sentences, this cancer, this human putrefaction, this excrement is still in our midst, its stench fills this city, this church, and has stifled the breath of this good, good man.'

Two of the men at the back started to shout and applaud until they were restrained by their more sober companions. The man in the double-breasted suit left angrily, pulling the woman after him but not before she made the briefest of eye contact with Dante. Adolfo stepped forward and attempted to usher his fellow priest away from the steps. At first he resisted then gave up the struggle and let himself be led back into the sacristy.

'Jesus, what came over you?' asked Adolfo, pouring

them both a substantial drink. Dante sat with his head in his hands. Francesca appeared at the door but was shooed away by Adolfo.

'We're well and truly fucked now,' he said. 'The moment those coffin carriers are out of the church they'll be on the phone to the bishop and goodness knows who else.'

'I don't actually care anymore.'

'You're not the only one in this parish. There are two of us.'

'I need fresh air,' said Dante, pulling the vestments over his head then buttoning up his cassock.

'Watch out for the men whose names we dare not mention.'

Dante stepped out into the midday heat. The conveyor belt of tourists was running more slowly as the visitors sought out open-air restaurants in the shade. Normally oblivious to the traffic noise, it was now driving away what rational thought remained in Dante's head. Multitone horns competed to produce discord. Two drivers, each enraged at some perceived impropriety committed by the other, fought a duel by horn. Long insistent bursts, palms flat on the steering wheel, were met with cheeky staccato retaliatory bursts. Sensing the rising tension, every other car in the vicinity joined in, arbitrarily taking sides and adding their own decibels to the growing feud. As he used to when his parents fought and shouted at each other, Dante put his hands over his ears and ran. Two small boys who moments earlier had been feeding scraps to a cat in a doorway in exchange for it standing on hind legs, abandoned the game and followed Dante down the street, imitating his run with their own hands also clamped to the sides of their heads. They eventually lost interest and went back to find the performing cat.

Dante slowed down as he edged past the hot horses waiting patiently by the tourist carriages that clogged the Quattro Canti. Steam rose from their flanks. The foremost animal turned a black baleful eye towards Dante that instantly made him think of Riccardo.

He left the main thoroughfare and entered the cool labyrinth of alleys. He knew this patch intimately, having visited the sick and consoled the bereaved in many of the single-roomed dwellings that opened directly onto the cobbles. Overhead, the lines of washing hung in the heat like faded trophies from an ancient battle. Vests past their best, pants the size of coal scuttles, football socks in the cheery pink of Palermo. Calmer now, Dante shook his head as he wondered how Adolfo had managed to get himself appointed club chaplain for the previous season. Leading prayers in the home changing room, and once, according to him, acquiescing to the chairman's request to curse the opponents' dug-out, 'Any time you want tickets...' He was consciously encouraging his mind to make these harmless connections. But these were failed attempts to distract himself. All he really wanted to think about, was not his eccentric fellow priest, not the football, but the sensuous mouth of the woman at the altar rail. He had touched her tongue, he was sure of it. He rubbed the side of his finger then raised it to his nose as if some small residue of her smell lurked there.He emerged at the start of the fish market and again used the change of scene to rid himself of the ridiculous lust that was seeping into his soul. The upper torsos of several swordfish squatted on a marble slab like grotesque toddlers, trays of pink sardines nearly slithered their contents onto his feet. Perhaps he was indeed a true fisher of men, harpooning the vulnerable with barbs through their lips, butchering the natural instincts of his parishioners. The flat fish lay piled on each other. He had heard that frustrated fishermen would rub themselves against the sexual organs that, apparently, could resemble female human genitals in certain lights. Appalled at this latest line of thought, he forced his way past the stalls and back into Via Alloro. He clenched his fists in his determination to resume control of his head and wrest it back from the demon that had wormed its way into his ear and was now happily regenerating itself in his brain. He crossed towards the gates of Giardino Garibaldi and consciously breathed in the air untainted by fish or lust.

An old woman in black slumbered on one of the benches with her mouth open. A small boy weaved his bike through the dusty path as if following an obstacle course visible only to him. Somewhere a bell sounded. The main feature of the park were the fig trees, astonishing almost prehistoric growths. Each tree had several intertwined trunks hanging with fronds and creepers that could have been appropriated from the bottom of a deep ocean. The outer branches had leant over until they touched the earth where they took root forming a phalanx of wooden statues guarding the many small passageways into the heart of the tree.

As boys Dante and his friends had often played in this park, hiding for hours from each other, and indeed the whole world, in the recesses and crevices of the miraculous trees.

After checking that no one was there to witness his regression, the old woman certainly seemed asleep, Dante approached the tree, resting his hand on one of the outer sentries, and consciously relived those innocent days that stretched for ever. Tales of the occupation were still current when Dante was a child. Parents would tell cautionary tales about hiding in the fig trees, as well as in the catacombs where they had to eat their rations under the scowls of long dead monks. Dante's father claimed he found several teeth in his panini. Dante asked if he still had them and his father mimed removing them from the back of his mouth.

In that moment, an arm emerged from the dark centre of the tree and dragged the astonished priest into its midst.

Fearing that he was about to be mugged, he grabbed the arm and twisted it until its owner gasped. It was not the gasp of a drug addict desperate for money, or the gasp of an opportunist thief; it was the gasp of a woman. Disconcerted, he relaxed his grip and in that moment the anonymous hand sought out his face and touched his mouth. Then a warm mouth covered his own, and he felt the tongue that he had touched so tentatively and electrifyingly at the altar rail. He started to protest but soon realised that coherent speech was not a possibility when his own tongue was wrapped around another's. In that split second he chose voluptuousness over salvation, surrender over protest; more than prepared to embrace an eternity of damnation for this one startling moment. His choice was soon rewarded as the woman lifted his cassock, pulled down his large underpants which he had recently purchased using his clerical discount card, and guided him into her. He came instantly and shouted for all he was worth. It was a cry of triumph, a war cry, a cry for help. She covered his mouth. 'Shh, Father, you'll wake the Vatican.'

She led him by the hand, from the tree and towards the seat which the old woman had recently vacated. They sat side by side. He looked at her and she smiled. 'Well, Father, how was that? Did the earth move? Do you think St Paul had as much fun on the road to Damascus? I watched you enter the gardens. I've followed you here before and couldn't believe my good fortune when you went to hide.'

'I've just had sex with a complete stranger in a tree,' said Dante, his knees shaking. 'I think I've just sold my soul to the Devil.'

'Thank you very much,' said the stranger. 'I think I've just helped the Devil out. He'd been trapped in you for years and needed a bit of a hand. And I'm less of a stranger than you think.' She pulled back the veil from her face. Late forties, early fifties, thought Dante, high cheekbones, wild

239

eyes. Yes, she was familiar. He had indeed met her twice before.

'Eleonora,' she said. 'From Monreale. My husband summoned you to the villa during the troubles. He paid for Riccardo's funeral by the way, an act of public contrition, he said.'

Dante rubbed the side of his head as if the memory needed some help to form. 'I remember now. He wanted to meet with a cross-section of the clergy, he said. Wanted to find out what made them tick, probe their weaknesses and discover how best to buy their silence. His bodyguards were thorough, I remember. That was probably the last time before today that anyone put their hands under my cassock. I thought then how the newspapers would report that a Capo had been garrotted by a heavy set of rosary beads before being disembowelled with a crucifix, and how the Carabinieri were scouring the hills for a band of rogue priests living rough.'

Eleonora smiled. 'Yes. I served the drinks then retired to the study where I listened to all that was said. Our paths crossed years later on the ship. You were there with your fat hobnobbing clerical friend. I was so pleased that you had survived. I assumed though you had sold out, made compromises with your God, made him see that pragmatic Christianity was the only way forward, explaining how bribes would ultimately benefit the parish.'

'No,' said Dante who had finally stopped his knees from shaking by pushing both palms down onto his thighs. 'I wasn't a hero, I just didn't care what he did to me. I was in the bleakest pit anyway, he couldn't have made it any worse. God was dead to me. Perhaps I wanted him to kill me, it would have concentrated the minds of the others... I can't believe you dragged me into that tree...'

'Get over it,' said Eleonora. 'Sometimes good things happen. You just stared at him, faced him down. He hesitated, forgot his words. He must have felt you could see into his soul.'

'I didn't care a spit about his soul. I just thought he was a cowardly runt of a man foolish enough to think that a suicidal priest would baulk at hearing threats of death.'

'You are a good judge of character, Father.'

'Call me Dante. Arguably we know each other, at least in the biblical sense.'

'No. You have been Father to me since I first set eyes on you, and Father you will remain. My husband was subdued that night, troubled, as if he had met his match. He shouted out in his sleep something about hell. He sat bolt upright in bed, got embarrassed, said it was the anchovies.'

Dante snorted. 'I too have been troubled by anchovies in the past. Your husband came to visit me on several occasions. Once at midnight he appeared at the vestry, said it was urgent. I was on my way to bed and didn't recognise him at first. He had two henchmen with him in standard issue long overcoats. I was petrified, to be honest. I had started to give God the benefit of the doubt again and was no longer immune to the prospect of death. The three of them embarked on a choreographed litany of ways to die. Like satanic plain chant. Completely emotionless, they each described a preferred method. Your husband started with an account of progressive mutilation supported by scientific research which demonstrated how much of a body could be removed before consciousness was lost. The freak on his left almost became animated when describing the subtle application of a blow torch to the genitals... Actually not too dissimilar to my recent experience in a tree now that I think about it...' Eleonora jabbed him in the ribs. 'Then the beast on his right extolled the virtues of dripping acid onto a naked body tied spread-eagled to a bed.'

'Not certain about the acid but I could cope with the spread-eagled bit,' said Eleonora.

'And then it became quite bizarre. Francesca, the house-keeper, had left a plate of macaroons for my supper. But she had recently been indisposed with a bout of sickness and diarrhoea, and not being known for her fastidious commitment to personal hygiene, I left the plate untouched. Your husband however had been casually stuffing them into his mouth. After delivering the shopping list of ways to die, he stared at me. I stared back, not out of steely courage, but because I was catatonic with fear. He then clutched his stomach and rushed out of the room. I heard him being sick in the vestibule.'

Eleonora stroked his wrist where the flesh was visible just below his cuff.

'They left but returned a week or so later. I had fallen asleep on the settee, not having managed to sleep properly since the first visit. Somehow they got inside the house. Sensing something seriously wrong, I dragged myself awake and opened my eyes. This time I could make out at least five figures standing either side of the doorway. No one moved. Complete stillness until the figure on the left moved to switch on the light. In that instant the room filled with sparks which arched from the wall into your husband's chest. The switch had been faulty for some time. Francesca had in fact stuck up a note warning of the dangers from the exposed wire. The man lit up like the Virgin Mary at a festa. He was eventually helped out of the room by the heavies, leaving behind a smell of burning.'

Eleonora laughed out loud. Dante looked at her. She was undeniably a good-looking woman. She stood up, kissed Dante on the top of the head, and still laughing, walked towards the park entrance. Dante held up both hands in her general direction in a gesture half pleading, half incomprehension. Eleonora turned, blew a kiss at him and walked through the gate. His half-flailing hand became still and hung in the air.

He felt something very like panic as the enormity of what had happened registered with him. This was a surreal but undeniable seismic occurrence, the consequences of which he could not yet foresee. Why had he surrendered his, admittedly tarnished, vow of celibacy for a moment of total, indefensible madness? Had it in fact happened? Furthermore, how on earth had he managed to conduct a conversation with the woman as if he had been on intimate terms with her all his life?

'A good day, Father?' asked Adolfo, pouring himself a second grappa.

'Unusual,' said Dante. 'I had sex in a tree with a stranger.'

'Fine,' said Adolfo. Perhaps there was hope for his housemate after all.

CHAPTER THREE

Dante understood obsession. He had been wedded to the concept all his days. At the age of ten he was scouring the hills and quarries round Perugia for fossils. The calcified shadows of reptiles, fish, bivalves, ammonites, echinoderms and crustaceans were all labelled and crammed into a shoebox under his bed. He dreamed of finding the palae-ontologist's holy grail: fossilised ambergris, also known as 'floating gold'. It was, according to the one specialised book available for his inspection at the public library, 'a solid, waxy, grey or blackish flammable substance usually associated with sperm whales'. He failed to interest either of his parents in this or any of his subsequent obsessions.

At the age of fourteen he became obsessed with Alfredo Bovet, winner of the Tour de France and the mountain trial. He took to wearing a bandana like his hero. He even affected deafness having read that a collision with an articulated lorry on a Savoie road had left Bovet's hearing damaged. His mother threatened to smack his good ear unless he stopped his nonsense.

He once sold a family bible handed down through generations on Alfredo's father's side to an antiquarian book dealer to realise sufficient cash to buy Bovet's autograph. Years later, he realised that the value of the 15th century bible would in fact have paid for the long dead cyclist to be disinterred and brought back to life. It was nearly a year before his father, hoping to find evidence of an aristocratic heritage hidden in its monogrammed pages, failed to locate the tome and eventually interrogated his son. By a fortuitous twist of fate, Dante's latest obsession was with God, an interest that rendered inappropriate any sustained accusations of theft. Instead his father devised a far from convincing scenario, part of which required the scapegoating of an itinerant band of Romanians who, years back, had acquired a wholly undeserved reputation for causing young brides to miscarry, and housebreaking.

The obsession with God had, with several significant lapses, including the current one, lasted all his days. At the age of sixteen, for the first time in his life, his mother noticed him. Prior to his calling he didn't actually exist. He was seen as no more than an extension of the mantle of duty that bound her to the home and an unwanted degree of penury. After he saw the light he was even consulted over his choice of meals. He was listened to as if he were a prodigy for whom canonisation was only a century or so away. Dante was sufficiently selfish to wallow in his new-found status. Perhaps this is what happened to good and holy people. The neighbours were unwilling witnesses to his emerging spirituality.

On entering seminary this obsession was stood on its head. He came to appreciate the profound self-deception and indeed fraudulence that had propelled him into the arms of the church. In short he became obsessed with his own sense of unworthiness. Only when he was certain that the chapel was empty would he enter and prostrate himself before the altar, begging forgiveness for his innate wickedness.

He embarked on various mortifications of the flesh including a spell of fasting that gave rise to real concerns about his health. He developed a related obsession, which still

245

lingered albeit in a perverse form, with all known Christian saints and martyrs. He measured himself against them and was appalled at his shortcomings. He had his favourites: he was intrigued by the legend that St Christopher was granted the face of a dog to ward off unwanted female attention. In later life he frequently encountered lonely parishioners who it seemed had been similarly favoured by God, and sometimes, when almost broken by his vow of celibacy, he found himself looking in the mirror for signs that he might be turning into a totally unlovable Pekinese. He also developed a soft spot for Saint Agata, banished to a brothel by a powerful but spurned potential lover. Thirty days of prayer kept her free of unwanted attention. At the end of this period, her frustrated suitor had her chained, whipped and stretched on the rack. Even at his most pious, Dante doubted if this had been the best solution to the situation.

Politics were to become the most formative influence on his priesthood. His finest obsession was with liberation theology. Finally, he had a cause that would stand up to any scrutiny, even in the dark moments when his belief in God wavered to the point of extinction. Only by embracing the poor could Catholicism look God in the face.

He incurred the wrath of his bishop when he organised a petition calling for the reinstatement of Leonardo Boff and Gustavo Gutierrez when they were silenced by Cardinal Joseph Ratzinger. In some respects his friendship with Riccardo was a legacy of that period of his life.

He had largely sold out since then, he knew that. As a young priest, not content with organising soup kitchens throughout Palermo, he had barricaded himself into a building, home to scores of the impoverished, which was threatened with demolition. It was this act, more than any other, which had first brought him to the attention of the mafia who had their own designs on the prime piece of real estate. He had accepted a sizeable donation from unknown

246

sources in exchange for his adopting a lower profile. Even then he was sufficiently canny to understand that he was fighting a lost cause. By accepting the money he could at least put the soup kitchens on a permanently firm financial footing.

But Dante had never known obsession until now. When clearing the steam from his shaving mirror with the back of his hand, it was her face that appeared in the glass. When reading the football pages in the Corriere dello Sport, a winning goal had been scored in extra time by a player called, improbably, Eleonora. When reading the latest revelations about Berlusconi he found himself wondering wherein lay the attraction of younger women. When visiting parishioners he looked at every dark alleyway lest she was lurking there in the shadows, waiting to drag him into her again.

Every hour or so he would revolt against the unwanted obsession and fight back with an onslaught of logic. He was a priest, and was under attack. For the first time since his ordination he understood Christ's temptations in the desert: Satan was offering not power, but sensual pleasure. He was being assailed by something similar. The very moment this thought had been formed, he despised himself for the arrogant effrontery, indeed heresy, of comparing himself with Christ. In this way lust became compounded by intense self-loathing. There seemed no way out. In his bleaker moments he even contemplated praying. Yet what form of words would adequately convey his remorse for the moment in the tree. But he felt no remorse. It had been one of the most extraordinary, glorious and life-affirming moments he had ever known. Without being able to acknowledge the wickedness of his sin, he could not reasonably ask his creator for relief from its consequences.

In the few waking moments when he was not thinking of Eleonora, he felt enveloped by a brooding sense of dissatisfaction. The cloud was dark and hung over all of the daily activities that he cultivated as sources of distraction. But the moment he became aware of the cloud and probed its soft underbelly, the old thoughts tumbled out and threatened to drown him.

A week after the tree episode, he was conducting a wedding in the church. He had known Paolo since he was a boy. A decade earlier his mother had brought the gawky teenager to the vestry and had declared that he had a vocation. Dante's heart had sunk. The boy was nervous and his leg shook constantly. Dante was aware of the unique opportunity he had to deliver, albeit retrospectively, advice to his earlier self. He listened as the mother extolled the boy's kindness to siblings, neighbours and stray animals alike. She even implied that he had the gift of prophecy. Paolo had allegedly forecast his grandfather's death. Dante tried to repress the thought that the man had been ninety-three and in poor health. He wanted to tell the deluded woman that the church needed priests, not soothsayers. Had he uttered the thought out loud? The woman's expression reassured him that his riposte had been for his internal consumption only.

He steepled the tips of his fingers and tried to look grave. 'The church is favouring older recruits,' he lied. 'In his latest pronouncement Benoit strongly recommended that no one should be considered for Holy Orders before the age of...' he looked at Paolo, 'forty-four.' The mother looked astonished and disappointed in equal measure. 'I mean twenty-four,' he corrected himself with a cough. Disappointment gave way to a stoical acceptance. Dante placed his hand on Paolo's head. 'Live well, my boy, God wants his soldiers to enjoy life's pleasures before they renounce them for ever.' Paolo's mother was looking dubious again. 'Only by savouring earthly joy can one make real sacrifices to God. I know the wait will be hard,' he offered by way of consolation, which was accepted by Paolo more readily than by his mother.

248

In the intervening decade Paolo had grown into an extraordinarily handsome young man much sought after by all of the young women in the congregation.

Six months later, after a solemn ceremony to celebrate the blessing of a relic purchased by the women's guild at great cost, Dante interrupted Paolo and a girl he didn't recognise, savouring earthly joy in a small room at the back of the church used for storing chairs. 'I really meant forty-four,' said Dante, closing the door behind him.

The girl, Felicita, became pregnant and the pair now stood before him at the altar. Dante looked at the front row where he intercepted a poisonous stare from the mother of the groom. 'In nomine Patris, et Filio, et Spiritus Sancti. We are gathered here today...' He paused. Eleonora's face had unhelpfully transposed itself onto Felicita's. She looked younger but still stunning. 'To celebrate the marriage of...' He was back in the tree again, he was touching Eleonora's mouth at the altar. Despite feeling quite unhinged, and physically unwell, Dante stumbled to the end of the ceremony. After the blessing he apologised to the couple and said that, regrettably, he would have to forego the festivities as he was sick and had to retire.

Back in the vestry he slumped onto the settee that had been left largely unused since Riccardo's death.

'A drink, Father?' said Adolfo who had been dozing on the seat nearest to the window. Despite the early hour, Dante said yes.

'What ails thee?' asked Adolfo, pouring a sizeable Martini. Dante sighed. 'Don't tell me, the old monastic accidie has you in its grip again. You are experiencing a frisson of existential angst, you are suffering from an ague brought on by excessive retrospection...'

Dante accepted the drink but waved his friend away. While appreciating that, beneath the irony, Adolfo was genuinely concerned, he couldn't confide in him, not now, not ever.

249

'Perhaps you should go back to the magic tree,' suggested Adolfo, without any appreciation of the pain caused by his well-intentioned humorous remark.

Yet this is exactly what Dante did. He excused himself, saying he felt better, and lurched into the sunlight. He knew that this course of action was utterly absurd. He felt panic, guilt and self-loathing in equal measure. He fully appreciated the sheer foolishness of what he was doing, but he was quite powerless. Several parishioners greeted him in Via Divisi but he failed to see them. As he was talking to himself they wrongly assumed that he was praying. Had they been closer they would have heard that the incantation had a more mundane focus, 'Please be there. Please be there.'

Of course, she wasn't there. The park was empty. Because of the hour the sun was directly overhead and there was no shade. He pushed into the centre of the tree, displacing a small cairn of Peroni bottles. A heart and several initials and a date had been etched into the wood. He put his arms round one of the central boughs as if it was the woman he sought, and rubbed his cheek against the cold bark.

He drifted through the next ten days resigned to sharing them with the dull ache that destroyed his appetite, made him restless and stole his sleep. Adolfo became genuinely solicitous and even put his acerbic wit to one side. Francesca eventually informed Dante that she would offer up prayers to St Jude as he was clearly troubled by a great burden. Dante thanked her and from nowhere resurrected the obscure fact that St Jude is the patron saint of the Chicago police department. Perhaps his crisis was passing.

Gradually, he was able to resume his parochial duties and concentrate on the worries of others and not exclusively on his own. He dropped into the geriatric dancehall in Via Carini and only felt a small pang of jealousy as the couples executed their arthritic tangos.

As he walked down the aisle to hear Friday night

confessions, he did check that there was no sign of Eleonora. He was safe. He wasn't certain that he wanted to be safe but was able not to dwell on the implications of that thought. He saw Signora Belcastro waiting patiently for him. She was the only one there. If he was honest he had actually missed her. He was a priest when all was said and done. His whole raison d'être was to succour the needy. The word did spark an unwanted pang which he just managed to ignore. He smiled at the Signora, stepped into the dark confessional, closed the curtain to the outside world and opened the small grille which always reminded him of the sliding door through which the police checked on, or taunted, their prisoners, depending on which film you were watching.

'Bless me, Father, for I have sinned...'

'I doubt that, Signora Belcrasto,' he intoned wearily.

'Indeed I have, Father. I murdered my husband...' Dante knew that the full tale, which was admittedly liable to occasional embellishment, normally lasted exactly twelve minutes...

'He was right to criticise as I was a bad wife...'

The curtain separating the confessional from the aisle was slowly pulled back. Dante looked up as Eleonora, her finger on her lips, slid into the box and sat on his lap. Horrified, he tried to dislodge her but she resisted and stayed where she was.

'Are you all right, Father?' asked Signora Belcastro.

'I dropped my missal,' said Dante, caught between incredulity, mounting lust and anger at this violation of the confessional, but unable to do anything about it. Eleonora giggled.

'Sorry, Father?'

'Continue, Sister.' Eleonora's face was inches from his own. The same perfume. Her breath sweet with peppermint. He could feel the full weight of her.

'I deserved to be beaten on account of my many misde-meanours…'

Eleonora fastened her mouth onto Dante's and dragged him into a kiss that lasted for most of Signora Belcastro's narrative.

'…and when I passed the bedroom I heard him chok-ing…'

Dante knew the feeling as he struggled for breath.

'Are you sure you're all right, Father?'

'Yes, yes, I've got a bad cold. Say three Hail Marys. Go forth, my sister, and sin no more.'

'Can't stop me,' whispered Eleonora right into Dante's ear. 'I'll be in touch.' With that she extricated herself from him, pulled back the curtain and left before Signora Belcastro could gather her handbag and prayer book.

Dante stepped out and looked at the departing figure of his loyal penitent. There was no sign of Eleonora.

'Jesus Christ!' he said. Something shifted in Dante's head after this latest encounter. He stopped pretending. He wanted Eleonora and unashamedly looked forward to their next encounter. His sexual fantasies about her were completely untinged by guilt. He even went about his priestly duties with renewed enthusiasm.

'Glad you're feeling better,' said Francesca, patting him on the shoulder as if he were a small boy recovering from a bad cold.

Signora Roatta had been on his conscience for some time. Now in her eighties and housebound, she was partially cared for by Piero, her learning-disabled child. In her prime she had been Dante's champion and had, on one occasion, led a delegation to intervene with the bishop who, embar-rassed by the priest's political activism, was arranging for him to be transferred to a parish in Milan. Furious at the bishop's intractability, she had chained Piero to a railing outside the episcopal palace with a large placard round his neck denouncing the occupier's wickedness. Piero had risen to the challenge and took to baying like a dog whenever anyone approached. Eventually the Carabinieri arrived.

Their sympathies however lay entirely with Piero on account of the Bishop's endless complaints, and increasing reluctance to pay backhanders. A photographer was duly summoned and Piero obliged by conjuring a bewildering array of facial expressions, baleful, vulnerable, and oppressed. Fearing a scandal, a compromise was reached and Dante was allowed to stay at Santa Caterina and promulgate his gospel of equality and sedition.

He really did owe her. The day was oppressive as he walked deeper into the labyrinth of back streets that spread out from the cathedral. The sudden switch from the blistering sunlight to the near darkness of the alleys left him blinded until his eyes adjusted. As he walked, he looked into the dark interiors of the tiny one-roomed homes. An old woman slept, head thrown back and mouth open. A child sat at the table tracing a pattern with a finger in the water he had spilt. TVs flickered and game show hosts elicited peals of canned laughter. Occasional cooking smells, garlic and oregano reminded him that he had forgotten breakfast.

Dante heard the sound of its engine before he saw the quad bike, headlight blazing, pummelling towards him. He looked round for a doorway in which he could flatten himself. Realising that the walls on both sides of the alley offered no shelter, he turned and fled. He reached the corner moments before the bike roared past him. It was being driven by a small boy, no more than nine years old. Clutching at his chest, Dante tried to compose himself. No sooner had he done so, than he heard the bike returning. Once again he caught sight of a tiny figure, its head almost resting on the handlebars, its infant hands revving the grips on either end. He was again a target, and again there was

253

nowhere to hide. He launched himself at a metal pipe that stretched across the alley and hauled himself upwards and onto it as the bike roared beneath him. He clung to the pipe, spread along its length, a pig on a spit waiting to be barbequed, a clerical kebab. A window opened and a woman looked out. 'If you steal my washing I'll rip your balls off!' Seeing his dog collar, she crossed herself, shook her head, briefly flapped her hand at the rising cloud of diesel, and retreated back into her room.

Still shaking, he eventually made his way to Signora Roatta's house. She welcomed him in, chastising him for neglecting an attractive old woman for so long, while Piero just beamed at the visitor.

'Matilda, I think a young boy just tried to kill me.'

'Still making enemies, Father, nothing changes.' As his mother fussed over a plate of biscuits, Piero removed the cushions and nestled up alongside Dante on the sofa.

'You missed yourself today,' said Adolfo, finishing his appetitive, then staring reproachfully at the empty glass. 'Some woman dropped by, said she was looking for you, in need of counselling evidently. Good looking, early fifties, a wicked glint in her eyes. She just invited herself in, asked where you normally sat, then walked out again. I think you've made a hit, Father, the old magic's still there.' Francesca, who had been polishing a brass candlestick as if the Devil himself had breathed on it, tutted audibly.

Dante, still traumatised after his quad bike ordeal, wanted to ask more but knew that it was best to keep quiet. His earlier mood of euphoric acceptance and partial anticipation of further remarkable encounters with Eleonora, had proved to be transitory.

'Hussy,' offered Francesca, reaching for the candlestick's identical twin. As Dante stood up to leave, Adolfo waved something in his general direction. 'Oh, she said to give you this.' He held the envelope between thumb and forefinger at arm's length as if it were a cigar.

Despite himself, Dante snatched it from him and hurried up the stairs to his bedroom. He sat down at his desk, oddly reluctant to open the letter. Fearful of its content, he tapped it against his lips and pretended to glance idly out of the window. The small boy he had noticed the other day was standing on the pavement opposite with a new red balloon. Unable to maintain a pretence of indifference any longer, he tore at the envelope and succeeded in ripping it diagonally.

Father, Father, I know you've been missing me. I saw you go back to the tree. I saw the look on your face when you realised I wasn't there. But I had been followed to the park and had to give my pursuer the slip. I'm afraid our liaison is no longer just our secret. Still I managed to see you which was good. You looked so lost, so forlorn, I wanted to take you in my arms again, hold you tight and make everything better. But I can't and things will only get worse. You see I have run away from Mario. And as you know, no one gets to leave the organisation, not of their own volition. Husbands may kill their wives, consign them in concrete to the bottom of the ocean but no wife willingly leaves her husband. If she does, she will be found and dealt with. Even if that husband developed a taste for sexually humiliating his wife, degrading her. Have you heard of such things in the confessional, Father? Are these the sins that the good parishioners of Santa Caterina bring to that small wooden box which, if you think of it – and I know you do – has generated its own small sins? If that wife had made her husband a cuckold then at least two deaths will follow. And the other one will be yours. Sorry to bring bad news. No, I'm not really sorry. There will be excitement, I promise you that. And I know you crave excitement, Father. So, I am on the run. He will catch me but for now I am the mouse that foolishly teases the cat. I will not give him the satisfaction of leaving Sicily. This is my island. I will stay in his own backyard which will make him mad. And yes, you are

now his victim too. I have put your life at risk. I should apologise,
prostrate myself at your feet, but I can't. I will however attempt to
make amends in other ways. I will look after my tortured priest, my
fellow rebel. Do not look for me. I will find you. Now destroy this
note, and think of me, Father, yearn for me, lust for me.
Your loyal parishioner,
Eleonora.

Dante crumpled up the note, wondering how best to destroy it. By tearing it into tiny pieces that the most assiduous criminal with time on his hands could reassemble? By burning it? But he had seen forensic programmes where scientists recreated whole manuscripts from ashes. By flushing it away thereby blocking the system, leading inexorably to the discovery of his secrets by a Sicilian plumber with mafia connections? He kept the note tight in his closed fist.

He lay back on his bed, stared at the multiplying cracks on the celling, and shook. The monstrous enormity of events struck him starkly. He felt overwhelmed. He wanted to regress to childhood and be with his mother again. He felt more guilt than he had ever experienced in his life. He felt self-loathing. He felt that in a moment's folly, he had thrown away everything that he at least half believed in. He wanted to confess, though God only knew to whom. Simultaneously he wanted to lose himself in total all-consuming lust. He wanted to live for ever in that moment in the tree when he forsook everything and embraced passion, spontaneity and unthinking damnation. He was sixty-five. There was simply no excuse, and certainly no expiation, no redemption.

In the past he had frequently advised troubled parishioners for whom there seemed no way out, to immerse themselves in work and the sustaining balm of routine. By adhering to some sort of structure, order would return. And so he slapped water on his face, glanced ruefully at the toilet pan waiting to receive his torn-up note, and went downstairs with as much normality as he could muster.

'Anything interesting?' asked Adolfo unhelpfully. 'One of your rich dowagers has left a fortune to the parish? You are being sued by Opus Dei for your liberal views? A billet-doux perhaps, inviting you to a deliciously guilt-laden rendezvous?' This last option was delivered with an expression that left Dante disconcerted, and the bizarre thought that before handing the letter over, Adolfo and Francesca had conspiratorially steamed open the envelope.

'I would be so lucky,' he said. 'Can you remember which ward is harbouring the wasting body of Signor Pascali?'

Normality dictated that he take the 27 bus to Place de Filumenanne; habit dictated that he walk down the left-hand side of the park towards the hospital thereby avoiding the sex shop and its lurid wares on the junction with Via Viande.

Over the decades Dante had developed an impressive familiarity with both the layout and personnel at the Ospedale Civico. He had briefly served as chaplain representative on the administrative board but soon resented his tokenistic role and resigned.

He recognised one of the nurses smoking outside the building as a former parishioner. Languidly breathing smoke in his general direction was the extent of her greeting. He nodded at her, she snorted. Dante vaguely remembered that she had been involved in some scandal but couldn't recall the details.

Outside of ward three he made eye contact with Sister Teresa, a tiny ancient nun whose arms seemed to be permanently outstretched as though embracing an overgrown child. She approached and nodded as if in expectation of a gift. Dante blessed her and moved into the room.

Signor Pascali was clearly pleased to see Dante. 'If you even think of sprinkling me with fucking holy water, I will rise from my deathbed and strangle the life out of you, Father.' The effort required to deliver this threat left him struggling for breath.

Signor Pascali was one of the few reminders of Dante's radical past. Formerly a steel worker from Milan, he had incurred the wrath of the factory bosses and the organisation. With a gesture, half bravado, half death wish, he had relocated to Palermo where he had apparently benefited from internecine rivalries between the northern and southern factions, and had bought a degree of immunity by informing on his previous tormentors.

Now in his eighties and dying from tuberculosis, the roles in the hospital seemed to be reversed. It was the frail old man who exuded a degree of serenity while his agitated pastor was the one in need of solace and reassurance. They held hands over the bedspread. 'Are you in trouble again, Father?'

'You could say that. I've upset someone. All my own fault. Do you remember when you would rant about how Satan and the church were collaborators exercising total control by perpetuating guilt and self-loathing among an essentially innocent population? Well, I am now the living proof of that particular theory.'

Signor Pascali squeezed Dante's hand then moved it above the covers until it rested over his groin. 'Finally, Father,' he said. 'All is still, all is quiet, no movement now in the rebellious regions for some time. I have turned into a geriatric teddy bear. All lust spent.' The two men laughed together. Signor Pascali's mirth precipitated a coughing fit which left him exhausted. He closed his eyes. He was asleep. 'Just to spite you, you old, lovely bastard,' said Dante, making the sign of the cross on his friend's forehead.

Eleonora's note had worried him. Why would his life also be at risk? Perhaps the old woman in the park had not really been asleep after all. To believe there were spies watching in Parco Garibaldi in case the spouse of a mafia boss had carnal knowledge in a fig tree was a leap into serous paranoia. Eleonora could of course have been followed into the church. He shook his head at the memory of the confessional. He was then struck by the possibility that she may have dropped hints as to his identity as part of her absurd game of power and manipulation. If so, he was indeed a condemned man walking. The thought made him extremely angry. If their paths ever crossed again, he would confront her, berate her for her selfish stupidity. What if their paths were never to cross again? What if he were never to see her again? The emptiness he experienced was akin to panic.

'Any phone messages?' Francesca shook her head and continued dusting the leaves on the monstrous Begonia plant that seemed to be taking over the day room.

'No billets-doux either,' said Adolfo, stroking his chin to gauge the success or otherwise of the expensive shave he had just treated himself to.

Dante was aware of his hypersensitivity. He had, many years back, experienced something similar at the end of a lengthy meditation led by a Benoitine monk at the San Galgano monastery. On that occasion he had passed, at the end of an intense day, into the mediaeval garden and become almost unbearably aware of the scents and colours of the flowers. He was held in a sixties psychedelic fantasy from which he had no wish to extricate himself. His clarity of vision and powerful perception took his breath away. But this present awareness was different in kind. It contained the contradictory elements of persecuted vigilance and desperate longing.

When he left the canonica every face he passed was appraised for signs that its owner might be seeking him, either to kill him if male or to make love to him if female. Every backfiring car, of which there were many, had an ominous and pressing significance. He tried to make out individual passengers on passing buses but found that having to move his own face at the same speed as the moving vehicle, was making him giddy.

Increasingly irritated with himself, he took a seat at Montefurio's café in Via Otagia and ordered an espresso. He must calm down, he must get a grip as this behaviour was bordering on madness. That would make two of them. He concentrated on the faded yellow poster, torn in one corner, of Teatro Thenola. He had performed there as a student, a walk on part in a passion play. A soldier charged with carrying the vinegar and a sponge to force into Christ's mouth. The waitress was polite and deferential when she brought his drink. A good Catholic, thought Dante.

And then she was there. Eleonora sat down opposite him. 'Good morning, Father.' She stretched and yawned, pushing her chair away from the table and arching her back. 'Sorry, not much sleep last night. I had not fully appreciated how tiring it can be, on the run all the time.'

Dante was in shock. 'What are you doing here?' His voice was too loud; they would be detected for certain. 'Were you followed? Why are you here? Why are you in my life at all?'

'If I'm not wanted...' Eleonora made as if to leave, unhooking her coat from the chair.

'No, no, stay, please stay.' He put his head in his hands. 'Well,' said Eleonora making a pattern with her fingers in the sugar she had spilt on the Formica tabletop. 'I may have been followed. Who can tell? We will know soon enough if his goons come in through the door with their coats draped over their arms. "Priest and Mafioso moll gunned down in café..."'

'Stop it!'

'"As he lay dying in his mistress's arms, Father Dante Corsini, 65, desperately attempted to administer the last rites to himself..." Can that be done, Father, you know, self-administration of sacraments in extremis? But could you absolve yourself? Do you always need an intermediary to intercede on your behalf? "Although a rebellious cleric with a weakness for women all his days, he did, when all is said and done, lead a good if not holy life..." Maybe the Vatican will have to meet in secret conclave to debate the issue...'

'What do you want?'

'To see you, my favourite priest, my chosen plaything.' She touched his hand with hers in a gesture half theatrical irony and half affection.' Any close shaves, Father, since we last met? Any small brushes with death?' She made small circular movements with her forefinger on his wrist, and pouted.

Dante waited until the coffee machine on the counter had spat its final hysteria of steam. 'A maniacal small child tried to mow me down with his quad bike but I'm sure it was a coincidence.'

'I doubt it very much,' said Eleonora. 'It wasn't a coincidence. More likely a warning. There will be others.'

'I'll be honest with you, I think I'm going mad. I'm having a crisis. It happens to priests in late middle age.' If he was expecting sympathy it was a failed gambit.

'Join the club, Father. Live on the edge. How many more years have you got anyway? What is the life expectancy for chubby Sicilian priests, especially for those whose drinking has increased incrementally over recent years?'

Dante looked at her. How did she know that?

'Do you want to die celibate in some old priests' home fawned over by drooling nuns, competing to empty your colostomy bag? "It's my turn, Sister Magdalena!"

"No, Sister Mayhem, it's my turn!" And then it bursts! Holy Shit everywhere!'

He smiled despite himself, wondering how she could articulate his own thoughts about mortality with such clarity and wit.

'Mercifully, Father, you have met your own personal angel of wickedness whose mission is to fill your final days with pleasure.' She struck a pose with hands clasped together and raised her eyes heavenwards.

'No, enough is enough,' said Dante, bringing his fist down on the table with more force than he had intended. He picked up the cruet. 'Yes, I enjoy the attention, the flirtation, and yes, that moment in the park was like nothing I have ever known but...'

'Suit yourself, Father,' said Eleonora who was standing and putting on her coat. 'So, I won't see you later this evening walking by the boats in the harbour.'

He also stood up and gestured after her as she pushed open the door and disappeared out of his sight. He was quite unable to conjure any words that could even approximate to the thoughts in his head.

CHAPTER FOUR

He had never really fallen out with Francesca before. Although there had of course been the occasional skirmish, he had certainly never been abusive to her face. But he was now. 'Stop that fucking cleaning! Why do you dust plant leaves, why do you pick up non-existent crumbs? Why can you never be still?'

At that moment the clock chimed a stern rebuke while Adolfo put down his copy of *Racing Post* and stared at Dante over his glasses. Francesca threw down the feather duster, spat on the floor and left the room.

'I've never seen her spit before,' said Adolfo.

Dante pursued her up the stairs to apologise but she slammed her bedroom door in his face and proceeded to pack a small brown suitcase.

Sitting on his bed, Dante opened his copy of St Francis' meditations and tried to read. To say the words swam off the page would not do justice to the sense that the typeface was turning to water and bubbling off the margins of the small book. He had been given it by a good friend in the seminary after completing the first two years of his noviciate. It had become a talismanic icon which had in the past sustained him through difficult times. It was not the words inside, for the most part banal, Dante had always thought, rather its worth as an almost magical object which would fit easily in his pocket and which he could touch as and when needed. He put it aside.

The only truth he knew was that in a couple of hours he would be wandering past the docks and towards the marina where Sicily's rich and aspiring rich moored their pleasure craft. He couldn't even pretend to himself that he might in the interim summon the willpower to resist Eleonora's siren call. He knew that he was already physically incapable of taking any evasive action that might, just might, preserve his sanity, his increasingly eroded sense of self, and indeed his life.

And so it came to pass. Rather than anticipate what delights or terrors awaited him, Dante found himself neurotically counting the number of containers that were stacked on the deck of the merchant vessel waiting to berth. Twenty-eight or twenty-nine depending on whether the furthermost were twice the size. Red was the most popular colour. And what of the contents? Cars probably, agricultural equipment. Possibly illegal immigrants from North Africa, stacked in rows, probably suffocated by now.

In the recent past when a score of half-drowned Somalians, clinging to wreckage from their overcrowded boat, were summarily imprisoned, Dante had visited the detention centre. Despite wearing only blankets, the men exuded dignity and a resigned despair in equal measure, while the women were sunk into themselves, probably mourning their dead children, thought Dante.

He had attempted to intercede with the authorities but had not a hint of success. In past times the mafia might have welcomed cheap labour for their sweatshops but now the money lay in cocaine and heroin not textiles. Which thought brought him straight back to Eleonora.

He looked over his shoulder at what might or might not have been pursuers. In that moment he felt that he left his body and was staring down at himself on a film set. It was, of course, film noir. The colours drained out of the picture. The camera focused on a small hunched figure glancing nervously behind him in the direction of his perceived enemies in the shadows. Dante wanted to fast forward the film and see its denouement but the projectionist would not collaborate; in any case he couldn't locate the final reel.

He changed cinema and in his mind's eye entered the sleazy porno house near to Via Flaco that he had never had the courage to visit, but about which he had often wondered. And again, he was the star. An aging stud with a much firmer body than the one he studiously avoided in the mirror. He was on a small boat that rocked with the rhythm of his and another's body as they writhed and groaned in syncopated ecstasy. Eleonora, for it was she, had torn off his cassock that lay discarded in a heap, and proceeded to explore his body with her tongue. And then the film juddered and gave up the ghost altogether with a painful sigh. The other occupants of the theatre extricated themselves from the raincoats spread over their laps and protested vehemently. Dante shuddered despite the residual heat in the day and crossed the cobbles towards the more open road that led to the marina.

He had no idea where to find her but supposed that she would do the finding. He remembered the failed finding in Giardino Garibaldi and baulked at the prospect of a similar disappointment.

There must have been upwards of two hundred craft of various sizes in the marina, organised according to a strict hierarchy of wealth. The larger vessels remained more aloof, while the humbler ones nestled up against each other at the quayside as if seeking mutual consolation for their relative poverty. The lights in the overlooking apartments created an uneven pattern as the buildings assumed the symmetry of illuminated circuit boards. There were lights too suspended from some of the masts.

He became aware of one light in particular that was flashing at intervals from a point some twenty metres from the edge of the water. He peered towards it and saw a figure, conceivably Eleonora, waving a torch at him. He ducked under a metal chain suspended across a floating walkway and moved in the direction of the light. The figure disappeared into the cabin as he got nearer. He almost failed to negotiate the gap between the jetty and the gunwale of the vessel and stumbled onto the deck.

Eleonora raised him to his feet and, holding his hand, urged him to mind his head as she led him into the cabin. Tea lights flickered on either side of the small space which was largely taken up with a mattress and a swirl of blankets. Eleonora squatted on her haunches with her legs tucked beneath her. Dante attempted the same pose but his arthritic knees prevented any similar manoeuvre.

'Drink, Father?'

'Please.'

'So, you came.'

'Evidently.'

'Why?'

'It must have been the prospect of unbridled, wild sex with the woman who has bewitched me.' Dante accepted a large glass. 'Champagne?'

'Yes. So, I'm a witch am I?'

'A pleasing witch.'

'You don't know that. I might not choose to please you.'

'Indeed.'

'Doesn't the notion of witchcraft somehow absolve you of all responsibility for what might or might not happen shortly? You will after all be under a spell. You will be powerless to follow your conscience.' She rearranged herself on the bed, stretching her legs out in front of her. 'Have you always sought excuses, Father?'

'Quite the reverse. Even when there were mitigating

266

circumstances for my behaviour that was less than exemplary, I have always refused to invoke them. I have always preferred to beat myself up, and then wallow in the guilt that follows like night the day.'

'You have self-knowledge, Father. I grant you that. But your ability to rationalise your thought processes is in itself disingenuous, isn't it?'

'Probably.'

'Oh, for God's sake kiss me, Father, I'm getting bored.'

Dante attempted to stand but hit his head on the roof of the cabin. He groaned and sank to his knees. They were both kneeling facing each other. Eleonora lifted a corner of the blanket and used it to staunch the blood that was trickling down his forehead. 'Wounded in the cause of love, Father.'

'I blame that fucking cupid.'

'When did he start using a harpoon?' 'I am the size of a whale under this,' said Dante, pulling at his cassock.

'I will be the judge of that,' said Eleonora, pulling her dress over her head.

Dante did likewise with his cassock then moved a hand self-consciously over his underpants. They knelt facing each other. Despite himself Dante thought of a painting in St Doninica of two penitents in similar mirror-image poses.

'Not a whale at all, Father, a small dolphin perhaps. Do you get hairy dolphins?'

'It was easier in the tree,' said Dante.

Eleonora pulled his face towards hers and kissed him.

After a full minute of pleasure, he was aware of her tongue becoming completely still in his mouth. He opened his eyes and saw that Eleonora was concentrating on something, listening. He listened too and also heard a low rumble of voices.

'You must have been followed. Come on, quickly.' On all fours she led Dante to the door of the cabin. He was about to speak but she clasped a hand over his mouth. Despite the darkness, he too could just make out the silhouette of two figures on the deck of a boat a small distance away. With an expression that brooked no questioning, she indicated that Dante was to follow her every move. With the stealth of a stalking beast, she pulled herself to the edge of the craft and dropped soundlessly into the water. Dante managed the same manoeuvre with considerably less grace. His inelegant belly flop must have alerted the two men. He was aware of being pushed under the water. He had barely had sufficient time to fill his lungs and struggled to reach the surface but Eleonora kept the pressure on his head. He could hold his breath no longer and swallowed hard.

Eleonora, aware that Dante was no longer offering any resistance, yanked his head out of the water. He spluttered and sank back. Eleonora grabbed hold of his underpants and pulled him above the surface. Spluttering, his eyes on stalks, he gradually became aware of what was happening. He attempted to speak but water not words dribbled from his mouth. The acute pain in his groin subsided as Eleonora relinquished her grip and placed both of his hands on the edge of the boat. He moved his mouth next to her ear, 'I never thought…' he whispered before gasping for air. 'That sex would be like this.' Shaking, and not just from the shock of the water, which admittedly was not too cold for the time of year, he realised that Eleonora had placed an arm around him.

'I thought dolphins could swim,' she whispered.

'Not if they are weighed down by body hair.'

The water lapped round their chins as they watched the two men enter the cabin. One of them emerged holding his cassock up to the light of the moon as if it was a trophy.

As they were some way from the quay, they pulled themselves slowly, hand over hand, from one vessel to the next, pausing only to glance back to see if they had been noticed.

At one point Eleonora kissed him on the forehead. He knew that she was smiling.

Finally they reached the iron ladder that led down from the quay. 'We have a small problem, Father,' said Eleonora.

'True,' he replied.

'And a solution,' she said. 'Wait there.'

'I'm fine, nothing beats a midnight swim in close proximity to murderers, but I will need a sauna soon.'

He watched as she relinquished her grip on the rung and swam towards a craft moored some yards away. She pulled herself on board and tugged at something dark suspended from a rail. Swimming with one hand, she pulled her plunder behind her.

'Wet suits,' she said, pleased with herself.

'I've always had a penchant for water sports.'

'You should avoid those websites, Father.'

She slapped the suits onto the quay and hauled herself out of the water before offering a hand to Dante. They stood dripping and half naked for a moment, looking at each other. Eleonora's gaze shifted back towards where they had last seen the two men. There was no sign of them. They ducked behind a parked car as two lovers paused under a lamp post and wrapped themselves round each other.

'All right for some,' said Dante shivering.

The lovers finally extricated themselves.

'Come on,' said Eleonora, standing on one leg while attempting to wriggle into the smaller of the two wetsuits.

'I don't think this belonged to a dolphin,' said Dante as he struggled to pull the suit beyond his middle. She assisted by tugging at the rubber folds.

'Breathe in.'

By placing a hand on his chest, Eleonora eventually managed to pull the zip over his torso.

'I prefer waxing.'

269

They faced each other and embraced. 'I never understood rubber fetishists before now,' she said.

'What now?' asked Dante, breaking away.

'Basically we are totally fucked, cooked, baked at gas mark 8. They know about us, they will come for you, Father. I will buy some time. I can tease the cat for a little longer, make him squirm. With every day that he fails to find me, his reputation suffers. Cuckolded by an aging priest. A laughing stock.'

'And me?'

'What do the Americans call it? Collateral damage? I'm sorry, Father. Become a hermit. A missionary perhaps. Hide in the Vatican. I can't save you. Perhaps I've used you, but I can't think about that.' She touched him on the cheek, turned and walked away.

'I'm not going anywhere,' he shouted after her but she didn't hear.

It was not the most comfortable walk back to the canonica. Apart from anything else he had no shoes, and for the first mile at least left a trail of water behind him. The streets were mercifully empty and he minimised the chances of meeting anyone by weaving his way through the labyrinth of small alleyways.

A drunk lurched into his path beyond Via Napoli. After a ritual dance, left, then right, then left again, the man stared at his dancing partner and recoiled into a doorway. A cat tried to attach itself to his feet before it was despatched with a kick. He could not think about what had happened, if indeed it had happened. The wetsuit dispelled that slight possibility. It had happened. A sixty-five-year-old priest dressed in rubber, running from failed sex with the unfaithful wife of a gangster in someone else's yacht. It made the encounter in the tree seem almost normal. One option was to revel in the existential aspects of revolt and rebellion. He was living, possibly for the first time in years. But for how much longer?

A parishioner recently confided that he had no fear of death, 'unless it was sore'. It would be sore, there was no doubt about that. He winced at the memory of the torture choices that had been dispassionately explained to him by Mario's henchmen. An emotion stronger than his fear was his anger towards Eleonora. How dare she? How dare she?

There were no lights on at the canonica which was a small relief. He felt for his door key in his back pocket then realised that he had neither pocket nor key. He rang the bell. What was the worst that could happen?

After a while an upstairs light was turned on and he heard Francesca shuffling and muttering her way down the hall. First one lock, then the other. Damn her obsession with security and her unshakeable belief that Satan and a tribe of salivating hobgoblins would sooner or later ravish them all in their beds. A single eye appeared round the partially opened door. This was followed by a shriek and the door being slammed shut. He tried speaking to her through the letterbox but she was away howling upstairs to waken Adolfo.

The door opened again to reveal Adolfo standing with a raised candlestick. Francesca would never forgive him if he broke it.

'I shouldn't have had that second grappa. Well, Father, have you taken up scuba diving? A few oysters for breakfast would go down well.'

After a fitful night during which exhaustion finally triumphed over anger and fear, Dante emerged bloodshot and weary into the day room. Francesca turned her back on him the moment he appeared. Adolfo looked over his paper.

'You look a bit rough, Father. Tell me, why was I not invited to join the over-sixties clerical midnight swimming club. I hope you weren't skinny-dipping, Father, such activities were expressly forbidden by the pontiff two back.

Noni puschini in mare sans vetebo, if I remember correctly.'
Although Dante was not in the mood to be teased, there
was a comfortable familiarity about the banter that made
him again entertain the possibility that the previous night's
exploits had been a bad dream. No, they had not been a
dream.

'I think, Father, you are possessed by an evil spirit that is
sucking out your heart.' Dante thought of Eleonora. 'I think
I'll apply to the bishop to carry out an exorcism. I'm sure I
can lay my hands on the black book of spells and incanta-
tions. I think it's hidden behind Francesca's collected set of
Men's Health in the library.'

Adolfo correctly interpreted Dante's silence and tried a
different approach. 'Is it something you can tell me about?

'No, but thank you. Sometimes Adolfo I think you are a
better priest than you would have us believe.'

'Remember I have contacts in this city who can solve
most problems.'

'Not this one.'

Francesca flounced into the room and thrust a large
paper-covered parcel in front of Dante.

'Special delivery,' she declared with a look normally
reserved for the Jehovah's Witnesses she had on occasions
passed in the street.

Dante opened the parcel and held up his immaculately
cleaned and folded cassock.

'Are my laundry services not good enough for you,
Father?'

Dante felt himself being pulled back into a very dark
place. The thought that he was probably several hours from
being killed was at best bizarre, at worst, terrifying.

'Don't forget your class,' urged Adolfo. 'The Seekers
After Truth are gathering.'

While welcoming the opportunity to leave the room
without having to explain either his exploits or indeed the

mystery of the immaculately laundered cassock, Dante nevertheless baulked at the thought of his weekly asylum seekers class. In its wisdom the Sicilian church had decided that in return for temporary shelter and food, the most recent arrivals must undergo instruction in the rudiments of Catholicism, before their inevitable deportation.

The room was full. Twenty sullen faces still showing the signs of trauma, and in some cases, shipwreck, stared impassively at this man committed to weaning them from the heresy of Islam.

After a half-hearted salaam, Dante embarked on the catechism that had been set for homework.

'Who made me?'

'Allah, blessed be His name, made me,' chanted the two women in the front row.

'Why did God... Allah, make me?'

'To know and love Him.'

'Good,' said Dante recognising that this particular torture would soon pass, unlike the real torture that could yet be part of his day.

An angry man in his mid-twenties stood up in the middle of the group. 'I do not want to know and love your god who take my children. They drown, my wife, she can't hold them all and let go.' The woman next to him burst into tears. 'They float away, my children. I do not love your god.' His outburst was received with a respectful silence from the rest of his peers, none of whom could speak Italian. Dante paused and considered his possible responses. He could of course explain that God works in mysterious ways. He could elaborate and explain that the concept of pain was inseparable from God's gift of free will, he could... He walked towards the man cowering under this perceived overture to violence, and held him in his arms.

'I don't know the answer to that question.' Dante left the class, all of whom shuffled away, relieved but mystified that their ordeal had been of such short duration. Nothing surprised them anymore.

Realising the futility of running away Dante decided the best he could do was wait with as much equanimity as he could muster until he was taken.

Lying on his bed, he decided to anticipate, and indeed make the most of that moment when his life would flash before him. The initial newsreels would almost certainly be in black and white. His father emerging from the grey back-cloth to wave self-consciously at the camera. His mother then entering from the left holding him as a baby in her arms. They were in the olive grove that surrounded their house. A few stills from the holiday album followed. Dante and his sister were on the beach at Realmonte. His mother was draping herself in the scarf she had bought from the hawker. His father opened another Moretti.

Gradually colour seeped into the film. He was on a hill somewhere at the end of a long string to which was attached a red balloon. He was running fast to see if he could leap and join the balloon as it sailed over the sea to a distant magical land. Dante was reluctant to let the image go and held onto it, like the small boy attached to the string, for as long as he could.

The next photos were formal and framed in dark wood. They had been taken down from the wall of the room reserved for feast days and funerals. They were taken at the seminary. He had a full head of hair and was smiling, like all the others, with a false joviality. He scanned the several rows. What had happened to Manfredo? Did he survive the dark nights of doubt that would claim him even then? Savino had been expelled after fornication with a village girl. And what of Carlo?

Why were there no photos of the years between then and now? There must be some good memories of his years as a priest? What about his work with the poor? There should

274

at least be a snapshot of the garden monastery where he had been, momentarily, totally happy? There wasn't one. Not a single one. In a panic he flicked through the empty pages of the album until he came across endless images of Eleonora. Pornographic images capturing, in close-up, their tryst in the fig tree, a picture, taken with flash, of their kiss in the confessional. The moment she knelt before him in the cabin...

There was a knock on the door.

'Come quick,' said Adolfo, 'the dance hall is on fire.'

CHAPTER FIVE

Dante dressed quickly, grabbed his coat and ran through the streets, following the flames, a moth attracted to its own immolation. The fire engines screamed with impatience as the cars wedged themselves up against the walls of the narrow streets. The smell of burning was in the air that also carried butterflies of ash. The curious crowd was proving an obstacle to the firefighters who eventually managed to rope off one side of the street. Their priority was to evacuate the adjacent buildings already besieged by imps of smoke. A firefighter emerged with an elderly woman slung over his shoulders, her arms beating an involuntary tattoo on his back. She was followed by a shirtless man rubbing his eyes like a crying toddler.

Dante forced himself to the front of the crowd. The flames, desperate for oxygen, punched their way through the window frames of the dance hall. The onlookers recoiled as they were hit by the wall of heat. Dante shielded his eyes as two firefighters carried a stretcher between them. He recognised Signora Albini, the caretaker who, despite instructions to the contrary, lived on the premises. Dante had long given up trying to persuade her that she couldn't live permanently in the tiny cupboard off the kitchen. 'There's plenty of space for a wizened soul, Father.' She took up so little room on the stretcher it could have been the body of a child.

Dante ducked under the restraining rope and ran towards the building. Two Carabinieri intercepted him but his forward momentum carried him past them. One of them grabbed him from behind. 'For God's sake, Father, there's nothing you can do.'

As he refused to cooperate, the police dragged him away from the building. He fought against them with such force that they had no alternative but to throw him into the back of a police van where he lay pummelling the floor with his fists. 'Jesus Christ, Jesus Christ!' It was a curse, not a prayer.

Who else had been in the hall? Gabriella and Marcella, both in their eighties, would arrive early to help Signora Albini decorate the tables. Donatella, a woman with a congenital illness who, despite expectations, had survived well into her fifties, would often drop by. She said she preferred dancing on her own and would glide silently across the empty space with a non-existent partner in her arms before the others arrived. Perhaps Pepe, homeless and habitually drunk, had been let in on the back of a promise to behave.

Through the side window Dante could only see the backs of the onlookers gawking at the fire. He started to catastrophise about the scale of the disaster. The only certainty was that he was wholly to blame. A horrible price was being extracted for his folly with Eleonora.

The Carabinieri delivered Dante back to the canonica. Francesca received him with a sniff and a shake of the head. Adolfo looked genuinely concerned as he slumped into his armchair. 'No fatalities yet,' he said. 'According to the radio they have taken three to hospital. Smoke inhalation.'

'It's all my fault,' said Dante.

'What do you mean?'

'I can't tell you. Just believe me. If any of my dancers die, I'll have blood on my hands.' Dante got out of his chair and paced round the room.

'Is there anything I can do? Don't worry, I'm not going to offer up prayers to Saint Jude. Unless you think it might help?'

'It won't help.'

'We may have to rethink our theology, Father. It does seem as if God is determined to punish you for your transgressions in this life rather than His usual practice of deferring punishment until the next. A more efficient system, I suppose. More through-put. The custodians of purgatory and limbo may find their jobs are at risk. Compulsory redundancy must be an option. I imagine Saint Peter may be sulking. His function has certainly been undermined by this new arrangement.' He paused and looked at Dante. His distraction gambit had failed, and his fellow priest looked even more agitated.

Francesca came back into the room. 'Another parcel, Father.' She dropped a thick jiffy bag onto the table with palpable disapproval.

'Are you running drugs, Father? You're not one of those mules are you?'

'In one sense, yes,' said Dante whose fingers shook as he opened the parcel. A smoke detector dropped onto the table.

When it came, the summons was almost a relief. Dante saw the car from his bedroom window. A white Mondeo with blacked-out windows. The chauffeur, wearing sunglasses, stepped into the street. Dante, having noted the clichés, didn't wait for the bell to ring. He walked down the stairs and opened the front door.

'Nice day for a drive,' said Dante. It's good to get out. A change of routine, and all that.'

'Shut the fuck up, lie on the floor and put the blanket over your head.'

The difficulties in lying on the floor of the car were almost insurmountable. The footwells were too small for

278

him to curl into, and the transmission made it impossible to lie across the available space. Eventually he adopted a crouching position which he hoped would meet the chauffeur's instruction. The blanket stank and Dante briefly entertained the disturbing thought that the last person it had covered had been dead.

He had frequently contemplated death both as a theological concept and as something deeply personal. He and Adolfo had debated the issue over many years. Dante's first real crisis of faith had occurred after the funeral of a child who had been killed in a hit-and-run accident. His consoling platitudes dropped like ashes from his mouth. The mother's rage had stopped him in mid-sentence. In that moment, he had a substantial sense of a nihilistic cavernous void into which all human life was destined to fall. That intimation had never completely left him.

The car braked suddenly and Dante was forced against the back of the seat. The chauffeur swore and accelerated angrily. The rapid changing of gears, and the fact that he was being thrown from side to side, reinforced the impression that they were climbing into the hills.

He thought of Eleonora. The anger he had felt on the quayside had completely dissolved. He just wanted her. Perhaps the blanket under which he now cowered would be lifted and she would join him again for another long wonderful anarchic kiss. He hoped she was safe. He hoped she was still winning her dangerous game of hide and seek. At least he couldn't reveal her whereabouts during whatever interrogation waited for him as had no idea where she was. This realisation raised the prospect of torture.

The car stopped on a gravel path. Dante was hauled out and frogmarched a short distance by the chauffeur, with the blanket held tightly round his neck. After walking for a few minutes he banged his shin against a bottom step and was made to climb three more. A door opened and he was thrown onto the floor. The carpet felt greasy. On opening his eyes, he saw not the interior he had anticipated. He was in a small ramshackle caravan.

Facing him across a desk overflowing with paper, sat a thin, balding middle-aged man nervously tapping a pen on a ledger. The walls were decorated with fading football posters and a large smiling portrait of the pope. 'Welcome, Father, you know of me, I am Mario, the husband of the woman you have been fucking. Apologies for the humble surroundings. Temporary accommodation, you understand. Obviously I am going to kill you but the manner and duration of your death depends on you telling me where I can find the delightful Eleonora. Did you find her delightful, Father?' He asked almost playfully as if they were men of the world comparing notes over an old flame they had in common.

He came round to the front of the desk, stood with his face inches from Dante's and screamed, 'Did you, Father? Did you?' Petrified, Dante stepped back into the arms of the chauffeur who held him in a bear hug. He was then dragged backwards down the steps, out of the caravan, and manhandled towards a barrel of rain water. The chauffeur grabbed Dante's tonsure of hair in a fist and pushed his head under the surface. Dante struggled against his own drowning, losing control of his bladder as he fought to hold his breath. He lost the fight and, in a terrifying moment of surrender, sucked the water into his lungs. Agony and burning panic.

In a moment he was again lying on the greasy carpet. 'No need to prostrate yourself before me,' said Mario. 'I do though appreciate the gesture. Put him in the chair.' The chauffeur did as he was told. Dante vomited a stream of water. 'Reminds me of *The Exorcist*. Did you see the film, Father? It was very good. Who was the star? Lee J Cobb, wasn't it? See it as a second baptism. Do you have evangelical tendencies, Father? Perhaps you've been born again.' He suddenly laughed. 'How ironic is that, given your current predicament! Anyway, I'm sorry about the mess but you must be getting used to the water now after your romantic midnight swim the other night. Strange behaviour for a priest, don't you think? It's not too late. I could have a word with the bishop if you like. I am sponsoring the festa at Monte Pellegrino this year. Tax avoidance really but still...' Leaning against the desk with legs crossed, he placed a cigar in his mouth and clicked his fingers. The chauffeur stepped forward with a lighter.

'Do you mind if I smoke, Father?' Dante shook his head and choked again.

'I've always thought there is something magical about the Feast of the Assumption, haven't you, Father? We all have mothers, long-suffering, self-sacrificing, deserving of the best, and God thought the same...'

Dante rallied. He was still shaking after the trauma but at least he could breathe again.

Regaining his equilibrium had nothing to do with courage. He was still petrified by the imminence of his death but he suddenly felt Eleonora's presence, there in the squalid caravan. All his days as a priest he had hankered to experience Christ as a living, comforting presence. He never had but this was close. Even as he looked round to see his love, he knew that she would not be there, her physical absence was irrelevant. It simply didn't matter. The relief he felt at realising that his lover, for a while at least, was safe, was accompanied by a longing that was more painful than his near-drowning. Perhaps this was, after all, a sort of courage.

'...which is why you must tell me where I can find the bitch.' In the moment of silence that ensued, Dante looked at his adversary and saw a sad, profoundly unhappy, bitter weasel of a man who had apparently sexually humiliated Eleonora and turned her into a maniacal fugitive.

'If I knew, I wouldn't tell you.'

'Oh, we will see about that,' said Mario, walking slowly towards Dante. When close he knelt down in front of him, pinned his wrist against the armrest of the chair, and ground the burning cigar into his flesh. He kept it there as Dante screamed. And kept it there some more.

'Shit, it's gone out,' he said, gesturing for the chauffeur to approach again with the lighter.

'The thing is, Father,' he said, getting off his knees, 'there will come a point when you will tell me, not to save yourself but to save others. By the way, did you hear that two people died in that unfortunate fire today? A simpleton woman and some old vagrant. Hardly a loss to the community, I would have thought.' He paused, smiling, looking at Dante for a reaction. There wasn't one.

'I'm bored with you now, Father. I will summon you again soon. That burn looks nasty, you should get someone to look at it. Take him away.

Numb with pain from his wrist and from his heart heavy with the news about Donatella and Pepe, Dante offered no resistance as he was bundled out of the caravan and into the boot of the Mondeo.

'Becoming something of a habit, 'said Adolfo, lifting Dante to his feet and helping him into the canonica.

The following day Dante woke with a strange inexplicable energy that made no sense after his ordeal. He considered the possibility that he was in delayed shock. Like the chicken whose head had been recently struck from its body, he still had sufficient residual life to run round the yard. Soon he might collapse in a pool of blood with his legs twitching in the air. But not yet. Perhaps the moment of epiphany, when he had felt Eleonora's presence, had galvanised him. His wrist throbbed but even that pain was bearable somehow.

'Your wrist, Father,' said Francesca, displaying something remarkably close to concern.

'It could be stigmata, stage one,' said Adolfo. 'There will be one on the other hand by tomorrow, mark my words. Pilgrims will be beating a path to our doors. Canonisation is only a hundred years away.'

Once Francesca had left to find a dressing for Dante's wound, Adolfo lowered his voice and changed his tone. 'Are you all right, old friend? Stupid question, I know you're not. But you won't let me intrude into your private hell. Let me in. Let the flames lick me as well. God knows I need it. Burn off the sloth, the incipient wickedness.'

'Adolfo, you are a good man but you really, really don't want to get involved. Trust me. Things are moving fast now. All will be well.'

The two men embraced, something they had rarely done in twenty years of sharing the same living space. Adolfo patted Dante on the back, partly in embarrassment, partly because he had never fully known what to do with his hand during an embrace with another man.

'There's much to be done,' said Dante, breaking away. 'I'm going to find out if Signora Belcastro has an existence outside of the confessional.

As good as his word, he retrieved her address from the filing cabinet and decided to cycle the few kilometres to the far side of Palermo.

He had to cycle one-handed as the pain in his wrist intensified when he gripped the handlebars. He dismounted when he saw his boys playing football on the wasteland. 'Il demente Padre!' cried the eldest. Dante leaned his bike against the wall.

'This is no longer a bicycle, it is the goal mouth at the San Siro. The score at full time is Inter 3, Juve 3. You each have to take a penalty against me. You are on a bonus of ten euros per goal.'

Shrieking with anticipation, the boys lined up. The first shot slithered through Dante's fingers. After hitting the ground in mock annoyance, he handed over €10. The next shot left him clutching at empty air and ricocheted off the back wheel. 'Ten Euros.' He parried the last shot before helping the ball to graze the saddle. 'Ten Euros,' he said, remounting and cycling off with a wave. 'See you in the final, boys,' he said.

He found Senora Belcastro's address but not before asking for directions several times.

'Great news, Senora,' he said, kissing her on both cheeks to her great astonishment. 'By a stroke of extraordinary good fortune I have obtained a holy relic from our own Holy Father. It is a bone from the foot of Saint Cecilia with miraculous powers of forgiveness.' He felt quite smug knowing that, despite his unshakeable belief that St Cecilia was one of the church's greatest frauds and charlatans, she had finally fulfilled a worthwhile function by featuring in his redemptive narrative. He carefully unwrapped the small chicken bone he had rescued from the garbage earlier that morning.

'Does it work for the greatest sins, Father?'

'It only works with the very worst sins.'

'Like…?'

'Yes, especially that one.' He put the bone to his lips and gently wrapped Signora Belcastro's hand around it.

'Go, my daughter, and sin no more.'

'Thank you, Father. Thank you.'

Signor Pascali was asleep when he entered the ward. Dante waited patiently. When he woke, Signor Pascali's initial bewilderment transmuted into pleased recognition.

'Hello, you old communist.'

'I thought for a moment, Father, you were one of Mussolini's henchmen come to take me away.'

'Who in their right mind would want to take you anywhere?'

'True, Father, but did I tell you about the time when I stood up for Matteotti at the party meeting?'

'Yes, but tell me again. It's one of my favourite stories...'

Dante's euphoric reconnection with life in general and his vocation as priest in particular, continued for the rest of the week. He baptised three bambinos despite his habitual reluctance to endorse the sacrament which he saw as denial of free will, a sort of abusive conscription of the young.

To his astonishment and delight, he celebrated the Eucharist on at least two occasions without being assaulted by the mocking devils of doubt who normally clambered onto the altar to get a better glimpse at his hypocrisy. He still braced himself on uttering the words '...corpus est,' and waited for the onslaught. But nothing. No mocking applause, no sibilant shrieking, just a short moment of calm.

He embraced each of his parishioners as they left the church after Mass, holding onto them for slightly longer than was his usual practice. His words of support and encouragement were sincere. He readily acceded to requests for additional prayers for the sick and dying, and gently returned the money discreetly passed to him for his services. The diocesan fund, skimmed from the collection plates each week, had accumulated to a considerable sum. Adolfo would normally deliver it personally to the bishop's palace on the first Monday of every month but he had been too busy ministering to the small fleet of oligarchs who had sailed unannounced into the harbour in a hedonistic flotilla. Dante had always pointed out that there was no difference between paying this unearned stipend to the bishop than paying pizzo to the organisation. There was no accountability, no financial transparency. God alone knew how the money was spent. Adolfo readily agreed that God himself was probably mystified as to which charities benefited from the money.

285

Dante opened the safe and put the money in the black case that normally carried the sacrament when visiting the sick.

His first stop was the hostel for the homeless on Via San Sebastian. Over the years he had come to find a sort of comfort in the warm smell of unwashed men. They were a community in whose presence he always felt at ease. Each temporary resident was allocated a locker located in a corridor that led from the dining hall to the dormitories. All of the locks had been broken a long time ago, leaving the doors to swing open on the personal detritus. Oddly, theft had never been an issue. There was a shared, respectful appreciation of the importance that these eccentric mementos held for whoever had accumulated them. After accepting an over-sugared coffee from Sister Angelica with whom he briefly flirted, he placed a bundle of notes in each locker and left.

The blind accordion player whose pitch was outside of the basilica was the next beneficiary of the bishop's unintended largesse. Alberto had a limited but invariably mournful repertoire. As Dante approached he was playing *O Sole Mio* with a spirited but controlled gusto that suggested that, in his mind's eye, he was performing an encore to a packed house. Rather than putting money into the open case, he put it straight into Alfonso's pocket. He stopped playing, smiled, and picked up the tune again.

Dante took a circuitous route back to the canonica, picking his way through the narrow passages. Game shows competed with domestic arguments. Football clashed with music. The cooking smells made him hungry. He paused briefly at each of the twenty or so separate residences whose single rooms opened directly onto the street. Where there were letter boxes, he posted money. Where there were no letter boxes, he pushed bank notes under the door or into the thin vertical cracks of light down either side. He walked quickly, not wanting to engage in conversation with any of the residents.

In other circumstances Dante would have been a fierce

critic of his own actions. He would have questioned his motives, and readily accused himself of burnishing his ego by dispensing largesse to the poor and needy. On this occasion he didn't care. He was dancing on the cusp of eternity. The moth was going to enjoy proximity to the flame before it devoured him. He knew full well that he would soon be taken by Mario, and that no matter how painful his demise might be, it wouldn't last for ever. Well, in one sense it would, and that too would be ok. He also felt secure realising that he could not ever betray Eleonora's whereabouts as he simply didn't know.

Would she eventually learn of his sacrifice? At one level he hoped so, at another he hoped not, as he had no intention to ever cause her pain. The thought that he would, most likely, never know what Eleonora's fate would be, gave him a moment's sober reflection. For the first time in days he felt that a plug had been pulled, and that the slightly hysterical euphoria that had sustained him might be about to drain away in a rush. Vulnerable again, he stood stock-still in the empty street and wished with every sinew of his soul that Eleonora would suddenly grab him from the shadows, and that they would, for one last time, embrace.

He was, at that very moment, grabbed from the shadows. And quickly beaten unconscious.

He woke in total darkness which he felt should have been illuminated by the electric pulses emanating from his brain. He was still alive but had no sense of whether that was a good or bad thing. The mustiness was familiar. Was he on the floor of the chapel at the seminary where he would prostrate himself in the early days of ecstatic penitence? Certainly there were stone flags beneath him. Why would anyone bring him back there? Had he been granted the chance to revisit his past and change all of the wrong decisions he had made? He would of course abandon the priesthood and return home. Marry someone, anyone.

Perhaps this was his old home, and this was the cellar, far more ancient than the rest of the house, where he would sometimes hide with a cycling magazine. His kidneys hurt. Presumably he had been kicked by his unseen assailant. He moved slightly and felt his side. He touched a hard rubberised object. He thought it might be the handle of a tool then felt the switch.

The torch cast a small puddle several yards in front of him. Dante stood up and redirected the beam upwards until it fell on a huge black figure. He dropped the torch. 'Holy Christ in heaven!' His curse echoed and returned to surround him. He knew where he was and knew who the figure was.

As a young priest he had been temporarily attached to the Convent of the Cappuccini. When both guides fell ill at the same time, he was quickly inducted into the role and was soon on nodding terms with at least some of the eight thousand dead inhabitants of the catacomb. That was nearly forty years ago. Nevertheless, he recognised the man in black as Bartolomeo Megna, fondly referred to as il Gigante. His hands were tied together with rope. The skull beneath the cowl was two-tone. The upper portion was white, the bottom half was brown. Dante recalled that during periods of rampant epidemic, the corpses were bathed in arsenic. His favourite had always been Giovanni Paterniti, American vice consul who had died in 1910. He was still there, staring out from over his handlebar moustache, looking for all the world as if he was recovering from a liquid lunch.

Why had he been brought here? To frighten him, presumably. The beating of his heart confirmed that, had this been the intention, it was at least partly successful. He turned off the torch. Was the darkness preferable? Realising this could be a harbinger of the perpetual darkness that was waiting for him, he switched it back on again. Now disconcerted, Dante felt compelled to illuminate each of the desiccated corpses in turn. He tried to create the mental curiosity of the tourists he had shown round in his earlier life. By replicating a detached, almost scientific interest he might keep at bay the terror that was, despite his familiarity with the environment, creeping up on him.

He remembered being told that the preferred method of embalming involved leaving the corpses to drain in a closed room after their internal organs had been removed. In a flash of quickly repressed horror he saw his own body hanging, dripping onto the floor. No. Concentrate. The bodies were then washed with water and vinegar, dried, and filled with straw before being dressed and displayed in the niches. How much straw could be stuffed into his own belly? Had Mario already requisitioned a bale or two from one of the many farmers whose land he 'protected'?

Move on, move on, be the tourist. He never, in the few months he worked there, became immune to the emotional impact of the saddest cadaver, two-year-old Rosalia Lombardo, embalmed using the latest pharmaceuticals and encased in a crystal coffin. Dante felt compelled to seek her out. He lowered the torch onto the stone flags which he followed to the altar in the Chapel of Santa Rosalia. She was still there with open eyes and auburn hair. He wanted to reach out and touch her innocent forehead and make the sign of the cross.

The wave of sadness that overwhelmed him was much more than an instinctive sentimentality on seeing a dead child. He was confronting a distillation of all the human suffering he had encountered during his years as a priest. All of the sick and dying, all of the bereaved and bereft, all of the lost and needy. Every comforting platitude, every solicitous cliché he had offered to the terminally ill, to widows, to grieving parents, merged into white noise in his head. The babel of well-intentioned but ultimately vacuous words became unbearable and he put his hands over his ears. He had assumed that he was well beyond spiritual crisis: a phrase he had always associated with an essentially self-indulgent state of mind beloved of angst-ridden noviti-ates. But what he felt now in the cold crypt was a demonic emptiness he had only ever experienced once before.

As chaplain to a school in Lombardo he had been sum-moned by a hysterical member of staff to an empty room where, she explained between sobs, some of the younger girls had conducted a séance during which, apparently, the Devil himself had put in an appearance. Dante walked into the room, cossetted by his scepticism, fortified by his faith, and was instantly enveloped in a tangible despair.

That moment had come again. He ran towards where he had remembered the door being. It was bolted shut and barely shuddered as he put his weight against it.

Determined to find another way out, although he knew there was none, he stumbled down the long aisles of the dead stacked and labelled in neat rows, past Marito and Moglie, the proximity of whose skulls suggested that their gossip had a conspiratorial component, past the anony-mous friar with the penitent's rope round his neck, past the lines of priests and nuns segregated by gender to prevent posthumous turpitude.

Eventually Dante slowed. To an extent the very familiar-ity of his companions had the effect of washing away his panic. Able to breathe again, he took stock of his situation. He was, after all, and despite the odds, still alive. Admittedly his time was running out and Mario, his puppet master, was playing games with him that could yet prove fatal. He hoped that Eleonora had managed to avoid detection, not only for her own sake but in the knowledge that he would be kept alive so long as Mario believed that he knew where she was hiding. Logically he knew too that he wouldn't be left here for ever. In a few hours the doors would open to admit the day's first tourists.

To ensure that his comparative equilibrium was maintained, he decided to keep walking through the catacomb; apart from anything else he was shivering with the cold. As he surveyed the row of pickled academics it occurred to him that he had always been comparatively at ease with the dead. On the occasions when vigils were held for late parishioners he would happily sit through the night. Francesca would provide him with a flask on these occasions. Always intrigued, despite his growing agnosticism, by the fact that a body loses 0.5 of a gram shortly after the moment of death, he would sit, half waiting for a glimpse of a soul rising, wraith-like towards the roof of the nave. He would speculate too, about the size, shape and colour of each soul. Some souls would be sad wisps shrivelled by a lifetime of mean-spiritedness. Others would be as large as an ox's heart, boldly journeying towards their Maker. Perhaps some of the weaker souls failed to complete their journey and, exhausted, sank back down again, left to be blown about the earth in an endless torment, or crept for shelter into the ears of sleepers bringing them nightmares too horrible to repeat.

He turned the corner and saw Eleonora hanging naked with her throat cut.

CHAPTER SIX

Adolfo was the first to visit but was told by the nurse that Dante was still heavily sedated. She had phoned the canonica at an early hour to pass on the news that Dante had been found wandering bewildered in the vicinity of the Catacomb dei Cappucini and had now been taken to a place of safety.

The Carabinieri had assumed that he was drunk. It wouldn't have been the first time they had rescued an inebriated cleric and returned him gently to his place of residence. But Dante was different. He was violent and seemed possessed of a strength that did not have its origins in the grappa bottle.

After staunching the blood from his broken nose, Inspector Ambrogi handcuffed the dangerous priest and bundled him into the back of the car. Between episodes of demented shouting, Dante took to headbutting the seat in front. This resulted in the other Carabiniero moving into the back of the car and holding the maniacal cleric in a headlock. Rather than risk further mayhem at the police station, they drove him directly to the Hospital of the Martyrs where he was summarily inspected by the admissions psychiatrist, sedated and given a bed in an empty ward.

In one of his dreams the dead and embalmed figures from the catacomb started to twitch, then stretch, shaking off the grey dust of centuries. They nodded in recognition of each other but their greetings were restrained. The process of reanimation was incomplete, skulls rather than faces stared from under the cowls and academic gowns. They stepped down from the niches that had held them for the last two hundred years and formed an unruly grumbling line in the corridor. Dante was at their head and at a cry from himself they stormed out of the cellar, choking and coughing in the fresh air, blinded by the sunlight.

Tourists screamed in horror and held tightly onto their children as the army of the dead stormed past them. The traffic stopped and vehicles bumped and nudged into each other.

The drivers hastily wound up their windows as a hundred monks and a hundred nuns and a hundred academics climbed over the car bonnets, leaving smears of dust on the windscreens as they marched relentlessly towards the object of their revenge.

Breaking into a run despite rheumatic, arthritic limbs they swarmed round the corner into Place dei Novitiates and crawled across the tables and chairs outside Café Claudio, a known haunt of the powerful. Patrons fled, waiters ran into each other in their panic. The owner emerged from his kitchen with a cleaver which he instantly dropped as the zombies ransacked his premises. A petrified businessman was cudgelled to death with a stave just in case he was a member of the organisation. A tiny shrieking nun held a huge vat of olive oil over her head, shaking its contents into the street. A wizened professor of rhetoric poked a bony finger at a terrified toddler trapped in his pushchair.

Other dreams were gentler. He and Eleonora lay on the banks of the Belice, differentiating, with closed eyes, the plash of the leaping salmon from the ripples brushing against the bank. He and Eleonora lay in the fields surrounding

Taormina, squinting in the sunlight to locate the ascending smudge of the skylark before it sang itself into infinity. Eleonora stared entranced at him from the foremost pew as he expounded from the pulpit about the love of God. His sermon was beautiful and compelling beyond imagining. His conceits were insightful and poignant. His paradigms were witty and compassionate. He conjured a vista of paradise that made the Garden of Eden obsolete and clichéd. From his garden, the writhing serpents of guilt and suspicion had been banished. In his garden, sensuality was a heavy scent alive with possibility. A musk, perhaps hinting at physical fulfilment, or cinnamon, exotic but redolent of pleasure. The light itself was a balm, healing and comforting, encouraging, permitting even, those over whom it washed, to go forth, find themselves and each other that they might lie in closeness and an endless anticipated joy.

After three days the Carabinieri had been permitted to interview him; after all there was the issue of assault and some damage to the inside of a police car. Dante had explained how he had been kidnapped, and how he had woken to find himself in the presence of a dead woman. The psychiatrist made meaningful eye contact with the officer who said that they had already spoken to the guide who had not seen anything amiss. 'They removed her body, don't you see?' said Dante who was patted on the shoulder by the nurse as the official party left the ward.

Dante knew from previous pastoral visits to the ward that psychiatric beds were at a premium and that in all likelihood any semblance of normality would be sufficient excuse to release him back into his life. Accordingly, he played the game, greeted Francesca like a long lost friend, behaved impeccably to all of the ward staff, and prepared himself mentally for his next meeting with his psychiatrist.

294

Dr Lombardi was a tall, languorous and deeply melancholic figure, not without compassion, who was increasingly confused by the existence of any theoretical line separating the mad from the sane. He sat on Dante's bed and rubbed some non-existent crumbs from his clipboard.

'You could argue,' said Dante, sitting upright in bed, 'that all adherents to religion are essentially deluded. The sustaining lie of immortality robs many adherents of their reason. How many saints would escape without attracting a diagnosis? Strange term, don't you think, Doctor, attracting a diagnosis? As if diagnoses are floating in the ether like so many lost souls eager to find a home and offer comfort to their unwilling host.' It occurred to Dante that he should not be too clever in his discourse as this could paradoxically be interpreted as him still possessing an overwrought brain in need of further therapeutic nurturing.

'I'm just tired and run down with it all,' he said, changing tack, aiming at projecting a more world-weary but reasonable persona. 'Lay people do not have a God-given monopoly on work-induced stress.'

Dr Lombardi smiled in acknowledgement of the ironic reference to the deity. 'If I let you out, can you arrange a retreat somewhere? Have all your needs met by the tender ministrations of nuns?' This time the ironic smile of recognition was mutual.

'I can go to a monastery for a few weeks. Should be easy if you write me a letter stating my need for respite and tender care.'

'No problem, Father.

Neither Francesca nor Adolfo quite knew what to do with Dante when the ambulance dropped him at the door of the canonica. They both hovered anxiously on the threshold of the day room and fussed over him, each of them competing to take his bag and offering him food and drink.

The housekeeper could not stop herself from inspecting the invalid for signs of raving lunacy that at any point could result in a murderous act. Having brought him his evening meal she made a special point of quickly removing his cutlery the moment he had finished eating.

Dante certainly felt murderous intent but not against Francesca. Never in his life, well with one exception, had he experienced such an overwhelming all-consuming emotion. He would, at the earliest opportunity, kill Mario. Of that there was not the slightest doubt. Somehow his anger was more manageable than his chaotic feelings for Eleonora. His hatred of Mario assumed a physical reality as he held both hands tightly clenched.

Noticing, Adolfo moved to the side of Dante's chair and lightly touched both of his hands until Dante released his fingers. He smiled, acknowledging Adolfo's kindness, and then resumed his inner scrutiny. There was something sacrilegiously liberating about the urge to murder. It was the dark corollary of what he had felt for Eleonora in Giardino Garibaldi. Its intensity precluded all traditional and habitual forms of thought. It contained not a soupçon of guilt. Its very amorality was exhilarating. God, religion, his entire time as a priest counted for absolutely nothing.

By way of distracting Dante from whatever demon was tugging at his heart, Adolfo resorted to the tried and tested gambit of provocation.

'Your favourite feast day tomorrow, Father. You must be on good form if you are to celebrate the glorious assumption of our Blessed Virgin Mother. Something special has been planned at Monte Pellegrino. Evidently a rich patron has bankrolled a spectacle "the like of which you will not see again in your lifetime". At least, according to the leaflets that have been plastered on every lamp post in the city.' Dante became attentive but not because Adolfo's tactics were working. He was trying to make a connection with something that was totally pertinent to his urge to kill but the link was eluding him. Believing that his ploy was working, Adolfo grew into his theme.

'I thought of you, Father, when addressing the women parishioners on the riveting subject of the Assumption. For some reason I heard you scoffing, and mocking my every word. Undaunted, I persisted. I did nod in the direction of paganism by acknowledging the link with the goddess Isis who was also born on August 15th according to mythology...'

Dante still looked as if he was at least tolerating the discourse. He was, however, concentrating on locating the link between the Assumption and his present preoccupation.

'At one level the ex-cathedra pronouncement of 1950 that "The Virgin Mary, having completed the course of her earthly life, was assumed body and soul into heavenly glory," remains deliciously ambiguous as you never tire of telling me. Christians certainly believe that Mary died a natural death, that her soul was received by Christ upon death, and that her body was resurrected on the third day after her death and that she was taken up into heaven bodily in anticipation of the general resurrection. However, Orthodox tradition is clear and unwavering in regard to the central belief in Dormition: the Holy Virgin underwent, like her Son, a physical death, but her body – like His – was afterwards raised from the dead and taken up to heaven...'

Dante clapped his hands, rose out of his chair, and to Adolfo's surprise embraced his fellow priest. 'I understand, I see the link now. Thank you.' With that he took his leave and retired to bed.

'Still not well,' said Adolfo to nobody but himself.

There was already a mood of celebration abroad when Dante stepped into the street. Keeping to the shadows on the far side, he managed to avoid the full impact of the sun until he crossed Papa Santo's Square and joined the queue waiting for the No.17 bus. He hadn't eaten but was too excited to think about food. His fellow passengers were clearly enjoying the day's holiday. The old woman was going to visit her daughter. Things had been strained since her marriage to a ne'er-do-well but, after all, it was the ideal time to build bridges what with it being such a holy day. The Virgin wouldn't fail her. Dante nodded his agreement. The man in front turned round. 'Children, who would have them? You're well out of it, Father.' Without elaborating, and assuming that what he had said was so obvious that further discussion was unnecessary, he went back to reading his paper.

An animated discussion broke out concerning the precise nature of the spectacle they had been promised in the piazza as part of the celebrations. 'A feast of roast boar, pigeons stuffed with quails, truffles by the bucket, cannoli for all of the children and the finest wines from the cellars of the Vatican for us,' suggested the passenger nearest to the driver.

'Quiet, you're making us hungry,' shouted someone from the back. 'I forgot my breakfast.'

'Perhaps there will be a miracle, perhaps all of the sick will be cured,' contributed an old woman with her Zimmer crammed into the aisle. Undaunted by the derisive laughter that accompanied her suggestion, she unwisely persisted. 'Perhaps the Virgin herself will appear.'

'Unlikely, she's fully booked for the next ten years, I heard. Berlusconi put in a bid.' The blasphemous voice was met with much shushing, and quick signs of the cross.

Predictably the bus ground to a virtual halt. The crescendo of horns and the noisy semaphore of hand waving were especially irritating given the urgency that Dante felt as he nursed his rage. There must be no equivocation, no pause for thought.

A Fiat three-wheeler nonchalantly blocked the bus's passage at right angles while the trader unloaded boxes of fruit and vegetables. A woman sitting on the other side of the bus started talking loudly in English about the wickedness of the Catholic Church, and the role it played in the suppression of women. She was ignored. Two other passengers, an older man and a younger woman, moved from their seats on recognising each other. They embraced in the aisle much to the delight of their fellow travellers. When the bus moved again they lurched into Dante. The woman's perfume was the same that Eleonora had been wearing in the confessional. He tensed.

The grinding of the gears and additional lurching confirmed that the bus had left the highway and had started on the long slow ascent. Other buses joined the pilgrims' convoy until, thirteen hairpin bends later, the vehicles stopped in a line next to the tourist stalls beneath the church. The midday sun was unrelenting and Dante regretted not having brought his hat. His subsequent thought concerned the absurd coexistence of murderous impulses and the realisation that he did not want his head to burn.

He sat at one of the many cafes and watched as an extremely large woman returned to the plastic table with her substantial burden of sweets and soft drinks for her three fat children. When she noticed that a priest was at her table, she chastised the largest child for no apparent reason and dragged his chair nearer to hers so as to give Dante more room. For what, he had no idea.

At an adjacent table another priest was holding forth to a party of very frail nuns on the beauties of paradise. Dante assiduously avoided eye contact with his fellow cleric whom he didn't recognise in any case, and hoped that the nuns hanging on his every sainted word would not be too disappointed when they arrived at the non-existent gates. He often thought it unfair that, given the nature of oblivion, not one of the millions of believers who had committed evil in the name of religion would ever be confronted with the folly and stupidity of their beliefs.

In the same moment he felt a small pang of sorrow for the nuns. And sorrow for himself, and Adolfo, and Francesca, and Eleonora. He stood up from the table, knocking over the fat child's plastic cup in the process. These thoughts would not do. He would not permit himself to be distracted.

Dante feigned interest in the cheap souvenirs at the first of the stalls. He turned a small glass globe upside down, releasing a snowstorm onto a plastic church. He inspected a dog's bowl festooned with Latin phrases, and a badly painted statue of Pope Francis. He then ran a hand over an array of souvenir knives and flicked one up into the sleeve of his jacket. Bizarrely the act of theft gave him a momentary pang of guilt, unlike the prospect of using the stolen item for murder.

Where was he? Dante knew that Mario would put in an appearance. He had evidently boasted quite openly about the contribution he was going to make at the festival. His reputation would be immeasurably enhanced, the clergy and the laity would marvel at his generosity. Only he could stage-manage the coup de théâtre that would be revealed on the piazza dominating the entire valley. His name was on everyone's lips. Dante even heard someone whisper to his neighbour that his wife had gone missing and that he was consumed by grief.

The church was emptying. One of the many priests who had conducted the service grasped the hands of each member of the congregation as they emerged. Those immediately behind were clearly anxious to claim a good seat in the piazza and were impatiently waiting for the hand-grasping to finish. The stairs down from the church were proving difficult for the older members who would only descend the steps with their good legs first and their sticks carefully positioned on the next one.

The path wound upwards from the church. The alleyway was narrow, obliging the crowd to elongate at the entrance. Dante found himself walking alongside a young woman in a tight leather skirt. He thought briefly of his love but was again determined to stay in control of his emotions at least until the deed was done.

The rectangle of blue sky at the end of the alley gradually grew in size until he and the woman spilled into the piazza. He was aware of those pushing from behind in their eagerness to see whatever spectacle had been prepared for their and the Virgin's edification.

There was a large structure made of scaffolding draped in a colourful tarpaulin that seemed to be moving with the small and welcome wind that had sprung up. There was though no indication as to what lay beneath the covering. A monument of some sort perhaps, thought Dante. He was becoming anxious mainly because of the crush. Fearing that he might not be able to move when the time came, he pushed his way towards the veiled centrepiece. Those he squeezed past initially resented being forced to one side until they saw that the person responsible was a priest. 'Prego, Padre. Prego.'

Eventually he stood at the foot of a ladder that led to a platform, also made of scaffolding. He looked above the crowd. Something was happening. He heard the singing first. And then saw the head of a massive statue of the Virgin being carried through the crowd that somehow squeezed itself even tighter to let the procession through. Dante saw the bishop's mitre before the man himself came into view. Too important to join in the hymn, he clanked the chain of the censer against itself, sending small clouds of holy smoke into the air. He was followed by various acolytes, some of whom Dante recognised. Father Davide was in their number, the cleric who had been sent on several occasions to convey the bishop's profound misgivings and displeasure at the alleged content of Dante's sermons. A mean-spirited man with a twisted mouth and an irritating high whine of a voice. But where was Mario?

Dante was pushed back as several officials linked arms and moved the crowd back to make room for the official party. Dante realised that his chin was practically resting on the arm of one of the men forming a link in the chain. The bishop led the way and the lesser clergy spread out from him on either side in descending order of importance. The bier holding the huge Virgin stopped at the foot of the ladder. Dante calculated that the statue must have been at least fifteen feet tall and yet she had been carried with comparative ease by four men. He could only assume she was made of polystyrene. This impression was confirmed by the ease with which one of the men lifted her bodily onto the platform, ducked under the tarpaulin and presumably attached her to whatever lay beneath. But where was Mario?

The bishop intoned several prayers with a gravity that belied his eagerness to get the proceedings over with so that he could enjoy the municipal feast that waited for him once all this nonsense was over and done with. He paused and looked above the crowd, all of whom turned to see Mario striding towards them along a human corridor, with a demeanour of smug self-depreciation. Dante gripped the knife tighter. Mario climbed the first three steps of the ladder and faced his admiring audience. He had placed himself so that it looked as if the massive Virgin behind him was welcoming him with open arms. He humbly motioned for the crowd to desist from its hubbub of respectful approval.

'Signore e signori, today you will witness a sight that will be remembered for decades to come. The marriage between the Holy Catholic Church and the men of the business community is one of the strengths that sustains our country.'

He lost his place in his notes and mumbled an inaudible curse before collecting himself and continuing. 'I sometimes think that Christ was a bit hard on the money lenders. You know, that time in the temple. All societies need the smooth flow of capital. Perhaps he got a row from his mother when he went home that evening.' He jerked a thumb over his shoulder at the statue and paused to milk the non-existent applause for his joke. Changing tack, he assumed a sad demeanour and with a wobble in his voice continued. 'Some of you know of the tragic thing that has happened to me. My beautiful wife, Eleonora, has gone missing. Perhaps I make enemies and now they punish me.'

A mood of embarrassed sympathy fell over the crowd. Dante gently lowered his head under the arm of the vigilante and moved deferentially towards the line of clergy who assumed he was one of theirs who had arrived late. Unnoticed, he climbed alongside Mario, took out his knife and pulled it swiftly across his neck.

At first no one knew how to react. After several seconds the silence begotten of disbelief, gave way to pandemonium and mayhem. Mario slumped forward, a profusely bleeding puppet whose strings had been cut along with his neck. Dante stepped upwards onto the platform he was now sharing with the Virgin Mary. Overbalancing slightly, he grabbed at the handle at his side. Instantly the tarpaulin was ripped away. He was standing beneath a cluster of several hundred blue and white balloons that shimmered and agitated in the breeze.

Then he left the earth for the last time.

He clung to the massive polystyrene Virgin but his arms were not long enough to circle her waist. For a moment the two of them hovered some twenty feet above the hysterical crowd. A massive Madonna and a tiny child caught in a pastiche of a sentimental icon. The upward-turned faces showed terror, disbelief and rapture.

A breeze caught the balloons, there was a jolt and his ascent continued. The piazza shrunk, the individual faces merged into an amorphous smudge. Dante experienced an ecstasy beyond anything he had ever known. The fabulous unreality of his situation was beyond comprehension. The balloons lurched sideways as if still reluctant to forsake the lure of the earth. He was being treated to a final tour of the region, a slow reverential flypast. Dante realised that if the contraption continued on this horizontal trajectory it would crash into the hills on the opposite side of the Conca d'Oro.

'It's you or me, Mother,' he said, looking to see how firmly the Virgin was attached to the platform. Her huge feet had been slotted into a stirrup. He administered a sharp kick to her heels, instinctively muttering an apology as he did so. She responded by tottering for a moment then keeling over. At the precise moment that she lost her footing and left the platform, a thermal caught her and held her motionless in the air, facing Dante.

'Holy Mary, Mother of God!' he exclaimed. At that moment the thermal released her and she floated down through the air. Dante, clinging to the trailing rope, leant over and watched her descent. 'This is the feast of the Ascension, Mother, you've got it all wrong!' He caught a final glimpse of the now tiny figure lying on her back on a green bier of foliage several hundred feet below, its arms still open in a gesture of benediction.

Relieved of its polystyrene ballast, the balloons stopped their sideways movement and climbed upwards. Wisps of cloud wandered past. The sun grew ever hotter, the air grew thinner and Dante's breathing became more laboured.

Gradually, almost imperceptibly, shapes emerged from

the opaque sky, became rounded and assumed human form. Riccardo was on his knees planting kisses on Orlando's neck. Signora Belcastro was gratefully clutching her relic and crossing herself. Signor Pascali, standing tall alongside his hospital bed, saluted. Adolfo offered Dante a glass of grappa. Francesca waved her duster. And Eleonora smiled knowingly.

EPILOGUE

We had been picked up on the outskirts of Edinburgh and driven to Peebles in a 4 X 4 with canvas seats chosen to reinforce the illusion of adventure and associated hardship. The trip was essentially a treat to myself intended to mark the conclusion of the balloon stories. Balloons have often featured in my own dreams but I have never been interested in whatever Freud might have said. There is simply no greater symbol of letting go, of going clear from earthly preoccupations and worry. Balloons represent respite, rescue and freedom. I understood why a former colleague with a diagnosis of a terminal illness wanted to experience a balloon flight. I suspect that in some way, for her, the flight was both a rehearsal and a type of acceptance for what was to come. Having conjured three fictional ascents, each grappling with the idea of exculpation and rapture, this excursion would draw a line and enable me to start another project.

On arriving at the public park the contents of the wicker basket were tipped out and we were charged with unravelling the balloon by hauling on the side ropes. We were fishermen hauling in a catch of laughter and anticipation.

The inert swathe of silk soon covered most of the grass. It was big enough to afford protection to a frost-threatened football pitch, or encourage the growth of a strawberry crop in a Perthshire field. The far reaches of the balloon were uniformly blue while the nearer sections had been quilted in many colours by someone detained in a therapeutic ward. The scale was exhilarating, and the expectation was real. A clutch of dog walkers and tired joggers, eager for respite, pointed at the sleeping skin.

An edge of the silk was lifted and the hot air blower was positioned. Ursule had experienced the same frisson on the concourse outside of the Gare d'Orléans. That was the moment when she knew she would eventually escape le Géant. She stared, entranced, as the sluggish folds of material roused themselves into a semblance of shape. Soon she would have to resume her place on the assembly line but not just yet.

We were told to stand back as the burners were lit. Twin tubes of flame with sharp edges roared into the space. Even from the designated place of safety, our faces felt the heat. Dexter watched helpless as the soldier pointed the flame thrower on the straw hut as if he were wielding a fire hose.

The names Dexter and Ursule had not been on the list read out by the leader in the Land Rover. I felt uneasy at their presence and was relieved when they scuttled away to the edges of the park.

The balloon assumed the bulges and curves of a vast figure stirring from a deep sleep. Her belly and hips, for it was a she, moved as if she was trying to get comfortable. The giantess had fallen asleep in her hippy regalia in the aftermath of a pop festival; hungover and reluctant to stir.

We were encouraged to peer into the prone kaleidoscopic tent; we had been invited to push open the doors of a large church into which the sun filtered through the stained glass windows. Dante was there making his way to the confessional box. All three, then, had been spotted.

The burners and the basket were dragged into an upright

position which in turn forced the balloon to stand up for itself. It did so unprotestingly, perhaps glad after all to be fully awake.

We were instructed on how to adopt the brace position with knees bent in the event of a difficult landing and were helped to climb into our allotted space in the basket which had been neatly divided into eight squares. Our heads bobbed free, like characters from children's TV. There was more laughter and bonhomie as the helper on the ground undid the restraining ropes.

The leader pulled at the cord and sent a several-second burst of flame roaring into the balloon. Then he switched off the burners. The precise moment when we left the earth was undetectable. Unhelpfully I thought of John Donne's poem *Valediction Forbidding Mourning* and how the relatives assembled at the deathbed cannot agree on the precise moment when the final breath was exhaled.

For a moment we hovered several feet from the ground, and then we drifted slowly and imperceptibly above the trees on the edge of the park. The onlookers waved and we waved back like excited children staring out of a carriage window. The TV comparison returned and I saw footage taken from a muted helicopter as the camera led us through deep green gardens towards whatever stately home was the programme's focus. There was a pleasing sense of unreality about the experience, and I had been right about the sense of serenity.

As I have explained in the Interludes, it was the idea of exploring the journey from serenity to rapture that had attracted me to balloon narratives in the first place. I had wanted a way to release my characters from the human miseries that assailed them, and evoke a sort of ecstatic consummation without being too specific about the religious connotations, or having to resort to the usual exigencies of plot. I heard what sounded like mocking laughter and for a brief absurd moment thought it was the three of them. But no, it was the middle-aged couple in the next wicker cell posing for a photo.

Floating over miniature homes, doll's houses and toy cars, I wanted to lean out of the basket and pluck up the church positioned at the end of the High Street. I would turn it upside down and look for the maker's name before putting it back. I could peel back the corners of roofs and see the people inside. I could get my revenge on all white van drivers by flicking their vehicles like Subbuteo players off the roads. This delusion was akin to that of writing fiction. The thought induced a small pang. We were drifting over the Tweed.

What if Dexter's flight had not transported him to some ill-defined ecstatic mental state in which he found complete absolution for his imagined crime against Jake? What if his improvised balloon lost height soon after its ascent and lowered him inexorably towards the nemesis of the river? The jungle sounds growing louder and louder, reaching a climactic cacophony at the moment that he dropped into the water. All his worst fears realised as he spluttered in the Atlantic Ocean once more.

I had perhaps miscalculated; I had possibly underestimated my responsibilities as an author, as a manipulator of imaginary lives. The thought was unwelcome and I shifted my eyes to the horizon. There were layers of hills, hills beyond hills. Those in the foreground were obviously green, those in the distance were much greyer.

Were they Tuscan hills? Did Dante loosen his grip as the cords dug into his wrists? Did he drop from the sky? Was he impaled on the rocks? Was he sufficiently conscious to realise that those snaking intestines lying across his legs were his? Did he become one of the martyred saints he despised, hung, drawn, disembowelled but not yet quartered? This was becoming ridiculous; he didn't exist. How could he feel either pain or disappointment, or indeed witness his own disembowelment?

The middle-aged couple were now wrapped in each other. They were real. Their pleasure in each other was real. This balloon was real. The man directly opposite was passing his hip flask around his fellow passengers who toasted each other. I did the same when my turn came. I hated brandy. What had Ursule accepted from Putois? Champagne, wasn't it? No, the champagne bottle had been broken during the take-off, it had been wine. Burgundy, I think. She would have become light-headed. She wasn't much of a drinker; she had left that to le Géant. What if they had landed behind Prussian lines? According to the records published by J Glaisher, several did. God only knows what would have happened to an attractive young woman like her. Other balloons drifted off course and wandered over the sea. Perhaps at the last moment Ursule's balloon unexpectedly regained height and soared northwards. Viewed from this perspective, a joyous reunion with Louis seemed much less likely than a death by drowning in freezing water. So much for rapture.

I was willing to accept that I had compromised my original intention of leaving all three characters on the cusp of an airborne epiphany that hinted at a reality more fulfilling than life as we know it, and certainly much more fulfilling than they had experienced. However, it was Ursule, more than the other two, who had refused to cooperate with this grandiose thematic purpose. It must have been a subconscious appreciation of her human potential that had made me bring her down to earth, her balloon brushing the trees. Realising that her tale had led me in an unexpected direction, I have since chosen to believe that Ursule's flight was in fact a life-changing rite de passage rather than an ascent into rapture. In which case, how dare I leave her story at that point? It was one thing letting myself be seduced away from my original intention, but it was another thing altogether failing to explain how life turned out for her.

Louis flicked through the pages of the journal. Ursule had always promised to let him see it, but had always shied away from letting him until now. She had gone to feed the calves in the barn. She had taken three bottles with her and said she would be back in an hour. He smiled as he flicked through the pages that described events before their unlikely but glorious reunion in a field near Limoges.

He didn't understand the drawing of the old man in the vineyard but would ask her about it when she returned. He liked the cartoon of the washerwomen fighting each other while a small boy ran away. The immaculately starched shirts that Louis always wore to the council meetings were a legacy of her earlier skills.

Best of all were the theatre drawings. Recently Ursule had returned to the journal and added colour to the black and white drawings. He particularly liked the depiction of an audience member falling from the box in his eagerness to get closer to the stage. He had recently suggested that the pair of them should visit the theatre in the neighbouring town of St Baptiste but she had firmly said no.

He must ask her why there were so many drawings of a railway compartment from the windows of which could be glimpsed various exotic locations. He must ask her if she really travelled as extensively as the drawings suggested. And who was her travelling companion?

If he were honest, Louis was hoping to find a drawing of le Géant. The previous week Ursule had woken screaming from a nightmare, and it had taken Louis several minutes to convince her that she was safe, and that there was not a large man at the window. But there were no drawings of Gérard though Louis noticed that several pages had been ripped from the journal.

The best section of all featured balloons. There were large ones, small ones. Balloons disappearing over a distant horizon. Balloons pushing against the girders in the roof in Gare d'Orléans. There were balloons of all colours, green, red, blue and striped. Here were several impressively detailed drawings of her final flight. Louis was genuinely impressed by the quality of his wife's draughtsmanship. The best of all showed Paris receding through the ropes that secured the basket. The Seine snaked its way across a foreground bisected by the Grands Boulevards and dotted with church spires.

Louis felt a frisson of excitement at the depiction of the distant night sky and, in the foreground, two slumbering figures illuminated by the light from a lantern. He laughed at the cartoon figure stranded in a tree while papers were blown hither and thither in the wind. Ursule had told him about the Very Important Man and his very important papers. The best drawing of all showed two tiny figures embracing in the corner of a vast field while a balloon and its basket bumped its way across the ploughed ridges. The last but one drawing featured the farmhouse where they now lived. It was one of the biggest houses in the area and had been purchased from the legacy that Louis' father had left them.

The last drawing had only been finished two days ago. Ursule's old school friend, Angélique, had come to stay. The women had laughed long into the night. Eventually Louis had left them to it, and had retired to bed. Ursule had sketched a remarkable likeness of her smiling friend.

I had embarked on the process now and there was no going back. I resented the thought; this trip was meant to be unalloyed pleasure. It was not meant to be hijacked by doubts about the completed stories. I chose to concentrate instead on the configuration of sheep seen from on high. This was not a perspective that had ever concerned me before. I could see a triangular flock moving slowly across a field. The black spots were sheep dogs skilfully maintaining the shape of the phalanx. Where was the farmer? There, some distance back on his quad bike.

I tried to tune into the explanation being offered by the leader in response to some anodyne question about his ability to harness winds and actually steer the balloon. I was in fact mildly interested but couldn't make out his reply which was muffled by another burst from the burners. I turned my attention to the symmetry of the woodland. The Forestry Commission was determined to march over most hills in the best regimental order with no single tree allowed to be out of step. The army again. Dexter.

So be it. Arguably Dexter came closer than Ursule to obtaining a nirvana-like state that was the perfect antidote to his phobias and guilt-ridden memories. During his hot ascent into the sky above the jungle, he was gently removed from both the narrative and the world. But annoyingly it didn't work. Any grandiose authorial hints that he finally obtained peace, counted for nothing alongside the host of unanswered questions. Basically, leaving aside his state of mind as he ascended, did he survive? Did he get back to the Country?

Transcript from the Court Martial of Private Dexter Warberg charged with desertion under the Military Code section 4, subsection 6b convened at Redmond in Washington State on 1st June 1967.

Final submission from Defence Council Donald Portersfield.

Your Honour, members of the panel, Dexter Warberg is demonstrably not a bad man; nor is he a coward. He has his demons, sure, but who

among our brave veterans is free from bad dreams
and memories of the hard things they witnessed
when serving this great country of ours? I know
there is scepticism among our colleagues about
the value of psychiatric evidence. Why, I agree,
it seems as if, on occasions, anyone can get a
trick cyclist to pull the wool over our eyes, and
make our hearts bleed for the few yellow-bellied
good-for-nothings who tarnish our fine military.
Just remember, Dr John Rosenberg, our expert
witness, served in World War II, he was decorated
for bravery. He is a man who, to quote Hamlet,
can tell a hawk from a handsaw, in short he can
tell a brave man from a weak one. And he recognised a brave man in Dexter Warberg.

You know, part of the problem here is that some
of us are struggling to accept that the unlikely
can happen; that God operates sometimes in mysterious ways. We must believe that the human
brain and the soul can work together to produce
remarkable results. We must have minds that
are open, open to the possibility that, to quote
Hamlet again, there are more things in heaven
and earth than are dreamed in your philosophy,
members of the panel.

I don't need to remind you of the derision that
this good man encountered when his tale leaked
out. Did you see the David Susskind show when
several supposed experts said it is impossible to
turn a parachute into a balloon? Did you see that
attempt in the television studio with the hot air
blower and the 'chute. Yes, it was funny, it sure
was. But yesterday you listened to a real expert,
Dr Dijkman from the army Department of Scientific Research and Innovation who explained

how it was indeed possible. The man did his god-damnedest to explain that formula, and I sure saw some puzzled faces in this room. Now, maybe none of us understood the science, but we have to believe a scholar of that standing. There is no scientific reason to believe that Dexter Warberg did not construct a balloon to carry him across the river that tormented his very soul. We have to make a leap of faith. As Dexter did into the hot sky above the Vietnam jungle.

Earlier you heard how the accused lived for a year in the company of dead men hanging from the trees. Now, who in their right mind would make up something as stupid as that? It was either true, in which case Dexter Warberg is deserving of our sympathy, or it was one of his delusions, in which case he is deserving also of our sympathy. In neither case does this good, troubled man deserve to be punished. I happen to think it was true. Remember, even in his fevered state he still recognised the authority of his dead colonel. He would report to him daily, he would seek advice before pursuing the enemy. These are not the actions of a man who despises his officers and who sneaks away in the dead of night to join the VC. What sort of society do we live in when a man achieves the impossible and is disbelieved?

This disturbed, heroic man, a survivor in the finest tradition of our pioneering forefathers, walked a thousand miles to freedom. Why would anyone choose to believe that he spent that time in the bosom of the enemy, telling them secrets, and swearing allegiance? And what was that other suggestion? Oh yes, I almost forgot. Some-where in that deep jungle, all the bad men, all the cowardly GIs live in a peaceniks' commune, smoking marijuana and stealing the local women, keeping them as their slaves, rather than return to the Country. So, did Dexter Warberg grow bored with the drugs and the women? Was he expelled from that strange club for taking more than his share, then hitched his way down the Mekong River? I think not, members of the panel.

Let us never lose sight of what Dexter Warberg carried with him on that journey. For eighteen months Dexter Warberg carried the letter from a dead colleague next to his skin. He endured tribulations and challenges that none of us can even dream of. He dragged his body racked with dysentery, plagued by insects through jungle and scrub. That letter became the sole reason for his survival. He had made a promise to himself that he would deliver the letter to the young widow in Connecticut. And that's what he did. Do you really believe he made that journey just to get himself laid, just to get a piece of ass? I'm sorry for my language, members of the panel, but it's difficult not to get carried away after hearing some of the terrible things said in this court about the brave man sitting over there. Don't tell me that Dexter Warberg lacks courage and commitment.

You heard from that young woman over there how she nearly called the cops when she saw a skeleton of a man in torn army fatigues standing on her stoop. She thought he was a mad man. And in one sense she was right, members of the panel. Dexter Warberg was mad for his country. He stood there shivering, barely able to speak, holding at arm's length the letter he had promised to deliver. Now, you all know how that story ended. They got married in the fall, and soon after Anne gave birth to their son, Jake.

I urge you, Your Honour, members of the panel, don't spoil the story, don't besmirch this good, good man's character by listening to that cruel little voice that says, desertion, cowardice. Silence that voice and give Dexter Warberg his freedom. He deserves it.

The leader shot two bursts of flame into the balloon. The noise from the burners brought me back to my own flight. Peebles had long receded. The ribbon of the North Sea was on the far horizon, and the sleeping Pentlands were visible through the balloon struts. The burners were shut down and again we drifted in silence. I felt more at ease with myself than at any time since finishing the stories and revelled in the exhilarating coldness of the flight, the views and, the serenity.

Dexter was found not guilty, how could things have turned out otherwise? This left the case of Father Dante. Of all of the characters, surely the most interesting. He was certainly the one with whom I could most easily empathise. Perhaps it was an age thing. Perhaps it was the nature of his splendidly outrageous and existential revolt. Like the character in Philip Larkin's *Poetry of Departures* he just went for it and walked out on the whole crowd.

On reflection, Dante was the only one of the three for whom the flight was genuinely transcendent. Although it is for others to judge, his story seemed to me to be the most complete. Obviously he would not have survived the ascent hanging on to several hundred balloons. Whether he fell to his death in the mountains or over the sea is largely irrelevant.

Had he managed to enter the ether, the cold would have induced a state of hypothermia, and ultimately he would have asphyxiated. We hope that his lapse into unconsciousness was accompanied by a lightheaded sense of euphoria rather than unbearable pain, of which he had surely endured enough in the last months of his life on earth. At the very moment of contemplating Dante's fatal ascent into the ether, the leader shot more heat into our balloon and we rose rapidly. The lens tightened and the earth shrunk. There was a slight curvature to the horizon and the detail on the ground became blurred.

'I've got a spare anorak if anyone is freezing,' said the leader. A thin woman travelling on her own accepted his offer and the garment was passed to her. She soon resembled the Michelin man and smiled her gratitude. The brandy bottle was completing its second round and I waited my turn. I realised that I was the only passenger not taking photographs: two of my companions had iPhones, two were holding up tablets, and a large man, I think he was German, was manipulating a camera the size of a bazooka. The pilot told us that official photos would be available when we landed. I could only assume that our progress was being recorded by passing angels. Religious pictures of the Assumption always featured angels with swooning eyes and hands clasped over their chests. Dante again.

Adolfo had gone to bed, tired he said, from leading a party of wealthy tourists round the piazza at Monte Pellegrino. Francesca switched on the lamp at the reading table and took out her scrapbook. Before pasting in the latest articles she ran her hand over the pages to check that they hadn't stuck together.

GIORNALE DI SICILIA – June 1
Protests at Mario's funeral
The Carabinieri were called to Sant'Orsola's cemetery after protesters wearing black balaclavas attempted to disrupt the funeral of Seniore Mario, a much respected local

businessman, who was recently murdered by Father Dante Corsini during a celebration of the feast of the assumption of Our Blessed Virgin Mary. Two men with spray-paint canisters were wrestled to the ground by the mourners. The men, whose identities have not been released, are said to be recovering at l'Ospedale Civico. Cardinal Fascoli was heard muttering, 'They know not what they do,' as he tried to pacify grieving family members. A statement later released by the Cardinal's office said, 'Only the emissaries of Satan would desecrate a solemn occasion such as this. Signor Mario was a good man who donated generously to the charities dear to Mother Church...'

LA SICILIA – June 3
Coastguards have abandoned their search for the remains of Father Dante Corsini. A spokesman said, 'If he landed in the sea he might well have been eaten by sharks. It is equally possible that the tides have carried him to the coast of North Africa. We have notified our colleagues in Tunisia.'

CORRIERE DELLA SERA – June 6
This newspaper is sponsoring a competition, open to all who live within twenty kilometres of Monte Pellegrino, to find the fallen Madonna. We will award 5000 Euros to whomso-ever is the first to find the Virgin. The polystyrene statue, four metres in height, is thought to have landed in the forest near the village of Villagrazia di Carni. An early reconnaissance by Signor Martini, a boar farmer, failed to find Our Lady. 'Perhaps it is a miracle,' he said. 'I know these woods like the back of my hand, and she's nowhere to be seen.'

LA SICILIA – June 12
The controversial memorial service held yesterday in Santa Caterina's for the late Father Dante Corsini will live on

320

in the memory for a long time. At least a dozen priests, rumoured to be members of the ultra-conservative organisation Opus Dei, held a demonstration in the street outside of the church. One banner proclaimed 'Hell is for murderers' while another declared that, 'The wages of sin are death! Romans 6.23'. Their protest however was short-lived as a horde of homeless men and their dogs swarmed out of the side streets and attacked the priests who were soon running for their lives…

GIORNALE DI SICILIA – June 15
It is rumoured that an emissary from the Vatican has arrived in Sicily for private talks with Cardinal Fascoli. The church hierarchy is understood to be alarmed by the cult that has grown up round the late Father Dante Corsini.

Corsini is being heralded as a hero who struck a fatal blow, not only to Mario but also to the hopes of a mafia resurgence in this part of Italy. Fervent followers of Corsini remain convinced that the priest, despite the evidence that he committed murder, should be sanctified. An online petition has already attracted over 20,000 signatures. The candlelit vigil being held outside of the canonica provides the clearest evidence yet of the fanaticism inspired by the late priest. Leading the prayers is an eighty-year-old woman, Signora Roatta and her son, Piero. 'Dante was a good, good man,' she said.

Signora Francesca smiled and closed her scrapbook.

I realised that the couple penned directly opposite to me were smiling broadly in my direction. This was because I had been smiling at my chain of thought and they had assumed I was being sociable. 'Great, isn't it?' I said, to reassure them. They put their thumbs up and smiled some more.

We had started on our slow descent. Individual farm-houses came back into focus, a different flock of sheep emerged from the indistinct fields. There was no sense of anticlimax, no intimations of loss as we drifted over fields whose hedges were now discernible. A picnicking family stood up and waved. We passed over a small river snaking through the jungle. A quad bike driven by a small boy puttered across a field. I felt a small tinge of apprehension but then reminded myself that this was neither Vietnam nor the back streets of Palermo.

The leader explained that the company had already visited most of the farmers in the area seeking permission to land in their fields if necessary. He also explained that this was just a courtesy as legally the balloon could land anywhere it wanted. Were there cattle in that field? Did we think that one was recently ploughed? He pretended to involve us in the decision as to the best place to touch down. For a moment it looked as if we would be landing in a clump of trees but a strategic bust of flame lifted us clear. I did though cast a glance in case there were any Very Important Papers hanging in the upper branches.

The noise from the burner frightened some sheep who ran frantically to the edges of the field. We were told to adopt the brace position and then, almost imperceptibly, made contact with the ground. We were dragged a few metres before coming to a stop with the basket completely upright. Part of me felt cheated by the uneventful nature of the landing but I nevertheless accepted a helping hand out of the basket. There was a smattering of applause.

We stood and watched as the dome of silk exhaled slowly before it slumped reluctantly onto the ground. The recovery vehicle entered the gate at the bottom of the field and ambled its way towards us. We worked together to bundle up the balloon which we lifted along with the basket onto the back of the Land Rover. In accord with established tradition, and as specified in the pre-flight publicity, the leader produced a bottle of Champagne. The late afternoon felt warm and I turned my face to the sun. I experienced a sense of well-being, a sense of acceptance, of being grounded. It wasn't rapture but it was good enough.

'Cheers!' I raised my glass to the leader, to the other passengers, and to my three fellow aeronauts.

We fell softly to the ground in a field not very far from Melun in front of those groups of trees which form the commencement of the forest of Senart. The wind drove us along for some distance over the ploughed land, the balloon bent over on its side, and we got covered with mud. It was like coming back to stern reality after a beautiful dream.

Gaston Tissandier's
The Ascent of the Union, 1868